WHAT OTHERS ARE SAYING ABOUT *THE SEVENTH DOOR*

The Seventh Door is truly a masterpiece of literature and one of Mr. Davis's finest pieces of art.

Jacob Howard (Age 15)

Seldom does a book move me to tears. This book was #1. I have never seen such character growth, faith, comic relief, and an author willing to openly talk about and display God and everything God is.

Sarah Kufrovich (Age 15)

The Seventh Door will have you absolutely riveted from start to finish. This book will build your faith and help you realize that we are all called to be "Lights in a Dark World."

Jacob Covell (Age 18)

The Seventh Door is the best book yet! It will keep you speechless with new plot twists in every chapter. It made me laugh and cry as I traveled with the gang through their incredible journey.

Jurnee Uetz (Age 17)

The Seventh Door is amazing, an unforgettable, emotional roller coaster. This book just adds to the amazing journey and sucks the reader into the pages.

Madi Olson (Age 15)

Bryan Davis has captured yet again the hearts of his readers with *The Seventh Door*! This thrilling adventure is filled with love, forgiveness, and a picture of the Ultimate Sacrifice.

Sarah & Abigail Rega (Ages 24 and 18)

The Seventh Door had my heart hammering with passion, slicked my trembling palms with sweat, and sent my spirit soaring with triumph while it burned with heartbreak, all at once!

(Age 15)

The Seventh Door is filled with unique tales of forgiveness, freedom, sacrifice, daring rescues, and seemingly impossible journeys. Bryan Davis has created another beautiful story that will be impressed upon my heart forever.

Elisabeth Robison (Age 17)

Once I started reading *The Seventh Door* I couldn't stop. There is only one thing left to say at the end of this book: WOW!

Zachery Anderson (Age 17)

Bryan Davis presents yet another stroke of genius! After only a few moments of reading, I found myself hopelessly bound up in this story world, racing side by side with each beloved character. The age-old tale of true sacrifice, undying love, and the quest for salvation shines anew in *The Seventh Door.*

Kayla Austin (Age 18)

In *The Seventh Door,* Mr. Davis mixed much-loved stories from the first Billy and Bonnie adventures with new twists. The incredible reconciliations and sacrifices grabbed my attention and set this book apart.

Sacha Gragg (Age 15)

Masterpiece is the only word that fully captures the essence of *The Seventh Door.*

Jonathan Peterson (Age 28)

A beautiful lesson in grace, forgiveness, strength, and faith, all wrapped up in an amazing novel that will keep you on the edge of your seat until the very end.

Michaila Cornwell (Age 15)

When you read *The Seventh Door,* it will enrich your faith in God, take you on awesome adventures, and pretty much build a friendship between you and the characters within the story. Like I tell everyone when I talk about this series, it blows the Chronicles of Narnia out of the water!

Christopher Meek (Author of *Blade Children*)

The Seventh Door is an exceptional thrill ride with a cliff-hanger ending that will leave you clamoring for more!

Kayla Gray (Age 13)

The Seventh Door is a masterpiece. The eloquence and overall beauty give the characters life and allow for a deep connection with them. As they grow alongside those who have faithfully followed Christ, they too learn the power of forgiveness and love that is everlasting.

Mitchell Leih (Age 19)

I didn't know I was so thirsty for a book that would not only inspire, but would awaken my heart to really seek after God. I saw sacrifice instead of selfishness, loathing turned into love, and reconciliation instead of revenge. This is by far the best novel I have read in a long time.

Priscilla Kwong (Age 18)

It is rare to find a book that brings me to tears, and even rarer a story with so much spiritual impact. This truly is a life-changing story that will leave you pondering your own walk with God long after you have read the last page.

Elizabeth Hornberger (Age 19)

The Seventh Door is 400 pages of action-packed awesomeness!

Danielle Lowder (Age 15)

Fantastic! *The Seventh Door* is beautifully written to combine fiction, the love of Christ, and the very real hope of redemption.

Benjamin Steward (Age 15)

The Seventh Door is quite simply the number one most gripping novel Bryan Davis has ever written. Don't miss out. You'll be taken on a wild ride.

Michael Tofte (Age 16)

Not since *The Bones of Makaidos* have I been so enthralled by a story. I felt like I was standing by the characters as they faced one impossible challenge after another.

Zachary Peterson (Age 20)

The Seventh Door will leave you on the edge of your seat! The spiritual journey is unmatched in any book.

Paige Passanisi (Age 22)

The many twists and turns in *The Seventh Door's* plot will make you not want to put the book down!

Tiffany Bennett (Age 17)

This book is amazing! It will capture you in the first sentence and keep you entranced until the end.

Makenna Pagniano (Age 12)

The Seventh Door has lifted my spirit to new heights, reminding me of God's truths and promises the world tries so hard to make me forget.

Jenalynn Weed (Age 17)

The Seventh Door is filled with constant excitement, suspense, and passion, a guaranteed favorite.

Jason Whiteaker (Age 14)

The Seventh Door demonstrates that without Christ in us we are powerless against our own desires; but with Christ's forgiveness and love we can forgive and love others. This insightful message is portrayed throughout this enjoyable and extremely suspenseful book.

Emily and Cheryl Mann (Ages 17 and 14)

The Seventh Door has mystery, plot twists, sacrifice, and love—you won't read another book like this in your life! It has given me a new identity in Christ.

Logan Brubaker (Age 16)

The Seventh Door is one of the most intense books in the entire Dragons In Our Midst world. It has a depth of emotion that can tug at anyone's heartstrings. A wonderful installment.

Caleb Breslin (Age 16)

Bryan Davis once again takes readers on an incredible journey. I relished every moment with my favorite characters as they suffered, rejoiced, sacrificed, and showed their faith through their trials.

Grant Brion (Age 17)

The Seventh Door is a book of unconditional love that brings us to the truth of God's love for us no matter where we are in life.

Chelsea Boling (Age 24)

Wow! Just wow! Bryan Davis has written another spectacular novel, this one with higher stakes than ever. The characters' struggles are so real, and you feel their gut-wrenching pain as they make life-or-death decisions.

Lydia Lyell (Age 16)

As the characters face unimaginable evils, the reader faces them as well. In this epic story of faith, love, sacrifice, and spiritual warfare, you will truly be changed.

Stetson Harper (Age 19)

Intrepid heroines and heroes, horrendous villains, incredible circumstances to overcome—*The Seventh Door* has them all. Self-sacrifice for the good of others gives meaning to this amazing tale.

Kaye Whitney

Our favorite heroes are back. With the threat of the apocalypse following them at every turn, they must team up with new allies and old enemies. This book is truly inspirational, my favorite of all of Bryan Davis's books.

Lissa Phillips (Age 15)

The Seventh Door is a spectacular book that I believe has one message, "Everything works together for the good of the Lord." This book is one that you will NEVER put down.

Hannah Santiago (Age 12)

The Seventh Door grabbed me the moment I picked it up. The action never stops and the characters come to life. I laughed when they did, got angry when they did, and most of all I cried when they did. Mr. Davis is a literary genius.

Hannah Young (Age 16)

From fast-paced battles to beautiful reunions and the return of characters that readers of the series will be ecstatic to see, *The Seventh Door* continues the series with just as many twists, turns, and the lesson of the love God has for each and every one of us.

McKenzie Young (Age 17)

The Seventh Door is undoubtedly Mr. Davis's finest book yet! From the beginning, this breathtaking book grabs you, pulls you into the story, and allows you to experience the emotional journeys of the characters.

Ansley Fetner (Age 17)

The best book Bryan Davis has ever written to date. I fell in love with the old characters all over again and met new characters who are fantastic. It is an amazing book.

Elizabeth Beard (Age 21)

The Seventh Door was great! I loved it! It was very action packed and kept me guessing through every chapter. The plot was great and had an awesome moral. I couldn't put it down!

Naomi Williams (Age 12)

Another beautiful edition to this story world. Masterfully written, it provides you with a whirlwind of emotion and imagination. God is so present in this book, and his presence encourages me to look through the trials of life and sacrifice myself, trying my best to become an Oracle of Fire.

Sarah Ball (Age 15)

Each page adds excitement and adventure, making the book nearly IMPOSSIBLE to put down!

Meredith Reeves (Age 20)

For the eleventh time, Bryan Davis mesmerizes us with the stories of Dragons in Our Midst. He takes us on an adventure even more exhilarating than dragon-riding.

Matt Kilens (Age 19)

The Seventh Door sends your head swirling in excitement, taking you on one of the greatest adventures yet.

Sarah Fenstermacher (Age 14)

With excellent character development and shocking plot twists, this addition to the Dragons in Our Midst world may be one of the best yet! It seizes your emotions and refuses to let them go even after the story ends.

Arianna Breslin (Age 17)

Bryan Davis has created characters you'll never forget, adventures that will linger with you for life, and inspiring moments that will strengthen your faith.

Hannah DeHerrera (Age 14)

I have never read a series like this one! Even though the books are fiction, the use of the Bible, God, faith, and forgiveness has changed my life.

Amanda Winter (Age 14)

Bryan Davis has done it yet again—written a book that pulls me in and refuses to let me go. I read late into the night, unwilling to stop reading until there was no more to read.

Lane Crouch (Age 17)

Mr. Davis has once again proved he is an amazing author with *The Seventh Door*. By far my most favorite series. A great read that I highly recommend.

Gretchen Riggle (Age 14)

The Seventh Door is an exciting and uplifting book that will keep you on the edge of your seat while encouraging you in your faith. Fans of the series will definitely not be disappointed!

Sarah Pennington (Age 16)

The Seventh Door shows us the power of redemption, God's never-ending grace, and the power of prayer. Grab your keys and get ready to unlock *The Seventh Door*!

Lacey Hilgen (Age 16)

Totally enthralling. The characters seem like real people and make you feel as though you're part of the action instead of a bird's-eye viewer. Yet another masterpiece from a great and brilliant author.

Keturah Goldsberry (Age 18)

The Seventh Door is packed with heart-stopping moments and breathtaking adventures that will leave you speechless and eager to turn the page.

Nichole Dixon (Age 14)

A fantastic journey through well-crafted parallels, vivid imagery, and stunning examples of faith. *The Seventh Door* is an absolutely brilliant installment in the series.

Brianna Tibbetts (Age 20)

Bryan Davis is a Master Bard in his own right, boldly proclaiming the Light of Truth in a dark world. This book is a beautiful example of spiritual strength and an insight into the tricks of Satan and his minions.

Kaitlyn White (Age 26)

The Seventh Door is by far the most engaging book in the series yet and will have readers eagerly awaiting the conclusion. This incredible tale of adventure, suspense, and all things fantasy brings to life in the imagination what only exists in dreams.

Lydia Frost (Age 18)

In all my years as a reader, I have never come across a story so full of selfless sacrifice, haunting tragedy, and unyielding faith even in the midst of despair. In all the previous books, even through the tears of sorrow and loss, the faithful have remained constant in their devotion to the Father, and *The Seventh Door* is no exception. Truly a job well done.

Courtney McDonald (Age 22)

Once again Bryan Davis leads his readers on a wild ride. There are amazing ups and downs, crazy turns, and breathtaking, heart-stopping cliff-hangers. Mr. Davis has taught me so many things about my walk with God. I can't wait to read the next book and continue this journey with all these characters I know and love.

Elizabeth France (Age 19)

The Seventh Door is an amazing addition to an already fantastic series.

Ben Vallance (Age 17)

An action-filled plot with a riveting ending, such as you've come to expect from the master storyteller, Bryan Davis.

Allison Desaulniers (Age 20)

The Seventh Door

Bryan Davis

The Seventh Door
Copyright © 2014 by Bryan Davis
Published by AMG Publishers
6815 Shallowford Rd.
Chattanooga, Tennessee 37421

Print Edition ISBN 13: 978-0-89957-882-8
EPUB Edition ISBN 13: 978-1-61715-109-5
Mobi Edition ISBN 13: 978-1-61715-045-6
EPDF Edition ISBN 13: 978-1-61715-194-1

The Seventh Door is the third of four books in the youth fantasy fiction series, Children of the Bard. CHILDREN OF THE BARD is a registered trademark of AMG Publishers.

All Scripture quotations, are taken from the King James Version (Authorized Text), which is in the Public Domain.

On pages 187 and 188, Bonnie sings a song. To learn how to perform this song, go to this webpage: http://www.daviscrossing.com/seventh_door.shtml

First printing—February 2014

Cover designed by Daryle Beam, Bright Boy Design, Chattanooga, Tennessee
Interior design and typesetting by Reider Publishing Services,
  West Hollywood, California
Edited and Proofread by Susie Davis, Sharon Neal, and Rick Steele

Printed in Canada
19 18 17 16 15 14 –MAR– 8 7 6 5 4 3 2 1

CONTENTS

xii

AUTHOR NOTE AND PARENTS' GUIDE

The Children of the Bard series is the culmination of a story that spans nearly the entire existence of mankind, from a few generations after the Garden of Eden to the dawn of a cataclysm that threatens to bring man's time on Earth to an end.

As an author, I pondered how to portray a world that has corrupted itself to the point that a righteous God would allow such destruction to occur. How can I explain depravity so that younger readers can understand why God would deliver so many to doom? In doing so, how can I shield their reading eyes from indelible images that might bring harm to their tender minds?

At the same time, I wanted older readers who are mature, who are trained to oppose corruption head-on with swords of the spirit drawn, to see clearly the evils they might have to face as they stand up for God and his kingdom.

This story is my attempt at balancing these desires. Each of the seven "doors" that the characters face provides a glimpse at a result of corrupting influences. While, for the most part, the graphic details are absent from the descriptions, mature readers will perceive the behind-the-scenes horror. My hope is that younger readers, who have not been made aware of such horror, will not be able to raise the mental images.

There is one exception. Behind one of the doors, a character finds a dead baby, the victim of an abortion (pp. 111–115). The text describes the baby briefly, so younger readers might be frightened or horrified at the mental image. I allowed this exception because of the present reality of this unholy slaughter that plagues our culture. Parents, please be aware that this scene exists and determine if your children are mature enough to read it.

My hope is that readers of all ages will benefit spiritually from this story. It is dark, to be sure, but such a journey through shadowed valleys makes the overwhelming light, blazing in triumph, that much more glorious. Readers of this story will become beacons in this dark world, as Isaiah said, "The people that walked in darkness have seen a great light: they that dwell in the land of the shadow of death, upon them hath the light shined." (Isaiah 9:2 KJV)

THE PROPHET'S GAP

(Ezekiel 22:23–31)

Beloved ground that calls for rain,
That cries for flooding wrath below;
Consume the priest, restrain the beast,
And raze the land with cleansing flow.

For lions tear the witless prey,
Conspiring prophets fill with dread;
The widows plead, their hearts still bleed,
While prophets' fingers drip with red.

They lie, they steal, they whitewash sin;
Obtaining visions straight from hell.
They rob the poor and shut their door
To strangers seeking ports to dwell.

A gap is torn within your hedge,
The pile of stones you trust to shield;
Protective wall becomes a hall
That channels wrath unless you yield.

I search for souls to seal the gap,
For holy ones to build the frame;
O come and stand before the land
Become the stones that block the flames.

Alas! No mason could be found
To set the stones the rampart needs;
The flames must rage upon this stage
And purge the land of choking weeds.

A final call I make today,
Will you become the stone that seals?
Will you command and take a stand
And call upon your friends to kneel?

The devil's darts awake to fly;
His priests repel the truth with scorn.
Yet still make haste, no time to waste,
For wrath will come upon the morn.

To my wonderful readers who have already passed through the eternal gates: Just as Christ <u>rose</u> from the dead, you have risen to eternal life and now reside in a place where neither flood nor fire can touch. I will look forward to seeing you in glory.

1

CHAPTER

RED DAWN

A winged shadow flitted by the motel room window, first one way, then the other, like an animated silhouette painted on the drapes. Matt lifted from his pillow and propped himself on an elbow. Was it a bird? If so, it had to be a big one, maybe an owl sweeping past. Yet, bird or not, something had ignited the danger alarm in his gut. No more sleeping, at least not until the sensation eased.

From the partially closed bathroom, a narrow shaft of light illuminated the area, revealing a TV, desk, dresser, and two beds. Matt lay in the one closer to the window, while his mother and Darcy slept in the other. The pairing seemed odd—a winged woman of incomparable faith slumbering next to a young prostitute fresh from a street corner—strange bedfellows indeed.

Thumps from the room above, squeaks from springy mattresses, and indiscernible whistles and clicks created a haunted-house sensation. Blown by the room's heater, window drapes shifted, making the persistent shadow undulate when it passed by, and muted light from the waning moon created an even spookier feel. If he were not well past the age to hide under a blanket on this cold Nebraska night, he might invent an excuse to awaken his mother. But after breaking into and out of a military prison, surviving a volcano eruption, and getting shot by an insane demon, a shadow was nothing to fear. It probably really was just a bird searching for crumbs or shelter from the wintry air.

Matt's danger sensors spiked. The bathroom darkened. The heater's fan fluttered to a stop. He sat up and stared at the window. The glass shattered. A winged beast burst through the drapes and leaped on him. He grabbed its neck, keeping its snapping jaws away. As the two thrashed, dark scales flew from the creature's skin, and thick fluid dripped from its sharp fangs to Matt's forehead.

Mom jumped out of bed. Darcy screamed. The door crashed open, sending wood shards flying. A dragon's head shot inside. Fire roared from its mouth and engulfed the beast's wings and back. A squeal erupted. Matt threw the attacker to the floor, leaped up, and flipped the light switch, but the wall fixtures stayed dark.

2

A man wearing a flannel shirt pushed past the dragon and burst into the room. "Stay calm," he said as he pulled a blanket from the bed and laid it over the flaming beast. "These creatures are dangerous, but fire kills them pretty quickly. We mustn't burn down the motel."

The first rays of dawn spilled in through the broken door, providing a good view of the man as he mopped his brow and brushed his hand on his faded jeans. "In any case ..." He bowed his head toward Mom. "It's good to see you again, Bonnie."

Mom straightened her shirt, having slept in the only clothes she had. "It's good to see you, Enoch."

Darcy rose from the bed and pulled Matt's cloak around her. "Hello, sir."

"Hello, Miss." Enoch bowed his head to her as well. "You must be Darcy."

"I am." She smiled, shivering. Although drapes again covered the broken window, frigid air seeped through.

"I'm Matt." He extended a hand. "Thanks for the help."

Enoch shook his hand firmly. "We were more than happy to offer assistance."

"Your timing was perfect," Mom said.

"Not quite perfect." Enoch picked up a long strip of wood from the floor. "If we had arrived earlier, we might have prevented all this damage. The innkeeper won't be pleased, especially when he sees the stain that foul beast will leave on the carpet."

"Your dragon friend looks familiar." Mom squinted. "Abaddon?"

The dragon's head bobbed. "I am able to appraise appearances, so I assume you wonder why I wandered from my world."

Mom crossed her arms and smiled. "Abaddon the alliterative angel has arrived."

"Pleased to be present," Abaddon said. "I was delighted to dispatch the demonic drone, but duties demand that a death-dealing dragon depart at dawn."

"Since dawn is nigh," Enoch said, "we must hurry with our explanations and purpose."

Matt pulled the blanket from the smoking carcass and picked up one of the scales the drone had shed during their battle. Slick and leathery, it smelled like burnt rubber mixed with wet dog and motor oil.

"You were being followed by a drone," Enoch said. "It is of demonic origin, one of Tamiel's minions. My guess is that it saw us and assumed that you had called for our help, which Tamiel would not allow. I suppose that he assigned it to track you, so others might be lurking."

3

Darcy scowled at the drone as it jerked in death throes—twisted and smoking. "It looks like a half-dragon, half-vulture … thing."

"And a dangerous *thing* it is." Enoch inserted the wood strip into the drone's mouth and pushed up its leathery lip, exposing one of its fangs. "When it bites, it injects venom that in low doses causes temporary paralysis, and in higher doses, death. A few drones have a different form of venom that slowly brings about irrational thoughts and behavior and finally insanity that cannot be cured by any medicine or therapy known to man."

Matt rubbed his neck. "Good thing you showed up before it got me. Thanks again."

"You are quite welcome. And now to explain why we are here." Enoch leaned outside, lifted two hard-shell suitcases into the room, and set them on the floor. "Clothing and other essentials. The heavenly grapevine told me that you are all in need of toiletries and proper attire, including something you can sleep in so you can launder your daytime clothing at night."

"Thank you!" Darcy touched a rose-colored suitcase. "This one?"

Enoch nodded. "That one contains your clothes as well as toiletries for all of you. Get dressed quickly while I talk to Bonnie and Matt, assuming, of course, you are able to do so without lights."

"No problem." Darcy picked up the suitcase and hurried into the bathroom.

When the door closed, Enoch lowered his voice. "No time for detailed explanations. The spiritual realm is bursting with frenetic commotion. Because of the weakness in Bonnie's song, demonic activity has escalated, and the vast majority of people have become your enemies, so you are in constant danger."

"And darkness will definitely dominate." Abaddon's tongue darted out and in. "As archangel of the abyss, I determine the day to distribute doom from my domain based on a barometer of barbarism. Calamity is coming quickly unless you conquer the corruption."

"Doom from your domain?" Mom said. "Aren't Sir Barlow, Tamara, and the Second Eden refugees still there?"

"Your comrades are currently commuting to Second Eden along with the returning refugees."

Enoch patted Abaddon's neck. "We have called upon Listener to help with evacuating the women and children. Although Abaddon's Lair will close, and resurrections to this world and to Second Eden will soon cease, I think combining Listener's diligence with Sir Barlow's strength will assure a good result overall. In the wake of Valiant's death and the volcano's destruction, Listener has taken a leadership role in Peace Village and has coordinated the rebuilding efforts. She has already proven to be a brilliant organizer and motivator."

Matt's ears burned. Just hearing about Listener brought a surge of mixed feelings. Such an amazing girl. But probably too old for him, and her wisdom and maturity definitely put her out of his league.

Abaddon blew a smoky sigh. "The interruption of my industry is inevitable, so I finished facilitating my fold. Now only a solitary statue stands by the streams."

Mom lowered her voice to a whisper. "Anyone I know?"

"For the moment it is merely a monument," Abaddon said, "a soulless slab of stone, though a symbol can be stirred. Still, a single statue is a satisfying situation. You see, Second Eden's birthing bed now blooms with babies, so it behooves Bonnie Bannister to bid for finer fates for her friends. Fatalities are frowned upon."

Enoch chuckled. "My dear, my draconic ally is saying that it seems of late that if someone you love dies, his or her soul ends up in Abaddon's Lair, though very few from the general population are resurrected. This revolving door, however, will soon stop turning, and resurrections will no longer spring from Abaddon's Lair. I do not know, however, when that change will take place."

Abaddon's eyes flashed blue. "Hear this admonition, unalliterated and unveiled. I have recently learned the reason for the many resurrections associated with you and your loved ones, but it would be impossible to explain in the brief time we have remaining. Suffice it to say that there is a reservoir that supplies the life energy for resurrections, and you and your friends have been among its suppliers in a way that I did not expect. A time will come when my realm will crumble and vanish, and this reservoir will be the only means of bodily resurrection." As his eyes faded to normal, he shifted his gaze to Matt. "If more information becomes necessary, then experience gained during your journey will provide what you need to know."

6

Matt averted his eyes. Abaddon's stare felt like a piercing knife. Why would he be so probing when he was obviously talking about Mom and her gifts? "Okay. Thanks for the info."

"Yes, Abaddon. Thank you." Mom gave Enoch a pensive look. "But what I really want to know is if you've seen Billy or Walter or the others."

Enoch shook his head. "The twisting spiritual planes have disabled my viewer. If not for Abaddon's keen sense of smell and excellent memory regarding your scent, we would not have been able to find you."

"My scent?" Mom asked. "Is it that strong?"

"Not strong. Distinctive. You have been in Heaven, Hades, and the Bridgelands, and you have collected a blend of scents that no one else has, an aroma that can never be washed off. The drones are trained to follow scents, which is likely why this one could follow you." Enoch pulled back a curtain and peered outside. "Much has happened since you've been gone, even overnight. You will find that the sun and moon aren't as bright as before. They both appear to be wearing a scarlet shroud. Plagues have killed millions, and most people cower in their homes in fear of a multitude of contagions, though some looters boldly steal whatever they can lay their hands on. The chaos is such that local authorities are useless. Most communications are down except for some that access satellites, so you can imagine the turmoil that is causing."

Matt glanced at the room's telephone. It hadn't worked ever since they arrived. "How about where we're going? Are things chaotic there?"

Abaddon spoke with a growl. "Mayhem is moderate in the Midwest, but chaos creeps from the corners as time ticks tenaciously. Soon the savage situation will spread from sea to sea."

"Correct," Enoch said. "It makes me wonder if the four horsemen are riding, and the trumpets are about to sound."

"The ones in Revelation?" Mom asked. "The end of the world?"

"Perhaps. If Earth's spiritual condition continues to deteriorate, I assume we are seeing the four horsemen of the apocalypse. If you don't stop Tamiel's plan to complete the corruption of mankind, at some point the great abyss will open and release a force that will torture the human race, and more calamities will follow. Then no one will be able to prevent the end of the world as we know it."

Matt blew out a low whistle. A real apocalypse. It all seemed too bizarre to be possible.

"No time to tarry," Abaddon said. "The sands are spilling as we speak. I must, however, take time to tell you this. If I arise from the abyss with my avengers, I will be waging war, and I will forsake friendliness." He withdrew his head from the room and shuffled away.

For a moment, everyone stared. Then Enoch waved a hand. "Don't worry about him. He's always filled with mysteries."

"That much I know," Mom said. "Sapphira and I had some, shall we say, heated conversations with him."

"To be sure. I will tarry for a little while, but since he is not a patient dragon, I will have to join him soon."

"So ..." Mom sat on Matt's bed. "If I go on this quest and hurt my song, I might hasten the calamity, and if I don't go on the quest ..."

"Then calamity is a certainty." Enoch's face took on a melancholy expression. "When I see the corruption that the people of this world have freely chosen, a battle rages in my heart. In one light, I feel sorry for them, and I wish to do whatever is possible to help them escape from their own foolishness. In another light, I long to deliver retribution, to punish them for their rebellion against the light."

"I feel that," Matt said. "How do you resolve the battle?"

Enoch sat next to Mom and patted the mattress. "Matt. Please."

When Matt joined them, Enoch continued. "I resolve it by realizing that desires for mercy and for justice are both motivated by love. Love for our fellow man desires rescue. Love for God desires justice. The conflict is resolved whether our efforts bring about repentance or are instead rebuffed. In the former case, our sorrows are eased, and joy results. In the latter case, only justice remains, and we are called to accept it, though sorrow and satisfaction are blended in a confusing whirlpool of emotions."

Enoch grasped Matt and his mother by their wrists. "Both of you have wondrous gifts from God. Bonnie, your eloquence will allow you to sing with words that will pierce even the most hardened heart, but they must spring from your own heart of love. Otherwise, your song will bounce off wooden ears. The lost and wandering people have heard it all before—lyrics without substance, poems without purpose, lofty platitudes that they assume no one really believes. Words of love must be matched with actions that demonstrate love. These souls must witness love in your outstretched hands as well as from your lips. Only this is true integrity. Words alone are not really love at all."

Enoch opened Matt's hand and ran a finger along his palm. "You have healing hands that will seal horrific wounds, and you have seen them work even for an enemy like Semiramis. Yet that miracle occurred in the relative purity of Second Eden, not on Earth. Unfortunately, the corruption in this world has diminished the range of your ability. Here, in the midst of depraved beings, your touch will be of no use unless all barriers to love are broken down. If there is the slightest stain of contempt for your patient, love will be squelched, and your touch will be nothing more than the abrasive scrape of a hardened callous." He released Matt's hand and sighed. "I hope you will ponder these words as you continue your journey."

9

While Enoch paused, Matt let the words sink in. They were deep and profound. Time would tell how they could be put to use, but for now they swam in a pool of scattered thoughts, adding yet more mysteries to the turmoil.

Enoch rose from the bed and nudged the other suitcase with a sandaled foot. "For reasons I am not at liberty to explain, this clothing is the only physical help we can provide, but I can give you one more prophetic word." When Mom joined him, he looked her in the eye and whispered, "Remember who you are and the seven trials you have already conquered. Your memories will be a shield of defense."

A light sparkled in Mom's eye, like a tiny flame that burst to life. "I'll remember."

"Do you have any questions for me?"

"Just one. When Tamiel kidnapped me, he said that he was able to see me because he was open and honest with me. Later I figured out that he must have been referring to the king's cap Billy applied to make me invisible to demons. Do I still have that covering?"

"That is highly unlikely. You were separated from Billy for too long. Perhaps you are semitransparent to demons now, and Tamiel meant that he could see you clearly. For practicality's sake, you should assume that you are visible."

Darcy emerged from the bathroom wearing hiking shoes, camouflage pants, and a thick long-sleeved pullover shirt—beige and closely fitting her slender, toned frame. She set the suitcase down and smiled. "I did the best I could in the dark. Do I look okay?"

10

Matt got up and fidgeted. "Um ... yeah. You look fine." Assessing her appearance felt awkward. With freshly brushed shoulder-length auburn hair, a clean angular face, and bright eyes in spite of the dim room, she really was attractive, in a good way, more like a neatly groomed college student than a tramp hunting for a victim.

"Well ..." Enoch clapped his hands together. "I'm glad everything fits."

"Are you sure they're not too tight?" Darcy ran her hands along her hips. "I don't want to look ... you know ..."

"Like bait?" Enoch nodded. "Fear not. This is a practical design. Because of the physical obstacles you will likely encounter, baggy clothes are not advisable."

She lifted her legs in turn, stretching the camo material. "Then they're perfect. Thank you."

"I almost forgot." Enoch reached into his jeans pocket and

withdrew a string of beads, each one a different color. "I recovered this for Bonnie." He draped it around Mom's neck and tied it in the back.

Mom touched a blue bead at the bottom of the arc. "Thank you. This is a precious heirloom."

"Yes, I thought so." Enoch nodded at each of them. "I have to go. My dragon transport is likely getting perturbed at my delay."

Mom hugged Enoch. "I hope to see you again soon."

"That is a certainty, though I know not if our next meeting will be in this world." Enoch backed out and swung the door to a closed position, though it wouldn't latch. The broken jamb created a three-inch gap that allowed a shaft of dawning light into the room.

Matt sat heavily on his bed and looked up at his mother. "An apocalypse?"

"Looks that way, but maybe it's an avoidable one."

"So what do we do?"

Mom picked up both suitcases. "We get dressed and go to the first destination." Without another word, she walked into the bathroom and closed the door.

"Wow!" Darcy scooted to the bed and sat next to Matt. "This is really scary sh—" She cleared her throat. "Uh … scary stuff, isn't it?"

"Pretty much." He looked away but watched her out of the corner of his eye. Sitting next to her felt like cozying up to a serpent. "And don't worry about cleaning up your language around me. I've heard every word in the book."

She folded her hands in her lap. "With all that's going on, I thought maybe I'd better … I don't know …"

"Change your ways?"

She bent her brow. "You're really quick on the draw, aren't you?"

11

"What do you mean?"

She touched herself on the chest. "You assume the worst about me; you're half cocked and ready to shoot."

"When you give me a good reason not to, maybe I won't."

She pressed her lips into a line. "Look. I did some terrible things to you. But that was years ago. And I'm sorry. I was a stupid kid. I was jealous because I wanted my parents to myself."

"Years ago? Tamiel said he picked you up off the street corner. Did jealousy drive you to that?"

"I had to walk from place to place." She crossed her arms tightly. "I play piano and sing at a couple of nightclubs. And I'm pretty good at it, if I do say so myself."

"Are you saying you never sold yourself to someone with a wad of cash?" Matt huffed. "Give me a break."

She looked away. "I don't have to sit here being interrogated. I said I'm sorry about what I did to you, and that's all you need to know."

"Yeah. Just what I thought." Matt rose, stalked to the window, and pushed the drapes to the side. Cold air wafted through the jagged hole, but that didn't matter. Darcy needed to cool off.

In the distance, a truck drove from left to right, framed by a layer of clouds painted red by the dawning rays, a bloody hue that seemed unearthly. The drill sergeant's words echoed—*Red sky in the morning, sailors take warning.* That maxim had proven true many times, and Enoch's warnings added a nightmarish mask to the horizon. Sunrise held no hope. Doom lay ahead—complete annihilation of the entire world. Only he and his newfound mother could stop it, and their efforts might even make things worse. It was like trying to disarm a time bomb by forcing the clock to tick faster.

Not only that, they had to worry about Darcy. She could be on Tamiel's side, pretending to be friendly while secretly plotting to destroy their efforts. Her presence would surely hurt Mom's song more. What other reason could Tamiel have for sending her along? Even now it seemed that she stared daggers into his back. She probably didn't like getting exposed as a cheap hooker. But that issue wasn't important enough to worry about. The end of the world was coming. He had to drop everything else and figure out how to stop it.

He let out a silent sigh. But how? The apocalypse seemed like a freight train, impossible to stop. And what would happen after that? Who would go to Heaven? Mom, for sure. Darcy? No way. But what about a skeptical military student who never really thought about faith until a truckload of reality smacked him in the face? It seemed that he balanced on a fragile boundary between Heaven and Hell, not knowing which way he would fall.

13

He closed the drapes, sat on the bed opposite Darcy, and stared at her. She stared back, her cheeks red and her eyes expressing a blend of fear and sadness. Pitiful. Pathetic. Mom would probably say that even Darcy could change. Maybe so, but she had yet to prove that she wasn't playing a part in Tamiel's drama.

Matt averted his gaze. It was better to assume that she remained the soulless, evil sister she had been before. And her presence could even be a benefit. The most obvious way to Heaven was to do the opposite of what a Hell-bound prostitute would do. Maybe, just maybe, her darkness would be his guiding light.

2

CHAPTER

THE STORM

The First Door —The Frauds. Matt silently formed the words with his lips. The label on the phone's GPS map seemed like an omen, a warning to stay away from the mysterious address. After Enoch's dire words, everything seemed surreal, like they were living in a nightmare.

In the backseat, Mom lounged at an angle to give her backpack room while Darcy sat in the front passenger's seat. Unfortunately, the clothing Enoch had provided for him matched Darcy's, making them look like twins. Mom's shirt, though consisting of the same materials, fit more loosely to allow for fastening Velcro attachments in the back. Without those, she would never be able to get the shirt around her wings.

As meadows and farmlands whizzed by in a monotonous collage of grass and corn stubble, Matt checked the Mustang's rearview mirror. A midmorning haze, dim and reddish, cast the western horizon in a crimson fog, a stark contrast to the scene in their eastbound direction on this rural two-lane road. Clouds boiled into towering thunderheads underlaid with purple floors and infused with dark green. Lightning flashes highlighted the ominous colors as if providing snapshot warnings to turn away, but the GPS provided no options. Their destination lay about an hour ahead, that is, if the storm didn't slow their progress.

Matt pressed the gas pedal. The faster they could get past the storm, the better. Still, they would have to endure Tamiel's demonic voice a while longer. During yesterday's evening drive, he had told them to wait until the next day to listen to the rest of his message. Any departure from his orders would be met with severe punishment for his captive, Billy Bannister.

"I guess I'd better turn the recording on." Matt pressed the mobile phone's Play button. An app transmitted Tamiel's recorded message to the dashboard speakers.

16

"Good morning, Matt Bannister," Tamiel said, sounding like a spy explaining a secret mission. "As you have discerned by now, I have conducted a good deal of research into your background. Since you enjoy old TV shows and potboiler genre novels, you recognize that those you call villains often tell their captives why they're being tortured, though divulging such information unfailingly leads to the captors' doom. Although it is risky, I, too, will explain my purpose, but I do so in order to increase the torture and further corrupt Bonnie's song, thereby enhancing my strategy."

"He's such a grandstander." Matt looked at his mother in the mirror. "I wish I could—"

"Shhh!" Mom set a finger to her lips. "No response. Not yet."

"The person you call God," Tamiel continued, "is the most predictable being in the universe. If you press the right buttons, you will always get the expected result. We knew of this predictability when we incited him to flood the Earth. We simply led the human puppets into temptation, provided intoxicants to take away their inhibitions, and let them corrupt themselves. And God, being bound by his overly zealous character to punish evil-doers, destroyed them. If you are a well-equipped student of the Bible, you know that Balak used the same method to bring a curse upon the Israelites when he tempted them with harlotry and idol worship."

Matt glanced at the mirror again. Mom gave him a nod. Apparently she knew that story. Tamiel was telling the truth ... so far.

"Now that the song of the ovulum has been reduced to a warped whisper, only a tiny remnant remains loyal to God, and his hand is ready to strike." Tamiel added a chuckle. "When the process of destroying the song is complete, even the faithful remnant will perish at the hands of those who once called them brothers. Then the wrath will come, though not by a flood of water. The angel of the abyss already awaits, and I am confident that your cognizant companion can conclude what I mean. Even if not, I won't reveal the answer. I leave it to you to ponder ... and worry about. The more worry, the more warping of the song."

He added another laugh. "Humans will all be dead, the image of Elohim destroyed. Then I and my colleagues will rule this domain forever."

Matt rolled his eyes. Nearly every word had been extracted from one of many novels. He was playing the role of the overtalkative villain flawlessly, except that he knew exactly what he was doing—mocking, taunting, and eroding faith.

"Pay careful attention as I describe your mission," Tamiel continued. "First, you must get a metal box that is attached under the dashboard. Pause this recording until you find it, but, for your own protection, do not open it until I provide further instructions."

Matt touched the Pause button.

"I'll get it." Darcy reached under the radio, patting beneath the dashboard as her hands shifted toward the glove compartment. "Here it is."

As she pulled, something ripped, like sticky tape peeling away. She set a gray box the size of a small paperback book on her lap.

Matt tapped the phone's Play button.

"Now that you have the box," Tamiel said, "I should warn you that the object inside will shimmer brightly when first exposed to air. Do not look directly at it for at least five seconds. By that time, it will sufficiently dim and not cause damage to your eyes. Again, you should pause this recording until you are able to look at the object safely."

"He's really pushing the drama envelope." Matt pressed the Pause button. "Let's do it."

Darcy set her fingers around the lid. "Everyone ready?"

Matt stared at the highway. "Ready."

"I'm ready," Mom said. "I'll count to five."

A flash lit up the car. Mom counted, and with every second, the light dimmed. When she reached five, Matt looked at the box. A silver ring the size of a palm lay in a preformed impression in a bed of purple velvet. A bluish glow spread across Darcy's hands, making her skin appear cadaverous.

"Look." Mom lifted her necklace. The beads glowed as well, each one emitting its own color. "They tell me it glowed like this when the dragons were resurrected in the seventh circle. It created a regeneracy dome for them. We assumed the beads have some sort of life-giving energy for those with dragon genetics."

"Then the necklace and this ring must be related. Maybe the ring energizes the beads somehow." Matt set his finger over the Play button. "Ready to restart?"

Mom nodded.

"One irritating demon coming up." He tapped the screen.

"The object in the box is a key ring," Tamiel said. "At each of the first six locations, my agents have left a key that will attach to the ring. When you find the key, it will be dull, but when you take it away from its sphere of influence, it will flash and glow. Again, be careful to avoid eye contact with the keys for a few seconds. While the key is still glowing, attach it by prying the ring apart and sliding the key on in the usual way."

Darcy used a fingernail to separate the two parts of the ring. "It's tight, but it works just like other key rings."

"You are likely wondering," Tamiel continued, "why I am pursuing this tedious methodology. I will explain so that you will be fully engaged in this quest and motivated to finish it without delay. As a former angel, I once had protective authority over these keys, but when I fell from Elohim's good graces, the keys lost their power and became dull. The only way for them to regain what was lost is for you to retrieve them from spheres of influence that Elohim considers evil. I cannot energize them myself because Elohim also considers me to be an evil influence. Once you collect these keys, you will be able to unlock the seventh door and finish your quest. Then I will release Billy Bannister unharmed."

19

Matt glanced at Mom again. She wore the same skeptical expression that he likely wore himself. Every word Tamiel spoke could be a lie, but as long as he held Dad hostage, they didn't have much choice. They had to follow the instructions, at least for a while.

"Now back to the addresses," Tamiel said. "You might have noticed that the seventh address is password protected. When the time comes, I will let you know how to get there, which means, of course, you will not be able to send someone to see what awaits at the final destination. Because of this lengthy journey, be sure to charge the phone at your lodging stops. You will find a power adapter in the glove compartment."

Darcy popped open the compartment and fished out a black cord with a plug on the end. "Got it." She wound it up and pushed it into her pocket.

Tamiel's tone became dark and serious. "Do not fail in this quest. At each location you will be able to do something that you will consider good and noble or at least learn something that will further your quest, which should be enough to motivate you to participate without delay. Yet still I warn you. Do not underestimate the pain I can inflict on Billy Bannister. If you depart from this path, I will see to it that he suffers greatly."

The message ended. Matt grabbed the phone and squeezed it. "I wish this was his throat."

"Matt." Mom reached from the backseat and touched his arm. "You have to stay in control."

"I know. I know." He set the phone down and gripped the steering wheel with both hands. "I guess we just have to go along with him, unless you have a reason not to."

"Tamiel is crafty," Mom said. "He teased with information but not quite enough for us to figure everything out, like providing a crossword puzzle with half the clues missing. We know about keys, but what will opening the seventh door reveal? We know that we can do good at the six addresses, but what evils will we face? We need to focus on the fact that everything we're doing is designed to help Tamiel and no one else."

"So what do we do?" Matt asked. "We can't just refuse. He'll kill Dad."

"Right. So at each address, we'll do the good, get the key, and move on, but that doesn't mean we'll give him the key later. I'll do my best to keep the evils from hurting my song. In the meantime,

20

we'll work on other clues Tamiel gave us. Maybe we can fill out that crossword puzzle."

"Okay. I'm game. What clues did you hear?"

"For one, he talked about how the world would be destroyed, as if daring us to try to figure it out."

"Probably just a red herring," Matt said. "He's too smart to give away much information."

"Maybe." Mom grasped Matt's shoulder. "There is something that is more obvious, but it's something Enoch said, that I need to remember the seven trials. When we get to the first address, I'll know if my suspicions are true."

"What suspicions?"

"I don't want to speculate out loud right now." Her loving smile brightened up the rearview mirror. "Let's just say that I have spoken to Satan himself face to face, so I have some experience dealing with evil intelligence. If we have a similar experience at the first address, then I'll tell you more."

"So what do I do with this?" Darcy asked, lifting the box.

Matt angled his body to raise his hip. "Attach the ring to my belt loop. That'll make it easier to access."

Darcy picked up the ring and slid it onto the loop. It continued glowing but not nearly as brightly. When she drew her hands back, she rubbed the base of her right ring finger.

"Did the glow cause an itch?" Matt asked.

"I don't think so." She covered her right hand with her left. "It's nothing."

Lightning flashed ahead. The storm clouds spread out to each side, now only minutes away. The ride could soon get pretty rough.

"Back to Tamiel's mystery," Mom said. "Since he didn't reveal how destruction will come, it could be a weak spot in his plan. If

21

we could figure it out, it might give us a clue about how to stop him."

"Okay." Matt mentally replayed some of the recording. The demon's words seemed to burn an ugly cattle brand in his mind. "He said something about destruction coming not by a flood of water, and the angel of the abyss awaiting."

"Right, and the Bible indicates that a final destruction could come by fire." Mom touched Darcy's arm. "Please brainstorm with us. Three heads are better than two."

"Sure." Darcy put the box on the floorboard and brushed a stray lock from her face. "I'm ready."

Mom raised a finger. "First part. Not by a flood. Why did Tamiel bring us to this location? How could it be destroyed by fire?"

"Well, we're still in Nebraska, but we'll dip south into Kansas soon, not that there's that much difference." Matt scanned the flat-lands—brown grass and cornstalk stubs. "Nebraska is the Corn-husker State. Not many trees. A lot of cattle." He nodded at the windshield. "And it's windy with plenty of storms and tornadoes."

"Speaking of windy …" Darcy pointed out the window. "Nebraska has windmills. Lots of them."

Outside, huge white blades spun on at least fifty mills. "Wind turbines," Matt said. "They're probably generating power for the area."

Darcy nodded. "That was my guess, but I don't see any build-ings or even wires to transmit the electricity."

"Maybe they're underground." Matt glanced at Darcy out of the corner of his eye. She was trying to be helpful, even friendly. Suspicions about her treachery felt pretty stupid, but he couldn't let his guard down. Not yet.

Mom leaned forward. "Matt, you said military thugs brought us here. What military interest is there in Nebraska? There aren't any borders to patrol, no seaports to maintain. Are there any potential targets to protect?"

A dust devil swirled in a field to the left, lifting grass into a twisting vortex, like a spinning column rising from the ground. The shape raised a similar mental image, another kind of column hidden from all nonmilitary eyes.

"Silos." A gust pushed the Mustang to the right, making the tires vibrate on the shoulder's rumble strip. Matt jerked the car back to the lane and kept a firm grip on the steering wheel. "Nebraska has quite a few silos."

Mom blinked. "Why would the military want to protect grain storage?"

"Not grain silos." Matt eased up on the accelerator. The speedometer digits now read 53. "I'm talking about underground missile silos. Nuclear weapons."

"Nuclear?" Darcy shuddered. "Now that's a real apocalypse."

Mom whispered, "Not by water but by fire. That fits perfectly."

Matt shook his head. "That's too easy. I've read at least five novels about nuclear war destroying the world, and since Tamiel talked about my reading habits, he was probably trying to lead us in that direction. And he knows about my military training. Missile silos are an obvious guess. It might be a wild-goose chase."

"That's true. But we shouldn't count it out just because it's obvious."

"Can't argue with that." Matt let out a sigh. "We'll keep it in mind."

"Okay," Mom said, "let's see where that idea takes us. How could Tamiel use us to incite a nuclear war?"

Darcy turned the phone her way and looked at the map. "Could one of the places we're going be a military base?"

"No clue." Matt shrugged. "The academy didn't teach where every base is located. I suppose some locations are top secret."

Mom settled against the back of her seat. "We need Larry or Lois. They could look up those addresses and give us the lowdown in a heartbeat."

Matt turned the phone back toward himself. "Thirteen miles to the next town. We can try to call them once we get there. Maybe we can borrow someone's phone."

"I suppose it won't hurt to stop at a restaurant," Mom said. "Tamiel knows we have to eat."

Matt jerked his thumb over his shoulder. "We have food in the back. It stayed cool in the trunk overnight."

"But we'll need a restroom."

"True." A few big raindrops pelted the windshield, promising many more. As windmills and harvested cornfields flew by, Matt imagined a stop at a gas station. To keep Tamiel from getting suspicious, any stop would have to be quick, but it might take a long time to convince someone to let him borrow a phone, especially with the storm likely pummeling the town. And with most communications now incapacitated, maybe cell phones around here no longer worked.

Not far down the road, an oncoming car pulled out into their lane, trying to pass a slow-moving truck. In seconds, they would collide with it head-on.

Matt swerved to the right. Their Mustang skidded onto the shoulder and grass, bouncing over the rough surfaces. When the oncoming car zoomed by, its horn blared. The driver stuck his arm out the window and displayed an obscene hand gesture.

As rain increased, Matt stopped the car at the side of the road, two wheels on the shoulder and two in the grass. He swiveled his head and checked his passengers. "You guys all right?"

"I'm fine." Mom gave him a weak smile. "Just a bit jostled."

Darcy blurted out, "That fool! It was his fault, not ours!"

Matt gave her a searching look. Was this all still an act? "Yeah. Pretty strange." He turned on the wipers and pulled their car back to the road. As he accelerated on the damp pavement, he looked at his mother in the mirror again. "I was thinking we could call Dad's parents' house to get some computer help, but he said some government geeks are monitoring all of Larry's communications, so we'll have to be careful."

"And clever." Mom leaned forward and clasped one hand with Matt's and her other with Darcy's. "So we'll pray for wisdom."

"Um … okay …" Darcy shifted nervously in her seat. "Praying is good."

As Matt stared at the road, prickles ran along his skin. "Sure. Go ahead and pray."

Mom grasped his hand more tightly. "Kind and loving Father…" She spoke in a normal tone as if addressing someone sitting in the car. "No matter where I have walked, whether on Earth, Heaven, or Hades, you have always been with me, so I have no doubt that you are with us now. The demon Tamiel is more powerful and crafty than we are, and without your help and guidance, we won't be able to defeat him. My song is fading, which means we are sure to be confronted by all manner of corruption as Earth dwellers flock to his side. This world is not our true home, so we will be viewed as aliens, because we will shine a light that will expose the deeds of darkness. And those in darkness will lash out to douse the light of truth.

"Of course we will do all we can to rescue those held captive by chains, and we ask you to step in and do what we cannot. We can change circumstances, but we cannot change people's hearts. We can shatter physical bonds, but we cannot make a dent in shackles of the spirit. We can give our lives in sacrifice, but we cannot give saving grace to those who plead for salvation. We three, therefore, confess our need for your assistance, because without you we are nothing, but with your help, we believe we can do anything."

She breathed a heavy sigh. "Dearest Father, I often sing part of Psalm one thirty-nine, but I rarely include the final two verses. As I do so now, I pray that each one of us will ponder the words until they are true in our hearts, so vibrantly real that we would reach out to you with pleading hands and beg you to heed our plaintive call." Her voice cracked with emotion. "Search me, O God, and know my heart. Try me, and know my thoughts, and see if there be any wicked way in me, and lead me in the way everlasting."

As tears flowed, Mom compressed Matt's hand. He returned the grasp. Darcy whispered, "Amen, Jesus. Take away my wicked heart. Lead me to everlasting life."

Matt resisted the urge to roll his eyes. Darcy had played the pity game so many times, and now she was trying to spear Mom with a sympathy harpoon. Obviously Mom's prayer was good and righteous, but a change of heart in Darcy would take more than a miracle.

"Well," Matt said as he released his mother's hand and reached for the radio. "Let's see if we can find something better than Tamiel's voice to listen to."

"A gospel station?" Darcy asked.

"Yeah … sure." Matt pulled back his hand. "If you can find one."

While Darcy fiddled with the radio buttons, Matt looked again at the mirror. His mother arched her brow and tilted her head. She seemed to be trying to transmit a silent question.

Matt gave her a mechanical smile. What else could he do? If he had grown up with her instead of meeting her only a short time ago, maybe he could have figured out her nonverbal cues. For now he would have to wait for some alone time with her. Maybe then he could warn her about Darcy's manipulative ways. Her eagerness to spout an *Amen* and her quickness to search for a gospel station would probably fool most people who hoped for a sinner's conversion. Mom needed to recognize Darcy's wiles. She had proven so many times that she couldn't be trusted—not then, not now. Too many lives were at stake.

Lightning crashed a hundred feet to the right and split a lone tree in a pasture. Thunder boomed and shook the car's frame. Rain poured. Pea-sized hail pelted the windshield. Gusts lashed the side door, making the tires slide.

Matt refastened his grip on the wheel and slowed to thirty-five. A billboard uprooted and flew onto the highway. The sign slammed against the road in front of the Mustang and flipped over the roof and onto the pavement to the rear.

27

For a moment, the noise settled. Music emanated from the speakers. A woman crooned with a gentle country twang, something about being in Heaven and singing to God—pretty and sweet, but not very practical, especially for people battling demonic forces on Earth.

Matt relaxed his muscles. Being so uptight wasn't helping. It couldn't hurt to listen while tuning out the words … and Darcy's presence … and try to unwind in spite of the chaos outside.

Darcy hummed along, her stare fixed on the raging storm, while Mom set an elbow on the back of the driver's seat as she gazed outside without a hint of fear. Her wings shifted in her backpack as if begging to stretch out and fly a recon mission.

Trying to balance between a safe speed and hurrying to get out of the storm, Matt accelerated to forty and crossed the Kansas border. A series of green signs reported the distance to the next town—eight miles ... five ... three. With lightning flashing, thunder booming, and rain blowing across the prairie in wind-driven sheets, every mile felt like a victory. At least no more cars came by. The storm must have chased everyone else off the road.

A blue light flashed in the distance. Matt slowed the car to a crawl, barely able to see through the driving rain. As he neared the light, a police cruiser came into view, blocking the road several yards in front of a downed power pole. Sparks flew near a transformer, and severed lines lay across the lanes. Beyond them, windswept rain drenched an electronics store, a McDonald's restaurant, a bank, and an ice-cream shop, all darkened.

Matt stopped the car within a stone's throw of the police cruiser and shifted to park. Now visible through the curtain of rain, several people ran back and forth between the electronics store and cars waiting at the curb. All carried boxes of various sizes as they ducked low and stashed their loads into the cars.

Matt tightened his grip on the steering wheel. "They're looting the stores."

"Yep." Darcy narrowed her eyes. "Someone paid off the cops, I'll bet."

"Or they don't want to be bothered." Matt peered past the beating windshield wipers at two officers in the cruiser's front seat as they sipped coffee and munched on pastries. "They might get rain on their doughnuts."

"Corruption is probably almost universal now." Mom leaned forward between Matt and Darcy. "People are taking what they want without remorse. Every guard on their moral foundations has fallen to the wayside."

"Now that you're here," Matt said, "maybe your song will affect them."

Mom shook her head. "Corruption deadens the ears and darkens the mind. It would take more than a song to do them any good now. I need to reach those who haven't already given in."

"Well, we can't just sit here and watch them." Matt opened the door. The rain had lessened to a gusty shower, still enough to get wet. "I'll be right back."

Keeping his head low, he hurried to the cruiser and signaled for the driver to roll down his window. When the glass lowered a few inches, Matt called, "Got a phone I can use?"

The driver shook his head. "Tower's down. Unless you've got a satellite phone, you're out of luck."

Matt glanced at the cruiser's rear seat. Several unopened boxes lay stacked there—laptop computers, widescreen monitors, and portable music devices. No wonder they weren't arresting the looters. "Is there any way I can get past the downed lines?"

"Sure." The officer pointed at an abandoned storefront. "Drive behind that building, and you can access the electronic store's parking lot. Go out the exit on the far side, and you can get back to this road past the lines."

"Thanks." Matt ran to the Mustang, hopped in, and shifted to reverse. "The cops got their own loot."

"Then we can't count on any help." Mom let out a sigh. "We're on our own."

Matt backed the car and turned onto the access road. After making his way to the parking lot, he dodged the scrambling looters. A few shouted curses. One pair dropped their boxes and threw fists at each other, though only briefly before scrambling to gather their ill-gotten gains from the wet sidewalk.

The illustration seemed all too appropriate. The Mustang felt like an ark in the midst of a swelling sea of destruction, surrounded by corrupted souls getting soaked by rain, except these people had no idea that they were drowning.

When they pulled back onto the street, Matt eased the car around a fallen tree. A bird's nest lay on the pavement along with a dead squirrel. Houses lined both sides of the road, some with missing roof shingles, others with flooded yards. Although the storm had wreaked havoc, now only a few wind-driven droplets pattered on the collection of fallen branches and puddle-strewn lawns. The worst appeared to be over.

"I'm not sure we'll find anything open to the public," he said. "If you need a restroom, we might have to knock on one of these doors."

"Or find a private tree." Darcy gazed out the window on her side. "People are scared. They might not be answering their doors."

"Good point. They might answer with the barrel of a gun."

Mom tapped his arm. "We can't get word out to anyone who can help us, but maybe someone else can."

"Like who?"

"Like anyone who has an Internet connection." She began pulling down a backpack strap. "Lower the top, and I'll fly around a bit. Let's see if we can get some cyber chatter going."

FOLLOWING BILLY BANNISTER

Lauren sat in one of *Merlin's* aisle seats as the aging Cessna flew in the midst of darkening skies. With an IV tube still attached at the crook of her arm and an IV pole at the tube's other end, moving around to view the storm clouds wasn't easy.

Not that she wanted to move much. A pounding head, burning nasal passages, and aching bones squelched any desire to lift more than a pinky, though cool air sometimes prompted a longing to put on her denim jacket. It lay draped over the back of the window seat, so close, yet so far.

She shifted her eyes toward the cockpit. In the two pilot's seats, Walter and Gabriel chatted and cracked jokes. They had taken turns flying the plane through the night and into the morning hours, tracking the chip in her dad's scalp as he rode captive in a helicopter to an unknown destination.

The chopper had landed a few times, only to take off again and follow another course as if trying to elude someone. *Merlin* had to refuel during a couple of stops, but it hadn't taken long to pick up the trail again.

Without moving her body, Lauren glanced at Ashley across the aisle. The super-intelligent healer bobbed her head, probably asleep. Good. She needed to rest. She had stayed up most of the night taking care of her volcano-victim patient.

Lauren couldn't help but smile. Ashley had tossed thoughts her way to ask how she was feeling, apparently not considering that such silent calls disturbed sleep just as surely as spoken words did. Still, since she couldn't hear thoughts unless an emotional surge switched on the tingling in her back scales, she had been able to sleep for a few hours.

Soon, however, she would have to force herself to perk her ears and listen for her mother's song, the song of the ovulum that only a Listener like herself could detect. Tamiel had kidnapped Mom, and no one else could track her down.

Lauren caressed the rubellite mounted in her ring—the scarlet symbol of the dragon blood coursing through her veins. All of her trials and troubles had risen because of her heritage. Yet, it made no sense to blame anyone. She was what she was, an anthrozil who only recently learned that her parents were Billy and Bonnie Bannister—offspring of former dragons.

The propeller's hum brought a relaxing sensation, though it could do nothing to quell the pain in her heart. She lifted the medallion dangling at her chest and read the engraved words— *My gift to you. My life. It is all I have to give.*

Eagle's sacrificial leap into the volcano flashed to mind, his body falling ... falling. When once again he splashed into the lava, she clenched her eyes shut. How many times would that memory

produce echoing images? How long might she lament the courageous young man who had given his life for hers?

The airplane bounced hard. Lauren opened her eyes and
gripped an armrest. The scales on her back tingled, sharpening her
hearing, but the propeller's drone washed out any hope of detect-
ing her mother's song.

Ashley grabbed her own armrest. "What's up, Walter?"

"Just turbulence." Walter twisted in his seat, a couple of feet
out of arm's reach of the front passenger row. "Check your belts.
Big storm ahead."

Gabriel jerked his seat belt strap, his wings folded tightly at his
back. "Those clouds look like doomsday. It's bound to get even
rougher."

Ashley leaned into the aisle and looked out the front windshield. "Let's hope the clouds don't interrupt Billy's signal."

"No worries." Walter touched a screen on a palm-sized gadget
attached to the front dashboard. "Looks like they turned parallel
to the storm. Probably too dangerous to fly a chopper through it."
His rolled-up sleeve revealed a toned forearm with a red scratch
from elbow to wrist and a burn the size of a quarter, wounds
earned when he climbed down a rope from a hovering airplane
and scooped a half-cooked Listener from the top of a pile of logs
that would have soon become her execution pyre.

"I'd better unhook Lauren." As more rough bounces rocked
the plane, Ashley unbuckled her belt and crouched in the aisle.
Wearing denim jeans and jacket that matched Lauren's, she
touched a bandage in the crook of Lauren's arm. "I don't want the
support pole to jerk the IV out."

Walter looked back at Ashley. "I'm turning with the chopper.
I hope they'll assume we're dodging the storm instead of tailing
them."

"I doubt it." Ashley withdrew a foil pouch from her jacket and tore it open, her hands adjusting with each bounce. "They're probably as wary as cats at a rocking-chair exhibit."

Walter laughed. "That sounds like one of my lines."

"It is. I'm borrowing it." Ashley tore away the bandage, pressed a sterile pad against Lauren's skin, and pulled out the IV tube.

Lauren winced, though the sting was minor compared to her other aches. "Can we fly over the edge of the storm and then turn? Kind of disappear for a while? That might put them at ease."

Walter touched a radar screen. "The thunderheads shoot higher than this bird will go, so I can't avoid them. *Merlin* took some hits to the outer skin yesterday and lost its static wick. I haven't had time to repair it, so we're vulnerable to lightning. One strike could easily take us down, so we'll just turn and follow the chopper from a safe distance."

"Let's not get fried." Ashley touched the ends of stitches at a wound in Lauren's forehead. "These look tight."

Lauren wrinkled her brow. "Yep. I can feel them. You did a good job, Doc."

"Just flying by the seat of my pants." Ashley carried the IV pole and bag toward the back. With each step, she set a hand on a seat to keep from falling. "I'll be right back."

Lauren tried to sit straighter, but pain forced her to stay put. She tuned her ears to the surrounding noises—still no hint of her mother's song came through. "Any word from Lois about Matt or my mother?"

"Nothing." Walter turned a dial on a dashboard instrument. "I'll check again."

"And see if Roxil's on her way," Ashley added as she staggered back up the aisle.

34

"Got it." Walter adjusted a microphone on his headset. "Carly, are you and Lois still patched in? ... Good."

Lauren strained her ears. Her enhanced hearing picked up a garbled voice leaking from the headset, but the background noise and the constant bouncing shook the words apart.

"We're close to a storm," Walter said, "so this will be quick. ... What's that? ... Okay, that's not cool. But good to know. What else? ... Uh-huh. ... Uh-huh. ... Now that's good news. Shoot me the coordinates." He picked up a handheld computer from the console and looked at the screen. "Got 'em, but we'd have to fly through the storm to get there. ... Right. So we'll split up. ... Where's Roxil? ... Good. She must've recovered quickly. Keep watching for Bonnie sightings and feed us the info."

Lauren leaned closer, but pain again forced her back. "Carly's heard from my mother?"

Walter raised a finger. "Right. We'll do that. Back at you soon." He slid off the headset and turned toward the cabin. "Here's the scoop. Lois spotted a few Internet posts about sightings of a winged woman flying over a Mustang heading east on a rural road not too far from here."

"She's doing it to attract attention." Lauren smiled, but even that hurt. *Way to go, Mom!*

"And Roxil's on her way," Walter continued. "Lois is guiding her to a rendezvous with us. Then we'll have to decide who chases Billy's chopper and who hunts down Bonnie and Matt. Lois says this storm has spun a few tornadoes, so it's too dangerous to fly through it."

"Maybe not for Roxil," Ashley said. "She's more versatile than an airplane."

"Exactly what I was thinking. Probably less prone to lightning strikes, too."

35

Gabriel poked Walter with the tip of a wing. "What about me? I've flown through a storm or three."

"With Ashley on your back?" Walter pushed the wing away. "Besides, I need you as a backup pilot."

"So," Ashley said, "Gabriel and you can follow Billy while Roxil takes me to hunt for the Mustang."

Lauren raised a hand. That didn't hurt … so much. "And me."

Ashley shook her head hard. "Not in your condition. You nearly got boiled in lava soup, and you can barely move, much less walk."

"I'll force myself. Give me a painkiller or something. No one else can listen for my mother's song."

Walter turned toward the front. "I'll let you two sort that out." He pointed at his jaw. "In the meantime, turn on your tooth transmitters. You can listen for Roxil. Elam has mine, or I'd do it myself."

"Have you heard anything from Elam?" Ashley asked.

"Not a word, but I wasn't expecting to. He doesn't want to take a chance that anyone can track him. I don't think we'll get an update until he's out of Fort Knox with Sapphira in his arms."

"You're probably right. He'll do anything to keep her safe." Ashley looked at Lauren. Thoughts streamed from her mind. *Will you let us keep you safe?*

Lauren forced a hand to her jaw and gave it a tap to turn on the transmitter. *If your mother were in danger, would a few burns and bruises stop you from trying to rescue her?*

Ashley firmed her lips. *Plus severe dehydration, possible scorched nasal cavities, and maybe a few cracked bones. We haven't X-rayed anything yet. You could fall to pieces in a gust of wind. Besides, Roxil will fly better with just one on her back. Two might be too heavy. I healed you the best I can, but without light energy from Excalibur, I can't penetrate your body to do more.*

Lauren broke away from Ashley's stare and looked out the front windshield. The dark clouds drew closer and closer as if annoyed at their attempt to avoid them. Lightning flashed—two bolts, then a third. Thunder rumbled, and *Merlin* bucked even harder.

Clutching her armrest more tightly, she tried to put on a conciliatory expression and turned back to Ashley. *So what am I supposed to do? I can't just sit here and twiddle my thumbs.*

You can call for Roxil and relay what she says to Walter while I talk to Lois about weather warnings. You and I are the only ones with working transmitters.

I suppose so, but even a trained parrot could do that. Lightning flashed closer, inciting a new round of tingles in Lauren's back scales.

Ashley pointed at Lauren's jaw. *Call Roxil. We can settle who goes with her later.*

Lauren heaved a silent sigh. Ashley was right about the physical trauma, but even her mind reading wouldn't be able to hear Mom's song.

"Roxil," Lauren said. "This is Lauren Bannister. Can you hear me?"

"I am able to hear you." Roxil's deep rumble sounded like distant thunder through the tooth transmitter. "I think I see your airplane. You must have been flying rather slowly to allow me to close the gap."

Lauren relayed the message to Walter.

"Kind of going in circles sometimes," Walter said. "The helicopter's been darting around like a dragonfly, if you'll pardon the expression."

Lauren repeated Walter's reply.

Roxil laughed. "Pardon granted."

"Listen," Lauren said, "we might need you to fly a passenger or two through a thunderstorm. Are you up for it?"

37

"Perhaps. Who are the passengers?"

"We're still working on who will go. Probably Ashley, and maybe me."

"I can carry both of you, depending on distance and rest stops, of course."

Walter gripped the steering yoke with both hands. *Merlin* pitched to one side, then dropped suddenly before catching the air again. "Tell Roxil it's getting really rough, so I'm going to land in a field. She should keep us in her sights and meet us there."

Again Lauren relayed Walter's message.

"The unsteady air is troubling me as well," Roxil said. "I will join you on the ground in a few moments."

Walter turned toward the cabin. "Get ready. It'll be rougher than riding on a drunk dragon, so pray for a safe landing."

"Will do." Ashley scooted in front of Lauren, lifted her jacket from the window seat, and sat down. "Aren't you cold?"

"A little." The thought brought a shiver and a smile. "Well, maybe a little more than a little."

"Here." Ashley helped Lauren put the jacket on. Although every move hurt, the warm material was worth it.

After buckling, Ashley hooked arms with Lauren and intertwined their fingers. *I assume you don't mind. I like close contact when I'm praying.*

Not at all. Lauren leaned her head against Ashley's. *You first?*

Sure. Ashley spoke loudly enough for Walter and Gabriel to hear. "Father in Heaven—" The plane dropped again, making them both gulp. After taking a deep breath, she continued. "We pray for safety in landing; for Lauren's healing; for success in our efforts to rescue Billy, Bonnie, and Matt—"

Blinding light flashed. An earsplitting crack ripped through the air. Sizzling energy shot around the cabin and knifed into Lauren

38

and Ashley. Their hands locked together. Lauren's teeth clenched; her skin burned; her bones felt like they were on fire.

The cabin darkened. Lauren's pain eased. In the cockpit, Walter slumped over the controls. As *Merlin* angled into a dive, Gabriel shouted, "Ashley! Lightning struck the plane! Walter's out cold. Autopilot's fried!" He grabbed Walter's shirt, pulled him back from the dashboard, and clutched the copilot's yoke. "Tell me what to do! I can fly this bird, but I can't land it!"

Ashley sagged to the side and leaned against the window.

"Ashley!" Lauren pried her fingers loose and shook Ashley's shoulder. "Can you hear me?"

A weak thought drifted into Lauren's mind. *I ... I can't ... wake up. ... Help Walter ... Gabriel.*

But I can't land it either!

Tell me ... what you see. ... I'll help.

Lauren unbuckled her belt and threw it to the side. She stepped up to the cockpit and grasped the two seats, balancing against the rocking plane. Breathless, she looked at Gabriel. "I'm mind speaking with Ashley. Tell me what's going on."

39

Gabriel touched a screen on the dashboard. His finger bounced as he spoke in gasps. "Altimeter's out. ... GPS is toast. ... Engine's running ... and so are hydraulics ... so we can steer. But that's it. ... I don't know ... about the landing gear." He swallowed hard and steadied his voice. "I managed to level off, but there's no telling if we might get zapped again. We need to land."

"We need our pilot." Lauren grabbed Walter's wrist. His pulse thrummed, fast and erratic. "He's alive, Ashley! Can you hear me?"

Lauren listened for thoughts, but none came through. "I can't hear Ashley anymore."

"Take my seat." Gabriel squeezed past Lauren and sat next to Ashley. His wings shuddered in a tight bundle.

Lauren slid into the copilot's seat and buckled. "What do I do?"

"Just hold the yoke—the steering column—and try to keep us steady."

Lauren grasped the yoke with both hands. "Got it."

Gabriel patted Ashley's cheek. "C'mon, Sis! Wake up!"

She mumbled something unintelligible.

A gust shoved *Merlin* down and to the side, jerking Lauren and pushing her body against the yoke. The plane dipped into a steep angle. Lauren pulled back on the yoke, but nothing happened. "I can't get it to come up!"

"Hydraulics are probably gone!" Gabriel scooped up Ashley. "Grab Walter. We're going to jump!"

"Jump?" Lauren snapped off her belt, then Walter's. "How?"

"You'll hold Walter. I'll hang on to Ashley and you." He hustled toward the door at the back of the cabin. "Get Billy's tracker and let's go!"

40

Lauren snatched the tracking device from the dashboard and stuffed it into her pocket. After sucking in a breath, she wrapped her arms around Walter's waist and heaved him into the aisle. Dragging him, she battled the incline until she reached the rear door and laid him on his back. "How can you hold us and fly at the same time?"

"Not fly. A controlled drop." Gabriel set Ashley down and opened the hatch. Wind swirled everywhere, batting their clothes and hair. He shouted, "It's either that or crash with *Merlin*." He grabbed a duffle bag from the floor and threw it out. It vanished as if swallowed by the air. "Walter's weapons stash. We might need it."

Lauren looked through the hatch. With no lip on the floor, anyone could fall right out. Below, the ground shot toward them. They had only seconds to live.

Gabriel slid an arm around Ashley's chest and held her aloft. "Hold on to Walter however you can, and I'll grab you."

Lauren jerked Walter to a sitting position, dropped to her bottom behind him, and wrapped her arms and legs around his torso. "Ready."

"Hold as still as you can." He bent his knees and pushed an arm around her chest. "Here we go!" With a leg thrust, he pushed himself and his load out the door.

They plunged. Clutching Ashley and Lauren, Gabriel beat his wings madly. Their descent slowed, but not enough. At this speed, they would all suffer broken bones, or worse.

Lauren relocked her arms around Walter. Fortunately the rapid descent made him feel lighter. Maybe at the last second she could lean back and be a cushion for him. At least someone might survive.

Gabriel let out a wail. His arm tightened around Lauren's chest and squeezed out her breath. The ground rocketed toward them. Five seconds to live. Three. One.

The ground shot away again. Gabriel screamed. Walter's body broke free from Lauren's leg lock. He slid down until she held only to his wrists with her sweat-slickened hands. The four jumpers floated nearly parallel to the ground, about ten feet above a cornfield.

Walter slipped away. Lauren cried out, "I lost him!"

They suddenly swooped low and tumbled on the ground, bowling over cornstalks. Lauren, Gabriel, and Ashley rolled until their momentum eased.

Lauren lay with her face in the dirt, her head dizzied. An explosion rocked the ground in concert with a loud boom. Fire crackled somewhere far away.

41

After a few seconds, she shook off the mind fog and climbed to her feet. Gabriel and Ashley lay sprawled over broken cornstalks, their bodies and arms intertwined and Gabriel's wings splayed. To the left, black smoke shot into the sky—*Merlin*.

But where was Walter?

Lauren searched the swath of broken stalks—no sign of him. The intact corn, although brown and withered, stood as a barrier, preventing a view of anything but the darkening sky.

Thunder rumbled once more. A breeze whipped across the tops of the stalks, making them bend and shake.

Lauren dropped to her knees and laid a hand on Gabriel's cheek, warm and moist. He breathed steadily. She shifted her hand to Ashley's cheek, then snapped it back. Hot! Worse than any fever. Yet she breathed easily. No sign of convulsions.

A loud rustle erupted in the cornstalks, growing louder and louder. After a few seconds, a dragon shuffled into view with Walter dangling from its teeth by his shirt.

Lauren swallowed. "Roxil?"

The she-dragon bobbed her head and gently laid Walter on a carpet of fallen stalks. "I watched where he fell and retrieved him. He is alive and appears to be relatively intact. I detected no severe trauma." She extended her neck and looked Lauren over. "I was able to release Gabriel at a low altitude, so I hope your spill did not cause too much injury."

"I'm okay." Lauren touched a rip in her jacket at the elbow. Something stung underneath. "Just some scrapes, I think." She gave Roxil a smile and a head bow. "Thank you for rescuing us."

"It was my pleasure. I regret that I could not arrive earlier to ease your landing even more."

"Oh, my head!" Gabriel sat up and massaged his scalp. "I'm never going to jump out of a plane while carrying three people again."

Lauren swung toward him. "Any other pain?"

"A few bruises." He blinked at Ashley as if seeing her for the first time. "Sis!" He leaned over and laid a palm on her forehead. "Wow! She's as hot as fire."

"I know," Lauren said. "How could fever spike so fast?"

"This has happened before. She gets hot when she ..." He stared at Lauren.

Lauren blinked at him. "Why are you looking at me like that?"

"You could barely move, but you hauled Walter out of the pilot's seat and hung on to him nearly all the way down."

"Adrenaline?" Lauren shrugged. "I didn't think about it."

"How are you feeling now?"

"Okay. Just a little banged up."

Thunder boomed, closer this time. The wind strengthened and batted everyone's hair into a frenzy.

Gabriel pushed Ashley's hair from her face. "She gets this hot when she's healed someone." He looked at Lauren again. "Was she touching you when that lightning struck?"

Lauren let her mind drift to the moment the flash of light shot through the cabin. "Yes, we were holding hands. Ashley had just prayed for ..," She whispered the rest. "My healing."

"She probably had the presence of mind to look at you. Beams from her eyes do the internal healing." Gabriel glanced from side to side. "We need water. Gotta cool her down."

Roxil stretched her neck high. "I will see if I can find some." In a flurry of wings, she took off.

Still on her knees, Lauren shuffled to Walter and grasped his wrist. Again his pulse throbbed—fast and jumpy. "His heart is beating in a weird way."

"He took quite a jolt." Gabriel flapped his wings and glided to Walter's other side. "The electrical current might have messed up the rhythm."

43

"That sounds dangerous."

"Potentially." He beat his wings again, rose above the corn-stalks, and looked around, as he hovered erratically in the wind. "No sign of the chopper."

"Right. I almost forgot." Lauren pulled the tracking device from her pocket and studied the screen. A stationary red dot flashed on a map. "The signal isn't moving. I guess they landed."

"Most likely. That storm's expanding too quickly. We couldn't get away from it." Gabriel rose higher. "I'm heading to *Merlin* to see if I can salvage the first-aid kit."

"Watch out for lightning!"

He winked. "I'll dodge the bolts."

When Gabriel disappeared beyond the stalks, Lauren muttered, "Watch out for lightning." She let out a huff. *My brain must have gotten scrambled.*

She sat close to Walter and held his hand. It felt cool and clammy. His face, partially covered by beard stubble, looked serene, noble, brave. "You risked your life to rescue me from the lava field, but I can't think of anything to do for you."

As her scales tingled, a voice entered her mind. *Nonsense, Lauren, you already risked your life by carrying him to safety.*

Lauren swung her head toward Ashley. She still lay on the ground, but now her eyes blinked. "Can you talk?" Lauren asked.

Ashley whispered, "Well ... a little, but it hurts."

Then stick with mind speaking.

Okay. Help me get close to my husband.

While sporadic raindrops tapped the fallen stalks, Lauren lifted Ashley to all fours and guided her toward Walter. Ashley's arms trembled, as if ready to buckle. When she reached him, she laid her head on his chest. *His heart is irregular, but it's not ventricular fibrillation. More like a bunch of premature contractions.*

44

Is it dangerous?

Not yet. Ashley rolled to her back and closed her eyes. *But I'm not so sure about myself.* She licked her dry lips and spoke out loud. "Ringing ears … febrile hallucinations … extreme vertigo." Her arms locked at the elbows, and her fists clenched. Her body jittered for a few seconds, then she fell limp, and her head lolled to the side.

"Ashley!" Lauren looked to the sky and shouted, "Roxil! Where's that water?" She cupped her hands, caught a few raindrops, and splashed them over Ashley's face, then repeated the process again and again and moistened Ashley's chest and arms as well.

Wind whipped the cornstalks. Lightning flashed once more. Thunder cracked. Rain burst from the sky and swept across the field in cold, horizontal sheets.

Lauren pulled Ashley's sweatshirt off and unbuttoned the top of her shirt to let the cool water penetrate. Then she settled on her knees and looked upward again, blinking at the driving rain. "Roxil!" she shouted. "Gabriel! Where are you?"

"Coming!" Roxil swooped low, carrying a wooden trough just above the bending stalks. A gust threw her down. The trough crashed and spilled a torrent of icy water across the human trio. Lauren gasped. Ashley sat up, coughing and spluttering. Walter groaned but stayed on his back.

Roxil belly-landed and slid a dozen feet, smashing cornstalks along the way. When she stopped, Gabriel flew into sight with a white box in his hands. He settled in a trot and dropped to his knees next to Ashley. "How is everyone?"

"Wet." Ashley peeled plastered hair away from her cheek. "But better."

"And Walter?"

45

Ashley pressed a hand over Walter's chest. After a few seconds, she nodded. "Rhythm is not quite normal, but closer." She took a deep cleansing breath. "And I'm picking up some coherent thoughts. I think he'll be all right."

"Good." While rain continued to pour, Gabriel set the first-aid box on the muddy ground and opened it. He spread his wings and shielded the contents as he withdrew a thermometer and a bottle of Tylenol. He pushed the thermometer into Ashley's mouth and opened the bottle. "Let's send Lauren and Roxil on their way."

Roxil lumbered toward them, her clawed feet splashing. "I am ready."

"Now?" Lauren asked.

Gabriel nodded. "Now. There's no time to lose."

"Lois has been giving me updates," Roxil said. "Reports of sightings of Bonnie and Matt are diminishing. They are likely in an isolated area now, so the longer we wait, the harder it will be to find them."

Lauren touched her jaw. "I didn't hear anything. Maybe the lightning bolt jolted my transmitter."

"Could be," Gabriel said. "They're pretty tough. It might have just shut itself off."

Ashley wrinkled her nose. "I think mine is cooked." She reached into her mouth, pried the wafer from her molars, and pulled it out. Squinting at it, she said, "Yep. It's a goner."

Lauren gave her jaw a tap. Sound returned, though static buzzed in the background. "I got mine to work, but it's kind of shaky." She looked toward the crash site. Smoke still billowed into the storm clouds. "How can you manage without *Merlin*?"

"I'll manage." He pulled the thermometer from Ashley's mouth and pushed three Tylenol tablets into her hand. "Take

46

these, Sis." He then squinted at the thermometer. "One hundred and six."

"A hundred and six!" Lauren's own cheeks heated up. "She needs to get to a hospital!"

Ashley swallowed the tablets. "Actually, that's not too bad. It was probably a couple of degrees higher than that before Roxil doused me."

"You still need to get treated. Roxil can fly you to—"

"No!" Gabriel rose, grabbed Lauren's arm, and lifted her to her feet. "Listen. Ashley, Walter, and I have been through a hundred fixes a lot worse than this. You're the only one who can hear Bonnie's song, and Roxil's the only ride you have." He smiled and pushed Lauren's hair back with a gentle hand. "Your mother and your brother need you. Trust me to take care of Walter and Ashley. I've been something of a guardian angel for a very long time."

47

Lauren stared at him through the driving rain. His words knifed deeply. She couldn't worry about everyone. She had to do her part and leave the rest to others.

"You're right." She handed Gabriel the tracking device and spun toward Roxil. "Let's go!"

Roxil lowered her head to the ground. "Climb onto my back and hang on. This will be the roughest ride of your life."

Rainwater dripping from her hair, Lauren hurried up Roxil's neck staircase and sat between two protruding spines on her back. The moment she settled, Roxil took off. As they rose, Lauren looked toward the ground. With every downbeat of Roxil's wings, Gabriel, Ashley, and Walter came into view, though sheets of water and bending cornstalks quickly drew a curtain across their forms.

Wet wind beat against Lauren's body and sent Roxil lurching to the side. With each gust, Lauren clutched the spine more tightly. Ahead, darker clouds loomed like a black awning undergirded by a purple wall.

A lightning bolt streaked from cloud to ground followed by a rifle-shot thunderclap. Lauren ducked her head. When the rumble subsided, she stayed low and stared at the monstrous cloudbank. If Mom and Matt traveled on the other side, why would God allow such a violent storm to block her from reaching them? Why would he allow lightning to disable *Merlin*, injure Walter and Ashley, and force them to go on foot? Why did evil seem to be in control?

She sighed and wrapped her arms around Roxil's spine. It didn't matter. She had made her choice to do whatever was necessary to stop Tamiel and rescue Matt and their mother, even if it meant jumping into a volcano ... or worse.

4

CHAPTER

A HITCHHIKER

Jared reclined on the rental RV's sofa. Any movement worsened a pounding headache that felt as if a lumberjack were splitting his skull instead of a log. Pain ravaged every inch of skin, muscle, and bone. The parasite that had invaded his body, as well as those of the other original anthrozils, had left behind toxins that still had to be flushed out, but they were leaving, slowly … too slowly.

With the help of a walking cane, he shifted to get a look at the lovely driver. While the stereo played an energetic jazz piece from a CD, Marilyn gripped the steering wheel with one loose hand, her hair tied back in a ponytail. The lush tail protruded through the back of a baseball cap and swayed at the collar of her navy polo shirt. Thin streaks of gray ran through her light brown hair, giving testimony to her decades of holding up under the worst stress imaginable.

Jared mentally replayed some of their adventures. During countless battles against demonic forces and during the trials of putting up with a husband who changed to a dragon, back to a

49

human, back to a dragon, and then back to a human again, she barely flinched. Her faith and loyalty seemed unbreakable. And now she drove this big vehicle like a pro, hour after hour, though she stopped from time to time to take advantage of the RV's kitchen and shower facilities and catch a short nap.

He angled his head to check the sky—no sign of rain. Earlier, they had barreled through a huge storm that whipped the RV with high winds, heavy rain, and hail. Besides that bout with the weather, this journey had been relatively easy, but mystery lay ahead. How difficult would it be to get the necessary data file and DNA sample from Larry? With government agents monitoring his data streams, it would be almost impossible. Almost.

Jared set his walking cane to the side, closed his eyes, and leaned back on a pillow. As the RV roared on, its tires rumbled on the pavement, raising a memory—a mother dragon's purr. How long had it been since that lovely sound had sung him to sleep? Too many years. That was so long ago, back in an age when mothers cared for their babies, even against the most fiendish attacks. Recent media reports, however, had turned that notion upside down.

50

Pushing the pain to the side, he called out, "Hey, gorgeous driver! Heard any news lately?"

"Nothing about Arramos's plans, or the Enforcers, if that's what you mean." She pushed a button that switched the stereo to the radio setting. A wailing signal pulsed through the speakers, prompting her to raise her voice. "The only station I can get ..." She turned the radio down and spoke at a normal volume. "The only station I can get keeps broadcasting an emergency alarm and plays the same warnings over and over. No one is allowed on the roads except for essential vehicles, but they don't define what those are, and I haven't seen anyone enforcing it."

"This country's too big for martial law. They're probably concentrating on helping the Enforcers round up children. It's a big job."

"It would be if they didn't have so much help." Marilyn squeezed the steering wheel as if wringing out a rag. "Can you imagine turning in someone's children? Or worse, your own children? And for what? A year's worth of food stamps?"

"I heard they were giving away televisions."

"Whatever. It's madness. Pure madness." She waved a hand toward the highway. "And it must be contagious. Even the weather is going crazy. A tsunami hit San Francisco, three typhoons are about to make landfall in Asia, and tornado warnings are up all across the central U.S."

"From the storm we just drove through?"

"Probably. We want to stay ahead of that monster, so I'll keep driving as far as I can." She yawned, then frowned. "Bad timing."

"Yep. You've got to be exhausted." Jared peered at the gauges. "How's the tank holding up?"

"Mine or the RV's?" She glanced back, smiling. "Maybe fifty miles. I saw a sign saying there's an open station at the next exit. We can check it out."

"Agreed. Open or not, I'd like to try to walk again."

"Good idea. You need to get your blood pumping."

"It already is. Arramos's scheme saw to that." Jared touched his cane. "If I'm able to walk without help, I'm sure I can drive for a little while, at least long enough for you to get a snooze."

"We'll see about that, Mister I'm-never-too-injured-to-go-full-steam-ahead."

After a few minutes, Marilyn stopped the RV and shut off the engine. Jared pushed a curtain aside and peeked out the window. She had pulled under the high roof of a Shell station's fueling island. Although its pumps appeared to be operational, only a solitary

51

pickup truck sat in the parking area. The ban on nonessential vehicles had cleared the roads, but the government had probably ordered some stations to stay open.

Jared grabbed his cane and pushed himself to his feet. Marilyn opened the side door and helped him down the stairs to the pavement. "I'll check out the store," Jared said.

Marilyn steadied him. "Need some help?"

"Better to fly solo. I need to test my legs."

"I'll pump the gas. Shout if you need me."

"Will do." After giving her the cane, he walked stiffly toward the station's store, his head low. Pain shot through both legs, but as his muscles loosened, each step seemed easier than the one before.

A man wearing patched jeans rushed out from the store and held the door for him. "You seem to be suffering quite a bit, sir."

"Not enough to keep me down. But thanks." Jared stopped in front of the oval-faced stranger, a shorter man than most. He wore silver-dollar glasses, and scars covered his face and scalp, likely from burns. "Mardon? Is that you?"

"I should have guessed that you would recognize me. I suppose I have some distinguishing characteristics that are memorable."

"You're memorable. That's for sure. I just didn't expect to run into you out here in the middle of nowhere. This can't be a mere coincidence."

"You are correct. When one of Tamiel's spies informed him that you and Marilyn had departed on this road trip, as it were, I deduced from your last known trajectory that you were on your way to your West Virginia home. A little research told me how much fuel this vehicle holds and where the open fueling stations were located, so I knew where you would most likely stop, and I simply waited for you."

"Care to say why you're tracking me?"

"All in good time. First I want to make sure you remember an important fact." Mardon gazed straight at Jared. "Do you remember when we first met?"

Jared nodded. "When your mother brought you to me in Second Eden begging for medical help. Deception has a way of sticking in my memory."

"That was not deception." Mardon touched a scar on his cheek. "My burns are quite real, though the pain has long since subsided."

"But I assume the scars remain in more ways than the obvious."

"You are a perceptive man." Mardon smiled, but it seemed forced. "My physical discomfort is far exceeded by the torture of never being able to conquer the beast who did this to me."

"You mean Arramos."

"Exactly the reason for my query into your memory. My mother and I vowed revenge on him that day, and our hunger to fulfill that vow has only increased over the years."

53

Jared looked him over. Since he had been able to open the door, he still had a physical body, even though he was dead ... sort of. "So, again, what brings you here?"

"My next step to fulfill my vow."

"A cryptic answer."

"Cryptic for now, at least until I judge whether or not you trust me enough to join me."

"Join you?" Jared half closed an eye. "Why would I want to do that?"

"I know you must also hope to destroy Arramos. Together I'm sure we can accomplish that goal."

"But you're dead." Jared nodded at Mardon's hand holding the door. "Though I see you're solid now. That means there's an open portal to Second Eden, unless you found some way to get a new body."

"I assure you, if I could get a new body, it would no longer be deformed." Mardon glanced inside the store, then to the sky before refocusing on Jared. "There is indeed an open portal to Second Eden. Since you seem to be unaware of it, I assume you cannot answer who opened it or how long the rift will remain."

Jared shook his head.

"No matter. I will take advantage of the situation while I can, which can also be advantageous for you."

"I see. You want to negotiate."

"The parasite has not fogged your mental acuity." Mardon gestured for Jared to enter the store. "Allow me to buy you something that will help you recover."

Jared walked in. To the left, a dark-skinned man stood at the register, his hands on the counter, one holding a pistol. Dressed in a khaki shirt, two buttons open to reveal a white T-shirt, he gave Mardon a nod. "Is this a friend of yours?"

"To be sure. He is no danger to you." Mardon walked to the counter. "Do you have any orange juice?"

The man gestured toward a line of refrigerated units embedded in the wall. "Should be some in there."

"Any vitamins? Vitamin C tablets?"

He shook his head. "There's a drugstore down the street, but I think it's closed. Looters took all the painkillers. They might have vitamins left, though. All I got was some laxatives and hair dye. It's not much, but you never know what'll sell in times like these."

"Quite true." Mardon opened one of the units, withdrew four glass bottles, and carried them back to the counter. After paying, he bowed his head. "Thank you for allowing me to wait here so long."

"No problem." The man smiled. His white teeth provided a stark contrast to his dark skin tones. "I enjoyed your stories. I think I'll tell some of them to my son."

When Jared and Mardon walked out the door, Marilyn bustled toward them. "The gas price is through the roof, at least tripled since—" She looked at Mardon and halted. "Oh! Hello."

Mardon nodded. "Hello, Mrs. Bannister."

Jared gestured toward him. "This is—"

"I know who he is. Mardon, the mad scientist who created the parasite that nearly killed you." Marilyn crossed her arms over her chest. "Why is he here?"

"To offer my services." Mardon pushed an orange juice bottle into Jared's hand. "Drink. Citric acid and vitamin C will counter the toxins the parasite left behind. If we come to an agreement, I can help you recover much more quickly. Unfortunately I don't have what I need to facilitate that recovery. Otherwise, I would help you right away simply on your word that we can cooperate."

Marilyn scowled. "Why should we trust anything you say?"

"Because I bring an offering that I hope will demonstrate my sincerity." He turned toward the pickup truck parked about a hundred feet away. "I will retrieve it."

As soon as he walked out of earshot, Marilyn curled her arm around Jared's. "Are you thinking about trusting him?"

"Not sure yet." Jared took a long drink from the bottle and drained the juice. After capping it, he tossed it into a nearby trash can. "Obviously he isn't motivated by any altruism, but we might as well hear him out. He wants to destroy Arramos, so I'm ready to hear his plan."

"Fair enough. I'm for anything that will stop the Enforcers."

Mardon returned from the pickup carrying a sword in a scabbard. Holding the hilt with a trembling hand, he withdrew the blade. An engraving on the flat of the blade showed a pair of battling dragons.

55

Jared whispered, "Excalibur?"

"This next step will prove the sword's identity." Mardon set the hilt in Jared's hand. The blade began to glow. "You are in Arthur's lineage."

Jared stared at his own reflection in the metal. How many centuries had it been since Merlin first wielded this sword and disintegrated himself in its transluminating light? Fifteen? And now here it was in his own hands, the great Excalibur!

"With the military otherwise occupied," Mardon said, "I was able to recover the sword without much difficulty. I now give it to you as a peace offering and as proof that I am dealing in good faith. You may keep it regardless of what we are able to agree upon."

Jared took the scabbard and slid Excalibur back in place. "Okay. What do you want?"

"To ride with you to West Virginia. I will explain along the way. If my proposal does not meet your approval, you are free to drop me off wherever you wish." He withdrew a cell phone from his pocket. "If you decline, I am able to obtain alternative transportation."

Jared gave Marilyn a quick glance. She replied with a nod, though skepticism still bent her features.

56

After they boarded the RV, Marilyn again driving and Mardon sitting in a captain's chair next to Jared's sofa, they headed eastbound on the nearly empty highway.

Mardon handed Jared another bottle of orange juice. "Since I have no love for Tamiel, and since I hate Arramos with a passion, I hope you will realize that I can be an ally."

"We both know that Arramos disfigured you," Jared said loudly enough to allow Marilyn to listen in. "We also know about your attempts to join Heaven and Earth, so we're aware of your desire to help yourself above all other motivations."

Mardon smiled weakly. "I see that you wish to push aside all pretenses."

"We'll save time that way." Jared took a sip from the bottle. "Just tell me what you want."

"Very well." Mardon settled back in his seat. "My mother and I want restoration. Morgan was able to keep our spirits alive in a wraithlike state, and my mother believes that Lauren's skin cells are the key to restoring our bodies completely. In the process, my scars will be healed and my youthfulness restored. My mother and I will no longer be wraiths who lose physical substance when the portals close between Earth and Second Eden. Theoretically, we could live forever, which was my ultimate motivation for uniting this world with the heavenly realm."

Jared capped the bottle and kept his gaze on the label. "You and Semiramis living forever isn't exactly a positive outcome, at least in our eyes."

57

"No, I expect not." Mardon pressed his fingers together. His lips twitched. "That is why I offer you a similar gift. Not eternal life, but certainly a better life. You see, when the government took control of your supercomputer, the officials gave me remote access so that I could search for secrets that they might not be able to locate."

Jared refocused on him. "And?"

"I found a file with no owner, no date stamp, and no description. When I tried to access it with every user ID in Larry's database, only yours requested a password. The others did not work at all, and the required security level indicated the highest secrecy. Breaking the encryption proved to be fruitless, but I soon found another way."

"Go on," Jared said with a nod.

"When I deduced where you were going, I assumed you hoped to retrieve the file on site." Mardon leaned closer. "Now you can tell me how to access it."

Jared narrowed his eyes. "Why would I want to do that?"

"A simple matter. Further deduction leads me to conclude that you want the file in order to provide for your own restoration. The only reason a very sick man is willing to travel so far and at such risk is so that he will find a cure for his sickness. Since I am the creator of the parasite that disabled you, and since I am the world's leading expert on genetic manipulation, I am certain that I can help with or even enhance your efforts."

Jared nodded. "In trade for Lauren's skin cells, I assume."

"That and one more request." Mardon glanced around as if concerned about a hidden recording device. "I gave Excalibur to you for a very important purpose. I know what the military has done to make Fort Knox impenetrable to Elam and the dragons who hope to rescue Sapphira. They will be stepping into danger beyond their ability to predict or defend against. They will either die or be captured."

58

"You might be underestimating Elam's wisdom. He has extraordinary discernment."

"No doubt. He has proven his mettle time and again. Yet no amount of discernment will be able to counter such brute force." Mardon nodded at the scabbard. "I am hoping you will be able to use Excalibur to rescue Sapphira."

Jared blinked. "So you *want* Sapphira to be rescued?"

"Very much so. You might find this difficult to believe, but I have had a soft spot in my heart for her ever since I fashioned her genetic splicing and rooted her in a pot of soil millennia ago. I knew she and Acacia were special, and I have taken a deep interest in her life ever since." Tears sparkled in his eyes. "When Devin killed Acacia, I vowed to destroy the efforts of all of his ilk—Morgan, Tamiel, Arramos ..."

"And your mother?"

Mardon stared at his wringing hands. "I realize that you place my mother in the same category." Sweat beaded on his forehead. "I want her to be restored, but when that happens, I wish to be separated from her and join Sapphira in Second Eden. I hope to be a research scientist or an advisor to a physician such as Dr. Conner, but I want to be near Sapphira for as long as I can. My mother can stay on Earth with Tamiel and do whatever she pleases, but I hope she never learns that our separation was part of my plan."

"Where is she now?"

"Tamiel has recruited her to do what she does best—deceive. She is supposed to play the part of Darcy, your grandson's former foster sister. Because of her wraithlike state and sorceress powers, she is able to manipulate her appearance enough to look the part."

"Why this charade?"

Mardon shrugged. "I am not aware of the details. We parted ways, and I have not been in touch with her in quite some time. But knowing Tamiel's purpose, I deduced that she will somehow cause your grandson great distress and contribute to the degradation of Bonnie's song."

"Jared," Marilyn called from the driver's seat. "I've been listening to conversations between Lois and others. The Internet has been abuzz with sightings of Bonnie flying over a Mustang. The driver fits Matt's description. No photos, but one person said a young woman with reddish-brown hair was riding in the front passenger's seat."

"Supposedly Darcy, I assume," Jared said.

"I cannot verify that assumption, but my mother has a similar hair color." Mardon stroked his chin. "She has worked remarkably quickly to take on her role as Darcy, so we have reason to believe that the deception is well under way."

"Lauren and Roxil are trying to find Matt," Marilyn said, "so we could relay a warning somehow."

Jared resisted the urge to cringe. Marilyn had just given away information about Lauren in Mardon's presence. "Go ahead and give it a try. Use the IP spoofing and the usual encryption."

"So," Mardon said, leaning closer to Jared, "we need Lauren's skin cells, not enough to do her any harm—just a graft, no more than what she might donate to cover a surgical scar. She will suffer no lasting effects from the surgery. And as I mentioned, I also want privileged sanctuary in Second Eden. In exchange, I will help you with the restoration that you are planning, tell you more about the trap at Fort Knox, and help you destroy Tamiel and Arramos once and for all."

When Mardon finished, the only sound came from the never-ending hum of tires on pavement and the motor's gentle roar. Jared glanced at Marilyn. She glanced back at him. No words were necessary. Mardon's entreaty held a treasure trove of riches, his motivations were somewhat believable, and the return of Excalibur seemed to prove his earnestness. Yet, one more piece of information could seal the deal.

60

"Mardon, when I was near death in the Second Eden hospital—"

"Jared," Marilyn said, "are you sure you want to tell him about that?"

"It's the only way to know for sure." Jared cleared his throat. "As I was saying, when I was near death, someone spoke to me about a scheme that Arramos is hatching. Do you know anything about it?"

Mardon nodded. "By your manner and tone, I assume you are saying that you heard a voice in the air, such as an angel, rather than a physical person."

"That's not important right now. Just tell me what you know."

"Very little. Only that if Tamiel fails to bring God's judgment by fostering corruption, then Arramos will dispose of him, a mere pawn in the larger game. Arramos knows how to bring wrath in the quickest way."

"And that is?"

"By inciting the already corrupted people to deliver their own children to the gas chambers, anyone too young to be put to forced labor. Something of an offering to Molech."

Jared tightened his lips. He could barely resist shouting. Marilyn's eyes lit up. She, too, celebrated this proof—proof that the voice was more than just a dream. Joan of Arc had really visited his hospital bed. Her entreaty for him to return to Earth to battle Arramos was true after all. Someone had to stop that evil dragon's plan to kill the children.

Mardon smiled, though tentatively. "May I assume from your improved countenance that my report was satisfactory? That perhaps ending Arramos's cruelty is now a common goal toward which we can strive together?"

61

"You may assume that." Jared clasped his hands together. "But I can't guarantee delivery of the things you're asking for. Whether or not you can stay in Second Eden will be up to Elam and Sapphira, and I can't speak for Lauren. She would have to donate skin by her own free will."

"I anticipated that, so I am willing to proceed on your word that you will personally appeal for these benefits."

Jared nodded. "I can agree to that. What's the next step?"

"To continue to West Virginia. Along the way, I will provide what I know about Fort Knox. You can then pass that information to Elam before he faces the danger."

Elam drove the van eastward, his mental map set for Kentucky, still a day's drive in the distance. With Yereq in the back and Makaidos and Thigocia curled tightly in a big trailer to the rear, the cargo felt like thousands of pounds of explosive power—a hazardous load indeed. It wasn't easy finding a trailer with a roof that opened to let sunlight in, but the hours of searching were worth it. The dragons, still recovering from candlestone wounds, needed the energy infusion. They all had to be ready for what likely would be an all-out war when they arrived at Fort Knox. The military would be more prepared this time, so everyone had to be healthy and well rested.

He looked in the side mirror and rubbed his fake eyebrows— still straight. Even this far from their destination, he couldn't risk being recognized. Now sporting a dyed-blond hairstyle and wearing a snazzy navy-blue military uniform along with dark sunglasses, maybe he could manage a stealth approach and infiltrate the compound before calling for dragon support.

"How's my photo ID coming?" he called to the back.

Yereq replied in his usual calm bass tone. "It will be finished in a few minutes. The embedded chip identifies you properly, and Lois says the encryption is up to date, but I still need to laminate it."

"Good work, Yereq." Elam touched a phone on the passenger's seat and turned the screen toward himself. No messages. Since the phone and his tooth transmitter could potentially be tracked, Carly and Lois were supposed to maintain silence unless something monumental happened, so no news was good news. Still, it would be reassuring to hear how Walter and Ashley were getting along in their pursuit of Billy, or how Jared was progressing in his secret quest, but his own mission had to stay secure.

Elam turned the radio to a news station and kept the volume low. Reports of fires, bombings, looting, and other mayhem dominated the broadcast, especially in cities on the coasts. It seemed that the people of Earth had lost their minds, but maybe that could be a blessing in disguise. If the violence spread to the Midwest, that could mean lower security at Fort Knox and easier entry. Maybe the dragons wouldn't have to face a battery of candlestone guns after all.

Elam blew out a sigh and whispered, "In your dreams."

"I am finished." Yereq's huge hand extended a plastic ID card over the seat.

Elam took it and read the information—Captain Andrew Moffett, security officer from the British Royal Navy. "How's my British accent, my good man?"

"I have heard several accents from the British Isles," Yereq said. "Yours sounds Welsh."

"Welsh will do, I suppose. I've practiced so much, I'm thinking in that accent."

"All for the better. We must make no mistakes."

"Right." Elam turned the radio off. His hand shook. He drew it close to his eyes and willed it to stop. *Stay calm. Stay focused.* Faith and its resulting serenity had been trusted allies for thousands of years. Only peace and a steady hand could pull off this rescue and bring Sapphira back into his embrace.

5

THE FIRST DOOR

Matt pulled the Mustang into a several-acre parking lot, perhaps three-quarters filled with late-model cars and sports utility vehicles, and stopped in a space next to a van marked First Community Church on a side panel. A paved walkway led from the lot to a huge off-white ovular sac that stood in a grassy field. A portico protruded from a crease in the sac's front, and a steeple stuck out through the top. White thunderheads loomed behind a cross at the steeple's apex.

With the convertible's top down, a warm, moist breeze blew across Matt's hair. The storm they had passed through was catching up, as if giving chase, and a distant rumble of thunder sounded like a dire warning to check this place out and move on.

Darcy straightened in her seat and looked over the windshield. "What is that thing?"

Mom leaned between them from the backseat, still breathing heavily from a recent flight. "It looks like a cocoon, like an enormous caterpillar spun silk around a church building."

Matt put the convertible top back in place and shut off the engine. "Let's see what's going on." He slid the cell phone into his pocket, opened the door, and stepped onto the lot's blacktop. Now on the east side of the violent cold front, warmth from the pavement radiated across his body. It felt good, but it wouldn't last.

After Mom and Darcy exited the car, Matt led the way to the portico and pushed the sac's fibers to one side, revealing a dark mahogany door with a welcome mat at the foot. When he stepped back, a few cottony strands stuck to his fingers, but the rest of the mass stayed where he had pushed it.

He grasped a brass doorknob and looked at his mother and Darcy, both standing behind him. "Ready?"

Mom nodded. "Go ahead."

Matt turned the knob and pushed the door open. A draft passed through the gap—moist air saturated with the odor of mildew. About twenty feet above the floor, several leaded-crystal light fixtures hung from a domed ceiling, all lit dimly.

He took three steps inside and stood on a carpeted aisle leading to a raised platform. A piano stood on the left side of the stage, a set of drums at the back, and a pulpit near the front. People sat in dozens of aligned pews, but only the backs of their heads were in view. They stayed motionless, as if entranced.

On a table near the stage's front edge, red pear-shaped fruit lay piled in three pyramids, each fruit about the size of a large apple. A huge spider perched atop the table, though he bore a man's clean-shaven face. In each of eight hairy appendages, he carried one of the fruits, clutched in a dragon-like claw. With his legs spread over the pyramids, he appeared to be protecting the fruit.

Matt steeled himself. With all the crazy happenings of late, he could handle this newest bizarre scene. "That explains the cocoon," he whispered to Mom as she and Darcy joined him. "I guess it's a spider's egg sac."

"Be bold," Mom said. "Let's walk straight toward the spider."

With Mom and Darcy following, Matt walked slowly along the aisle, dodging fruit cores strewn across the carpet. Men and women wearing dressy-casual attire sat on long cushions in each row, some with Styrofoam cups raised as if ready to drink. One woman with long red hair sat with a pen poised over an open three-ring binder, apparently ready to jot down a note.

Matt grasped the shoulder of a man sitting at the aisle and gave him a shake. He moved with the force, but his stare remained locked on the spider. He didn't even blink.

As Matt continued walking toward the front, Mom picked up a Bible from a space between two seated women, both undisturbed by her reach. Wrapped in a fabric carrying case, the Bible was like many others dotting the seats and sitting on the floor at the congregants' feet—all closed, all out of their motionless owners' view as they gawked at the spider.

"Interesting," Mom said as she returned the Bible to its place. "I've never heard of mass hypnosis this powerful. And where are the children? I don't see any, not even a baby."

"A nursery?" Matt asked. "A separate service for kids?"

"I suppose so, but usually some children stay with their parents."

A hissing voice slid from between the spider's lips. "Welcome, friends."

Matt halted in front of the stage, his head even with the table-top. "How do you know we're friends?"

67

The spider set an "apple" on top of a pyramid. "Because you have entered my church. I consider all who enter this sanctuary to be my friends."

Mom strode forward, Darcy a step behind her. "Who are you?" Mom asked.

"I am the pastor of this church." The spider bowed his head. "And who are you?"

"An inquisitive visitor." She gestured toward the congregants. "Why is everyone sitting like they're frozen?"

The spider skittered a foot or so to the side and looked past Mom. "Their state is a temporary reaction to the fruit I provided. They will recover soon, and they will find that they have received everlasting life."

Mom nodded at one of the pyramids. "That fruit looks very familiar."

"It is from the tree of life." The spider extended one in a clawed hand. "Do you wish to receive eternal life?"

"The tree of life, you say." Mom bent her brow. "How long do you plan to continue this charade?"

"Charade?" The spider let out a hissing chuckle. "My dear woman, I have no idea what you're talking about."

"Really?" Mom set her hands on her hips. "I encountered similar fruit in the first circle of Hades, and this is Tamiel's first door. Someone offered me fruit there, and now you offer fruit here. I'm not as stupid as you suppose."

"Are you not?" A leathery tongue darted from the spider's mouth, then zipped back in. "Then why are you taking the time to speak to me?"

"So I can do this." She flew up to the stage and shoved the table. It flipped over, sending the fruit flying. The spider hopped up, shot a silky strand to the ceiling, and hung from it. As he swayed, the fruit and cores vanished.

The spider grinned. "You are not quite as predictable as I was told. Yet I think I know you well enough. You will make an attempt to revive these fools, so I will amuse myself by watching your vain efforts." He rode the thread to the ceiling, crawled to a corner, and clung to the rafters.

Matt looked at his mother. "Now what?"

"We find the key." Mom pushed the table to the side. A finger-length key, silvery but lacking a glow, lay on the stage floor. She picked it up and handed it to Matt. "We'll see if it flashes when we leave this place, but first we have to try to wake the people."

Matt slid the key onto the ring at his belt. "But that's exactly what the spider wants you to do. The longer we stay, the more damage to your song, especially if we can't wake them."

"We have to take that chance." Mom glared at the spider. "Let's look around for clues. If the fruit put them to sleep, maybe something else will wake them."

"I'm on it." Matt climbed the stairs to the stage, stood next to the pulpit, and picked up a small stack of typewritten notes. A title said, The Gates of Hell Shall Not Prevail! A subtitle in small letters spelled out, The Church Triumphant.

Darcy joined him on the stage and strolled across it, her head swiveling from side to side. "This is like Sleeping Beauty. Everyone was frozen until Prince Charming kissed her."

"Or some twisted version of Sleeping Beauty." Mom walked up the aisle and eyed a few of the mannequin-like faces. "They have a purplish residue around their lips."

"Probably from eating the fruit," Matt said.

69

"Most likely." Mom stopped next to a pew and wiped a bit of the residue from a woman's cheek. The woman didn't flinch. "I don't think a kiss is going to work. It's like they're in a coma."

"Music, maybe?" Darcy walked to the piano, sat on the bench, and began playing "Amazing Grace," complete with scale runs and other embellishments. Her fingers flew across the keyboard. With every vibrant chord, furrows dug deeply into her brow. Her body swayed in time with the rhythm.

Matt stepped closer. Darcy mentioned playing for nightclubs, and she had played piano while they lived as brother and sister, but never like this. She seemed enraptured by her own performance. But was it real emotion or just show?

The lights above flickered for a moment, then continued burning dimly.

70

"I learned this while working at a bar," Darcy said as she continued at a quieter volume. "I played drinking songs and rock mostly, but one day a street preacher came in and put one of those gospel tracts on the piano, then he sat next to me and taught me 'Amazing Grace.'" She ended with a soft chord and laid her hands in her lap. "But when we finished, I made a dirty comment about his anatomy, and when his cheeks turned as red as a beet, the customers laughed him out of the bar." A tear sparkled in her eye. "I wish I could take it back and tell him I'm sorry."

A man fell from the end of a pew and rolled into the aisle, spilling coffee on the carpet.

Mom rushed to him and helped him rise.

Still carrying the pulpit notes, Matt hurried off the stage and joined them.

When the man stood upright, Mom let him go. "Are you okay?" she asked.

"I think so." The man stared at the empty cup in his hand, then at the floor. "Pastor will be furious."

"No, he won't. It was an accident." Mom brushed a coffee droplet from the man's white sleeve. "What's your name?"

"Stan." He glanced around the sanctuary. "What's going on here? Why is everyone like a statue?"

"I was going to ask you that," Matt said.

"I have no idea." Stan laid a hand on his forehead. "The last thing I remember was Pastor beginning his sermon, but I can't remember what he said."

"Maybe this will help." Matt read the first line of the notes out loud. "Decision of the board of elders concerning the Enforcers."

"Oh, yes, yes. I remember." Stan looked around again, now smiling. "This is a dream, right? Things like this don't happen except in dreams."

"Stay focused." Matt rattled the pages. "What's this decision about the Enforcers? Are they still trying to find dragon children?"

"I guess you haven't heard the news. The Enforcers have expanded their net. They're now rounding up all children who fall below minimum standards."

"Minimum standards?" Mom asked, anger rising in her tone. "What standards?"

"Strength and intelligence standards. If children are physically weak or are, shall we say, significantly behind in intellectual development, the Enforcers take them to a training camp where they will be brought up to the standards. Obviously the parents aren't capable of providing what these children need."

"Aren't the parents protesting?"

"Some are, but they have no legal recourse. That's where the decision by the board of elders comes in. A few church members say that we should hide the neglected children from the Enforcers, and even from their parents if those parents are willing to turn their children over to surrogates."

"Good," Mom said. "That's courageous. The Enforcers are evil, and we have to protect the children."

Stan tilted his head slightly upward. "Be that as it may, the Enforcers are still our authority. We have to obey them. That's why the board decided that we will not support hiding the children or the parents, and we will expose any who do."

Mom's eyes seemed to flame. "What? Expose them? That's the devil's work!"

"Stay cool, Mom," Matt whispered. "Tamiel wants you to get worked up."

She took in a deep breath and nodded. "Good reminder."

"Yes, we must always use gracious words." Stan smiled in a condescending way. "Some in our church forgot to follow that rule. They actually accused Pastor of being like those who turned the Jews over to the Nazis. Fortunately those rebels are probably gone for good. They walked out and took their children with them."

"So there *was* some sanity here." Mom scanned the congregation. "Speaking of children, I don't see any."

"They're downstairs." He nodded toward a door to the left of the stage. "They have more fun in their own services."

"I'll check on them." Darcy hurried toward the door.

"People who prefer being away from their own children." Mom crossed her arms. "It's no wonder everyone is in a coma."

"They do look that way," Stan said. "All the more reason to believe this is just a vivid dream. I'm sure I'll wake up soon and have a good laugh."

Mom's eyes flickered again. "Those parents and children you're persecuting won't be laughing."

"Don't be ridiculous. We're not persecuting them. We're just not hiding them from the authorities." Stan curled his hand and looked at his fingernails. "Besides, these children need help. Those parents, as loving as they might be, aren't capable of providing what their children need. We are doing them a service."

Mom's cheeks flamed. She closed her eyes and took in a couple of deep breaths. Soon, the color faded. "Stan, maybe you're better off thinking you're asleep. Just stand here and snooze with the rest of them."

Stan grinned. "It's amazing what my brain comes up with. I am imagining my own opposition. It's quite entertaining."

"If delusion is entertaining." Mom turned to Matt and whispered, "I'm not sure there's any hope for these people. It sounds like the only ones with any sanity already left."

Darcy jogged through the doorway and joined them again. "I found cribs and toys in one room and a bigger room with drums and guitars on a stage, but I didn't see anyone, not even nursery workers." She lifted a fragment of black leather pinched in her fingers. "But these were all over the place."

Matt touched the fragment. It looked exactly like a scale from the drone that attacked him at the motel. Could drones have abducted the children? "Very strange. Maybe—" The cell phone chimed in his pocket. He drew it out and answered. "This is Matt."

"According to the tracking devices," Tamiel said, his tone cocky, "you are parked in the church lot. I congratulate you on arriving on time in spite of the storm, but I am disappointed that Bonnie decided to make a spectacle of herself. It was a clever ploy, but you should have known that I would have noticed the Internet chatter about her antics. You may tell her for me that her little stunt will cost her husband some pain. Nothing more than a broken toe or two, because I did not specifically warn her about flying

73

above the car, but she now must travel with her wings always hidden in her backpack. I won't be so merciful the next time you pull any tricks to thwart my will. Do you understand?"

Matt looked straight at his mother. It wouldn't do any good to pass along the news about Dad's suffering. That would just warp her song further. "Got it, Tamiel. No more tricks. She'll hide her wings."

"Now turn on the speaker and allow everyone to hear my next comments."

"Mom, he wants you to listen." As she stepped closer, Matt looked at the screen, found the speaker option, and toggled it. "Okay. You're on."

"Bonnie Bannister …" Tamiel's voice came through tinny though clear enough. "Now that you are inside this exquisite example of God's house of love, drink in its bounty of generosity. Take note of its crystal, its marble, its fine woods. Surely the people here give and give to their noble cause." He laughed. "The cause of building an ecclesiastical empire out of expensive finery. Surely this vine has borne plenty of delicious fruit."

"What is this fool talking about?" Stan crossed his arms tightly. "We have charitable funds. Lots of them."

"Who is that?" Tamiel's voice turned harsh. "Who has joined you?"

"His name's Stan," Matt said. "He was sitting in the church and woke up from a trance."

"He woke up?" A deep sigh filtered through the speaker. "This is unexpected. We will have to take corrective action."

The lamps above flickered. Still clinging to the ceiling, the spider crawled closer until he perched overhead. He lowered himself on a silk line, dropped onto Stan's shoulder, and wrapped his legs completely around his torso.

74

Stan screamed and tried to pry the hairy legs off to no avail.

"Let him go!" Matt punched the spider's head, but the blow didn't faze him. Fangs protruded from his mouth and, like a striking serpent, he dug them into Stan's neck. Instantly, he collapsed. More silk shot from the spider's abdomen. With his legs acting like high-speed knitting needles, he began spinning a web around his victim.

"Your time here is finished," the spider said as the sac thickened. "You must now travel to your next destination or else Billy Bannister will suffer the consequences."

In a flash of legs and white webbing, he ascended toward the ceiling, Stan's sac in his grasp.

The lights brightened. Silence descended. Matt sucked in a breath and let it out slowly. The air felt thick and heavy.

"Well," Darcy whispered, "that was ... strange."

"That's putting it mildly." Matt read the phone's destinations. "And this is just the first address. We have six more to go."

Mom scanned the room. "We'd better not risk waking anyone else."

"Right. No more arachnoid abductions." Matt grasped his mother's arm and began guiding her toward the door. "Let's go."

"Wait!" Darcy stepped in front of a pew, opened a woman's purse, and began fishing through it.

Matt stopped and glared at her. "Now you're stealing from sleeping churchgoers? Didn't you make enough money turning tricks?"

"Matt!" Mom said. "Don't!"

Darcy's lips tightened. She threw the purse down to the pew, though she kept something partially hidden. Her arms rigid, she stalked up to Matt and held out her hand. "Give me your phone," she said, her tone firm.

Matt raised it in his palm. "Why?"

Darcy snatched it, resumed her tight-fisted march, and stormed out the door without bothering to push the webbing to the side.

When she disappeared, Mom grabbed Matt's sleeve, her jaw tight as she whisper shouted, "What were you thinking, insulting Darcy like that?"

"You saw her go through that purse." Matt pointed at the door. "Mom, she's a prostitute! A hooker! She sells herself to anyone with a heartbeat and a twenty-dollar bill."

"And you're throwing stones at her."

Matt's ears heated up. "Throwing stones? I'm just telling the truth. You didn't seem to mind giving Stan a few verbal jabs. And I thought you were great. You exposed him for what he is. Shouldn't we do the same to a prostitute?"

"Not in this case. Stan was self-deluded. He needed a cold slap in the face to wake him up." Mom pulled him close, almost nose to nose. Although her cheeks continued to flame, her tone softened. "Matt, Darcy isn't deluded. She knows what she was, and she knows it's wrong. She doesn't need you to shake her chains. I've already had long talks with her while you were asleep, and she's knocking on the door to freedom, but you answered by spitting on her."

Matt pulled away, suppressing an emerging growl. "Mom … listen. You don't know Darcy like I do. I saw for myself how devious Semiramis is. Darcy's her clone. Semiramis helped Listener and pretended to be your friend, but it was all a ploy. You never trusted Semiramis, and you were right. Darcy's the same. I know from experience. I've seen this act too many times before."

Mom's tone sharpened again. "She was your sister!"

"Yeah, an evil, twisted sister. What do you think we did together? Walk hand in hand through the snow? No! Her idea of winter fun was hanging me out a window by a rope!"

Mom nodded in a conciliatory way. "She did terrible things to you, but you'll never reconcile with someone you choose to hate. Hatred is a cancer that will devour you. It consumes its victims like a raging fire. No one can be saved who harbors hatred in his heart, not Darcy, not Semiramis, not even you."

"Semiramis?" Matt blinked at her. "Do you think Semiramis can be saved?"

She set a fist on her hip. "You're changing the subject."

"No. Seriously." Matt lowered his voice. "You're trying to get me to trust Darcy, but you never trusted Semiramis. What's the difference?"

Mom let out a long sigh. "There's a big difference between Darcy and Semiramis. Semiramis is a sorceress who is already dead, so she can never turn to the light. Darcy is a living human with a precious soul, and she can change her ways. If you don't allow her a chance to repent, maybe she never will."

77

"And if we keep trusting her, we'll end up dead, or at least look like fools when she turns against us." Matt averted his eyes and stared at the open door. It would sound stupid to give away his suspicions that Darcy might actually be Semiramis in disguise.

After echoing his mother's sigh, he looked at her again and continued in a calm tone. "Mom, we have to focus on what we're doing. Recognize who our enemies are and who our friends are. Tamiel sent us here so you'd get upset about this corrupt church and their stupid self-centered members. He wants to warp your song so the world will get even worse. You need to stay in control and not let him get to you."

"It's not Tamiel who's getting to me. It's—"

The lights flickered again, then stayed dim.

Mom squinted at Matt and used her thumb to wipe the side of his lips. When she withdrew her hand, purple residue stained her thumb. As she stared at the stain, she whispered, "We need to go."

"Where did that purple stuff come from? I didn't eat any fruit." Matt tried to lift his legs, but they wouldn't budge. "What's going on?"

"Something evil." Mom wrapped her arms around Matt's waist, beat her wings furiously, and zoomed toward the door.

Matt gasped. His heart raced. He could do nothing but hang on and let her carry him.

When they burst through the mass of fibers, Darcy came into view in the parking lot. A short, bearded man wearing dirty jeans and a greasy T-shirt held her wrist and pointed a knife at her throat.

Mom hurtled straight toward the attacker. When they drew close enough, Matt broke free, hit the ground with his feet, and lunged. Lowering his shoulder, he plowed into the man, and they both sprawled backwards. The knife flew from his grip and skidded across the parking lot.

Matt crawled to the knife and grabbed it. "Stay where you are!"

The man, a fortysomething tramp, sat up and scowled. "Playing cop, are you boy?"

"I'm no cop." Matt pulled his hand back, ready to throw the knife. "But I can embed a blade in a tree from a hundred feet."

"Well, goody for you." The man spat. "Go ahead. Kill me. I don't have the guts to do it myself."

Mom stood with an arm around Darcy. "What were you looking for?"

"Listen to the winged freak. She can talk." The man sneered. "You need someone with a machete to slice you into a normal person."

"If you need food, we can—"

"I wasn't looking for food." He climbed to his feet and began walking away. "I'm outta here. Go ahead and stab me in the back if that's how you get your high."

Matt lowered his hand. Straining to get his numbed legs to work, he climbed to his feet and staggered toward his mother. "I guess we should get going."

"What's this?" Darcy picked up something leather from the pavement. "It's that guy's sheath for his knife."

Matt looked it over. Although dirty, it was in pretty good shape. "Well, he's not getting it back."

"No, but …" Darcy slid the sheath over the knife, still in Matt's hand. "Maybe we can use it."

79

Mom angled her head and pointed at Matt's belt. "The key is glowing."

"Good." Matt lifted the ring, still attached to his loop. The key radiated a bright blue aura. "I guess that means we're done here."

Darcy held the phone out. "It's already set to the next address."

Matt picked it up. "Why did you want it?"

"To leave a clue." She showed him a phone with a pink-and-purple cover. "I took this one from that purse, and I copied all the addresses from your phone into it. And I wrote a note about what we're doing and that the seventh address is missing. I thought we could put it in an easy place to find, you know, in case someone figures out we came here. Since Bonnie can't risk flying anymore, it's the only way someone can track us down."

Keeping his gaze on Darcy, he picked up the second phone. Her eyes seemed to beg for affirmation, for just a kind word. Distrust of her felt more and more stupid every second. "Yeah. I guess that's a good idea."

"It's a great idea." Mom took the phone and flew to the church door. She tore away some of the fibrous material, compressed it into a short rope, and hung the phone from the doorknob. As she hurried back, her wings again boosting her, she smiled. "Let's pray that helps."

Matt opened the front passenger door and gestured for Darcy to enter.

"Your mother should be next to you." She opened the rear door, slid onto the backseat, and tossed the empty backpack to the front.

Matt shrugged and gestured again, this time looking at his mother. "Shall we?"

Her lips taut, she sidestepped past him, picked up the backpack, and began tucking her wings inside. As she kept her stare on him, her nimble wings helped her hands maneuver the backpack into position. In less than a minute, she looked like a hiker with an overstuffed load.

She ducked into the front seat and settled in place. "I'm ready, Matt Bannister."

Matt blinked. Why the last name all of a sudden?

Thunder rumbled across the sky. The dark edge of the storm front rushed closer. He closed the door and hurried around to the driver's side. After settling in his seat, he looked at the mirror. No residue appeared on his lips. Since the fruit disappeared, maybe the stains were all part of a hypnotic image.

He laid the sheathed knife in the middle console pocket, propped the phone against the dashboard, and started the engine. "At least we have a weapon now. Maybe it'll help down the road."

Darcy picked up the sheath and drew the knife out partway. "It's serrated. Very sharp."

"Yeah. Someone could do a lot of damage with it."

"I'd rather have my Glock or my shotgun." She hooked the sheath to her waistband. "But this will do."

Matt raised his brow. "You have guns?"

"I didn't until I moved to Vegas. I needed protection, so I carried a Glock in my purse and kept a shotgun in my closet. I take them both to the range every chance I get. Actually, I'm a pretty good shot, especially skeet shooting."

He smiled. "Okay, your coolness factor just surged."

"Coolness is good." She gave him a thankful smile. "Glad to have your approval."

"And Mom," Matt added, "I loved how you threw that table over. You didn't even flinch."

She nodded. "I saw no reason to fear him."

"I wish I had your confidence." He pushed the stick into gear. "We'd better go. We still have to find a motel, and I'd like to stay in front of that storm." He pulled out of the parking space and onto the highway, following the phone's directions.

In the backseat, Darcy remained quiet. The urge to glance at her in the mirror seemed overwhelming, but he resisted. No matter her posture, no matter her expression, his distrust, even hatred, would boil again, and Mom would notice. She always noticed. And that would further break down her song.

Darcy whispered from the back. "I'm sorry, Matt."

He tensed. "Sorry for what?"

"When you thought I was stealing, I said some awful things about you in my mind, so ... I'm sorry. I'm trying to change, but it's hard, so I hope you'll be patient with me."

81

He looked at her in the mirror. She rubbed her ring finger again, probably a nervous habit. "You're right to think that way," she continued. "That I might be a thief, I mean. No one should trust someone like me. No one. I'm not worth a nickel."

"Not worth a nickel?" Matt said. "Where did that come from?"

"It's something one of my bosses used to say whenever I made a mistake. I guess I picked it up. But it's true."

"Well ..." Matt glanced at his mother. She stared straight ahead, her lips moving silently, probably praying for this actress who continued playing her pity-inducing role flawlessly. Even though showing Darcy a bit of compassion felt like petting a rabid dog, he could grit his teeth and bear it, for Mom's sake.

He exhaled. "I'm sorry, too. I guess I misjudged you. You really came up with a great idea."

82

After a moment or two of silence, Darcy extended her hand over the seat. "Friends?" Her hand seemed to hover in place. How could he refuse? Rejecting a peace offering would make him look like the most vindictive person on Earth.

Twisting in his seat, he grasped her hand and interlocked their thumbs. "Friends."

As Matt drew his hand back, Mom cocked her head and looked straight at him but said nothing.

He shifted uneasily. Mom was smart, probably too smart to be fooled by his apparent quick change of heart. "Is everything all right?"

"I'm just trying to read you. You're a puzzle sometimes."

"Sorry. I guess that comes with the territory. You know, being separated from you all these years."

"Maybe. I just want to be sure you're ready for the second door."

"Uh ... sure. I think so." He blinked at her. "Do you think I might not be?"

"Hard to say." She turned and looked forward. "I've got a feeling that Tamiel started us out with an easy one. The second door is likely to be a far bigger challenge than the first."

6

WHEN IT RAINS

Walter sat up in the cornfield. Everything swirled in the midst of driving wind and rain. Ashley lay next to him, a hand over her eyes, while Gabriel stood nearby bending over Billy's tracking device. Although his wings protected the tracker from the rain, water dripped from his hair to the screen.

"Where's the chopper?" Walter called loudly enough to be heard over the storm.

"Oh! You're awake." Gabriel strolled closer and pointed into the field as he stared at the tracker. "Billy's signal stopped about a mile to the north. They've been there maybe twenty minutes."

Ashley rose to a sitting position and clutched Walter's hand. "Feeling all right?"

"I feel like I plugged myself into a hydroelectric plant. It's the only explanation for being fried and soaked at the same time."

"I guess you should know," Gabriel said. "You've done that before."

Ashley slowly pulled her hand away. "I sense a new presence. Someone's coming this way."

"Friendly?"

"Not likely." Ashley looked toward the north. "Four ... no, five people. Searching. Getting closer."

"I haven't found the weapons duffle, so we don't have a gun." Gabriel slid the tracker into his pocket. "We're sitting ducks."

"Then we have only one option." Walter climbed to his feet, helped Ashley up, and pushed her toward Gabriel. "Take her and get out of here."

"What?" Ashley shook her head hard, slinging hair and water. "I'm not about to leave you."

"Don't let emotions cloud your thinking," Walter said. "I'm too weak to run. Gabriel can't carry both of us. And if I'm captured, I'll probably be with Billy, so you can still track us. If we're all captured, we've got nothing."

Her eyes wide, she whispered, "I need to be with you. I ... I ..."

"I love you." He kissed her and pushed wet hair from her eyes. "With Billy and me back together, we'll figure out a way to mess up their plans."

She nodded. "I know you will."

"Keep track of us." He patted Gabriel on the shoulder. "Go!"

Gabriel wrapped his arms around Ashley from behind. With a burst of flapping wings, he lifted her into the air. As they ascended, Ashley cried out, "I love you, Walter! I will always love you!"

He blew her a kiss. Gabriel zoomed away to the south and flew low over the bending cornstalks. In seconds, he and Ashley were out of sight.

Walter turned toward the north and straightened his body. Numbness in his fingers and toes proved that the electric shock still lingered, but he couldn't let potential captors know about it. Confidence had been a great ally for years, always a useful stalling device. Maybe Gabriel and Ashley could get far away before anyone would bother to look for them.

A stout man in a wet soldier's uniform broke into the clearing and aimed an M16 rifle at Walter. "Hands up."

Walter raised his hands. "If you're here to steal corn, you're a bit late for the harvest."

"Shut up!"

"Oh, I get it. You don't want corn. You're just stalking me. Well, I understand that. My mother always said I was outstanding in my field."

The soldier lifted the rifle to his shoulder. "I said shut up!"

"Whoa! There must have been a kernel of truth in my comment for you to get so—"

"This'll keep you quiet." The soldier turned the rifle and belted Walter across the cheek with the butt.

Walter staggered backwards but quickly regained his balance. Although pain ripped through his skull, he refused to touch the wound. At least the distraction worked. The soldier hadn't bothered to look for the obvious signs that other people had been here.

As rain continued to pound the field, four more men tromped into the clearing. Three soldiers carried rifles, and a short, thin man dressed in black held an umbrella over his head. Tamiel. No one could mistake that demon's sinister mug.

Tamiel brushed a dark boot along a depression where Roxil had rested. "Where are the others?" he asked without a hint of emotion.

Walter blinked innocently. "What others?"

Tamiel's lip twitched. "Your fellow travelers and the dragon."

"A dragon?" Walter laughed under his breath. "Mister, my plane just crashed, and I'm kind of woozy, but ... a dragon?"

Tamiel pointed at Walter's legs. "Shoot his kneecap."

"Wait a second!" As the first soldier aimed, Walter backed away. "If you shoot me, you'll have to carry me to—"

The soldier fired. The bullet ripped across Walter's knee, tearing his pants and skin. As pain roared, he dropped to the carpet of wet stalks and curled on his side, clutching his knee. He bit his lip hard to keep from crying out. Blood trickled between his fingers. Warmth coated his cold skin. Although the torture was awful, it seemed that the bullet hadn't broken the cap, maybe just grazed the knee.

"Now," Tamiel said as he stepped closer, "where are the dragon and your traveling companions?"

Walter rolled to his back and spoke through clenched teeth. "I don't know, you cowardly snake! And even if I did, I wouldn't tell you."

"So be it." Tamiel withdrew a handgun from his jacket and aimed it at Walter. "You are worthless to us." He fired. The bullet slammed into Walter's chest just below his shoulder.

Walter gasped. Pain throttled his mind. Blood poured from the wound. As the world grew darker, Tamiel and company marched into the cornstalks. Seconds later, everything faded to blackness.

Lauren kept her head low and her wet hands tight around Roxil's spine. Sheets of rain swept across the gap between their flight level and the ground, which seemed to shift like a bucking bronco about a hundred feet below. Lightning streaked by and crashed into a tall pine. An earsplitting boom shook the air itself.

Lauren strained her eyes. Every building appeared fuzzy, impossible to identify. With these terrible conditions, who could hope to find anything, especially a specific location that some blogger mentioned on the Internet? Even though Lois had read the post to Roxil word for word, that didn't help much. Supposedly, a mugger with a knife accosted a trio that included a winged woman, but the only helpful detail was that it occurred in a parking lot next to a church with a cocoon spun around it. At least a cocoon would be hard to miss if they happened to fly directly over it, but with only the closest town's name to go by, they had to search a huge area.

Lauren regripped Roxil's spine and shouted, "Do you need to stop and rest?"

"Not yet, but soon." A gust knocked Roxil to the side, but she quickly adjusted. "My weariness might be affecting my judgment, but I am beginning to wonder if the blogger's report might be inaccurate. Perhaps she was frightened by the sight of the mugger."

"Maybe so." Lauren brushed water from her eyes and continued scanning the ground. The cocoon did sound kind of crazy, but they had to follow the lead. Besides this one, sightings of a winged woman had dried up.

After a few more moments of dips and swerves, Roxil called out, "I think I see something white, or perhaps off-white."

"Does it look like a church?"

"A steeple is evident, as is a parking lot. Since it is nearly filled with vehicles, perhaps a service is under way."

"Let's land and take a look." Water spewed from Lauren's lips as she spoke. "At least we'll get out of this storm for a while."

Roxil shouted, "Hang on!"

Lauren wrapped both arms around the spine. Roxil bent her wings and angled into a dive. As needlelike droplets stung Lauren's cheeks, she squinted to protect her eyes.

After a few seconds, Roxil leveled out and skidded on a grassy area between a parking lot and what appeared to be a grayish-white cocoon with a protruding porch and steeple.

The moment they came to a stop, Lauren slid down Roxil's wet flank and ran toward the porch, water dripping from her hair and hands. When she reached shelter, her feet slipped on stone tiles. Still on her feet, she slid through the edge of the cocoon, slammed her hands into a door, and fell to her bottom.

Lauren rubbed her wrist—sore but probably not sprained. At eye level, a phone with a pink-and-purple cover swung from a fibrous rope attached to the doorknob. She grabbed the phone and stretched the rope until it broke. "Now this is strange."

Roxil pushed as far as she could under the porch and shook her wings. Water scattered everywhere. "What did you find?"

Lauren showed her the phone. "It was hanging from the knob."

"Are you proficient at searching the device for messages?"

"Most likely, but I might not have time. I banged the door pretty hard. Someone's bound to come and check it out."

"I hear nothing from within the church," Roxil said, "so it seems that your noisy arrival went unheeded."

"Then I can probably take a minute." Lauren unlocked the screen. The app icons appeared. One flashed to indicate a new message. She brought the message up and read it out loud. "This church is address number one. Check the address book and follow us. We are supposed to go to each place but not sure of the schedule. Maybe one each morning. Bonnie, Matt, and Darcy."

Lauren leaned her head against the door and whispered, "Thank you, God."

"Clearly the Maker is guiding our way," Roxil said.

"There's no other explanation." Lauren thumbed through the contact list. "Any idea who Darcy is?"

"I am not familiar with that name."

"And I don't recognize any of the names on this list."

"Perhaps this is a borrowed phone," Roxil said. "It would not have familiar entries."

"But Matt or Mom could have entered their number. I could just call them."

"We can only speculate. We do not even know if they have their own phone."

"True. I jumped to conclusions." Lauren eyed the signal meter. Nothing. "We can't call anyway. There's no signal." She switched to the address list. "If the list is in order, their next destination is a town called Mobley. If we fly straight to it instead of following the roads, maybe we can catch up."

"Does the message indicate a time it was written?"

Lauren flipped back to the note and nodded. "About a half hour ago."

"And what direction is the address?"

"Can't tell. The GPS won't work without a signal, so we'll have to ask Lois." She touched her jaw. "Lois, have you been listening? Can you tell us where Mobley is in relation to where we are now?"

"I have been listening." Low static buzzed through her reply. "I have not been able to get the GPS function in either of your transmitters to work, so I have to base my estimations on your latest reports of roads in your area."

"Sure. That should be close enough."

"The town of Mobley is nearly due east, approximately two hundred ten miles by the route most likely taken by Matt."

Lauren winced. "Roxil, did you hear that?"

"I heard." Her wings wilted.

"Lois," Lauren said, "what about a direct flight?"

"Two hundred three miles, give or take a mile depending on how closely you follow the line."

Roxil settled to her belly. "I am already nearly exhausted. I could not fly three more miles, much less two hundred, especially in this storm."

"It's already pretty late," Lauren said. "Maybe they'll stop somewhere for the night."

Smoke rose from Roxil's nostrils. "If they are ahead of the storm, they will probably drive as far as they can. With multiple drivers available, tiredness will not be a factor."

"So what do we do?"

"Rest." Roxil touched the church door with a wing tip. "After I dry you off, you could go inside and see if anyone is there. Perhaps they will provide a place to sleep. I will be fine under this roof. Just call if you need help. When I am rested, I will awaken you."

92

Lauren nodded. "That sounds good."

"Stand, spread out your limbs, and close your eyes."

Lauren peeled her wet shirt away from her skin and spread her arms. A jet of warmth blew across her body, shifting from head to chest to legs, then from hand to hand. After Roxil inhaled and repeated the process several times, Lauren ran her fingers along her warm, dry clothes. "Thank you. That felt wonderful."

Roxil dipped her head. "You are welcome. Now go inside before you become wet and cold again."

"And I'll see if they have a food pantry for the needy. I'm sure we qualify."

Roxil settled to her belly. "If not, I will try to find a stream and capture fish for roasting, but not until morning."

"Fish for breakfast would be great." Lauren set her hand on the knob. What might be inside a church-like structure that had been wrapped in a giant cocoon? Her back scales tingled. No wonder. This felt like stepping into a bizarre nightmare.

She opened the door. A foul stench drifted by, something rotten blended with mildew. Darkness shrouded the massive room, and with the storm allowing only a dim glow through a window on each side, the sanctuary's pews appeared as shadows aligned in rows that faded into darkness toward the front.

Since her scales had activated, her own glow had probably turned on as well. Standing in the dimness, she would look like a beacon, an easy target.

She found a wall switch and flipped it up. Lights flickered, illuminating a huge hole near the apex of the domed ceiling. Raindrops fell through, though not as heavily as outside. Maybe cocoon fibers sheltered the opening.

A bulb popped, then another, then dozens more. Glass rained over the pews, and the chamber fell dark. She shuddered. Her uncontrollable ability to interfere with electrical equipment had probably disrupted the circuits.

93

Trying to ignore the stench, she left the door open and tiptoed along the carpeted floor to the back pews, one on each side. Someone sat in the aisle seat to the right, motionless and quiet. A homeless person who found refuge from the storm? Maybe.

Lauren leaned close and touched the person's shoulder. "Excuse me. Are you awake?"

The person stayed silent. As Lauren's eyes adjusted, the form took shape. A skull protruded from a suit coat's collar, and bony hands extended beyond the sleeves.

Lauren gasped. She staggered backwards and propped herself on the pew across the aisle. She grasped an armrest, but a skeletal hand was already there. She jumped away and called, stretching out her words, "Roxil, there are dead people in here."

Roxil's head and long neck appeared through the door. She spewed a low flame from both nostrils and lit up the sanctuary. A few hundred skeletons wearing suits and dresses occupied the seats. They all faced the front, their ivory-white jaws hanging open and their vacant sockets staring.

When Roxil's flame fizzled, she blinked her fiery eyes. "Obviously these skeletons will not endanger you, but whatever force caused their deaths might still be lurking. You should rest under the porch roof with me."

"No argument here." Lauren exited with Roxil and closed the door, and the two settled on the portico's concrete floor, Lauren with her back against Roxil's flank. Rain pounded the roof. Wind howled and tossed a cool spray over Lauren's body. She crossed her arms and shivered. "It's getting colder."

"Indeed." Roxil covered her with a wing. "Try to sleep. I will contact Lois so she can relay our news. Perhaps she has heard from Ashley and company by now. When the storm subsides, we will search for food together."

"That's perfect." Lauren closed her eyes and rested her head on Roxil's scales. Although tough and slick, they were warmer than expected. A whirr deep inside the dragon's body sounded like an electric fan with a blade tapping the frame. It resurrected memories of summer nights in Nashville, nights too early in the season to run the air conditioner but too warm to sleep without a fan. The fan would oscillate, first sending a cooling stream along her body that rippled across her thin nightgown, then angling away to tease her until the next arc through the cycle.

She sighed. Those were good days, days when the only worries were school tests, volleyball drills, clothing choices, and girly gossip. Back then those worries felt like steep hills, but they were just

94

bumps in the road, nothing compared to the unscalable mountains of recent days.

But why would a girl her age have to climb these impossible peaks? There were plenty of strong men who would gladly step up and try to save the world. It didn't make sense to send a high school volleyball player to do a trained soldier's job.

She submerged herself in her imagination. If only she could go back to those simple times. After a good-night kiss on the forehead from her foster mother, the soothing fan could blow the cares of the day into oblivion. They really didn't matter. Morning would come, and all would be well. Her adoptive mother and father would be alive, breakfast on the table—oatmeal with cinnamon and raisins. They would eat, share news, laugh—a normal day, back when normal didn't include constantly racing against time to defeat a scheming devil.

"Roxil?"

"Yes?"

"Did you ever have easy times, I mean, before all this crazy stuff broke loose?"

Silence ensued. Even the inner rumble quieted. Finally, Roxil shifted her body, and the gentle fan blades restarted. "A very long time ago. Goliath and I became mates, and for some years we lived together in peace and contentment. I gave birth to Clefspeare, who later became your grandfather in his human form."

"So you're my great-grandmother," Lauren said.

"On the dragon side of the genealogy, yes."

"Interesting." Lauren gave Roxil a nod. "Sorry. Please go on."

"Very well." Roxil took in a breath. "While Clefspeare was a youngling dragon, we lived in bliss. We played flying games, staged mock battles, and went on long journeys to hunt big game. He proved to be the most proficient hunter and warrior any of us had ever seen. I was as proud as I could be."

She exhaled loudly. "I had no inkling that Goliath would turn on me and allow the slayers to kill me. Bitterness poisoned my soul, and I became a tyrant queen in the dragon afterlife. I persecuted those who resembled the white-haired underborn who was prophesied to destroy my little kingdom, but that is a long story.

"Although I obtained the blessing of resurrection and returned to sanity, nothing has been the same. Even after Elam appointed me as an ambassador between Earth and Second Eden, tension persisted at a high level. I could tell that most humans disdained dragons and the mere existence of Second Eden. The tenuous alliance crumbled, and I am sure you know the rest. Trouble and turmoil have been my constant companions, and a return to those days of bliss seems like an impossible dream."

"I know exactly what you mean." Lauren ran a finger along the mainstay of Roxil's wing. "If you could bring back one part of those blissful days, what would it be?"

A soft laugh shook her body. "It is funny that you should ask, because while you were quiet, I was pretending that one precious gift had been restored to me. I felt the happiness with such realism, it restarted my contentment flutter."

"I heard that. Is it like a cat purring?"

"It is similar. It rather surprised me. That purring, as you call it, had been silent for centuries."

"What awakened it? What were you pretending?"

Roxil patted her head with her other wing. "That you were my little Clefspeare sleeping at my side."

Tears welled in Lauren's eyes. "That's ... that's really nice, Roxil. I'm glad I could bring back the memory for you."

"And I am thankful for your precious gift."

Lauren pulled on Roxil's wing and covered more of her body. After a few moments, the contentment flutter strengthened.

"Lauren," Roxil said, a hum in her voice. "I wish to ask you the same question. What part of your past days would you restore?"

"That's fair. Let me think." Lauren blew a puff of white vapor. With cool air settling in and with Roxil's gentle flutter, the soothing fan from those warmer evenings didn't seem important enough to serve as her wish. No, not tonight. Yet one part of those blissful days was still missing, that tender kiss good night, a seal of love, a promise of protection. The beloved comforter who delivered that kiss would never forsake her, would carry her over the impossible peaks, would never let her fall. At least that was the kiss's message, and she believed it. Never doubted it.

Yet mentioning the kiss would likely cause Roxil to want to deliver one, and it wouldn't be the same. Yes, she would provide protection, but dragon lips couldn't communicate intimate touch or provide a vulnerable connection. Their scaly faces were incapable, no matter the sincerity of their love and compassion. Still, Roxil asked. It wouldn't be right to withhold the answer.

"What I really miss," Lauren said, "is my adoptive mother's kiss good night. I can still feel her brushing my hair back and her tender lips touching my forehead. Every time she did that, I knew I was loved. She would say good night and I would say, 'I'll see you in the morning.' For some reason, my words were a promise, and they comforted me. I knew I would survive the night no matter the nightmares. I knew the sun would rise and I would awaken to a new dawn. The promise was like a shield, an oath spoken by a guardian angel. I could go to sleep without fear."

Again silence ensued, though Roxil's flutter continued. After another moment, Roxil shifted her wing and covered Lauren up to her chin. "You have your mother's gift of eloquence." She then heaved a sigh. "I will be your shield tonight, but I cannot deliver the kiss. It would not generate the feeling you remember."

Lauren nodded. "That's okay. I was thinking the same thing. And thank you for being my shield."

"Yet I will give you what I can. It is a dragon's equivalent." Roxil breathed across Lauren's face. The warm air caressed her cheeks and brushed through her hair.

Lauren closed her eyes and imagined her mother's fingers pushing back her childhood bangs again and again, the warmth of her breath when her lips drew near, the whirr of the fan blades. Yes, this would do just fine.

"Good night, Roxil."

"Good night, dear girl."

After taking a deep breath, Lauren whispered, "I'll see you in the morning."

98

Tamiel sat on the church's stage, his stare fixed on the entry door, a nearly invisible passage in the dimness. Lauren had just rushed outside to escape the morbid collection of skeletons, an amusing sight and perfectly orchestrated. Now she would stay out there with the mother of Clefspeare and not disturb this peaceful sanctuary. Fortunately, the hole in the ceiling and the exploding bulbs had kept her from noticing who sat on the stage, a benefit for her. Making eye contact with Arramos would probably have resulted in her death by dragon fire.

Within arm's reach, Arramos perched on his haunches. A scowl on his face, his head swayed at the end of his draconic neck. "The Listener is gone, but will she be able to hear us?"

"It is unlikely," Tamiel said. "The storm will overwhelm her senses and drown out any sounds we make in here."

"Then you may proceed."

"Very well." Tamiel waved a hand toward the ceiling. "Vacule, begin the procession."

The huge spider descended by a silk string and landed on the first skeleton Lauren had touched at the back row. With his legs wrapped around the skeleton's neck, Vacule sank his fangs into its skull. Seconds later, a reddish light began pulsing at its chest, barely visible through its clothes.

When Vacule skittered over to the next skeleton, the first rose and walked slowly toward the stage on wobbly legs. As it proceeded, it stripped off its suit coat and shirt, revealing a throbbing heart behind its ribcage. The second skeleton followed and a third. Soon, a line of skeletons, both male and female, paraded toward the front, all removing shirts and blouses to expose ivory bones surrounding a beating heart. Pants and skirts dropped from their scant waists, along with shoes from their bony feet, and made a trail of clothing that the marching skeletons tromped over.

The first skeleton stopped in front of the stage. It reached under its ribs and pulled its heart out. Cradling the still-pulsing heart in both hands, it extended its bony arms toward Arramos as if presenting an offering.

The skeleton's jaws moved, but only a stream of mist emerged. The skull cracked. Jagged lines ran down the shoulders, along the arms, and finally through the ribs and legs. Then, the entire frame crumbled into a heap. The heart fell along with it and splattered, blood mixing with bone dust.

A breeze swept up the moistened powder and tossed it into a swirl that lifted to the stage. A whisper rode in the spinning air. "I give you all, my master—my heart, my soul, and the fruit of my body." Then, the swirl ascended through the hole in the ceiling and disappeared.

Arramos laughed. "The judgment seat will soon be inundated with souls whispering their allegiance to me. Elohim will not be pleased."

"To be sure," Tamiel said. "Yet, it is a fitting tribute, both to you and to him."

As the next skeleton in line made his offering, Arramos focused on Tamiel. "Lauren drew dangerously close to you. Why do you allow her to continue pursuing her mother and brother? I could easily do away with her in a flash of fire, and I greatly desire to destroy her dragon companion."

"Because we need Bonnie to witness Lauren's death. That will be a sharp and deep dagger straight into her heart. To this point, Bonnie has not suffered enough. Her song is waning, but not quickly. Her resolve is great."

100

"Which is why your plan is so fragile. You are depending on the reactions of someone who obeys our opposition. My plan avoids that problem."

A skeletonized woman collapsed in front of the stage. As her whispered tribute passed by, Tamiel waved a hand and batted away the swirling dust. "Our plans are not at odds. While your forces continue collecting children, the degradation of Bonnie's song will make the process easier. Betrayers will multiply. Parents will forfeit their natural love. You will have tens of thousands of children in the camps in short order."

"We have already seen such forfeiture, but I am concerned about another issue." Arramos's head snaked closer to Tamiel. "Have you set the plan in motion to neutralize Second Eden?"

"I have. Semiramis planted the device when she was last there."

Arramos spewed hot jets from his nostrils. "And you trust that sorceress? She has been plotting my destruction for years."

Another skeleton crumbled. More whispered words of allegiance breezed by. Tamiel scooted farther from the front of the stage. These fools were getting annoying. "I don't trust Semiramis unless she is motivated by her self-interests. She is cooperating with me in order to get an opportunity to kill you. When she comes to the sixth address, she plans to splash you with a potion that will strip away your dragon body and leave you vulnerable. Instead, I will simply take the potion and use it on any dragons that might come to help Bonnie and her allies." He patted a shirt pocket. "Semiramis supplied the device coordinates. Second Eden will soon be conquered."

"If Semiramis is not lying to you." Arramos grumbled as he spoke. "I assume you still have not located the portal. We have no way to send your nuclear missile to Second Eden."

"No, Excellency. Elam has hidden the portal well."

"A pity. I prefer relying on brute force than the word of that sorceress. Until she is cooking in the fiery lake, I will have no peace."

"As soon as I verify the location of the Second Eden device, we can get rid of her. In any case, my missile will not go to waste. Everything is proceeding according to plan."

"Make sure you limit it to only one explosion. A nuclear war is unacceptable. I want the worldwide destruction to come from the hand of Elohim, not from the folly of mankind."

"Understood, Excellency. Taking over a nuclear wasteland is not my idea of a reward for a job well done."

"If you hope for a reward," Arramos said, "I suggest that you speed up the process."

"I can do that, but why the hurry?"

"I want to convert the detainment camps as soon as possible. The gas chambers are already in place. If your plan does not succeed in bringing Elohim's wrath, then mine surely will."

"Very well. I will adjust the schedule." Tamiel lifted his brow. "Anything else?"

"You should not wait long to kill Lauren. If you cannot easily arrange for Bonnie to witness the killing, you should forfeit that part of the plan. You must protect yourself from the Listener's wrath. If she reaches the sixth door, she could do great damage."

"Indeed. I fear that she is well aware of her potential. The question is whether or not she has the courage to fulfill it."

"I think she does." A growl rumbled in Arramos's voice. "I should at least eliminate Roxil while she sleeps. A quick kill of a dragon will further my cause greatly."

"Don't worry. If Lauren begins traveling toward the sixth door, we will be able to eliminate both of them. She and Roxil will spend a lot of time in the air, and since Lauren frequently glows, a fighter jet will find them easily. A heat-seeking missile is quite effective, as Legossi learned not long ago."

102

"Then Makaidos and Thigocia will be my only remaining rivals." Arramos shot his head forward again, bringing his snout within inches of Tamiel's nose. "I trust that it is quite clear that every dragon must be destroyed."

Tamiel forced a calm demeanor. "Of course, Excellency. You will be omnipotent, as planned."

Arramos breathed a hot blast across Tamiel's face. "Never forget that I could roast you with a single puff. And do not assume that your schemes can deceive or thwart me. I am no fool."

"I would never presume otherwise." Tamiel slid away from the scalding flow. "What have I done to raise such suspicions?"

"Your alliance with Semiramis is enough. She has a potion that can neutralize me and the means to deliver it, all because of your desire to manipulate Bonnie's song. I find the entire setup to be suspicious."

"Yet I freely told you about it. When she comes to the sixth address, you can avoid her until I take the potion and use it on the other dragons. Semiramis assures me that it is extremely potent. We need only to get the dragons to sniff the vapor, and they will weaken enough to be easily killed."

"You are skilled in persuasion, but I will continue watching you carefully." Arramos rose to his full height. "I will put the next step of your plan into motion—that is, if I can locate Bonnie."

"You should not have a problem. Although her king's cap is still somewhat effective, I have heard from my agents that she is visible enough. Also, her scent is easy to detect."

"Then I will rely on my nose if I have to."

Tamiel raised a finger. "Wait until Bonnie views the hostages. That is crucial."

"I understand. I will wait."

"And since her song is able to break her bonds, you will need a candlestone to keep her weak. The candlestone bullet that was once inside her proved its ability to sufficiently sap her strength. She was unable to break free."

"I have taken that issue into consideration. Securing her in a candlestone's presence will be a difficult procedure for a dragon, but I will manage."

Tamiel rose to his feet. "And I will continue monitoring Elam's journey. We expect him and his allies to arrive at Fort Knox soon. We are ready to intercept him, but our timing has to be perfect. Altering his course will be the most delicate part of this operation."

Arramos's eyes began to flame. "That leaves only Jared Bannister and Mardon."

"Yes." Tamiel pulled out his phone and read the screen—no reports from any agents. "My messengers lost track of them, but they are of no importance. The last I heard, Jared is still quite sick.

If he or Mardon emerges from hiding, I will hear of it. Since I don't trust Mardon, I didn't tell him the truth about Fort Knox or the missile's target."

"So Mardon is likely neutralized, but I will not be at peace until the former Clefspeare is dead under my claws. He is not one to cower and hide during times of turmoil."

"True, Excellency. We should not underestimate him."

Another skeleton, perhaps number fifty or so, lifted a heart and crumbled in the same way as the others. The whispered pledge whisked by, and the bearer's body and soul ascended to the skies. As more followed, one by one, Tamiel smiled. "Only a few days remain. Just as Noah had seven days of warning before the flood, the human pestilence has only days until the ultimate destruction arrives. Soon you will have your victory."

"And there is no ark to save the species." Arramos unfurled his wings. "We will reconvene at the sixth door, earlier if complications arise." He launched from the stage, circled the sanctuary once, and disappeared through a hole above.

Tamiel turned toward the parade of skeletons. With hollow sockets and gaping mouths they continued marching over their clothing—tailored suits, silky gowns, impeccable skirts, high-heeled shoes, fashionable ties, and other accessories that once covered their naked bones.

Tamiel laughed. Such comedy! Such a pathetic display. The Son of Elohim was right when he said, "Woe unto you, scribes and Pharisees, hypocrites! For ye are like unto whited sepulchres, which indeed appear beautiful outward, but are within full of dead men's bones, and of all uncleanness." These fools probably read those words a hundred times, yet they played them out every Sunday, blinded to their own folly.

When the final skeleton collapsed and blew away, Tamiel nodded toward the spider, now perched on the front pew. "Your work is done here, Vacule. Gather the drones and send them to the sixth door."

"I will." Vacule shot a thread to the ceiling and quickly ascended.

Tamiel extended his wings and flew toward the ceiling. He pushed his fangs over his bottom lip. So far the plan had proceeded without much violence. Soon it would be time to shed more blood—Lauren's blood.

105

7

CHAPTER

The Second Door

A scream sounded from far away, bloodcurdling and desper-ate. Where had it come from? Hadn't everyone just gone to sleep in the motel?

Matt opened his eyes. Standing on a wooden platform that was attached to a rope, he hovered over a void. A pulsing red glow radiated from the depths and illuminated the surroundings. A cylindrical wall of uneven stone reached to an open top at least a hundred feet above and plunged downward out of sight. Shadows shifted on the wall's surface, like doors opening and closing. The grinding of rock on rock added to the image.

High above, a woman lay at the edge of the cylinder's top holding the other end of the rope. Hot air blew from the void and across Matt's sweat-slickened skin and saturated shirt. He grabbed the rope and tried to focus on the woman. She looked like Darcy, but it was too dark to be sure.

An image flashed—a younger Darcy looking down from a bedroom window as he dangled by a rope. While she laughed, he swayed helplessly in bitterly cold air.

Matt shook himself back to reality. But how could this be reality? The red glow swelled upward, growing closer and closer. More hot air surged. The platform cracked and splintered between his feet. He twisted the rope around his fist and held on.

The wood crumbled and scattered in the upwelling breeze. He dropped. The rope tightened, slowing the plunge, but he continued downward in rhythmic pulses.

An echoing laugh filled the cavern, cruel and feminine. A loud crack sounded. The rope suddenly slackened. Matt fell into the void. As he dropped, he flailed in darkness, unable to scream. A voice whispered into his ear. "Trust me while you have nothing to lose. I will wait until everything is on the line. Then I will stab you in the back."

Matt shot up, gasping. He sat in his motel bed, his T-shirt drenched with sweat. Darcy lay curled on the other bed, apparently asleep, but Mom no longer lay next to her.

Framed by dawning rays passing through the draped window, a human shadow with a lump on its back crossed from left to right outside. The lock clicked, and the door swung open, revealing Mom wearing a backpack.

She cocked her head. "Are you all right? You're sweating."

He peeled the moist shirt away from his skin. "A nightmare. I guess I got a little warm."

Mom closed the door. "Well, it's freezing outside. That storm came through and brought in some cold air."

"What were you doing out there?"

"Praying. And singing. I hoped to strengthen my inner song, and I didn't want to disturb anyone. But it's dawn now. Since we have to be there by eight, we should get going."

Matt shook away the mental haze. Last night's text message from Tamiel flowed to the forefront. *Be at the second door by eight a.m. From now on, proceed to the rest of the doors without seeking a motel unless I say otherwise. I wish to accelerate the collection of keys.* "Right. We'd better hustle a bit."

Darcy stretched her arms. "I slept really well. Sorry to hear about your nightmare, Matt."

"Well ... no worries. Dreams are just dreams." He threw off the bedcovers, exposing the sweatpants and loose T-shirt Enoch had provided for sleepwear. "I need a shower."

Mom rubbed her hands together. "Darcy and I both showered after you conked out last night, so we'll see if this place has anything for breakfast. If they don't, we'll get something from the box in the car."

"Okay by me."

After Darcy hurried into the bathroom and changed from her own sweatpants and T-shirt, she joined Mom at the door. Mom pointed at a motel room key on the dresser. "I have the other one. See you in a few minutes."

After showering quickly, Matt put on the new camo pants and beige long-sleeved shirt. He unplugged the phone from the adapter, picked up the car and motel keys, and hurried out the door to the sidewalk that ran between their room and the parking lot. A brisk, cold wind bit through his clothes, but it didn't matter. His inner furnace always kept him warm.

To the east, a hazy ball of dull red peeked through the overcast sky and painted the thin clouds crimson once again. Matt breathed a sigh. "Sailors take warning." His words puffed out in clouds of white.

He pushed the phone into his pocket and hustled along the sidewalk toward the motel lobby. As he drew near, his stomach tightened. Danger?

He halted and looked across the street. The GPS pointed to a building half a block away as the address of the second door, a medical facility with a sign that read Women's Health Clinic.

Matt shuddered. Those words seemed cryptic. The phone's address label had called it *The Second Door —The Forsaken.* That only added to the mystery.

After meeting his mother and Darcy and eating a breakfast that consisted of cold biscuits and hardboiled eggs, they walked out to the street, leaving the Mustang in the motel parking lot. When they arrived at the clinic, Darcy pointed at a sign mounted on the door that displayed their hours of operation—7 am to 3 pm today. "They should be open. We can just walk in."

"Isn't that early for a medical facility?" Matt asked.

Darcy shook her head. "Probably doing surgeries. They always start those early."

Matt reached for the doorknob, trying to ignore the fact that Darcy knew so much about a place like this. Better not to ask.

He pushed the door open and walked into a small waiting room. Six metal-framed chairs with seats and backs of beige fabric ran along three walls. Next to an interior door, a closed sliding window provided a view of a cramped office, but no one seemed to be inside, only a wraparound countertop, a copier, and a few floor-to-ceiling filing cabinets.

Matt tapped on the window with a knuckle. "Anyone here?"

From a side door, a slender black woman in a flowery nurse's smock bustled into the office. She slid the window open, her head tilted. "No walk-ins today." Her tone was firm but not harsh. "The doctor is out. We canceled all appointments."

"No surprise," Matt said. "Lots of weird stuff going on."

"You're telling me." She offered a halfhearted smile. "Maybe things will settle down soon. Call for an appointment."

110

"We don't have time to call—"

"Nonsense." The nurse glanced at Darcy. "Your girlfriend can't be more than a couple of months, tops."

When she began sliding the window closed, Darcy rushed forward. "Wait!"

The nurse pushed the window back a few inches. "What?"

"I'm just here to ask you to check my temperature. I want to make sure I don't have an infection."

"Oh. You're post-op." The nurse narrowed her eyes. "I don't recognize you. When was your surgery?"

"Not long ago. It must have been your day off."

"Wednesday, then." The nurse pushed a button. The door in the waiting room buzzed. "Come on in. I'll check you."

Darcy pulled the door and held it open. "Snoop around while I'm in there. I'll try to delay her as much as possible. If you find the key, then give me some kind of signal, and I'll come out."

Matt nodded. "Got it."

When Darcy walked into an interior hallway, Matt caught the knob, then peeked inside. The nurse led Darcy around a corner and out of sight.

Matt waved for his mother. They padded noiselessly to the opposite end of the hall where a closed room stood on each side. He touched a knob and whispered, "You check the other one."

She nodded and went inside. A light flickered on, and she closed the door behind her.

Matt entered his room and flipped a wall switch. Ceiling lights flashed to life. He let the door close with a gentle click.

Trash pails and bags lined the side walls, and two tall refrigerators bordered a window at the back. Red drops marked a trail from the room's entry and split into several branches leading to the pails and toward the rear wall.

Matt crouched and touched one of the brighter drops—blood, tacky but not wet. Brushing the blood on his pants, he rose and followed the freshest trail to a metal trashcan. When he pressed the can's foot pedal, the lip popped up, attached by a hinge.

A choking stench rose from the can. Matt held his breath and crouched. Inside, a plastic bag fastened with a twist tie rested on the bottom, yesterday's date marked on the side with a dark pen. The size and shape of a small pumpkin, it was probably nothing more than someone's discarded lunch, but that didn't explain the odor. Could a sandwich smell this bad after only one day?

He picked up the bag. A gray key lay underneath. He snatched the key and set the bag back in place. The key was the same size as the first one, but would it prove itself?

As he rose, he averted his eyes. A flash lit up the room. When he looked again at the key, it glowed with an orange hue. This was the sign. It had moved out of the "sphere of influence," whatever that meant. With the first key, he had to hurry out of the church, so it was impossible to determine the boundary of that sphere. Maybe this would be a good chance to learn what sort of influence kept the key from glowing.

Matt attached the key to the ring at his belt. Crouching again, he reached into the pail and began untwisting the metal tie. With every turn, something pinched his gut. Danger? No. Something different.

He dropped the tie and spread the top of the bag. A baby's tiny body lay curled inside, no bigger than his hand.

Matt sucked in a breath. The stench burned in his nostrils and tightened his throat. Nausea churned. Bile leaked into his mouth, but he swallowed it down.

Trembling, he lifted the baby's petite arm and closed his thumb over the perfectly formed hand. So soft. So delicate. The picture of perfect innocence, torn from a mother's womb and tossed into a waste can. Human trash.

Matt shot up and backed away. The lid fell closed. The ringing of metal on metal hammered against his skull. Heaving shallow breaths, he looked around the room—a disposal area, a garbage dump.

Anger burned. Dark spots flooded his vision. Have no use for something? Throw it in the trash! Used band-aids, banana peels, and babies!

The room began to spin. He staggered to one of the refrigerators and grabbed the handle to keep from falling. What else might these demons be hiding?

He opened the door. Two plastic bags fell out, the same size and shape of the one in the pail. At least twenty more had been crammed into the refrigerator, each one labeled with a date.

113

Matt's heart pounded. He tried to breathe, but his throat locked. Gagging, he stumbled toward the door. It opened. Mom appeared, her eyes wide. She rushed in, threw her arms around him, and guided him to the hallway.

The moment he crossed the boundary, his throat loosened. He sucked in fresh air, trying to stay as quiet as possible. "Mom …" He swallowed. "Mom … I …"

"Take your time," she whispered as she patted him on the back. "My room was just an examination room. I didn't find anything important. No key."

"I found the key." Matt swallowed again, but he couldn't avoid a lamenting squeak. "And I found dead babies."

Her cheeks flushed bright red. "Dead babies?"

His breathing stayed fast and shallow. "In bags. In a pail. In a refrigerator. A bunch of them."

"I knew this was an abortion clinic, but I didn't know we'd find dead babies." A growl rumbled in her voice. "Tamiel knows how to make my heart bleed."

"What are we going to do?"

"Do?" Mom asked. "You got the key. What else do you have in mind?"

He clenched a fist so hard, it shook. "We can't let them keep killing babies here. It's madness. It's murder."

"Of course it is, but this happens all over the world every single day, and what have we done about it? Protest? Vote? Write letters? Sure, but nothing ever happens. The butchers keep killing babies, and the politicians ignore us."

"That's because they haven't held a dead baby's hand." Matt spotted the door leading to the office. "Darcy asked for a sign when I found the key. Well, I'm going to give her one."

114

He stalked to the door, flung it open, and grabbed a desktop computer. Jerking the wires and cords, he hoisted it to his shoulder and flung it through the window. Glass shattered. Shards rained over a flowerbed outside. The computer landed on the sidewalk and slid to a stop.

Rage stormed within. A jagged dark frame pulsed around every object in the room. He threw a filing cabinet over, then another. File folders scattered across the floor. Papers spilled and flew everywhere.

The nurse ran in and screamed, "What are you doing? Get out!"

Matt picked up an armful of files and tossed them into the air. "I'll get out when I'm finished."

"I'm calling the cops." She picked up a phone and punched in 911.

"See if I care!" Matt scanned the room. Another computer hummed against the wall. Nearby, a printer slid out a page. "Where's the circuit breaker box?"

"You think I'm crazy?" She turned to the phone. "Hello? I need the police."

"I'll find it myself." Matt stormed into the hall.

Darcy caught his arm and held on. "Matt!" He pulled her along for a second, but she set her feet, halting him. "You have to stop!"

Red-stained spots flooded his vision. "Why should I? They murder babies in this place!"

"I know they do." She slid a hand into his, interlocked their thumbs, and looked into his eyes. "Matt. Listen to me." Her voice purred, soft and soothing. "We need you. Any minute, the police will show up, and they'll haul you to jail. Then where will we be? Do you want your mom and me to face Tamiel's other five doors by ourselves?"

115

Matt's inner heat ebbed. Darcy's watery eyes seemed to douse the flame.

Mom joined them and took his other hand. "We have to go."

His head spinning again, Matt nodded and followed their lead outside. When they reached the sidewalk, he pulled away. "I'm okay. I'm fine."

Mom half closed an eye. "Are you sure?"

"Yeah. I'm sure." He looked back at the broken window and the nurse still talking on the phone. "We'd better haul out of here."

Mom pulled a motel key from her backpack. "Darcy and I will get our stuff while you start the car. Pull it right up to our room."

While Mom and Darcy jogged across the street toward their motel room, Matt angled toward the parking lot. A siren drew close, maybe just a mile away. When the police arrived, it would take at least a minute for the nurse to tell the story, so they might have time to sneak away, but it would be close.

As he ran, the two keys on the ring clinked together. Tiny sparks flew at the contact point, as if electrified, but they didn't seem to cause any damage to each other.

He jumped into the Mustang, started it, and drove slowly toward the room. When they arrived the night before, the lot had been packed, forcing him to park pretty far away. Now only five or six cars remained—plenty of space.

He parked parallel to their room's door, popped the trunk, and jumped out. Just as he reached for the knob, the door flung open. Darcy charged out with one suitcase, and Mom followed with the other. "You prepaid with the credit card," Mom said as she breezed past. "Let's go."

116

Mom and Darcy threw the suitcases into the trunk. Matt closed the motel room door and hopped into the driver's seat, while Mom slid into the front passenger's seat and Darcy jumped into the back.

Matt drove to the street. At the clinic, two police officers stood at the front doorway, one taking notes on a pad while the nurse talked. Matt drove slowly onto the road in the opposite direction. His heart thumped hard. Would the police notice? Give chase?

Now that his rage had subsided, questions surged. Did he have the right to ransack that place? Definitely. After all, it was a house of murder. But a soldier should never lose his cool, never stray from discipline, no matter how noble the motivation. He had probably forced that clinic to close for a day or two. They would use their blood money to clean up the mess and be back to killing babies all too soon. What had he done but make a huge mess and risk their freedom to complete their mission? Still, he had sent a message. Murder brings wrath. But was that enough of a reason to deliver that wrath himself?

He sighed. Too many questions and not enough answers. And with the third door on the horizon, another avalanche of questions would soon bury him.

Lauren, this is Lois. I have a report for you."

Lauren shook herself out of a light doze and touched her jaw. "Yes, Lois. I'm here." Lying curled on her side and covered by a blanket, she glanced around. The church's portico still provided shelter, though it couldn't keep out a chilly breeze. Roxil was nowhere in sight. "What's the report?"

"Marilyn Bannister sent an encrypted message to one of our cyber mailboxes. I ignored it at first, because it was not marked properly as being from her and Jared, but when I went back over the mailboxes again, I found that she made a simple typing error and—"

117

"It's okay, Lois. No need to explain." Lauren sat up and draped the blanket over her back. "Just tell me what the message says."

"Matt is being accompanied by his mother and a young, auburn-haired woman. We have reason to believe that the woman is Semiramis posing as Darcy, Matt's former foster sister. Marilyn believes she could be a potential betrayer or perhaps is accompanying them simply to gain information."

"And I suppose Matt doesn't know who she really is."

"Nor do we. It is only a theory."

"This is getting really complicated." Lauren pulled the cell phone from her pocket. "Lois, I'm going to read more addresses to you from that phone we found. The address Matt was supposed to go to this morning was too far away for us, but maybe you can tell us where we can intercept him by dragon flight."

"Very well. I am ready."

Lauren pulled up the list and read the addresses for doors three, four, five, and six out loud. "The seventh one just has a note saying it's missing, so I guess that one's a bust."

After a few seconds, Lois spoke up again. "When I include the address you provided last night as well as the church's where you are now, the six together create an interesting pattern, a rough circle. Matt's course will take him back toward your current location eventually, which means that the sixth address is the closest.

"If you fly there, you will intercept him easily. If you wish to do so earlier, the fourth address is within reach. Assuming high motivation will cause Roxil to fly twenty percent faster than usual and require fifteen percent less rest than recommended, you should be able to arrive at address number four sometime tomorrow, but that does not mean that you would arrive while he is still there. You could expend much energy and miss his presence by mere moments."

"What about number five?"

"It is an outlier from the circle, making it the same distance as number four. You could choose to fly toward number six and adjust to navigate toward one of the other addresses if we learn more about Matt's location and determine that a change of course is reasonable."

"That sounds perfect." Lauren slid the phone away. "Can you guide Roxil on the best course to number six?"

"Since I know your precise location now, I should be able to guide you, but I will again need frequent reports of landmarks such as roads, bodies of water, and significant ground formations. I will also schedule appropriate places to rest and find food and water."

"Do you know where Roxil is now?" Lauren asked. "I haven't seen her this morning."

"She has been at a nearby lake roasting fish and is returning to your location. She asked me to awaken you, and she should arrive at any moment."

"Have you heard from Ashley or Walter or Gabriel?"

"Nothing, though that does not necessarily reflect the status of their health or safety. According to my records, they do not have working tooth transmitters, so they do not have any means of communicating with me."

"Right. Ashley's got cooked by the lightning."

"If I receive contact from them, I will let you know." Static entered Lois's reply for the first time that morning. "I am monitoring hundreds of frequencies."

"How about Elam? Have you heard from him?"

"He and his team are intentionally avoiding all communications in order to ensure complete secrecy. They will call for help only if necessary."

"I understand. Thank you." Lauren clutched the blanket and rose to her feet. Her knees and ankles popped. The colder air and the concrete bed had stiffened everything.

As she stretched her back, she leaned out from under the portico and scanned the sky. Against reddish haze, a flying dragon came into view about a mile away. Roxil would arrive in moments.

119

Lauren walked to the church entrance, brushed back the cocoon, and peered inside the sanctuary. The skeletons were gone, vanished except for a pile of clothes lining the center aisle. What could it all mean? Had they died of a flesh-eating disease? No. A disease couldn't work that quickly. A sudden firestorm? No again. The discarded clothing seemed to be intact.

In a flurry of wings, Roxil settled in the parking lot, carrying in her teeth a wicker basket filled with a half dozen blackened fish. She shuffled to the portico and set the basket down. "I apologize for their scorched appearance. I already ate several, and they are tender and juicy on the inside. I will carry you to the lake for a drink when you are sated."

The aroma ignited a rumble in Lauren's stomach. "Thank you." She picked up a fish, perhaps a trout, and bit into it, careful to avoid bones. Even without any salt or spices, it tasted wonderful. Her body likely craved nourishment.

While Lauren chewed, Roxil nudged the blanket with her snout. "This and the basket were lying on the ground in a park. Storm debris, I assume. I used my breath to warm the blanket for you. Also, the church area seemed secure, so I thought it safe to let you sleep. After your ordeal, you need plenty of rest."

Lauren swallowed a hunk of fish. "The skeletons in the church are gone. Did you hear anything strange during the night?"

"No, but I felt a heightened sense of danger now and then, nothing truly alarming."

"Very strange." Lauren touched her jaw. "Did your transmitter pick up Lois telling me where we could intercept Matt?"

"Every word, but we cannot simply fly and collect Matt and your mother. Tamiel must know by now that we are on the trail. We will need a plan to counter his schemes to capture or destroy us should we appear at one of the addresses."

"So we need to get there secretly to see what's going on."

Roxil bobbed her head. "Which means that I cannot fly all the way there. I am far too visible. I should land close to the destination, and you should travel the final part of the journey alone." Roxil examined Lauren's hands. "Are you adept at any form of weaponry?"

"I shot a rifle to save Gabriel, but I think I got lucky." Lauren painted a mental picture of herself holding a gun, this time aiming at Tamiel. He had been shot before but soon recovered. Since he was a demon, the weapons of this world likely wouldn't do any permanent damage. It would take much more than a bullet to kill him. "Don't worry ..." A rush of tingles ran along the scales on her back. She took a deep breath to keep her emotions in check. "If I run into Tamiel, I'll know what to do."

121

CHAPTER

THE THIRD DOOR

After getting well out of the policemen's sight, Matt accelerated to the speed limit. "I think we made it." He pulled out the phone and handed it to Darcy. "Can you map our route?"

"Sure." She brought up the next address and leaned the phone against the dashboard. The label flashed at the top of the screen: *The Third Door —The Flyers.*

Matt mouthed the words. The meanings of *The Frauds* and *The Forsaken* had become obvious, but only after opening the doors.

"Any idea what it means?" Darcy asked.

"Maybe." Mom leaned forward. "Billy and I saw a lot of strange things in the third circle of Hades. Morgan's home stood on top of a strange hill, and a swamp filled with venomous serpents surrounded it. I flew across the swamp while Billy waded. Me flying is kind of a remote connection to *The Flyers.* It's not much, but it's something."

"Maybe we'll find out more soon," Matt said. "It's only thirty miles away. Since Tamiel hasn't sent a message, we're probably supposed to go straight there instead of finding a motel."

"That's my guess." After a few moments of silence, Mom touched Matt's shoulder. "You know, maybe we already have more clues about what's going to happen."

"What do you mean?"

"This might sound unrelated, but I've been thinking about your nightmare. Do you feel like telling me about it?"

He shook his head. "Like I said before, dreams are just dreams. They don't mean anything."

"Sometimes they do." Mom pulled a band from her pocket and fastened her hair back. "Lauren and I are dream oracles. We sometimes dream true events, though that hasn't happened to me since I returned to Earth, I suppose because of my weakened song. Anyway, I thought you might have the same gift."

"Well, now that you mention it, one time I had a dream that seemed to be coming true word for word. I mean, what was happening in real life was exactly what happened in the dream, so when it came time for me to say something that I said in the dream, I said something else."

"Why?"

He shrugged. "So the dream wouldn't control me, I guess. I don't want to be a puppet on a string."

"So you *did* see something that was going to happen, but you were able to change it." Mom nodded thoughtfully. "Interesting."

As Matt sped along, the farm landscape slowly gave way to a marshland. Water birds poked long beaks into ponds between grassy islands. A heron lifted its head and stared at them, its grayish-blue body awash in the eerie red sunlight. It ruffled its feathers and looked around, as if nervous. It seemed that the birds knew

124

something twisted was going on. Even the water appeared bloody in the scarlet glow.

While they drove, Mom told Darcy a few stories about her adventures, beginning with her recent escape from jail then shifting back several years to when the Enforcers hunted for her and Dad in order to kidnap their twins. During those precarious days, they sometimes communicated using sign language when they suspected that their dwelling had been bugged. Walter and Ashley learned the language as well so they could make plans in silence and in secret.

Mom then focused on her dark hours trapped inside the candlestone, apparently hoping to encourage Darcy with the amazing tale of protection and rescue from what seemed to be an impossibly forsaken dungeon. When Mom mentioned meeting Sir Barlow there, she told tales of his steadfast courage. Matt added the details about how Colonel Baxter shot Sir Barlow and how they were both transluminated. To this day no one knew what happened to them.

125

"While I was in prison," Mom said, "I had a vivid dream about Sir Barlow. He had a romantic interest in Tamara, a former dragon. It seemed like a perfect match. Tamara has difficulty speaking, and Sir Barlow loves to talk, and if anyone needs a good woman at his side, it's Sir Barlow. The last time I saw them I got the impression that they're lonely for companionship. And since they are both centuries old ..." She finished with a smile.

"How romantic that would be!" Darcy closed her eyes and inhaled deeply. "I love a good romance story. If only everyone could find the perfect person for them."

"Yeah," Matt said. "That would be great, but maybe not everyone needs another person."

Mom and Darcy sat quietly, as if not knowing how to respond.

Following the phone's directions, Matt turned onto a dirt road, barely wide enough for two cars. A thick cluster of trees lay about a mile ahead, apparently a dense forest that looked like an oasis in this wilderness of marshlands. Based on the GPS map, the cluster had to be their destination.

He stopped the car a couple of hundred yards short of the forest. "No buildings in sight."

Darcy picked up the phone and scrolled across the screen. "We didn't miss any texts, and we're getting a signal."

"Then we'll just go on." Matt pressed the gas pedal. As they drew near the forest, his danger sensation skyrocketed. Something sinister lay within those woods. "Mom. Darcy. My meter's clicking in red zone. Just letting you know."

"We'll keep our eyes open," Mom said. "We have to go on."

When they entered the forest, the overhead canopy veiled the sun. The road weaved around dark water and cypress trees. Their trunks looked like crooked forks poking into the marshy soil. After a couple of miles, the road ended at a tree-lined path, too narrow for the car to navigate.

Matt stopped and shut off the engine. "I guess we go on foot."

"How's your danger meter now?" Mom asked.

He laid a hand on his stomach. "About as bad as it gets." He slid the phone into his pocket and opened the door. "Let's go."

As they hiked the path, Matt led the way. He grabbed hanging vines and jerked them down, though they really weren't an obstacle. Exposed roots crisscrossed the uneven ground, becoming more numerous as the trail meandered through the darkening forest.

After several minutes, the path led up a slope and into a clearing. Grass spread across a quarter-acre expanse, nearly choked with dandelions and thistles. A four-story house constructed with huge red and yellow stones and gray mortar stood at the center, more

126

like a castle than a normal home. The stones, along with the sun's light, gave the entire house an orange hue.

"A house on a hill," Mom whispered. "Like Morgan's."

Matt walked between a pair of tall gardenia bushes and up to the front wall. He touched a thick vine that zigzagged along gaps between stones from the ground to a parapet at the roof's edge. "This place has been here a very long time."

"No doubt." Mom ran her foot along the grass. "It seems familiar."

Darcy picked up a shiny penny. "The date is last year. Someone has been here recently."

"Good find." Matt stepped to a window and grasped one of five black iron bars running vertically in front of the opening. With no glass or frame, the window mimicked a medieval castle's venting hole. "Can't get in this way."

He sidestepped to a massive wooden door and turned a black knob that looked like a beetle, similar to an Egyptian scarab. The door pushed open without a sound. "So much for security."

"Tamiel's expecting us," Mom said.

Matt walked in, Mom and Darcy following. Windows on each wall allowed plenty of red-tinted light into an enormous room. With long rows of blooming flowers and other plants growing from parallel openings in the floor, and with a garden hoe lying between two rows, the place looked like a greenhouse of some kind, though framed paintings on paneled walls and a fireplace on the left gave it the feel of a museum.

He crouched next to the closest flower and touched one of its red petals. "The plants aren't fake. No one's taking care of the lawn, but someone must be watering these."

"They're poppies." Darcy pointed at a row of greenery. "And that's marijuana."

"So this is a drug farm." Matt rose and crossed his arms. "The third door. The flyers. Drug users get high."

"That could be it." Mom scanned the garden. "I see more parallels to the circles of seven. In the third circle, Morgan sprayed me with a drug when she kidnapped me. And did you notice the doorknob? It looks like the passage beetle that bit Billy in the second circle and sent him to the third."

Matt nodded. "So the doors are still in parallel with the circles. How can we use that knowledge to our advantage?"

"Maybe we can't. It's just too obvious. Probably a red herring, or maybe the parallels are there to remind me of the tortures Billy and I endured. It's another song killer." Mom walked fully inside and inhaled deeply. "I recognize the scent."

Darcy inhaled. "Lilacs?"

"Yes. I smelled them in the place Tamiel imprisoned me." Mom pointed at the fireplace. "I heard flames crackling over there, so …" She marched to an oaken door to the right of the fireplace and touched the front panel. "Tamiel kept me locked up in here." She laid an ear against it. After a few seconds, she whispered, "I hear something. A voice. But I can't make out any words."

Matt hurried to her side. "Another prisoner?"

"Most likely."

Matt turned the knob and pulled, then pushed, but nothing would budge.

Mom banged on the door with a fist. "Is anyone in there?"

A pair of muffled wails sounded from the other side, one deep and one high-pitched.

"A man and a woman." Matt thrust his shoulder and hip into the door. Again, it wouldn't budge. "Tight as a drum."

Darcy dropped to her knees and peered underneath. "I can't see anything. The door's maybe six inches thick. No one could break it down without a battering ram."

"Let's find a window to that room." Matt strode to the interior garden, picked up the hoe, and jogged outside and around the house. When he reached a window on the side, he stopped and looked between its iron bars into a dim room, illuminated only by daylight. Two figures, one wearing jeans and the other a calf-length skirt, hung by their manacled wrists, suspended by chains attached to the ceiling.

Dark bags covered their heads, and their bare feet dangled several inches above a rectangular hole that appeared to be about ten feet long and five feet wide. As the captives twisted one way, then another, water splashed over the edges of the hole and spilled onto the tiled floor.

Matt leaned back and shouted toward the front door. "Mom! Darcy! Over here! Hurry!"

Seconds later, they appeared at the corner and ran to join him. Mom peeked inside. "They can't survive like that for long."

"I know. This setup is recent. Tamiel knew when we would get here."

Darcy looked over Mom's shoulder. "Something must be in that water to make it splash so much."

"Nothing good, I'm sure." Matt leaned the hoe against the wall and pushed his shoulder between two bars, but his chest wouldn't fit. "My name is Matt Bannister!" he shouted. "I'll get you out of there somehow!"

The male prisoner moaned, and the female grunted several times as if trying to speak.

Matt pulled back from the window. "They must be gagged."

"I'll try to slide through." Mom began shedding her backpack. "I lost a lot of weight in prison, but my wings might get stuck."

"Maybe I can fit." Darcy slid her slender arms between two bars. She exhaled and wriggled her chest through, then, bracing on the stone sill while Mom pushed, she thrust her hips past the bars and dropped to her hands and knees on the floor.

"Great work!" Matt pointed at the interior door. "See if you can let us in."

While Mom continued stripping off her backpack, Darcy leaped up and ran to the door. She grabbed the knob and pulled, then pushed to no avail. She bent over and peered into a keyhole below the knob. "It must be locked. I don't see a key anywhere."

Matt picked up the hoe and extended it between two bars. "See if you can get those bags off their heads."

She hurried back to the window, grabbed the hoe, and walked to the edge of the hole in the floor. Standing on tiptoes, she leaned over the water and pushed the hoe's handle under the woman's hood. After three tries, she lifted it over her head. When the hood fell, gray hair spilled down to her shoulders. Muted by a tight gag, she wrestled against her bound hands, her eyes wide as if trying to shout with her expression.

"Mariel!" Mom grasped two bars. "The other one must be Thomas!"

"The missing anthrozils?" Matt asked.

Mom nodded. "I've never met them, but I've seen photos."

"Obviously Mariel's trying to tell us something. I sense danger, but that's been constant ever since we got here."

"Mariel can see down into the water." Mom pushed her face between two bars and shouted, "Darcy! Get away! I think she's trying to warn you about something!"

Darcy stepped backwards. Something splashed in the water. A serpent-like appendage slithered over the edge of the hole and snaked around her ankle. It jerked her toward the opening and knocked her to her knees. The hoe flew from her hands and clattered to the floor. As the tentacle slowly dragged her toward the

water, she lunged for the hoe but merely brushed it with her fingertips.

Matt shook the bars. "Darcy! Hang on!"

"We'll tie some vines together!" Mom ran toward the woods,
but just as she neared the trees, a red dragon swooped down and
grabbed her jacket by the shoulders. Flying parallel to the ground,
it swept her across the clearing. "Matt!" she screamed as she beat
her wings to fight back. "Help!"

"Mom!" Matt sprinted after her, but the dragon lifted her out
of reach. Within seconds, the beast had carried her over the tree-
tops.

As they began shrinking in the distance, Matt shoved a hand
into his pocket and jerked out the car keys. Just as he turned to
sprint toward the Mustang, Darcy screamed, "Matt! I can't fight
it much longer!"

He froze, his mind numb. The call sounded like a distant
siren, a fire engine wailing in the night—someone else's concern.

Darcy cried out again. "Matt! Please!"

He shook away the numbness. "I'm coming!" He scooped up
some of the vines he had broken earlier. With trembling hands he
began tying them together as he lumbered back to the house.

He halted at the window, breathless. His heart raced. Sweat
poured. As he glanced at the dwindling forms of his mother and
the dragon, he tightened his jaw. He had to focus on his training,
not let emotions interfere again—be a soldier, not a boy.

Working quickly, he coiled several yards of the vines into a
loop. Inside, Darcy clung to the hole's edge, only her arms and
head visible. As she clawed at the tiles, water splashed over her
head and across the floor.

"Catch!" Matt tossed the loop. It fell over her arms. She
grabbed it and wound it around her wrist. Bracing his feet

against the wall, he leaned back and heaved with his entire body. The vine tightened and twisted. As Darcy clutched the other end, desperately pulling hand over hand, thin vine fibers snapped and curled. She slid forward on a carpet of puddles, her eyes trained on the hoe.

With every inch of progress, Matt regripped the vine and pulled again. Darcy's chest cleared the edge of the hole, then her waist, legs, and feet, the monster's tentacle still wrapped around her ankle. Darcy's facial muscles strained. Both arms stretched. Soon, her hands drew even with the hoe.

Letting go with one hand, she reached for the handle. The vine broke with a loud crack. Matt flew backwards. His head slammed against the ground, and he slid across thistles and sharp grass.

He blinked at the sky as it spun in a swirl of scarlet. The dragon and Mom were nowhere in sight. As dizziness overwhelmed his senses, it seemed that resolve to go on began leaking from his pores.

132

Then, danger spiked once more. Adrenaline kicked in. Darcy! He flipped over to hands and knees. He crawled back to the window, braced his hands on the opening, and climbed to his feet. Inside, Darcy stood holding the hoe, her shoulders sloped. Blood dripped from the blade, and a foot-long tentacle section lay wriggling next to her foot.

With the hoe's blade dragging on the floor, she shuffled toward him. Her clothes clung to her thin frame, and hair lay plastered across her face. When she bumped into the window frame, she dropped to her knees and whispered a tired, "Thank you."

"Yeah." Matt swallowed. No more words would squeeze through his tight throat.

She swiveled back toward Mariel and Thomas, still dangling over the tank. "What'll we do?"

"I ... I'm not sure." Matt grasped a bar tightly. "See if you can get the other hood off and untie their gags. Whatever that monster is, it likely won't try to grab you again. It doesn't want to lose another tentacle."

"Okay. I'll try." She peeled a lock of hair away from her eye. "What are you going to do?"

He let his gaze drift to the inner room's ceiling. The prisoners' chains passed through holes in the paneling. "I'll try to find a stairway and see if I can get to the room above this one."

"Good idea." Darcy wrapped her fingers around Matt's hand. "Thank you again for saving me."

Matt resisted the urge to jerk his hand back. The words *you'd have done the same for me* came to mind, but they hung in his throat. "I'm glad you're all right."

He slid his hand away and ran to the front. When he entered, he scanned the room. The locked door seemed to be the only passage out of this strange greenhouse. The ceiling, consisting mostly of windows, lay well out of reach. The only remaining option seemed to be to climb to an upper floor from the outside. Maybe the windows up there wouldn't be secured by bars.

Something clicked. The interior door creaked open, and Darcy stepped through the gap holding the hoe and a key ring. "I found this ring in a hole in the wall."

A barrage of thoughts whisked through Matt's mind. She just happened to find the keys? Now? When she couldn't find them before? Had Tamiel orchestrated every event, including a fake monster to keep him from chasing the dragon? Was Darcy part of the conspiracy?

He shook the thoughts away. No time to worry about crazy ideas. He hurried into the room and looked up at the dangling pair, Thomas still hooded and Mariel still gagged.

133

"I didn't try to reach them again," Darcy said. "I found the keys, so I thought I would tell you—"

"You thought right." Matt walked to the edge of the hole. It appeared to be the top of an enormous aquarium. A pair of huge, sharklike shadows swam in the depths, turning this way and that and agitating the water.

He took the hoe and hustled to a wall. Using the corner of the blade, he pried a long panel loose. When it fell to the floor, he gave the hoe to Darcy. "Get another one."

While Darcy tugged at the next panel, Matt pushed his over the aquarium hole, making a bridge. He slid a foot out onto it. It bent slightly, too flimsy to support his weight. "We need more."

"Sure." Darcy grabbed the edge of another panel. "Where did your mom go?"

Matt dug his fingers under the panel and jerked it free. "A dragon took her."

"What?" Her eyes shot wide open. "A dragon?"

"Yeah. A big red one." He inhaled a deep cleansing breath. "I didn't recognize him."

"I'm so sorry. I noticed she was gone, but ..." Her face reddening, Darcy grabbed a panel and pulled. "I don't know what else to say. The whole world has gone crazy."

"Just keep working. We'll figure out how to save her later."

During the next minute, he and Darcy tore away several more panels and built a two-layer platform over the water. This time when he stepped onto it, the panels held firm.

He extended a hand. "Give me the keys." As soon as she dug the ring out of her pocket, he snatched it away, ran four keys along the ring, and stopped at a small brass one. It looked just like the handcuff keys the military police used. "Now to unlock the manacles."

"How are you going to get up there?"

"By climbing." After clamping the ring between his teeth, he stepped to the middle of the bridge, reached up, and held Thomas's belt with both hands. "Sorry about this," he said, his voice hampered by the ring. "I'll try to be quick." He jumped from the platform and grabbed Thomas's arm, then climbed up to the chains and held them to support his weight. Thomas grunted with each move, but he didn't cry out.

Matt called, "Darcy, get ready to catch him."

She stood on the bridge and wrapped her arms around Thomas's legs. "Ready."

Releasing the chains with one hand, Matt reached down and pulled off Thomas's hood, revealing a bald, age-spotted head and a white goatee. Matt spoke in a soothing tone. "Almost done. Get ready to drop."

Still holding to the chains, Matt unlocked a manacle. When it popped open, Thomas's arm flopped to his side. When he unlocked the other, Thomas fell. Darcy let him slide through her arms until his feet settled on the bridge.

Now holding the weight of two people, the panels bent, and water sloshed onto the surface. A shark swam under the bridge and bumped it hard. The panels shot upward. Darcy leaped with Thomas, and they rolled safely across the floor.

The bridge panels bobbed in the water, some bearing cracks. A dorsal fin sliced through them as if sending a warning.

Darcy hustled to her feet while Thomas sat massaging his arms. "What now?" Darcy asked as she untied Thomas's gag. "Build another platform?"

"Just get ready to catch Mariel." Matt climbed higher and jumped to the other set of chains. After twisting them around his legs, he dropped upside down and grabbed Mariel's wrist. With

135

his free hand, he unlocked her manacles. When they popped open, he began swinging her in a slowly increasing arc. "On three."

Darcy braced her feet and spread out her arms. "I'm ready."

"One ..." Matt glanced at the aquarium. The dorsal fin sliced through the surface again.

"Two ..." His body slid down the chains, making Mariel's toes clip the water at the bottom of the arc.

"Three!" On the final upswing, he let Mariel go. Darcy caught her and let her spin slowly to ride out the momentum.

Matt untwisted the chains around his legs, swung upright, and flung himself over the edge of the water. He landed on his feet and trotted between Thomas, who still sat on the floor, and Darcy, who stood with Mariel, rubbing the elderly woman's arms. Mariel's gag now lay in a puddle.

Matt turned slowly, blinking. For the last few minutes, he had been in rescue mode, oblivious to the absurdity of the situation. And now? The objects in the room seemed like a series of stunt props for a really bad movie. Dangling chains? Sharks in a subfloor tank? Seriously? Tamiel's spy-novel mimicry had gotten way out of hand.

Darcy, shivering in her wet clothes, stepped back from Mariel. "What do we do now?"

Matt peeled away his own moistened shirt. Since the windows here didn't block the outside air, Darcy would soon freeze.

He fished the car keys from his pocket. "Start up the Mustang and turn on the heater. I'll wait here with Thomas and Mariel until they feel up to walking. But if you see any sign of my mother or the dragon, come and get me."

She took the car keys. "What about the third key, the one we're supposed to find here?"

"Right." He lifted the ring that held the key to the manacles. One of them shone with a green hue. "That's weird. It's glowing.

It wasn't before, or I would've noticed it. I guess it flashed when I released Mariel." He slid it off the ring and fastened it to the one at his belt. When the three clicked together, they sparked, but only slightly. "Done."

"Good." Darcy gave him a weak smile. "You were amazing the way you rescued them. Just like a movie hero." She trudged toward the door, leaving a trail of water in her path.

"She was amazing, too," Mariel whispered to Matt.

Matt glanced from Mariel to Darcy. When Mariel's comment sank in, his cheeks flashed hot. "Darcy. Wait."

Now at the interior door, she turned. "Yes?"

"You were great. I mean, really great. I couldn't have saved them without you."

She smiled broadly. "Thank you." Then, with a livelier gait, she hurried toward the main door.

Matt crouched and looked at Thomas and Mariel in turn. Mariel, large boned but not obese, looked back at him with bright red eyes in the midst of a sea of scaly skin that covered her forehead, nose, and cheeks. Her hands, however, appeared to be normal. Thomas stared at the floor, his bald head glistening with sweat, no dragon features apparent.

"I'm Matt. Are you two feeling okay?"

Thomas nodded. "Physically speaking, I am merely sore and feeling like I have been strapped to a medieval rack. My old bones are not accustomed to such stretching. Spiritually speaking? I am still evaluating my condition based on internal sensory perception."

Mariel batted Thomas's shoulder. "Don't be so mysterious. Matt probably has no idea what you're talking about."

"True. I apologize." Thomas looked up at Matt. His eyes were completely white—no irises, no pupils—just white. "Since I am physically blind, my visual perception is limited to what I sense internally. Yet my dragon heritage has gifted me with prophetic vision that is often sharper than mere eyesight. I am told that the original Arramos—not the evil copy who now claims that name—had similar insight, and I believe I am the only anthrozil ever to inherit his gift."

Mariel swatted him again. "But you haven't learned his humility."

Thomas grinned, revealing a gap in his upper teeth. "And you are always nearby to keep my head from swelling."

"In any case, we have both been rude." Mariel extended her hand. "I am Mariel, and this is Thomas."

"Glad to meet you." Matt shook their hands in turn.

Mariel looked toward the window. "Did I hear you say a dragon took Bonnie? I saw her a few moments ago."

Matt nodded. "I wanted to chase them, but ..." He swallowed his words. Making them feel bad wouldn't help.

"The dragon was Arramos," Thomas said. "I thought I felt his presence. I could never mistake the presence of Satan himself. He is pure evil."

Mariel rolled her eyes. "A child could have guessed that. Arramos is the only remaining dragon who would capture Bonnie. Still, since you say you are able to feel his presence, maybe you'll do something besides sit around on your duff and instead lead Matt to Bonnie."

"With all your browbeating, you're going to make Matt think you're a nagging, shrewish, ungrateful witch of a wife." He winked. "But you're not my wife at all."

"No woman in her right mind would marry you. After one hundred years with you, I ought to know."

"Wait a minute," Matt said. "How old *are* you two?" He cringed. "Sorry. I shouldn't have asked that."

"Don't be silly." Mariel gathered her thick white hair and pushed it behind her back. "Old folks like us enjoy a bit of bragging about how many years we've managed to survive. After all the two of us have been through, I think we're just too stubborn to die." She pointed at Thomas with a thumb and whispered, "Especially him."

"I heard that." Thomas felt for Mariel and patted her on the back. "My dear friend here is more than one hundred fifty years old, but she is a spring chicken compared to me. In fact, I have forgotten how old I am, so I just say I am three hundred and leave it at that."

"Your memory lapses always seem to benefit your ego. You're not a day over two hundred."

"I should know how old I am. I was born——"

"Oh, stop it. We've been over this a thousand times. I'm sure Matt has a lot more important things on his mind." Mariel looked up at him. "Don't you, Matt?"

139

"I do. Like you said, I have to find my mother." Matt glanced out the window. Darcy probably had the Mustang good and warm by now. They should hurry and join her, but this might be the only chance to get a look into her soul.

He seated himself and touched Thomas's shoulder. "Real quick, so you can leave this place and get warm in the car. Since you have spiritual perception, what kind of feeling did you get from Darcy?"

9

Parallel Circles

A feeling from Darcy?" Thomas stroked his chin. "Strong girl for her size. Her arms felt a bit thin, but she handled me quite well, and I'm no scarecrow."

"You're half a scarecrow." Mariel's scaly brow bent. "If you'd listen to me, you'd be strong as an ox, but you just eat grass … grass and that curdled yak milk, when you can get it."

"Bean sprouts and yogurt."

"Whatever. You'll never get any muscle on those old bones if you don't—"

"I don't mean to interrupt," Matt said, "but I wasn't asking about how Darcy felt physically. Did you get a feel for her … spirit, I guess?"

"Her spirit?" Thomas stared at Matt with his blank eyes. "My dear Matthew, the young woman risked her life to save mine. Why should I probe into the secret chambers of such a sacrificial soul?"

141

"Well …" Matt's cheeks turned hot again. Thomas's question made his own sound really stupid. "To see if she's acting, I suppose. You know, pretending to be something she's not."

"Acting?" Thomas continued his blank stare for a moment, then stroked his chin again. "Forgive me. At first I thought you daft for questioning the character of such an obvious heroine, but as I sense your anxious feelings, I now have a better understanding. You believe you might have an accomplished deceiver in your midst who is skilled enough to realize that a sacrificial act is the best way to achieve confidence in her pretended loyalty."

"That's exactly what I mean." Matt leaned closer and whispered, "Do you know about someone named Semiramis?"

Thomas nodded. "We have heard stories about her. We came out of hiding for a short time, and Bonnie sent us a copy of her journal to let us know what has been happening over the years."

"Then you know how deceptive Semiramis can be," Matt said.

"True. Semiramis is one of a kind. If, however, you are wondering if I can determine if Darcy is such a wolf in sheep's clothing, then it depends on how accomplished she is as a deceiver."

"I'm wondering if Darcy *is* Semiramis … in disguise, I mean."

Mariel's red eyes pulsed. "That would be an extraordinary disguise. Semiramis is several years older, at least she presents herself that way."

"I know it's far-fetched, but …" Matt waved a hand. "Never mind. It's stupid. Forget I said anything."

"Don't worry, Matt." Mariel patted his hand. "I'm sure Thomas will do what he can."

"Of course I will," Thomas said. "When I am with her again, I will conduct a test or two to see what I can learn."

"Great. Thank you." Matt climbed to his feet and helped Thomas and Mariel to theirs, then guided them toward the Mustang.

Mariel held Thomas's hand every step of the way, warning him of roots and divots on the path, though Thomas seemed capable of avoiding every obstacle Mariel didn't mention.

When they reached the car, Darcy was sitting in the front passenger side with the engine running. Once Thomas and Mariel had settled in the backseat, Matt jumped in and looked at the phone's next address—pretty far away.

Darcy passed around snack bars and bottles of water she had retrieved from their supply box. While Matt drove back to the main road, he related the details of the seven-door journey—everything that had happened so far, including a blow-by-blow account of his mother's recent capture.

When he tried to explain Darcy's role, he drew a blank for a moment and chewed on his snack, a sticky blend of granola, peanuts, and chocolate. During the pause Darcy described Tamiel's interrogation, how he had grilled her for information about Matt, silly things like what movies and books he enjoyed. She also added Mom's observations that the doors paralleled the circles-of-seven adventure.

After finishing his last snack bar, Matt tapped his thumbs on the steering wheel and glanced at the mirror every few seconds to see his backseat passengers. "So now we're like a kite that's been cut loose. Supposedly Tamiel wanted us to go to each place so Mom's song would get hurt, but now she's gone, so maybe we need to do something else. Of course we still have to find my mother, but where?"

"Maybe she'll be at one of the addresses," Darcy said, "so she's like bait to keep us going."

Thomas raised a finger. "My advice is to proceed to the fourth door. Since Tamiel is likely behind your mother's kidnapping, and since he also provided you with instructions to follow, you should continue following them until he tells you not to. Doing otherwise could well lead to your mother's harm."

"Unless we gain new information," Mariel added. "Like if Thomas senses Arramos nearby."

"Of course. Of course. But I have to be fairly close to Arramos to detect him, and he isn't likely to show himself." Thomas touched Mariel's shoulder. "Perhaps we should tell them our story. They might benefit."

"There isn't much to tell." Mariel settled back in her seat. "I'll start at the point when Thomas went into hiding to run from Devin, who had already killed his mother. Thomas escaped to an industrial part of Zurich and began working for a garment manufacturer. Although he was blind, he was able to feel the quality of the raw materials and recognize if vendors had delivered the right fabrics."

144

"And I was good at it." Thomas wiggled his fingers. "They said I had magic hands."

Mariel sighed. "Thomas, dear. Who's telling this story?"

"You are." Thomas slid away from her. "Go ahead."

Mariel lifted his hand and kissed it. "Anyway, I went into hiding when Devin killed my mother. Since I have scales on my face, I have a hard time protecting my identity. I would always wear heavy makeup, a scarf, or even a burqa whenever I could, but I raised a lot of suspicion."

Thomas nodded. "A burqa in a Swiss park will do that."

"Hush." Mariel pushed his arm. "So when Devin began closing in on me, Thomas and I met at a restaurant in Zurich. I agreed to be his nurse and guide in exchange for protection. Since he is able to detect the approach of evil, ours turned out to be a successful arrangement for many years."

"Quite successful. And I must admit that she is an excellent cook, though she often complains about my dietary choices."

"That's because you're a vegetarian one week and a carnivore the next. I never know what to buy at the market."

Thomas waved a hand. "Go on with the story. You're off topic again."

Mariel rolled her eyes. "Anyway, we came out from hiding fifteen years ago after the victory in the great battle in Second Eden, but only to contact our birth mothers so they would know we're alive."

"Kaylee and Dallas are their human names," Thomas said. "Their dragon names were Alithia and Firedda."

"Right," Mariel continued, "but we didn't reunite physically with them. Thomas's gifted perception warned that all was not well, and he was right. Relations between Earth and Second Eden deteriorated, so we went into hiding again. Only this time, we were unable to avoid Tamiel, who turned out to be much cleverer at pursuing us than Devin was. Apparently he doesn't transmit the same kind of evil signals other villains do. Since Thomas relied on his usual skills, Tamiel was able to capture us last week."

145

"So what did you do during all those years of hiding?" Matt asked. "Did you help Thomas at the garment factory?"

"For a little while. Later we worked with Sir Patrick and his spies. We coordinated getting messages to surviving anthrozils and put out false information to mislead Devin. We also made arrangements for Bonnie's transfers after Devin killed her mother."

"So you hid my mother from Devin." Matt nodded. "That's cool."

"And from her own father. Devin attacked Irene on December thirtieth, and we whisked Bonnie out of the state very soon afterward, but we left clues that she was still in Montana, including registering her in the Montana foster system in March of the next year. That kept Bonnie's father and Devin searching in that state for quite some time while Bonnie was getting settled in West Virginia."

"So why did she keep her first name? Wouldn't that be an easy way to find her?"

Thomas cleared his throat. "Well, that objection sounds familiar. You see, she was registered in West Virginia under another name. She just went by 'Bonnie Silver' at school, an idea that I warned against. The prevailing thought was that she would be safe because the chances of word getting back to Devin were practically nil. As it happened, Devin, in his search for Jared Bannister, became the principal at Billy's school. Since Bonnie and Devin were both looking for the Bannister family, it stood to reason that they might cross paths. People thought I was just being paranoid." He shrugged. "But being the kind and humble person I am, I refused to say 'I told you so.'"

"You are kind," Mariel said, "but when humility rained from the sky, you put up an umbrella."

Thomas laughed. "And you were struck by the lightning bolt of nagging."

"Then the bolt charged me with keeping you humble, which requires more energy than even Excalibur can deliver."

"Okay, okay." Matt smiled, though their banter sounded like fussing children. "Can we get back to the story?"

"Certainly," Mariel said. "Besides taking care of Bonnie, sometimes we didn't have much of that kind of business to do, so we also helped with Patrick's orphanage network—picked up lost and forsaken children, found homes for them, that sort of thing. We stayed quite busy."

"I'm sure." Matt turned onto the main road. The destination lay a couple of hours to the north in Nebraska. They still had plenty of time to talk. "Do you two know much about my mother's adventures in the circles of seven? My father told me he carried my mother through the seventh circle of Hades, but if you know the other parts of the story, maybe we can figure out how the fourth door might be similar to the fourth circle."

"We know quite a lot," Thomas said. "As I mentioned before, we had a copy of Bonnie's journal. Mariel read it to me, and, of course, I memorized it after a single reading. The parallels are striking. In the first circle, Arramos tempted your mother with forbidden fruit, and, as you might expect, she refused. Now she witnessed an entire church that gobbled the fruit gladly, which was designed to cause her great grief."

"And hurt her song," Mariel added.

"Of course. I don't plan to explain the obvious. Matt and Darcy are smart enough to—"

"Just go on," Matt said as he glanced at them through the mirror. "Please."

147

"Glad to." Thomas raised a pair of fingers. "In the second circle, Billy and Bonnie met the Caitiff, savage beasts who prey on children. At your second door, you discovered a so-called medical clinic that preys on unborn children. In the third circle, in addition to the parallel your mother mentioned, Billy had to wade through a swamp filled with dangerous serpents. Here you had to overcome a shark tank, a parallel dangerous creature in the water."

Mariel poked Thomas's ribs. "And Morgan kidnapped Bonnie in the third circle and separated her from Billy, and now Arramos kidnapped Bonnie at the third door and separated her from Matt."

"I was just getting to that." Thomas looked straight ahead. "According to Bonnie, Morgan kidnapped her because she was making Billy's journey too easy for him. He needed to face the perils and gain strength. Morgan wanted him to be prideful by the time he reached the seventh circle, but Bonnie thinks God wanted Billy to learn about himself through trials and thereby become wiser and stronger." In the mirror, Thomas's blind eyes seemed unearthly. "Does that portion have a parallel in you?"

Matt shrugged. "Not that I can think of. I'm about the same age my father was then, and I have the same ability to sense danger, but since I don't know what he had to learn, how can I figure out a connection?"

"Bonnie didn't provide those details in the journal," Thomas said.

"Too personal," Mariel added.

Thomas nodded. "Too personal."

"What happened in the fourth circle?" Darcy asked. "Maybe that could be a clue."

"Yes, of course." Thomas spoke with a lyrical hum. "The child of doubt will find his rest and meet his virgin bride, to build a world of love so blest, forever to abide. For Arthur has a choice in hand to choose this lasting bliss, or fly again to troubled lands and toil through Hell's abyss."

"Naamah's song," Mariel said. "Billy met a lovely songstress in the fourth circle who entreated him to join her in a blissful union of everlasting pleasure and peace. Because of the circumstances, the magic of that place, and Naamah's stunning beauty and unmatched acting abilities, Billy's trial was very real. Even though he was not bound to Bonnie by marriage, he stayed true to her, as well as to his commitment to purity. So he rejected Naamah, even as she wailed that she would die in that place without him."

Matt painted a picture in his mind of a girl on her knees, begging for help. "That last part would be hard for me—the wailing, I mean."

"The first part wouldn't?" Thomas asked. "Even for a blind old coot like me, the thought of a beautiful nymph propositioning me is enough to make me sweat. Don't you find girls attractive?"

"Oh, hush," Mariel said to Thomas. "Haven't you got any sense at all?"

Darcy stared intently at Matt, as if anxiously awaiting his answer, but she didn't breathe a word.

Matt's cheeks heated up. Of course girls were attractive, but Darcy had injected a suspicion of all females. Lauren was the first exception, then Mom and Listener. But present company made that topic untouchable. "What I mean is, I can't imagine just walking away from someone who says she'll die without my help."

Mariel reached forward and patted Matt's shoulder. "Of course not. You're a courageous young man who would never want to see a girl suffer." She elbowed Thomas. "Now tell him the rest, and be more polite this time."

"I *am* being polite." Thomas folded his hands. "Naamah turned out to be a wraithlike creature who could turn into a bat. Her pleas were all part of her act. If Billy had given in, he would've been vampire bait."

Matt nodded. The words *no surprise* almost slipped out. "I'm glad to hear that my father could see through her charade."

"Oh, he didn't see through it, at least not until later. He just knew he couldn't accept her offer. He chose to follow principle in spite of appearances."

"Yeah, I get that. After all I've seen in the last few days, I know you can't trust appearances." He glanced at Darcy out of the corner

149

of his eye. She brushed a tear from her cheek. Yes, appearances could be deceptive.

"So," Thomas continued, "you should prepare yourself for a similar trial. Perhaps you will meet a seductive beauty who shows unusual admiration, or a pathetic child who begs for rescue from danger. Whatever it is that would attack your vulnerabilities the most, that is what you will likely face."

"Then we should make sure I'm with you, Matt," Darcy said. "Maybe I won't be vulnerable to whatever you're vulnerable to." She looked away, her face reddening. "I didn't mean to imply I'm stronger or anything. I'm sure you're stronger in places I'm weak."

Heat spread to Matt's ears. It took all his willpower to avoid thinking about Darcy's cruel "strengths." He firmed his lips and nodded. "I guess everyone has strengths and weaknesses."

150

"True," Thomas said. "And Darcy's suggestion is valid, but we don't know if she will be able to accompany you. Since Billy entered the fourth circle alone, perhaps you should expect to enter the fourth door alone."

Mariel grasped Darcy's shoulder. "Allowing Darcy to go along makes perfect sense. Most women are able to see straight through the wiles of other women. I'm sure Darcy is quite aware of how deceptive some women can be."

The words *I'm sure she is* came to Matt's mind, but he kept them locked inside.

"I grant you the point," Thomas said, "though begrudgingly. We would all have come up with a plan to include Darcy when we reached the fourth door."

Mariel wrinkled her nose. "It takes brains to plan in advance."

"Then if you're so smart, why would Arramos capture Bonnie if his goal is to ruin her song? She won't be around to witness the remaining tests."

"Tamiel is mimicking the circles. Morgan placed Bonnie in the sixth circle where she met a virtual copy of herself."

"Shiloh," Thomas said. "Of course. I know that."

"Then be quiet and listen. I'm not explaining this for your sake." Mariel shifted her hand to Matt's shoulder. "While Billy marched on through the circles, Bonnie endured her own test. When she sacrificially provided a way for Shiloh to escape her prison of forty years, Bonnie died, and, as you learned, Billy had to carry her to the seventh circle where he hoped to find a way to resurrect her."

"So my mother and her song will suffer while I'm staying on this course," Matt said. "She'll be worried about me, and that's a song killer."

Mariel squeezed his shoulder and settled back in her seat. "Exactly."

"Then what's the point in me going to the rest of the doors?"

Thomas lifted a finger. "Suppose Tamiel's obsessive mimicking extends to the point of killing your mother. Perhaps he will bait you with the idea that the only way to raise her from the dead is to go through the seventh door."

"And I'll need all the keys to open it." Matt nodded. "It's diabolical, and that fits his perverted style."

"He also put us all together," Mariel said. "While he was having a couple of thugs chain us to the ceiling, he mentioned the circles of seven a number of times. Obviously he wanted us to tell you about the parallels."

Matt squinted. "Why didn't he tell me about them himself? Is he playing a game?"

"Yes," Thomas said. "A game. This is fun for him. It's hide and seek. It's blind man's bluff. I wouldn't be surprised if more puzzles and intricacies continue to be revealed. We are dealing with high intelligence. Evil intelligence, to be sure, but we should not under-estimate his mental prowess. By threatening your father and removing your mother, he has provided all the incentive you need to visit every door."

Matt sighed. "And there might be more people to rescue. I can't just leave them hanging."

Thomas laughed. "A fine choice of words, considering our own predicament."

"I guess so. But I wasn't trying to be funny."

"Don't worry." Mariel patted Matt's shoulder. "If we can't laugh at ourselves, we will be sour people indeed."

"So," Thomas continued, "you have triple incentive—your father, your mother, and anyone who is Tamiel's next victim. And besides, where else would you go? It seems to me that Tamiel is giving you a lot of leeway. For some reason, he is allowing you to make decisions as long as you don't stray too far from the path."

Matt glanced at the GPS map. "Well, we have to decide about where we're staying. We have quite a few miles to go, so I'm guess-ing we should find a motel for the night. Tamiel didn't mention adding passengers, but like you said, he knew I'd try to rescue you and I wouldn't just leave you behind."

"Then all is well." Thomas nudged Mariel. "I told you so. Even when all seemed lost. Even when they were ready to hang us over those man-eating sharks. Didn't I tell you so?"

Mariel let out an exasperated sigh. "Yes, until they gagged you. You are as insightful and insufferable as ever."

"And handsome." He grinned. "I told you that, too."

Mariel groaned. "Maybe leaving him behind isn't such a bad idea after all."

CHAPTER

FLIGHT PASSENGERS

Billy sat in the helicopter's rear passenger compartment, his legs chained to the bench's frame. He gnawed on an asbestos rag stuffed inside his mouth, unable to spit it out because of a gag tied securely around his jaw. Saliva had long ago dried up, making his tongue feel like sandpaper.

Dehydration racked his body. Pain hammered his skull. His captors didn't dare remove the gag for fear of his fiery breath. They mentioned the possibility of an IV once, though they never followed through. Instead, they broke the two smallest toes on his left foot without bothering to explain why. Pain from those breaks matched the dehydration headache throb for throb.

Lack of information added to the discomfort. Why were they just flying around? It seemed as if they were waiting for a call to do something, and in the meantime they flitted from base to base like a stray dog searching for a handout. The soldiers wouldn't talk, not even to each other. They seemed like robots, programmed to obey without question.

The propeller buzzed, adding to the pounding hammer in his head. He raised a hand along with a cuff and massaged his temple. The motion jingled the chain attached to manacles around his ankles, a chain that ran to Ashley's ankles and then to Walter's and Gabriel's.

Ashley squirmed a bit as she dozed, but the slight jingle didn't faze Walter. He was asleep and sat with his head leaning against Ashley's.

Billy closed his eyes. Earlier, Walter explained last night's events in his usual rapid-fire manner. As Billy replayed Walter's account, he let his mind follow the action in vivid pictures.

154

"The pseudo-goth freak shot me." Walter touched the blood-stained bandage around his chest. "When he and his goons left, I blacked out for a second, but rainwater ran up my nose and woke me up. Then Ashley and Gabriel came zooming back like angels sliding on greased ice. Well, Freak and his friends must've been hanging around in the cornstalks, playing Farmer in the Dell for all I know, because they came back with guns ready and with a pro-posal we couldn't refuse—basically that they would let Ashley dig the slug out of me if we came along without a fight. Well, you know how much Ashley loves to do dangerous surgery, especially with lightning flashing and cold rain spilling into my open chest cavity, so she agreed, though Gabriel made it easier by making an umbrella with his wings. Anyway, since Ashley's healing touch was working great and since I'm too ornery to die, I survived. We kind of ruined that part of the cornfield, but I left a big blood donation on the ground as payment. I hope the farmer appreciates it. I don't want to give blood in vain."

Billy smiled in spite of the corny pun. Good old Walter. No matter how much he suffered, he never lost his sense of humor or his confidence. Whether facing dragons or demons, he always stood his ground. Now having him close brought a boost. He was a survivor, a valiant warrior, a loyal friend.

From Walter's other side, Gabriel leaned forward and winked but said nothing. Across a narrow gap on the opposite bench, four quasi-soldiers sat with automatic rifles on their laps. Three slept while one kept his stare on Gabriel, perhaps thinking that a winged man would be the most capable of escaping.

Billy massaged his temple again. During an overnight stop to refuel, use the facilities, and get some food, he had thought he could pry information from one of the soldiers while the other three were guarding Gabriel, Walter, and Ashley at the restroom. When he asked a simple question, a whack to the skull with the butt of a rifle silenced any further communication. At the time, it seemed that dehydration had one advantage, the lack of a need to use the facilities, but the new headache chased that thought away.

Ashley's handcuffs rattled. Her eyes still closed, she spread out her right hand between her thigh and Billy's. Then, one by one, she folded her fingers in, as if signaling a countdown.

Billy nodded. She was awake, ready to read his mind. Then she would use sign language to answer. They had employed that routine several times years ago when worried about eavesdroppers.

When the final finger curled down, Billy called out mentally, *Have you been able to read anyone's mind to figure out what's going on?*

Her closed fist nodded almost imperceptibly. Then she spelled out, *They always knew we were following you. Sprang trap to catch us all. Wanted Lauren but missed her.*

Where are we going?

She spelled, *Unclear. Something about the sixth address.*

Interesting. Billy looked through the side window. The worst part of the storm had long passed, and now snowflakes fluttered by the dirty glass. *Any idea how many addresses there are?*

Ashley spelled out, *Seven, I think. Hard to know.*

Sixth address out of seven. There are seven circles in Hades.

Ashley nodded with her fist.

Bonnie was imprisoned in the sixth circle. She died there, and I had to carry her body to the seventh circle, hoping to get her resurrected.

Are you worried she will die again?

Definitely. Can you blame me for that?

She laid her first two fingers over her thumb, the sign for *no.*

Any thoughts out there about her? Billy asked.

Ashley's fist nodded. *Trying to think of a way to tell you.*

Just … He bit his lip. *Just tell me.*

Her fingers flew. *Arramos captured her and took her somewhere. Unclear.*

Captured. A painful lump swelled in his throat. *But Bonnie will manage. She always does.* He looked past the guards and eyed the helicopter pilot as he guided the craft through thin clouds. *Any other clues? Maybe about where Sapphira is?*

Mysterious. Picked up chatter through headphones. No one is at Fort Knox. Deserted. Elam is heading that way. Thinks Sapphira is there.

A trap?

Her fist nodded. *But what kind?*

The worst kind. When the rats desert the ship, you know it's going to sink. Billy looked at Walter, then at Gabriel, then at the rifles in the soldiers' hands. *When Walter wakes up, we need to hijack this chopper. Think he'll be up for it?*

Ashley smiled. *Think you could stop him?*

Not a chance. Billy locked gazes with her. The fire in her eyes proved that she was ready to fight. *Gabriel knows sign language. I've seen him use it with Shiloh.*

Her fist nodded once more.

I'll formulate a plan. Then you can let Gabriel in on it.

She slid her hand into Billy's and used her other hand to spell out. *We should pray for your plan.*

Thanks for the reminder. Give me a minute. As they held hands, Billy closed his eyes and leaned his head back. Years ago, prayer was just a collection of words spoken at a meal or before bedtime. Talking to God seemed out of reach. Memorized phrases bounced off the ceiling unheard—rote requests unanswered by a deaf deity.

And then came Bonnie—a miracle gift bestowed on the wings of a prayer. Even though she had suffered so much at the hands of a slayer, even though she had bounced around from foster home to foster home, even though fears and doubts assailed her during dark hours in the candlestone, even after sitting in a cold prison cell for fifteen years, her faith endured. She never lost hope. And now, in even darker hours at the sunset of Earth's existence, she needed help. Her song was fading.

Billy took a deep breath and exhaled slowly. *Father in Heaven, I pray for my beloved wife. Years ago, through heartfelt words in her journal, she showed me your light and love and how to wield a spiritual sword and shield. Not long after that, she shone the same light to Ashley and led her to your saving grace.*

Ashley compressed Billy's hand.

But her light was more than ink on paper. She lived out her words. She was like a beacon in everything she did. She was a living song that expanded until it eventually fed the entire world with a holy influence.

He let out a silent sigh. *And now her song is faltering. The corruption in this world is sending a cacophonous blast of twisted noise that tortures her heart. She needs your help. She needs encouragement. Just like you sent Merlin to remind her to sing while in the*

157

*candlestone, she needs another uplifting voice. She needs a lifeline
from the heavens. She needs to know that you are at her side.*

Ashley spelled out, *And that we love her.*

Billy nodded. *Amen.*

High above the ground, Bonnie dangled from Arramos's grip.
Although one claw pierced the shoulder of her shirt, the
other clutched her hair and pulled, stretching her skin and making
it impossible to tear the shirt and fly away. With every gust of
wind, he refastened his hold, sometimes clawing her scalp. Blood
trickled down both sides of her head. Pain roared from ear to ear,
and her underarms ached from her body weight straining against
her clothes.

Below, farmland stretched out for miles and miles, cut into
squares by dirt-covered access roads. At times, people stepped out
of a farmhouse and looked up, unable to do anything to help as
they gawked at the strange sight—a dragon carrying a winged
woman. One farmer ran back in and emerged seconds later with
a rifle, but after taking aim, he lowered his weapon. Apparently he
didn't want to risk harm to the helpless captive, or maybe he was
worried about facing the fiery wrath of an angry dragon.

Finally, an expanse of water came into view, a lake that carved
a circular oasis in the midst of the endless squares of dark soil.
Arramos descended toward a small island near the lake's center.
With just a few trees and a perimeter of dark mud, the island
appeared to be no bigger than a convenience store parking lot.

Arramos orbited the island twice at a low elevation, then
released Bonnie near one edge. She dropped several feet, beating
her wings to keep from tumbling headlong into the mud. When
she touched down with her feet, she jogged along the lakeshore
until her momentum eased.

Arramos whipped around and blew a jet of flames over her head. "Stay on the ground!"

Bonnie ducked just in time to avoid the fire. When Arramos landed next to her, she glared at him. Although questions bounced around in her mind, she said nothing. Speaking to the devil might be risky.

As Arramos stared at her, his head swayed. "I assumed you would demand to know why I brought you here. Has the troublesome wench lost her eloquent tongue?"

Bonnie crossed her arms and maintained her silent glare.

"Answer me when I ask you a question!" He swatted her jaw with the end of his wing. "I have put up with your haughty arrogance for far too long!"

Bonnie staggered backwards and splashed into the lake's shallows. Blood dripped from her chin to the water, creating a red circle on the surface. The wound stung terribly, but she refused to grimace. "I answered you, but you were too dull of hearing to realize it. Even as I stand here, I speak with the tongues of angels. My song is my answer, and I have not lost it. You can slap me with your wings, spear me with your spines, or burn me with your flames, but you cannot silence my song. It is a song that has existed since the creation of the world, a hymn that called light out of darkness, that commanded fullness from the void, that brought order out of chaos." She crossed her arms again and stood erect. "I am the eighth ovulum, and to those who have not chosen deafness, I am never silent."

Arramos's maw spread out in a hideous smile. "Pretty speech for a weakling hominid whose eloquence comes from her dragon nature."

"Stop with the psychological games. You lost that contest years ago."

159

"But I will not lose this one." Arramos used his wing to detach a leather bag and strap from a spine on his back. He lowered the bag and let it dangle in front of Bonnie's eyes. "This is a tablet computer programmed to display crucial events. Since you are a woman of prayer, I assume you will want to view the events so that you can pray for those involved in what you see."

"Don't pretend you're trying to help me." Bonnie grabbed the strap and pulled the bag away. "You don't want me to pray. You just want to show me things that will hurt my song."

"Quite true, but you will not be able to resist the desire to look. For a short time you will battle between the responsibility to protect your song and the need to pray for those you love, but curiosity will be the deciding factor. Your final motivation will not be love or prayer or song preservation. It will be an insatiable inquisitiveness driven by your lust for self-gratifying knowledge."

160

"My decision to look at the computer or not will be driven by love, not selfishness." Bonnie laughed under her breath. "You keep trying your accusatory games, but your slithering tongue has no power over me. You waste your time with your rhetoric."

"Perhaps so. I cannot delve into your mind to learn your motivations, but I do know that the vast majority of humans give in to their lusts every day, especially now that the song of the ovulum is so weak. If you choose not to watch, your song will weaken because you will know that Matt is struggling through the trials without you, and you will suffer in a state of tortured ignorance. If you do choose to watch, you will witness his failures, because he is woefully unprepared." Arramos shifted his head closer. His rancid breath stung Bonnie's nostrils, but she stood her ground. "You know your son lacks the spirit that empowers you. You know that he harbors hatred and bitterness. You know that such hostility of heart will lead him to calamity, especially since the tests we have in store were designed with such weaknesses in mind."

Bonnie forced herself to maintain a confident stance. Arramos had spoken the truth this time, but letting him know that his words had hit the mark would give him a psychological advantage.

"Your song will weaken as you travail from afar," Arramos continued, "whether you watch or not. Either way, I win, and you lose."

Bonnie clutched the tablet bag tightly. For some reason, a new, low-grade pain coursed through her body. "We'll see about that."

"Indeed, we will." Arramos shuffled toward one of two scraggly oaks. "Now to address the matter of keeping you here. I do not have time to stay and guard you, so one of my agents should have provided—Ah! Here they are." He used a foreclaw to lift a pair of chains and manacles, though his foreleg trembled, as if weakened by the weight. "I am faster and more powerful than you are, so let us not waste time with a chase and capture. One way or another, I will chain you here."

161

Still holding the bag, Bonnie walked to the closer oak. With each step, the pain increased, and weakness weighed down her arms.

Arramos snapped the manacles around her ankles and quickly backed away, aided by his wings. Bonnie examined the manacles— brass cuffs, each embedded with three dime-sized candlestones. No wonder Arramos appeared somewhat weak. All dragons were susceptible, even Satan in dragon form.

The chains snaked around the foot-wide trunk as well as the smaller trunk of the other oak, making it impossible to slide the loops up and over the branches. A hefty lock secured the tangled mess. She jerked on the chains. They held fast.

"You should feel fortunate," Arramos said from the lakeshore. "I suggested that I burn your wings and fill the water with venomous serpents, but Tamiel was concerned that you would perish and bring about the curse. It seems to me that he is too softhearted for this pursuit."

Bonnie sat heavily on the ground, making the chains rattle. Although pain rippled across her skin, she had to keep her composure. "Softhearted wasn't the word that came to my mind."

Arramos snorted in a laughing sort of way. "Actually, Bonnie, I admire your courage. Throughout the millennia, I have met only a few humans who possess your unfailing faith. Yet, since you lack my experience, you have no way of knowing the evils of the despotic being you call God. You worship a cruel tyrant."

Bonnie leaned back against the tree and breathed a tired sigh. "You can cut the theatrics. You're used to dealing with easily manipulated puppets. I'm not one of them."

162

"Are you not?" Arramos unfurled his wings. "We shall see how long your resolve lasts." With a beat of his wings, he lifted into the air and flew away.

When Arramos faded from sight, Bonnie touched one of the leg irons. Recently it seemed that her song had been able to open locks. Maybe it would work on these as well.

Pain tightening her throat, Bonnie lifted her head and tried to sing a note, but only a scratchy squeak came out. She shook her head. It wouldn't work. When Tamiel shot a candlestone bullet into her body, she had tried a hundred times to sing herself out of captivity, and it hadn't worked then either.

She let out a pain-streaked sigh. At least she could see what Satan and his head minion were up to. She opened the bag, withdrew the tablet computer, and set it on her lap. After finding the power switch, she turned it on. White letters scrolled horizontally across the black screen—*The video will play when activity begins. Leave the computer on. It will shut down to power-save mode and awaken on its own at the proper time.*

Bonnie laid the tablet down and looked up at the sky. The sun poured reddish beams through thin clouds and painted the surrounding water with a scarlet tint, making it look like a placid pool of blood. No breeze shifted the foliage in the imprisoning tree. Birds, if any were around, stayed silent. It seemed that the entire world had quieted, as if waiting for something to happen. But what might that be?

A performance? Had the surroundings become a polite audience that sat in wait for the curtains to open?

She nodded. The world was waiting for her to sing. Years ago such a thought would have felt too proud, too self-focused. Imagine thinking that anyone cared to hear her voice! But now God had bestowed a gift and granted a responsibility. She had to sing in spite of the pain and in spite of past failures, for the sake of the world and all of its inhabitants. Knowingly or not, they were counting on her. She had to summon the energy to infuse the air with a remedy for their ills. And maybe this time the effort would unlock her own chains.

163

She took in a deep breath and forced out a soft note—a smooth one that didn't squeak. Soon the words would come, just as they had a thousand times before, whether in a dark candlestone, on a lonely rooftop, or in the depths of Hades. The song in her heart, a gift from God, would rise to the surface and emerge from her lips.

Yet, no words came to mind. When she tried to change the note to create a melody, her voice cracked and faltered. Her throat tightened worse than ever. A new squeak signaled the end of the effort. No song emanated from the ovulum.

A tear spilled from one eye and trickled down her cheek at the same rate that at least three streams of blood and sweat coursed along her skin. All three liquids met at her chin and dripped to her shirt, pink droplets of toil and misery. Billy had been captured and even now endured torture. Matt continued on a dangerous journey without an experienced guide. Beset by anger and distrust, he was really a spiritual cripple. And the world's culture crumbled as it pounded away at its own foundations, unaware that it was responsible for its coming demise. People were dying. Innocent children suffered. Evil blew a trumpet of triumph from horizon to horizon. Who could sing while being stabbed from all sides with so many daggers?

Bonnie closed her eyes and whispered, "God of my love, you have proven yourself faithful so many times before. You are the composer of my song, the writer of my verse. Without you, I am nothing but a clanging gong. So I ask you to be the great composer once again, because I am empty, breathless, void of any poem or melody. I need a musical miracle, for these troubles plague my heart, and these candlestones shackle my body."

164

She inhaled and continued in a soft voice. "While I wait for your help, I will speak what I know, the timeless truth that you taught me during the dark days when I was transferred from foster home to foster home, sometimes waking up in a strange house and not remembering where I was. I had to hold on to my anchor—you, my Lord, who never left me for a single second."

She opened her eyes, gazed at the scarlet sky, and whispered,

Whither shall I go from thy spirit? Or whither shall I flee
    from thy presence?
If I ascend up into heaven, thou art there: If I make my bed
    in hell, behold, thou art there.

If I take the wings of the morning, and dwell in the utter-
 most parts of the sea;
Even there shall thy hand lead me, and thy right hand shall
 hold me.
If I say, Surely the darkness shall cover me; even the night
 shall be light about me.
Yea, the darkness hideth not from thee; but the night shineth
 as the day:
The darkness and the light are both alike to thee.

When she finished, she let out a satisfied sigh. "And thou art
here on this lonely island, so I wait for you to help me sing again,
my Lord, my stronghold, my salvation."

165

CHAPTER

THE FOURTH DOOR

After spending the night at the only open motel in Smithers, Nebraska, Matt, Darcy, Thomas, and Mariel climbed into the Mustang once again and drove along a two-lane rural highway. Fortunately, the motel had toast, juice, and coffee—not much, but enough to fill their stomachs, Thomas being the only exception. He chose a carton of prunes from the supplies box, a snack that he claimed would be plenty, though Mariel chided that he would soon lose his pants if he got any skinnier.

"You are what you eat," Mariel had warned him, but he paid no attention.

Light snow fell from a gray blanket above. Although the air crackled with cold, no breeze disturbed the sparse flakes. Weather probably wouldn't be a big problem.

Matt propped the phone against the dashboard and read the address label: *The Fourth Door—Friend or Fiend.* A text message from Tamiel during the night had said they needed to arrive by

10 am. No problem. The destination lay only an hour from the motel.

At around nine thirty, Matt turned onto a dirt road and drove for several miles before stopping the car in front of a one-story farmhouse. Dark shutters covered two windows that bordered the front door. A barn stood a hundred yards or so to the left. With bright red walls and a silver roof, it looked newer and more modern than the house, certainly more inviting.

A silo loomed tall and straight on the closer side of the barn. With stubs of brown stalks all around, it was a good bet that corn filled the gray cylinder.

"This is the place." Matt turned off the engine. The phone beeped. He picked it up and read the message out loud. "Go into the barn. Your companions may relax in the house. You will find a fresh supply of food and more clothing there."

Thomas snorted. "The villain is feeding his pets, I see."

"Or maybe poisoning them," Matt said.

Mariel clicked her tongue. "No worries. Thomas can sense danger as well as the best of them. No one can poison us."

"Do you feel any danger now?" Matt asked. "I don't. At least not yet."

Thomas raised a hand, his palm outward, and moved it slowly in a wide arc. Finally, he stopped. "Great danger lurks in that direction. All other angles are safe."

"The barn," Mariel said. "The house must be all right."

"Then let's get going." Matt grabbed the phone and hopped out of the car. While he helped Thomas and Mariel, Darcy got out on her side and looked around, her eyes narrowed. Snowflakes settled on her hair and painted a stark contrast—white speckles on dark auburn, somehow profound. She shivered, casting off some of the flakes.

As they walked to the house's front door, Thomas and Mariel at the rear, Darcy stayed close to Matt's side. "Like I said before, I'd like to go with you," she whispered. "To the barn, I mean."

"Why?"

"Even if you don't think I can be strong where you're weak, at least let me give you moral support."

Matt tightened his lips. Moral support? He squelched the urge to laugh. That would be harsh. He had already been too eager to question her every move and motive. "Let me think about it."

"Sure. Think." She lowered her voice further. "But just remember. You shouldn't walk straight into danger without someone to watch your back."

"Let's get Thomas and Mariel inside, and we'll talk." Matt opened the door to a foyer that led to a furnished sitting room straight ahead and a kitchen to the left, complete with a stove and refrigerator, both avocado green, an eye-straining contrast to the blue-and-red striped wallpaper.

169

While Matt held the door, Mariel walked straight to the kitchen. "Let's see what I can whip up in this cozy little cottage. It might be quite a while before we can get a cooked meal again."

With Darcy staying close behind, Matt guided Thomas to an overstuffed sofa in the sitting room where a collection of jackets and sweatshirts lay, some for men and some for women. Several weather-proof boots of various sizes stood on the floor.

When Thomas sat down, he rubbed his lips together. "Darcy, would you be a sweetheart and find a tube of lip balm I left in the car? It must have fallen out of my pocket."

"Sure." Darcy hurried out the door.

Thomas tugged on Matt's sleeve and whispered, "It did fall out of my pocket. On purpose, if you get my meaning."

Matt leaned closer. "Did you get a reading on her?"

"Nothing definitive. I didn't detect anything malevolent at all, but if she is who you suspect, I could be wrong. Sorcery has unpredictable effects on my gifts."

Matt nodded. "I understand. Thanks for trying."

When Darcy returned with the lip balm and gave it to Thomas, she picked up a fuzzy dark coat with a fur-like collar. "So these are for us."

"Tamiel said they are." Matt gave her a come-along nod. "It's muddy outside, so grab some boots."

Darcy put on the coat and a pair of calf-top boots, while Matt chose a sturdy jacket and ankle-high lace-up boots. He quickly put them on and fastened them in place.

As they passed by the kitchen, Mariel carried a package of bacon and a carton of eggs to the stove. "When you come back, I'll have a hot lunch ready. I hope Thomas decides to be a carnivore, or I'll have to send him out to graze like an old goat."

Matt forced a smile. "Sounds good."

When he and Darcy stepped outside, he closed the door and looked her in the eye. "Listen, I appreciate all you've done so far ..." His lips seemed to stick together. How could he tell her to stay here without letting on that he simply didn't trust her?

She grasped his wrist. "Matt, I know you don't trust me, but even if I'm just protecting my own interests, I'm going to make sure that the only physically capable guy in our group doesn't get his head blown away. I want to survive." She gave him a dismissive wave. "Go alone if you want, but I'm going to follow you anyway. You can't stop me."

"Okay, okay." He let out a heavy sigh. "Come to the barn door with me, but stay outside until I'm sure it's safe. Thomas said there's danger, and I don't want you to get hurt."

"Perfect." She curled her arm through his. "Okay with a show of unity? It's the first step toward trusting."

Matt resisted rolling his eyes. Even her gesture was an act of manipulation. Only a hard-hearted cynic would refuse. "Sure. Let's go."

They walked together across the house's sparse lawn and into a field of flattened cornstalks, coated with a glistening layer of ice that cracked under their weight. With snow falling more heavily now, the new bad-weather clothing was already coming in handy.

When they reached the barn's front, they stopped at a closed door, similar in size to the house's entry door. Matt slid away from Darcy and quietly turned the knob. It rotated easily.

"Okay," he said as he pivoted back to her, "are you warm enough to stay here while I look around?"

She tightened a belt around her coat. "I'll be fine."

"Good." Matt opened the door and walked in. Daylight illuminated only a few feet of concrete floor, aided by a small lamp glowing atop a desk that abutted the adjacent wall. He searched for a switch for an overhead light but found nothing.

Following the lamp's glow, he padded to the desk—a two-person workstation. He touched the back of one of the chairs and gave it a slow spin. When it stopped, he sat and studied a set of dual monitors embedded in the wall. In a gap between them, a metal key protruded from a circular depression, the same size and shape as the other three keys on the ring. This had to be number four.

Matt pinched the key, averted his eyes to avoid a blinding flash, and pulled it out. Although no burst of light came from the key, ceiling lights flickered on throughout the barn. He spun in the chair and scanned the spacious interior. Burlap sacks of grain stood in uneven piles along with a haphazard array of shovels, rakes, hoes, and coils of rope. Yet, the tools were clean and new, as if on display at a hardware store.

Something hummed at the workstation. On the monitors, lines and lines of indecipherable letters and numbers ran across several program windows, though one window displayed a map with a target grid centered on a rural section of Nebraska, as if this were a weapons station of some kind.

Matt ran a finger along a gray keyboard but dared not touch the keys. An array of telephones, maps, and warning labels practically shouted out affirmation of his guess, including a digital clock above the two units that displayed bright red numbers—00:00:00.

A voice emanated from the workstation. "Launch sequence initiated."

The numbers changed to "00:15:00" and began counting down … "00:14:59" … "00:14:58."

Matt shoved the key back into the hole and tried to turn it, but it wouldn't budge. The clock's digits continued changing.

The cell phone rang. Matt jumped from the seat and jerked it out of his pocket. "Hello?"

"Congratulations on your accomplishment," Tamiel said in a cheery tone. "You are now the potential cause of the first nuclear disaster in many years. You have less than fifteen minutes to figure out how to stop it."

Matt's heart raced. "I put the key back in. That didn't work."

"The key is of no use in stopping the launch. It is yours, and you will need it when you get to the seventh door. The nuclear missile is hidden in a fake corn silo, but the target is not anywhere in this world. The grid on the screen points to the location of a portal through which the missile will travel. Elam must have known that I could discover the presence of an open portal because of my two agents who can detect it simply by whether or not they have solid bodies. I'm sure he thought the societal chaos here would keep military forces from exploiting the opening, which is technically true. I had to persuade a nonmilitary weapons expert to set this up for me."

Matt attached the key to the ring at his belt, then glanced at the digital clock—13:23. When would this insane demon get to the point? And even if he did, could anything he said be trusted? He swallowed to keep his voice under control. "So what am I supposed to do?"

"You are free to do nothing. Rest for a while at the farmhouse in peace, knowing that the missile has vaporized Second Eden. Or you may want to figure out how to stop the launch. You must decipher your surroundings and make the correct decisions."

"My surroundings?" Matt let his gaze dart from place to place, but the same items appeared—grain, tools, and rope. "I don't see anything."

"Look for a red switch under the keyhole."

Matt found a vertical rocker similar to a light switch. "I see it."

"Flip it up."

Matt touched the switch. Following Tamiel's commands felt like a fool's errand. "Why should I do what you say? You're trying to launch a missile."

"Then don't flip it. If you know of another way to abort the launch, feel free to try it."

Matt pushed a computer mouse. Letters flashed on both monitors—*System Locked.* After a few seconds, the message disappeared. He tapped a key on one of the keyboards. The message returned, again flashing. He picked up the keyboard and smashed it against the desk. It bent in the middle, but nothing changed on the screen.

Laughter crackled in the phone's earpiece. "I can hear your attempts at violence, but they will do you no good. We programmed the missile so that it will detonate immediately if it loses connection with the guidance system. If you manage to destroy the workstation, you will be vaporized."

Matt rolled a hand into a fist. Tamiel had cornered him. No options remained.

He flipped the switch. Something hummed at the center of the room. An object covered with a silver tarp rose from the floor. When it reached chest height, its motion stopped. Another hum awoke at the ceiling. Three security cameras descended—one trained on the tarp, one on the control station, and the third on the entry door.

"Who's watching me with the cameras?" Matt asked.

"A singer." Tamiel laughed. "Oh, by the way, we will kill whomever you choose to leave behind."

"Leave behind? What do you mean—"

The phone clicked. Matt banged his fist on the console. This impossible mission was getting more insane by the second!

The clock ticked down to twelve minutes. He shoved the phone back to his pocket and hurried toward the tarp. One of the cameras whirred as it followed his progress. He pinched the tarp's edge and pulled it away. A young woman clad in jeans and sweatshirt sat in a chair, her arms and legs bound and her mouth gagged. She stared at him with wide eyes and shouted through her gag.

Matt squinted at her. With auburn hair and slender, angular features, she looked exactly like—

He swallowed hard and whispered, "Darcy?"

She nodded vigorously.

His hands trembling, Matt untied the gag and let it drop to the floor. She blew out a breath. "Matt!" She sucked in air, gasping. "That desk over there controls a nuclear bomb!"

His throat tightened. She sounded exactly like Darcy, even her tone and cadence. "I know—less than twelve minutes to launch."

She struggled against her bonds. "The creep who tied me up told me you'd come, but I'm sitting on some kind of pressure-sensitive gizmo. If I get up, the missile will launch in ten seconds, but he said if you replace me with something of the exact same size and weight, you'll stop the launch completely."

"Replace you? Why would he want ..." Matt looked at the door. This couldn't be the same Darcy he left waiting outside. "And what happens if the replacement moves from the chair?"

"Immediate launch. Really bizarro, isn't it?" She nodded toward one of her arms. "Untie me, and we'll figure out what to do."

175

Matt stared at her. Could she be the real Darcy? Was the other Darcy really Semiramis after all? Or was this woman Semiramis?

She scowled. "Matt, don't just stand there with your mouth gaping. Untie me!"

"Okay. Just don't get up yet."

"Don't worry. I'm not stupid."

Matt winced. Her tone echoed dozens of sarcastic comments from years gone by. Could anyone imitate her bitter tongue so well? The other Darcy certainly hadn't. She seemed gracious by comparison.

He untied rope sections binding her arms to the chair. When they dropped, she reached for her legs and jerked at one knot, then the other. "They're tight." She looked up at Matt. "Can you untie my legs? It's hard to reach, and my fingers are still numb."

"Just a second." He glanced at the clock. A few ticks more than ten minutes. "How much do you weigh?"

"About one twenty." Her brow bent, and a growl spiced her words. "Matt ... untie my legs."

"Soon." He hustled to a big sack of grain and lifted it over his shoulder. "This is probably about a hundred pounds, but it doesn't have a label. I can't be sure."

Her frown deepened. "The guy said the replacement had to be within five pounds."

"Five pounds! What kind of game is he playing?"

Darcy rubbed her other wrist. Her tone grew more threatening. "This isn't a game, and if you don't untie my legs—"

"Yeah, yeah. Keep bullying me. I'm used to that from you." Matt set the bag on the floor and walked closer to her. "How did you get here? Where did they find you?"

"Okay, I'll play nice." She rocked her head in a condescending way. "I'm a teller at a bank in Des Moines. At least I was. With the whole world going crazy, I'm not sure I have a job anymore. Anyway, when I was getting off work two days ago, a couple of guys grabbed me and threw me into the back of a van. They drove me here, and I've been sitting in this chair since early this morning."

"A bank teller?" He leaned within reach and studied her eyes. "Not a prostitute?"

"A prostitute?" She slapped his face. "How dare you!"

Matt backpedaled a few steps. His cheek stung. How could he explain? Should he bring the other Darcy in? Let them both try to prove that they're the real Darcy?

"You're gaping again." Darcy folded her arms tightly across her chest. "Matt, stop acting like the stupid brat I remember and grow up. Untie me right this minute or I'll hop off this sensor thing, chair and all!"

She braced her hands on the chair's arms, but Matt grabbed her wrist. "Wait. Give me a second. Let me show you why I'm acting so weird."

As he walked to the door, her voice followed like a foul wind. "You always acted weird."

The words stabbed his heart. A tear welled. Why did he care so much? She was a witch, an acid-tongued hellcat. Several brutal retorts came to mind, but he brushed them away. She would learn soon enough.

He opened the door. Darcy #1 stood nearby, her hands deep in her coat pockets as snow continued to fall.

She lifted her brow. "Is everything all right in there?"

"Not exactly, but …" He gestured for her to follow. "Come on in."

When they entered, Matt glanced between the two Darcys. The moment they saw each other, their mouths dropped open.

Darcy #2 clutched the armrests. "Matt, who is this?"

"She claims to be Darcy. Tamiel … he's the mastermind for all of this … he says he picked her up at a Las Vegas street corner. But a sorceress named Semiramis might be pretending to be the real Darcy."

"A street corner?" Darcy #2 gave him a knowing nod. "I see. That's why you mentioned the prostitute thing."

"Matt," Darcy #1 said, "Did you tell her I was a prostitute?"

"Not really." Matt gave her a quick explanation of the situation, including the pressure-sensitive trigger and how a replacement would stop the launch, though the replacement would have to stay put and later be killed by Tamiel. "So," he concluded, "she just put two and two together. I wasn't trying to criticize you or anything."

"What a con!" Darcy #2 smirked. "The hooker has reformed. A story to tug at your heartstrings. This imposter has you wrapped around her finger with a pathetic I-got-religion game."

"Religion?" Matt narrowed his eyes. "I never said anything about religion."

"It's just an idiom, Matt." She nodded at Darcy #1. "Just look at that penitent posture. It's a con game. I've seen it too many times before."

Darcy #1 straightened her sloping shoulders and shot Darcy #2 a sharp glare. "Listen, honey, I know what a con game is. I stood around night after night using myself as a billboard pretending I liked any man who opened his wallet. But I hated them all, especially their eyes, the way they looked at me. In their minds I was a medium-rare steak they wanted to sink their teeth into. But I just smiled, took their money, and played the game. I was the ultimate con. So don't tell me about con games. For the first time in my life I'm being true to myself. I have faith."

"Faith is the ultimate con." Darcy #2 touched herself on the chest. "Matt, do you seriously think I would grovel at the feet of a god? Don't you remember? I was the president of the school atheist club."

"I remember." Matt squinted at Darcy #1. "Do you?"

"Of course." She raised a finger. "I told Tamiel about that. He must've asked me a thousand questions, but I don't remember all of them. I think they drugged me to make me talk."

"What a dodge!" Darcy #2 altered to a mocking tone. "They drugged me to make me talk!" She then growled. "Matt, don't be an idiot. Grab that faker, untie me, and put her in this chair."

He tightened his fist. "Give me a second to think about it."

"Think about it? It's obvious! Who's acting more like me?" She jabbed a finger at Darcy #1. "This imposter doesn't know squat."

"We'll see about that." Matt grabbed Darcy #1's arm. "Listen, do you remember pushing me out the window one morning?"

She covered her mouth. "I'm so sorry, Matt. It was a terrible thing to do."

"Yeah, whatever." He riveted his stare on her. "Do you remember what you said to me while I was hanging by the rope?"

"I remember." She looked away. "I said, 'Enjoy the snow.'"

Matt swiveled back to Darcy #2. "She got it right."

Darcy #2 rolled her eyes. "And then I said, 'I'll unlock the door for you in a few hours. Maybe even you will be cold by then.'"

Matt winced. That *was* what Darcy had said. Both women could quote the evil sister from the past, but Tamiel couldn't have prepared Semiramis for every possible memory.

Tears sparkled in Darcy #1's eyes. Of course, her visible emotions could be part of the act. Darcy #2 glared at him as the real Darcy would, but what if the real Darcy had changed? Still, might Semiramis have chosen to act like a repentant Darcy because she didn't know the real Darcy well enough to imitate her?

Matt glanced at the clock. Just over two minutes to go—no time for a detailed interrogation. One question for each of them would have to do. He pulled Darcy #1 closer to #2 so he could look at both of them at the same time.

"You." Matt pointed at Darcy #2, still tied to her chair. "What was your mother's middle name?"

"Gladys," she replied without hesitation. "Matt, this interrogation is wasting—"

"Shut up!"

A voice from the control panel announced, "Silo blast door opening. Two minutes to launch."

He shifted his finger to Darcy #1. "What was our street address?"

She bit her lip. "Nineteen something? On Violet Way, I remember that."

"It was Violet Way," Darcy #2 said, "But it was eighteen forty-five."

"Yeah, yeah, I know." Matt ran a hand through his hair. "I have to think of another question."

"Another question?" Darcy #2 clenched a fist. "I swear, Matt, if you make a stupid decision and leave me here, I'll—"

"You'll what?" Matt growled. "What will you do? If you're the real Darcy, you made my life a living Hell. Why shouldn't I let you stay here? Why shouldn't I let Tamiel kill you? You deserve it!"

"Matt," Darcy #1 said, her voice tortured. "I'm the one who did those things to you. She didn't, so maybe ..."

180

"Maybe what?" Matt leaned closer to her, almost nose to nose. "If you did those things, then the other Darcy's a sorceress, and she deserves to die!" He spun toward the control panel. Forty seconds left. He had to make a decision and make it now.

12

A Song in the Air

Bonnie smacked her dry lips. Acres of fresh water beckoned only ten steps away, though for a woman shackled to a tree, the vision of refreshment might as well have been a photo on a billboard.

She stretched her arms and let out a yawn. Her elbows and shoulders popped. Sleeping on hard ground littered with tree fragments had been a challenge, especially with odd noises drifting through the air—splashes, growls, squawking birds, among others. In the middle of the night an owl perched in her tree and hooted once in a while, as if announcing the time every hour. In spite of its sleep-depriving call, at least it probably kept mice and snakes away.

Fortunately, the chains were long enough to allow for occasional visits to the opposite side of the tree. The conditions there weren't any better, but at least it was downwind and worked as a serviceable restroom. Yet, no matter where she walked or sat, the

181

candlestones in the manacles were always there, like angry dogs gnawing on her legs.

Now sitting, she touched the wound Arramos had inflicted on her jaw—swollen and sore. A crusty clot had stopped the flow of blood.

Something beeped. She turned toward the computer tablet, still lying on the ground. A video played showing a silvery tarp draped over something in a large room. Matt appeared. His eyes wary, he walked slowly toward the tarp.

She grabbed the tablet and set it on her lap. "Matt …" She touched his face with a shaking finger. "Where are you?"

He pulled the tarp to the floor. A young woman sat in a chair, her wrists and ankles bound and her mouth gagged. His voice came through the tablet's speakers. "Darcy?"

The woman nodded.

Matt untied the gag and let it drop to the floor. Her face aflame with terror, Darcy called out, "Matt! That desk over there controls a nuclear bomb!"

"I know," Matt said. "Less than twelve minutes to launch."

As the conversation ensued, Bonnie drank in every word, every emotion. When Matt brought an exact replica of Darcy into the room, Tamiel's sinister plan became clear.

Arramos's words returned to mind. *You know that he harbors hatred and bitterness. You know that such hostility of heart will lead him to calamity, especially since the tests we have in store were designed with such weaknesses in mind.*

"Matt," Bonnie said out loud, "don't be blinded by hatred. Don't let bitterness skew your thinking. Semiramis will poison you with her deceptive portrayal. I can't be sure that the Darcy who traveled with us is the real one, but don't let anger veil your heart to the idea that she really can change."

She spread out her wings and looked toward the sky. "Father in Heaven, please help him. If I were there, I could offer counsel. My guess is that Semiramis would never think to pose as a humble, contrite woman. She would seek to further embitter Matt's heart with savage memories. I would suggest to Matt that the entire setup is a ruse. Maybe the nuclear weapon is real, but Elam would never be so foolish as to allow an open portal that an enemy could find. If Elam had made such a mistake, Tamiel would attack it immediately without resorting to this charade."

Bonnie lifted a chain and shook it. The reason for the shackles became obvious. The candlestones weakened her physical song, and watching Matt struggle through this decision was designed to stifle her inner melody by smothering her heart with grief.

She covered the screen with a hand. Arramos's prediction about her dilemma had come true. Should she keep watching? She couldn't do anything to help. Yet, not watching might have the same song-stifling effect. She would wonder how Matt was faring. The fate of millions lay in his hands—inexperienced hands guided by a volatile mind that shifted between love and fury depending on who pulled his strings.

Her lips quivering, she cried out, "Father! He's my little boy! My darling son! I cuddled him for only a few short months! My baby who was torn away from my arms before he was even weaned! He and my sweet daughter fell into the jaws of vicious predators who feed on hatred, who gnash their teeth at righteousness, who want nothing more than to corrupt your perfect image, the imprint of your divine nature on the human heart. They hate your holy counsel. They despise your light, your law, and your love. They sow seeds of rottenness by spreading the great lie that you are not powerful enough to bring light to darkness, to cleanse from all sin, to completely heal the soul."

As she exhaled, her entire body shook. "And the corruption in Matt's soul eats away at him. He doesn't believe in your regenerating power, that a harlot like Darcy can kneel in humility and anoint your feet with her tears and dry them with her hair. The wounds she inflicted upon him won't let him understand your gentle hands, that you offer grace to everyone—even to Darcy, though her back deserves a whip."

She sniffed to suppress a sob. "And that's why Matt suffers in darkness. That's why he is unable to reach out to you and embrace your forgiving heart. Unless he learns to forgive Darcy, he will never understand the mercy you offer. He needs to witness the blazing miracle of sacrificial love, or else he will remain shackled in the dark dungeon of misery and bitterness forever.

"And Father ..." Bonnie swallowed. Racing thoughts transformed into shattered words that squeezed through her narrowed throat. "And Father, Matt's blindness is the world's blindness. People don't understand how God could be loving and still allow millions upon millions to suffer, whether at the hands of a cruel sister or at the hands of a domineering tyrant. How can a God of justice allow the wicked to oppress the innocent?" She pounded the ground with her fist. "Why doesn't God come off his high horse and do something about it?"

Weeping, she took a breath and continued. "Such is their misdirected anger. They don't understand that your gift of free will is both a blessing and a curse, that it can be as beautiful as Heaven itself or as corrupt as the depths of Hell. Some are ignorant. Some are simply evil and rebellious. But they all need my song ... your song ... the song you sang when you called light into being, when you shaped mankind from the dust of the Earth, when you delivered your precepts on tablets of stone, when you visited us in a manger and later shed your blood on a cross. It has always been a mercy song, a song to strengthen your friends, for they need your guiding light, and a song to call your enemies to repentance, for love is a beacon that keeps wayward ships from crashing into the rocks."

She sucked in a breath and held it. Silence ensued again. When she exhaled, air came out in halting gasps—sobs that seemed to punctuate her emotions.

"Bonnie, that was so beautiful."

The voice came from above, feminine and lyrical, as if the wind itself had spoken. Glittering specks appeared in the midst of crimson clouds. They collected in a swirl and swept toward the island. The spin broke into twin cyclones and rotated a few steps away.

Still holding the tablet, Bonnie climbed to her feet. As the cyclones slowed, human forms took shape, though transparent, like phantoms. Seconds later, the swirls settled, and the phantoms' faces clarified. Joran and Selah stood before her, dressed in loosely fitting brown tunics and ankle-length trousers—the same clothes they had worn in her dream, back when they hunted demons alongside Makaidos. Although semitransparent, every detail of face and form was clear.

Bonnie brushed tears from her cheeks and smiled. "Joran. Selah. What are you … I mean … how did you—"

"Don't be alarmed, Bonnie," Joran said, raising a glowing hand. "We were taken up to the skies and have now been called to help you."

"Help me?" Bonnie glanced at the tablet screen. Matt was now interrogating the two Darcys. The pain in his face tied a knot in her stomach. "How can you help me?"

"You need to sing." Selah lifted a lyre. Multicolored strings vibrated from top to bottom. "The God of our fathers has not abandoned you and will not allow you to be tested beyond what you can endure. So he sent us to this lonely isle to bring you spiritual sustenance. The battle for the human heart is hanging by a burnt thread. You must fill the cosmos with your song."

Bonnie nodded, though her heart felt like a lead weight. "There are candlestones in my ankle cuffs, and they're draining me dry. I have no strength to sing, no spiritual energy. I'm an empty shell."

"The candlestones should prod a memory," Joran said. "When you were inside one, even though you felt lost and abandoned in that dark place, you forced yourself to sing, and that built your defenses."

"And do you remember how you defeated the influence of a candlestone in Second Eden?" Selah asked.

"I heard a voice, a song that strengthened me," Bonnie said. "It carried the tune I often used to sing Psalm one thirty-nine."

Selah smiled. "And the voice also encouraged you with these words. 'Let no shackles bind this valiant daughter of the lamb. Let no darkness overcome the light within an Oracle of Fire.'"

"You broke those chains in Second Eden," Joran said, "where corrupting influences have been but fleeting thoughts, thereby making them less able to enslave hearts and minds. Now you must break the chains in this world where corruption is a consuming cancer, and the influences that bind hearts are much more powerful."

Selah strummed the lyre. "The world needs you. Matt needs you. Even if you sing from the ashes of grief, your song will be like a balm to needy hearts. Just pour out your soul. Your prayer for Matt will be like a prayer for the world. Speak your heart, and we will find a melody."

"I'll do what I can." Tears again trickling to her chin, she sat and looked up to the sky. A cool breeze wafted from the lake, drying tears, sweat, and blood. She let her mind drift to places far away and times long past, pleasant memories when life was simple, when cares were nothing more than how to hide wings in a backpack. "I am on Mount Hardin once again. I seek refuge in the God of comfort, and I cry to him from the depths of my wounded heart. My soul has been stabbed with a cruel dagger. The evil one, the enemy of all that is good, the father of lies has poisoned the stream of truth with his deceptions, and mankind has eagerly lapped the defiled water."

Selah played a note, then three more. Colors radiated from the strings and vibrated in the air as they ascended into the sky. Joran hummed along, his voice as beautiful as peace itself.

As the lyre's notes collected into a haunting melody, Bonnie's words conformed to the tune as if they had minds of their own.

> From the ashes I call to you, O God;
> From the canyons of grief I beg for light.
> Darkness covers me, evil ensnares me;
> I need your love to cast away the night.

187

While Selah continued playing, Joran added a descant that felt like pure energy. Bonnie's voice strengthened and poured forth, filling the air with luxurious song.

> You are the one who spread out your hands;
> You are the one who cleansed all my blight.
> You bled on the cross; you purged all my dross;
> You transformed my scarlet into white.

She pressed her hands over her heart. Her tone altered to a mournful lament.

My dear son is lost in the wilderness;
He bears no shining light from above.
Let him see kindness; heal his dread blindness;
And touch his darkened eyes with love.

You understand the mysterious plan,
Never confused by the turns;
You see from the skies with experienced eyes,
Always knowing my concerns.

From ages to ages, from ashes to glory;
You know all the stages, you know my whole story.
And now my appraiser, who purged all my dross,
Come be my trail blazer, I look to the cross.

188

Bonnie rose to her feet and lifted her hands.

I rise from the ashes to praise your name;
I shout from the darkness to shine your light.
You are always near; my words you always hear.

My spirit revives; my soul takes flight.

My spirit revives; my soul takes flight.

My spirit revives; my soul takes flight.

When the words finished, she continued humming the tune. Selah added embellishing notes, while Joran harmonized with hums of his own.

Something clicked below. The manacles had unfastened and lay loose on the ground. As Bonnie stooped and lifted a chain, new tears flowed. "God of my deliverance!" she called out. "You have truly set this captive free—body, heart, and soul! Let the wicked bring their ropes and chains! Let them shout their lies! Nothing compares to your power! Nothing compares to your love!"

Breathless, Bonnie spread out her wings. "I have to go. I have to find Matt."

"Not yet, Bonnie." Joran nodded at the computer tablet. "Wait to see how God answers your prayer for Matt. You can no longer be his crutch. He must find the light on his own or else it will be merely a reflection of yours. The fire must burn within his own heart."

Brushing away more tears, Bonnie nodded. "I understand." She lifted the tablet so Joran and Selah could watch with her. Again, she set a finger over Matt's face. "Peace be with you, my son. Settle your mind. Listen for the song as it arrives on angels' wings. Let God's love reach into your heart and set you free from your chains."

189

M att stared at the two Darcys. He could ask more questions, but time was running out. As sweat trickled down his cheeks, a hummed tune filled the air. He looked at the door, now closed to the snowy landscape. "Did you hear something?"

"Nothing," Darcy #2 said, her hands tight on the chair's armrests. "No time for distractions. Just get me out of here and put that imposter in my place!"

"I'm not an imposter!" Darcy #1 shouted. "She's the imposter!"

Darcy #2 lifted a hand. "Matt! I just remembered. This is the ring you gave me when we first met, the one from the Cracker Jacks box. I told you I threw it away, but I really saved it."

Matt looked at her finger. Yes, it was the exact ring.

"No!" Darcy #1 rubbed her finger. "Tamiel must have taken it from me. I've been wearing it ever since you left."

His thoughts spinning, Matt blinked at Darcy #1. Her story could be true. She had been rubbing that finger. That couldn't have been a ploy, could it? Only if the imposter knew about the ring. If so, the imposter would have taken it, which meant the Darcy in the chair had to be the liar.

He glanced at the clock. Fifteen seconds! He had to retie the imposter's arms, but she would fight tooth and nail. Maybe a quick punch to the jaw would knock her out.

Darcy #1 whipped out her knife, leaped for the chair, and sliced through the remaining ropes. She grabbed Darcy #2's arm and jerked her from the seat. A siren squealed. A mechanical voice called out from the control station, "Thirty seconds to launch."

Darcy #1 threw off her coat, sheathed her knife, and sat heavily in the chair. Covering her face with her hands, she wept.

The siren died. The speaker announced, "Launch terminated."

The words echoed in the barn. Silence took over except for gentle sobs from the former prostitute now sitting in the chair.

Matt gaped at her. He couldn't breathe. What had she done? She had to stay put or the missile would launch. And Tamiel would eventually kill her.

Darcy #2 crossed her arms. "Now that was a surprising move. The ultimate play for your sympathy. I suppose when the people who planned this crazy system come back, they'll turn off the launch system and let her—"

"Shut up!" Matt punched her in the mouth. She staggered backwards and slammed against a wall.

As she slid down to her bottom, her eyes rolled upward. Seconds later, her cheeks, forehead, and chin morphed into the familiar face of Semiramis.

190

Matt charged, grabbed her by the throat, and threw her on her back. Straddling her on his knees, he set a fist in front of her eyes. "Listen, witch! I want to hear only one thing from you. How do I get Darcy out of that chair without launching the missile?"

"You ..." Her eyes wide, she swallowed. "You can't. The system is locked. If she gets up, the missile will launch. It's impossible for anyone but Tamiel to turn it off."

The hummed tune again drifted in the air—soothing and peaceful as it cleared his mind fog. "Elam's not stupid. He wouldn't leave his defenses down. Where is the missile really aimed?"

She glared at him, her lips thin and pale.

Matt tightened his grip around her throat and shouted, "Tell me!"

She gagged as she spoke. "You wouldn't believe me even if I told you."

"You're probably right." He loosened his hold. "I can't even trust that the missile is real."

"No, you can't trust anything." She stared at him with hate-filled eyes. "You are such a fool, a simple pawn in this game. Every step has been designed to weaken your mother's song. Some things you see are real. Some are merely deceptions. What matters is that we silence your mother."

"But my mother's not here. She—" He looked at the cameras on the ceiling. One still aimed its lens at him. A red diode on the front silently blinked. "Oh. I get it. She's watching us right now."

Semiramis smirked. "So you plucked one grain of truth. As you will learn, the truth can be an effective dagger. It plunges straight to the heart."

"What do you know about truth?" Matt snatched the ring off her finger and stuffed it into his pocket. "I'm going to show you some truth." He grabbed a fistful of her hair and jerked her to her feet. While she struggled, he hauled her to the chair and collected the pieces of rope.

"Matt," the real Darcy said. "What are you going to do with her?"

"Semiramis is about to learn how truth can be a dagger." He dragged her to the exit, flung the door open, and threw her outside, sending her sliding through the snow-covered cornstalks and up against the silo.

"Matt ..." Semiramis sat up, her back to the silo. "What do you have in mind?"

"You'll see." Matt flung the silo's access panel away and peered inside. A blast-door hatch lay open on the concrete floor of the otherwise empty cylindrical shell. The missile appeared to be ready to launch immediately.

Semiramis scrambled to her feet and tried to run, but she slipped on the wet stalks and fell. Matt grabbed her hair again, dragged her into the silo, and laid her next to the blast door. Using the rope sections, he tied her wrists and ankles as tightly as he could. "Don't go anywhere."

He ran to the barn, picked up a coil of rope, and hustled back to the silo. As he tied one end around Semiramis's waist, he spoke in a calm tone. "Remember how I lassoed you in the tank? That's nothing compared to the ride you'll go on when I release Darcy."

She spat but missed his face. "You wouldn't dare!"

"I looked at the map. The target is in a remote area, far from any farms or towns. Even if the missile is real, Elam is smart enough to be ready for it, and maybe it won't hurt too many people. Whatever happens, at least we'll be rid of one of the worst blights in the history of the world. ... You." He jerked the knot tight. "The truth plunges straight to the heart."

192

"Matt ..." Her glare melted into a weak smile. "Let's be reasonable about this."

"Keep your demonic tongue moving long enough to tell me how to stop the launch." He tied a slipknot loop at the other end of the rope and began lowering it into the silo. "I'm listening. It might take me a minute to attach this end to the missile."

"Matt, I ... I don't know how to stop the launch. Only Tamiel does."

He slid the loop around a metal protrusion on the missile's cone. "Really? I'll bet your son set it all up."

"Yes, of course, but I don't understand what Mardon did. I'm not a scientist."

"Oh. Right. I've seen this movie. You're playing the part of the sleazy seductress in this team of stupid lackeys."

"Lackeys? Tamiel is—"

"Tamiel is a clown. He thinks he's in control, but Arramos is just pulling his puppet strings. Tamiel says that God is predictable, but he's the one who's following a script." Matt pulled the rope, testing the attachment. It held fast. "Since he can't see me on the cameras, I'll bet he calls me in less than a minute."

She snarled. "You're so cocky. You have no idea how powerful Tamiel is. He is the Silent One, an angel who resisted the tyrant of Heaven and was cast down because he dared to question the Almighty's despotic reign."

"Keep talking. Maybe someone will listen to your blabbering when little pieces of you scatter with the wind."

Her lips trembled, and her whole body shook. "Matt. Listen. Please. I'm just a mother who is trying to get revenge on Arramos for what he did to my son. I've been going along with this plan so I can get close enough to kill him. Even now I am carrying a potion that will destroy him, but I won't have the opportunity until we're all together at the sixth door."

Matt tested the rope again. It still held perfectly, but maybe delaying would keep Semiramis talking long enough to give something away. "Why should I believe someone who lies for a living?"

She breathed faster, shallower. "I have information, vital information that will save Second Eden. It has nothing to do with the missile. It's a different danger. Release me, and I will tell you everything."

"Tell me. If I think it's valuable enough, I'll let you go."

"But it's the only bargaining chip I have. How do I know you'll keep your word?"

"I suppose someone like you doesn't understand trust." The cell phone rang. Matt smirked. "He's right on time." He climbed to his feet and fished the phone from his pocket. "Tamiel, it's so good of you to call."

"Matt Bannister, it seems that you failed to identify the correct Darcy, and your former sister is now trapped in that chair. Will you leave her there for me to kill when I come, or will you take her with you and allow my missile to launch?"

"Oh, I'm definitely taking her with me. I'm not cruel like you."

"I assume you understand the ramifications of your decision. Second Eden will be in grave danger."

"Yeah. Semiramis told me. I'll let her tell you more." He turned on the speaker and aimed the phone at Semiramis. "How about a little dose of truth?"

"Tamiel!" Semiramis called. "Matt tied me to the missile. If it launches, I'll go with it."

Silence ensued. After a few seconds, Tamiel's voice came through the speaker. "A most ingenious solution, Matt. Your awareness of her value to me over the years has provided you with significant leverage. Congratulations."

"Stop stalling. Tell me how to disable the missile, or it will soon rain glowing bits of Semiramis over the fields of Nebraska."

"So be it. Such debris will not harm the corn crop too severely."

"What?" Semiramis shrieked. "After all I've done for you over the centuries? I survived Morgan and Naamah and Goliath and Devin. I am your most trusted servant. I will do anything to help you. And you'll need me at the sixth door. When Lauren arrives, only I can protect you. You can't trust Arramos."

"Your appeal was elevating my sympathies until you questioned Arramos's loyalty. Your fate is now sealed. And I do not fear Lauren. Her self-preservation instincts will overrule her courage. All will be well."

"But you said yourself that Arramos is expendable! You need me to eliminate him!"

195

"Nonsense. Such a desperate accusation against my loyalty is truly vile." After a brief pause, Tamiel continued. "Matt, if you want your father to stay alive, proceed to the fifth address. It is only four hours away, so there is no need to spend the night anywhere. Be there by sunset."

Semiramis gasped. "Matt. Listen. I will give you part of a numerical string—four, four, zero, three. The numbers are part of coordinates where I hid a lethal device in Second Eden. If you release me, I will give you the rest."

"Is that so?" Matt spoke into the phone again. "Tamiel, Semiramis just gave me the numbers four, four, zero, three. What do those numbers mean to you?"

Tamiel laughed. "I heard. She is quite desperate, isn't she? Those digits are part of my phone number. I assume it was all she could think of at the moment."

"He's lying!" Semiramis shouted. "He's a demon! You can't trust a single word he—" She closed her mouth and swallowed. "What I mean is—"

"What you mean," Matt said, "is that I can't trust him or you."

"But ... but ..."

A click sounded. Matt looked at the screen. The call had ended.

"I guess that settles that." He shoved the phone back into his pocket. "So much for all those centuries of service."

"Matt, he's ... he's just calling your bluff." Her voice shook like a withered leaf. "He knows you wouldn't really—"

"I'm not bluffing."

Semiramis choked on her own saliva as she whispered, "I can help you save Second Eden. Trust me."

"Trust you?" Matt crouched in front of Semiramis. "You're nothing but a dead sorceress. A wraith. You told me yourself some things are real and some are deceptions. Maybe you're not even real, so I'm not going to bother figuring out if you're lying about Second Eden or not. Maybe the missile isn't real either, and you have nothing to worry about." He pointed toward the barn, his arm shaking. "But I do know Darcy's real, and I'm going to save her life. I'll take my chances with the rest."

Matt stalked out of the silo. From within, Semiramis wailed. "Matt! You can't do this to me! Have mercy!"

His jaw firm, he marched back into the barn and picked up Darcy's coat. "It's still snowing out there," he said as he held it open. "You'll need this."

"Matt?" She looked up at him. Tear tracks stained her cheeks.

He grasped her wrist gently. "Let's go."

"But the missile ..."

"We'll let the missile take care of itself." He pulled her to her feet. "I have to take care of you."

The siren blared. "Launch sequence commencing."

Matt wrapped the coat around her and patted her on the back. "Ready?"

As she smiled, tears flowed anew. "Ready."

Matt turned to the ceiling camera and blew a kiss. "I love you, Mom. Thanks for everything."

He offered his arm to Darcy and whispered, "I'm not saying I trust you yet, but let's keep up the show of unity, for my mother's sake."

"I understand." She hooked her arm around his. "We'd better hurry."

With the siren still blaring, they ran from the barn into the snowy field, the farmhouse in sight. A tremor shook the ground. They slipped and dropped to their seats. Matt pivoted and looked at the silo, now about fifty paces away. The metal façade fell to the sides, revealing Semiramis curled on the floor.

A silvery missile shot out of the ground and hurtled toward the sky. The rope pulled taut and jerked Semiramis upward. Fiery exhaust shot along the ground in all directions. Matt threw himself over Darcy. A wave of mist roared by, rattling the surrounding cornstalks, but it felt no hotter than a steamy shower.

He rolled off, and the two looked up. Semiramis's body dangled at the missile's midsection and banged against the hull. The missile adjusted its trajectory and zoomed onward, leaving a white smoke trail.

Darcy stared with wide eyes. "What will happen to her?"

"Hard to say. I'm no rocketry expert. The missile might eject part of its body, but since I tied her to the warhead, she should go along for the full ride. I'm guessing the computer will keep adjusting the course no matter how much her weight affects its balance."

Darcy breathed a whispered, "And she'll go up in a mushroom cloud." A new tear slipped to her cheek.

"Are you okay?" Matt rose and helped Darcy to her feet. "She's already dead. She's a wraith. A demonic sorceress. My mother said there was no hope for her."

"I know." Darcy brushed water from the seat of her coat. "It's just that ..."

Matt looked into her eyes. It seemed that every thought came through loud and clear, as if Mom's song carried emotions on the snowy breeze. "It's just that you were kind of demonic, too."

Biting her lip, she nodded.

"I get that. Sometimes I feel the same way about myself. It's like two wild beasts fighting inside me, and I'm not sure which one's going to win."

"I know that feeling. But I think the battle's over now, at least for me."

Matt lifted the key ring at his hip. The fourth key glowed red. As it clinked against the others, it threw off scarlet sparks. "I wish I could say the same for myself."

"Maybe I can help." She extended a hand. "The show of unity was the first step. Will you take the second with me?"

He stared at her hand. "What's the second step?"

"Just pretend you like me, at least for a while. A wise person once said to me, 'Be kind to those who cast shadows on your soul, and soon the light of love will drive the darkness away.'"

"Let me guess. My mother."

She nodded. "It's worth a try. You already saved my life, so why not?"

"I guess it can't hurt. But first …" He pulled the ring from his pocket and slid it onto her finger. "It fits perfectly."

She rubbed the ring with her other hand. "I wore it to remind me to be nicer to people. … And to remember you."

"I saw you rubbing your finger. Why didn't you tell me about it earlier?"

"I thought I had just lost it." She gave him a hesitant smile. "Would you have believed me if I showed you a bare finger and told you I had been wearing your Cracker Jacks ring all this time?"

"I guess not." He slid his hand into hers. "But now I'm ready for the second step."

She clutched his hand gratefully. "Hungry?" she asked, her smile brighter than ever.

"Starved."

She led him toward the farmhouse. "Let's see if Mariel has those bacon and eggs ready. It's too cold to go grazing with Thomas."

He laughed. "Now you're talking."

Matt and Darcy walked hand in hand toward the farmhouse, their arms swinging as light snow collected on their heads.

199

Bonnie dropped to her knees, the tablet still in her hands. She lifted her head and shouted, "Praise the God of Heaven and Earth! You have answered my prayer! You sent my song to my son's ears and pricked his heart. He witnessed love, the love of a forgiven harlot who is now a saint. He saw Jesus in her sacrifice." She brushed tears from her cheeks. "And now his heart has been softened. Now he can receive your grace and be forgiven himself, because he has seen your handiwork. He has witnessed the results of the fire that burns away every trace of dross."

Selah crouched in front of her. Her intangible body glowed. "When Arramos hears what happened, he might come back to get you."

"You're right." Bonnie touched the tablet's screen. Matt and Darcy were no longer in view, just a toppled chair in an otherwise empty chamber. "Lord, I pray that you will continue to reach out to Matt. Allow me another chance to speak to him about faith in you. Now that the blinding shadow of hatred has been cast away, maybe he will be ready to hear about the greatest sacrificial act of all time."

After taking a deep breath, she rose and looked out over the lake. Snow began falling, veiling the distant shores in a silky shroud. "While Arramos carried me here, I tried to keep my bearings, but with all the farms stretching out for miles and miles, everything looked the same."

In the distance, something pierced the clouds and flew toward the lake. As it zoomed higher and higher, a silvery cylinder took shape. Something dark flopped against the cylinder like a loose garment, though it was too far away to distinguish. "It looks like ..." Bonnie squinted. "A missile!"

"Tamiel wasn't bluffing," Joran said. "Taking Darcy from the chair must have triggered the launch."

"Dear God," Bonnie whispered, "please protect everyone at the target and in Second Eden."

After it flew past, Bonnie gazed at the exhaust trail. The missile had drawn a path to its launch site—straight to Matt!

She stretched out her wings. "I'd better go before the wind blows that smoke away."

Selah looked up. "It's already starting to fade."

"Then I have to leave right now." Bonnie bowed her head. "Thank you for helping me with my song. I hope to see you again."

"Maybe you will," Joran said. "But not likely in this world. The ushering in of the sunset of this age is quickly approaching, and it's possible that nothing can stop it."

"I refuse to believe that." She beat her wings and lifted into the air. "I'll see you in my dreams!"

As she ascended, Joran and Selah dissolved into swirls of light. Seconds later, they dispersed and vanished.

Bonnie flew up to the missile's trail and followed it toward the source. With snow pelting her eyes and a breeze scattering the smoke, the task seemed impossible. She picked a point in the distance where the trail seemed to originate and locked her stare on it. Even if the smoke disappeared completely, she had a target. Matt would be somewhere nearby. Somehow she would find him.

201

MUSHROOM CLOUD

Lauren clung tightly to Roxil's spine. The she-dragon had flown for hours, stopping only for water and food as directed by Lois. After getting a long rest in an abandoned airplane hangar the night before, Roxil's energy had skyrocketed, which also increased her metabolism. With just a few lakes and streams, fish had been scarce, but her sharp eyes had spotted several rabbits and a deer that made wonderful roasted meals for both of them. Fortunately, her fire-breathing quickened the cooking process considerably.

Snow swirled in a cold, gusting wind. Roxil curled her neck back and breathed on Lauren from time to time. That helped a lot. This journey was proving to be far less painful than expected. In fact, constant lifts and falls in time with the wing beats, jerks to the side from gusts of wind, and beautiful farmland vistas proved to be exhilarating. Emotions surged, and, as usual, Lauren's back scales tingled, enhancing her hearing.

She parsed the sounds in the wind—whistles, a dog barking, a rumbling engine, and ... a song? Mom's song?

"Roxil! I hear it! My mother's song!"

Roxil called back. "Can you figure out where it is coming from?"

"I hope so. I mean, I'll try."

"Guide me. Slap my left side to go left, my right to go right. Pull on my spine to straighten."

"Got it." Lauren slapped Roxil's left side. As their angle adjusted toward the song, Lauren pulled back on the spine. "That's it. Perfect."

Lauren then touched her jaw. "Lois, we're going off course. I'm following my mother's song."

"Wait a minute," Carly said through the transmitter. "I ran out of gas, so I couldn't leave Lois plugged into the car battery for very long. I carried her to an abandoned warehouse and climbed the stairs to the roof for better reception. I was just about to plug her in to an extension cord I found, but it's kind of frayed so …" She grunted. "There. … Coolness. Her lights are flashing, and no sparks, so she should be good to go in a few seconds."

204

"How far did you have to carry her?" Lauren asked.

"About a mile, I think. She's pretty heavy, so I had to rest a few times. It took about an hour. You should have seen the looks I got from drivers passing by, but no one stopped to ask why I was carrying a Sputnik or even offered to help."

"Are you exposed to bad weather where you are right now? It's snowing here."

"Not bad here at all, but I heard that a storm front is coming. I can haul her to the stairwell if … Oh. She's up. Tell her again what you want."

Lauren spoke slowly and evenly. "Lois, Roxil and I are flying a bit off course. I'm following my mother's song."

"Because of my recent shutdown," Lois said, "I no longer have an estimate of your current location. Be sure to tell me about highways and landmarks you pass, and I will pinpoint your site and trajectory."

"Perfect. And Carly?"

"Yes?"

"Thanks for all you're doing. I hope you're getting enough food and sleep."

"Food's not a problem. I have a backpack full of munchies. And sleep? I'll take a fifty-hour nap when this crazy stuff is finished."

Lauren yawned. "I'm with you on that."

As Roxil flew onward, Lauren scanned the ground about two hundred feet below. She described every road, stream, and rocky protrusion to Lois. With each passing minute, the song grew louder. It seemed that they were chasing a chirping bird and gaining on it second by second.

Soon, a winged form came into view far ahead. Lauren jabbed her finger toward it. "There she is! My mother!"

"I see her." Roxil beat her wings harder. As they closed the gap, Roxil let out a deafening roar, but the wind caught the sound and threw it back in their faces.

Tears formed in Lauren's eyes. Mom didn't slow down at all. But they would catch her—only a few minutes to go.

When they drew within a hundred yards, Roxil roared again, louder than ever. Mom arched her neck and peeked back. Her mouth dropped open. She smiled, spun in the air, and hovered in place, her wings beating furiously.

As Roxil drew near, Mom began flying slowly in the same direction. She lifted higher and settled on Roxil's back just behind Lauren.

205

"Mom!" Lauren twisted and hugged her tightly.

As they embraced, Roxil called, "I will contact Lois and get us back on course."

Mom released Lauren. "No! Wait!"

Roxil curled her neck and brought her head close. "Yes?"

Mom pointed over Roxil's right shoulder. "We need to go that way. That's where Matt is. At least that's where he was a little while ago."

"Very well. Guide me. Lauren will demonstrate."

After Lauren showed her mother how to adjust their flight direction, she reached back and held her hand. "It's so good to see you again. You wouldn't believe all we've been through." She laughed. "Well, I guess you would. The craziest things seem normal now."

"You're right about that," Mom said. "Less than an hour ago I was stuck on an island watching a video on a computer. Matt was trying to decide whether to allow a nuclear missile to launch or to let Darcy die."

"I saw Darcy's name on a phone message she left at the church, the one with the web stuff covering it. Who is she?"

"I guess I have a lot to explain." For the next several minutes, she filled Lauren in on their travels to the four addresses, their discovery of Thomas and Mariel, her abduction by Arramos, the restoration of her song with help from Joran and Selah, who Darcy was, and Matt's apparent change of heart about her.

After a couple of hours, a column of smoke appeared, rising from the ground and into the clouds. Mom pointed at it. "That direction is about right. Let's see what's going on."

Roxil curled her neck and looked at them. As she blinked, her ears wilted. "I concur. I am growing quite weary. Even if it is nothing important, I will be able to rest."

Several minutes later, the source of the smoke came into view—a burning pile of cornstalks between a red barn and a farmhouse. In the midst of falling snow, Roxil landed in a slide several paces away from the fire.

As soon as she stopped, Lauren and her mother hopped down. Keeping her ears perked for any unusual noises, Lauren looked around. She picked up a fallen cornstalk and shook off a thin coating of snow and ice. "How could someone burn these on such a cold, wet day? Making a fire would be nearly impossible."

"Matt could do it," Mom said. "I'm sure he's an expert in survival skills and signaling for help."

"True. But since the fire's still going, he couldn't have started it very long ago." Lauren dropped the cornstalk. "So what now?"

"The video looked like the camera was in a big room." Mom nodded toward the barn. "Let's check it out."

While Roxil rested near the fire, Lauren and her mother jogged across the wet, furrowed field. When they drew close to the barn, they passed by sheets of metal on the ground surrounding a blackened concrete pad. At the center of the pad, a hatch stood open, also bearing the signs of a scorching blast.

207

Lauren walked to the hatch and looked in. Nothing but darkness lay below. "Just a hole. I can't see anything."

"Let's go inside." Mom opened a door to the barn and waited for Lauren to join her. When they entered, Mom turned in a slow circle under a bank of ceiling lights. "This is the place." She walked to a toppled chair and touched its leg. "Semiramis sat here, and then Darcy. I saw Matt take Darcy, but I don't know what happened to Semiramis after Matt punched her."

Lauren smiled. "I love that part of the story. I'm so proud of him."

Mom touched her shoulder. "Let's see what's in the house."

They ran across the field. After pausing for a moment to tell Roxil what they had found, they hurried to the farmhouse. Once inside, Lauren stopped in the anteroom and inhaled deeply. The aroma of bacon permeated the air.

Mom passed her and stepped into a small living room. She picked up a sheet of paper on a sofa. As she scanned it, she smiled. "It's from Matt."

Lauren joined her and looked over her shoulder. Hurried script written in dark blue ink covered the page.

Mom read out loud. "Whoever finds this, Thomas, Mariel, and Darcy are with me, and we're all safe. I now have four keys, and I'm on my way to the fifth address. I copied that address and the sixth one on the back of this sheet, but I still don't know number seven. A missile launched from a silo here. Tamiel says it is nuclear and will go through a portal and destroy Second Eden, but I don't believe him. I'm not even sure it carries a real warhead. The computer map in the barn is tracking the missile. At first, it was targeted on someplace in Nebraska, but last time I checked, the target had drifted eastward like someone's controlling it remotely. The missile had flown a few hundred miles, but I didn't have time to stay and watch it. I have to go to the fifth door before sunset and then the sixth door, maybe tomorrow morning. Everything's accelerating. My danger sense tells me that something terrible is about to happen. Maybe it's the missile. Maybe it's what's waiting at the next door. I'm not sure. But I do know everything will eventually be okay."

208

She turned the page over and continued. "Mom, if you're the one reading this ..." She sniffed and wiped a tear. "Your song made all the difference. I don't know how you did it, but thank you. I'm not sure if that missile will detonate or not. I figured Tamiel could launch the missile later no matter what I decided to do. He has control over it. I had to take care of what I had control over. Saving Darcy. I have no regrets."

Biting her lip, Mom folded the page. "I guess we should check the addresses to see if they match what's on the phone."

"Sure." Lauren took the note and slid it into her back pocket. "We should have a look at the computer map, and Roxil can ask Lois how long it would take to fly to either address."

"Good plan."

After informing Roxil, Lauren and her mother hurried back to the barn. They each chose a chair at the computer station and looked at the monitors. On one of the screens, a flashing missile icon moved across a map with an arcing trail of illuminated dashes behind it. A small bull's-eye target icon sat on the right-hand side of the screen.

Mom pointed at the target. "Matt said it was drifting, but it looks like it's staying put now."

"Can you tell where it is?" Lauren leaned forward and squinted at the screen. "I can't find any labels."

"I see state borders. It looks like it's heading for north-central Kentucky, maybe a bit south of Indiana." Mom tapped on the screen. "Isn't that where Louisville is?"

"It is!" Lauren flopped back in her chair. "And so is Fort Knox!"

Mom blinked at her. "What's so important about Fort Knox?"

"That's where Elam thinks they're holding Sapphira! He's on his way there now!"

Mom's expression turned vacant. "Tamiel is that evil. He would slaughter thousands of people just to kill Elam."

"And Yereq and Makaidos and Thigocia. They're all with him."

"Can we get word to him?"

"I'm not sure." Lauren tapped her jaw. "Lois! Can you hear me?"

"Quite well. You seem to be distressed."

"I am." Lauren took a deep breath and exhaled slowly. "Can you get a message to Elam? It's urgent."

"Elam provided a way to send an urgent message, but his parameters for urgency might be more stringent than yours."

"A missile with a nuclear warhead is about to hit Fort Knox. Is that urgent enough?"

"Affirmative. I will send the message. Give me a moment."

Lauren breathed a frail whisper. "But will it get there in time?"

Lauren and her mother stared at each other. Although Mom's song had been loud and clear earlier, it now faded with every passing second. There was no need to talk. They both knew the possible outcomes. Even if Lois reached Elam in time, a nuclear blast would kill Sapphira and obliterate any nearby town. Countless lives might soon be snuffed out.

After a few minutes, Lauren whispered into her tooth transmitter. "Lois? Any luck reaching Elam?"

"I sent the message. I am awaiting confirmation of reception."

Lauren kept her voice low. "If a nuclear bomb hits Fort Knox, how many people would die?"

"It depends on the type of warhead. Do you know the yield in megatons?"

"No. Just assume it's a big one. And please answer as quietly as you can. I'll be able to hear you."

Lois's reply came through at a barely audible volume. "Assuming fifty megatons, the number of fatalities would initially be fairly low because of the relatively rural location, perhaps seventy thousand. Long-term deaths due to fallout could reach more than three hundred thousand. These estimates are based on a population reduction that has already occurred due to rampant crime and riots in Louisville."

"Any chance the U.S. military will see the missile on radar and somehow stop it?"

"The chance is low. The military branches are in disarray, though the missile defense system has procedures that allow for a counterattack if authorization is given. It takes only a few highly ranked personnel to trigger retaliation."

Lauren strolled away from her mother. "Since the launch came from within the U.S., would they retaliate?"

"According to my knowledge base, authorities would attempt to determine if a terrorist accessed the launch site and if a foreign government directed the action. If so, retaliation would be likely, though the investigation would create a gap in time before the counterstrike."

211

"If the military is in disarray, could they investigate at all?"

Static filtered into Lois's reply. "My artificial intelligence engine is unable to predict the response of human personnel in the wake of such a disaster and the pressure of a terrified populace demanding answers and retribution. Perhaps the authorities would believe that their entire nuclear arsenal is compromised, and they might launch all remaining missiles in order to keep them from striking additional domestic targets."

As Lauren walked toward her mother, she whispered, "Nuclear war."

Lois began a reply, but static drowned her out. Lauren massaged her jaw. Maybe the transmitter was deteriorating, or maybe her tendency to disrupt electrical equipment had again come into play. "Lois, would you repeat that, please?"

"Certainly." The static settled to background noise. "Nuclear war is a possible outcome, though I cannot predict the likelihood of such a response or how long the U.S. military would wait to proceed."

Lauren sat down again. "I understand."

Mom wheeled her chair closer. "I heard some of your side of the conversation. I can imagine the rest."

Lauren smiled weakly. "I didn't want to hurt your song."

"If we have nuclear war, it won't matter much." She grasped Lauren's hand. "I need to talk to you about something very personal."

"Sure. Go ahead."

"I might as well be blunt." Mom leaned toward her. "Has anyone talked to you about faith in God?"

212

"Definitely." As Lauren compressed her mother's hand, she let her smile grow. "My dross is purged. Just like you, I am an Oracle of Fire."

Tears trickled from Mom's eyes. "Then you're safe, no matter what happens."

Lauren stood and pulled her mother into her arms. As they embraced, Lauren whispered, "Safe. We have nothing to fear, not even death."

The tingles in her scales spiked. Lights on the ceiling flickered. The monitors at the workstation flashed and buzzed, and the cameras began spinning wildly.

Mom wrapped a wing around Lauren. A monitor exploded. Glass pelted the wing's membrane. Shards pierced and stuck on the outer side. The overhead light panels burst. More glass rained on their heads.

Then, darkness enveloped the room. The workstation continued buzzing. A barely visible glow on the remaining monitor, just a fading ghost, spelled out, "Connection Lost. Assume Detonation Sequence Activated."

Elam yawned. After driving through the night and taking only a couple of short naps, the final hundred miles lay before him, though it seemed like a thousand. The eerily reddish sun had passed its high point and now sank toward the horizon, a fireball in the exterior rearview mirror. Soon it would be dark enough to stop and let Yereq and the dragons out for a stretch before driving into Fort Knox.

The cell phone chimed as it lay on the passenger's seat. He furrowed his brow. One ring and then silence. So far, so good.

It chimed again—once, twice, three times, then silence.

Elam called to Yereq. "Did you hear that?"

"I did." He pushed up from his reclining position and sat against the van's side wall. Wearing a medieval tunic and trousers that Tamara sewed for him years ago, he looked perfect for the villain's role in Jack and the Beanstalk. "We wait one minute for a double ring."

Elam pointed ahead. "There's an abandoned gas station. I'll pull in there and alert Makaidos and Thigocia. We'll see if they detect any danger."

Something thumped three times in the trailer.

"I think we have an answer already," Yereq said. "That was not a call to stop for bladder relief."

Elam drove the van into the gas station's parking area, an old Stuckey's travel center. Weeds grew from cracks in the pavement, and wide strips of paper tape drew huge X's across the windows.

When he stopped, he scooped up the phone, hopped out of the van, and jogged to the back of the trailer. He grabbed the rear gate's handle and swung the door open.

Makaidos immediately extended his neck and pushed his head out while the rest of his body stayed tightly curled with Thigocia's. His eyes seemed to flame. "I sense horrific danger."

"We guessed that." Elam waved an arm. "You'd better get out so you can fly if necessary."

While the two dragons untangled themselves and climbed out of the trailer, Yereq exited the van's side door and joined them.

Elam looked at the phone. About ten seconds remained until the expected third signal.

Makaidos stretched his neck and looked at the sky. "The danger is up there. It is not close, but it is of such magnitude that proximity is not a factor."

The phone chimed ... once ... twice ... then fell silent.

"That's it." Elam punched in the designated emergency number and held the phone to his ear.

A woman answered. "Castlewood Chamber of Commerce. How may I help you?"

"Activate voice encryption," Elam said.

The phone began a low hum. "Encryption activated."

Elam paced in front of Yereq and the dragons, his head low. "Lois, what's going on?"

"A missile with a nuclear warhead has been launched. The target is Fort Knox. I estimate that it will arrive in eight minutes."

Elam stopped. His heart thumping, he whispered, "Eight minutes?"

"Affirmative. I concluded that the situation was sufficiently urgent to initiate contact with you."

"Of course. Of course." Elam looked up. No smoke trails appeared in the scarlet-tinted haze. "We're still a hundred miles away, but if Sapphira's there …" An image of Sapphira being incinerated by an inferno blast pulsed in his mind. "How sure are you of this information?"

"The confidence is quite high. We have an eyewitness who saw the missile in flight, and we have two eyewitnesses who have seen the targeting map on a computer workstation. The eyewitnesses have a reliability factor of one hundred percent."

"Who are they?"

"Bonnie and Lauren Bannister."

"More like two hundred percent." Elam gazed at the eastern horizon. "If the missile hits Fort Knox, how much danger are we in?"

"That depends on the payload, but considering the prevailing winds are in your favor, it is not a deadly threat unless you enter the fallout zone."

Elam looked at the dragons. Both Makaidos and Thigocia shifted uneasily. Why would they sense such great danger if the missile wouldn't cause them any harm? Maybe the danger was so extreme for others, it somehow bled into their own radar screens. He quickly summarized the warning for them and Yereq.

"My security algorithm indicates that we should end this call," Lois said. "I will send an encrypted text that will provide all updates I have at this time."

"Very well, Lois. Thank you." Elam pressed the Disconnect button. A series of unintelligible text scrolled across the screen. When it finished, a new series began—the translated version. Elam read the note and summarized it out loud. "Bonnie and Lauren are going to try to intercept Matt at an address that Lois included in her message. They call it the sixth door. No word from Billy.

Walter, Ashley, and Gabriel went down with *Merlin* in a plane crash, but they survived."

"What is the address?" Makaidos asked.

"Someplace in Nebraska. Take a look." He held the phone close to Makaidos so he could read it.

A brilliant light flashed in the eastern sky. It shot outward in concentric rainbows that shattered in sparkling colors. At the center, a mushroom cloud blossomed high above the ground.

"Cover them!" Makaidos shouted.

The two dragons shoved Elam and Yereq down. As Elam lay with his cheek on the cold pavement, Thigocia's wing blanketed him. Seconds later, the leatherlike canopy rippled over his body as if blown by a violent wind.

After a few moments, the wing lifted. Elam and Yereq climbed to their feet. The redness in the sky appeared pink now, as if someone had spilled antinausea medicine from horizon to horizon.

216

Elam brushed gravel from his pants. "That wasn't eight minutes. Not even close."

Makaidos bobbed his head. "The explosion occurred high in the air."

"Then the missile didn't make it all the way to Fort Knox." Elam breathed a sigh. "There's still hope for Sapphira."

Yereq sniffed. "What is that odor? Garlic?"

Elam inhaled deeply. A blend of garlic and camphor tinged the air, a familiar odor … too familiar. "It smells like one of Morgan's concoctions. I had to endure that foulness too many times in the mines of Hades to ever forget it."

"And now Semiramis is Morgan's successor," Yereq said. "She has proven herself to be an expert potion brewer."

Thigocia stretched out her wings, but they quickly drooped. "How strange. I feel so weak."

"I feel it as well." Makaidos snorted a thin flame through his nostrils that immediately died away. "This must be the danger I sensed. Something is sapping our strength."

"That explosion delivered a payload of Morgan's magic." Elam patted Thigocia's neck. "You and Makaidos had better get into the trailer while you can still walk."

The two dragons climbed through the open gate and settled in their intertwined position, breathing in fitful gasps.

Yereq stroked his beard. "This incident makes me wonder if Sapphira is really where we think she is. The missile appeared to be aimed at Fort Knox, but this explosion could have harmed her or us, which would not help Tamiel's cause."

"Because he needs her and me both alive to gain access to Second Eden," Elam said.

Yereq nodded. "She is the ransom bait, and you are the only one who can pay the ransom. Killing either of you would be foolhardy."

"Then why the bomb? Why detonate it in the sky?" Elam began pacing again. "Using a nuclear weapon to deliver Semiramis's potion seems too risky. How could they know the potion wouldn't be instantly burned up? You don't launch a computer-guided missile and then detonate it in the sky. They missed us. They missed Fort Knox. They basically just blew a hole in the air."

"To open a portal?" Yereq asked.

Elam stopped and looked toward the west where the portal to Second Eden lay. "You can't open a portal that doesn't exist. If you know where one is, it's possible to move it. Sapphira's done that. But you can't just blow up a bomb in the air and hope it cracks a dimensional doorway. I have to believe Tamiel knows better."

"Then what was the purpose?"

Elam shrugged. "Maybe there was no purpose. Maybe it was an accident. We shouldn't conclude that everything works perfectly for our enemies. They're clever, but they're not infallible."

"So do we go on to Fort Knox?" Yereq asked.

Elam turned toward the east. A multicolored aura hovered over the horizon, intermixing with the expanding mushroom cloud. "I don't think so. Radioactive fallout has to be terrible there, or at least it will be soon."

"Then what about Sapphira? If the missile was an accident, then she might really be at Fort Knox."

"No, no. The missile itself wasn't an accident. The accidental part was that the missile blew up in the air. Tamiel intended to destroy Fort Knox before we arrived. I think he wants to redirect us to where Sapphira really is."

"Perhaps to capture us in an ambush," Yereq said. "With our dragons incapacitated, we are easy prey."

"Which gives us more evidence that something in the explosion caused their weakness."

"A poisoned payload," Yereq said, "but it might not be deadly. Whatever was in it must have dispersed greatly."

"We can hope." Elam looked at his phone. The screen was dark. "If our theory is true, we should expect Tamiel to try to contact us to provide a new destination." He pressed the Power button, but the screen just flashed and turned black again. "Strange. The phone's not working."

"Because of the explosion?" Yereq asked.

Elam scanned the sky, still pink with shades of blue and green. "I've heard that a nuclear blast high in the atmosphere can cause powerful electromagnetic pulses that travel for hundreds or even thousands of miles. They can knock out anything electrical."

"That complicates things." Yereq eyed the phone. "We have no way of receiving a message. Tamiel cannot redirect us."

"Let me think." Elam began pacing again. With each step, memories from previous centuries flowed like visions from above.

Enoch's voice echoed as if calling from a canyon. *Methuselah inherited the oracle title from me, but the flood created the need to pass the Ovulum to Sapphira Adi, a special kind of oracle whose true mission has not yet begun. Now that she has been set on her path, the Ovulum is yours, and as my descendant, you are the rightful heir.*

Elam whispered his reply from that day long ago. "So am I an oracle?"

The echo continued, though fading. *That mantle is yours to be grasped, but time will tell if you are able to wear it with authority.*

When the vision disappeared, Elam stopped and looked at Makaidos and Thigocia in the trailer, then at Yereq. They all had ancient, sagacious eyes. Only they and Sapphira could understand both the benefit and the burden of witnessing so many centuries of life—some wonderful … some terrifying … some lonely. Thousands of years of experience had infused them with wisdom, but Enoch had singled out only one as a prophetic oracle—Elam, son of Shem, son of Noah. He had to seek God's insight and make a decision for everyone.

After taking a deep breath, he stood close to the trailer gate and spread out his arms. "When we battled evil forces on Second Eden, it seemed that God called every ally to come to our aid. Our paths converged then, and they are converging now. We should travel to the address Lois gave us. Since Bonnie and Lauren are trying to meet Matt, then we should add our strengths to theirs. We are a small army, but, with God on our side, we are a mighty one."

Yereq clapped his huge hands. "Well stated!"

Elam held up the phone. "Makaidos, I can't turn this on to get the address. Do you remember it?"

"I do," Makaidos said, his voice weak. "But how will we locate it?"

219

"The old-fashioned way. We'll go to an open gas station and get a map."

After Makaidos recited the address, Yereq closed the trailer gate, and he and Elam reentered the van, Elam again in the driver's seat. When he pushed the key in and turned the ignition, nothing happened. The starter didn't even click.

Elam leaned back in the seat and heaved a sigh. "The electro-magnetic pulses must have cooked the van's electronics."

"Could we try to find another vehicle?" Yereq asked from the back.

"Maybe. For obvious reasons, I'd have to search alone, maybe hitchhike, but there weren't many vehicles on the road before. After that blast, they all might be malfunctioning."

"Allow me to guide Makaidos and Thigocia into the woods while you search. Then you can return with your findings. Even if I accompany you to the rendezvous and we have to leave the dragons behind, they should be safe."

"I definitely want all of you to come with me." Elam climbed out of the van and hurried to the back of the trailer. After opening the gate, he explained the situation and Yereq's idea to Makaidos and Thigocia. The dragons agreed to the plan, crawled out of the trailer again, and shuffled alongside Yereq toward a nearby cluster of trees.

Elam watched the trio shrink in the distance. How could he possibly transport such a cargo? Even if a car stopped to pick him up, it might not have a trailer hitch or the ability to pull that much weight. A tractor-trailer combination, maybe? Or a flatbed truck?

He retrieved a bag that held his normal clothes, then tore off his fake eyebrows, brushed his hair back, and straightened his uniform. At least he looked presentable. With so much turmoil in the world, maybe someone would stop for a military officer.

CHAPTER

ESCAPE

Something nudged Billy's ribs. Half asleep, he blinked his eyes open. After spending another night on this bench, everything felt stiff, especially the broken toes. His mouth, still stuffed with asbestos, ached.

Ashley's hand lay next to his thigh. She spelled out, *Something is up. Might have to act now. Walter is awake. He is feeling good. I guess my healing touch worked.*

Billy sent a thought her way. *What have you heard?*

Atomic weapon. Potential war. Pilot flying to base for safety.

He nodded. *Better to face a few goons here than a bunch of them at the base.* He leaned forward and looked at Gabriel and Walter. They stared straight ahead, both with bent brows. On the opposite bench, the four soldiers shifted nervously, fingers twitching on the triggers of their automatic rifles. This wouldn't be easy.

He shifted his gaze to Ashley, keeping Walter, Gabriel, and the window beyond them in view. If worse came to worst, Gabriel might have to bail out and fly to safety. *Ashley, I'll let you give the*

221

*signal to attack when you think they're the most distracted. With cuffs
on, it will be hard to grab their guns, so we can try to—*

A brilliant light flashed in the sky. Rainbow arcs expanded
from the center, and a mushroom cloud rose in midair, as if
birthed by the colors. The interior lights blinked off, and the helicopter's engine sputtered. The whirring blades slowed, making the
chopper descend, while sparks and smoke erupted from the cockpit's control panel.

When the soldiers turned toward the pilot, Ashley jerked
Billy's gag down. He blew the rag out and launched a ball of flames
at the soldier in front of him, then bashed him in the head with a
two-fisted punch. Ashley clawed at the eyes of the next soldier,
while Walter and Gabriel grabbed the rifles of the other two and
tried to wrestle them away.

Walter's guard head-butted him, but Walter kept fighting like
a wild animal—kicking, punching, and biting.

His eyes bleeding, Ashley's guard grabbed her hair and twisted
until her body arched backwards.

Billy wrapped an arm around his opponent's neck and jerked.
Something cracked. The man fell limp. Billy snatched away his
rifle and fired at Ashley's guard. The bullet plunged into his shoulder. He crumpled in place, releasing Ashley. She punched Walter's
guard in the nose and thrust a knee into his groin.

Billy aimed the rifle at the other two soldiers. "Surrender or
you're dead!"

Just as the soldiers gave the guns to Walter and Gabriel, the
pilot twisted in his seat and fired a pistol at Billy. The bullet nicked
his shoulder. He fired back with the rifle and struck the pilot's
neck.

The pilot fell to the side, coughing as smoke filled the cockpit.
The chopper's descent accelerated and bent into a sharp angle.

Billy set his feet and aimed at the two remaining soldiers. "Unlock us!"

The closer soldier took a key ring from his belt and unfastened Gabriel's handcuffs. Gabriel then grabbed the ring and unlocked the other three sets.

After they shook the cuffs loose, Billy shifted the rifle back to the soldiers. "Now unlock the leg irons. Then I'll see about flying this bird."

Walter wrinkled his nose. "What is that terrible smell?"

The pilot pushed himself upright. Bleeding from a gaping hole at the side of his neck, he shouted into his headset. "Mayday! Mayday!"

The engine fell silent. The propeller stopped, and the chopper dove into a near-sideways plunge. Everyone toppled toward Gabriel, but the free fall kept their bodies from pressing against the side door.

223

Gabriel grabbed the latch and pushed, but he seemed unable to overcome the outside air pressure. Billy aimed the rifle at the door's window and fired. The glass shattered and flew through the cabin along with a rush of foul-smelling air.

With a loud grunt, Gabriel shoved the door open. Holding the leg chains with both hands, he forced his way out and pulled Walter, Ashley, and Billy along. When Gabriel cleared the door, he set his feet against the fuselage and dragged his companions the rest of the way out, Billy still holding the rifle.

All four drifted away from the falling chopper. Gabriel beat his wings and shot upward while the helicopter continued plunging. The chains tightened. Walter, Ashley, and Billy dangled from his grasp in a vertical line of flailing bodies. They began falling again, though much more slowly, as if suspended by a perforated parachute.

Seconds later, the chopper crashed in a dry ravine and exploded. Smoke shot up from the site and enveloped them. Grunting loudly, Gabriel lurched to the side and dodged the choking fumes. His face locked in a tight grimace and his wings beating madly, he seemed to be guiding everyone toward a nearby bog of mud and swamp grass. "Brace yourselves!" he shouted.

Billy tossed the rifle and twisted until he faced upward. He splashed into thick muck and submerged. Three more splashing sounds erupted, one immediately after the other.

Billy turned his body upright and stood in waist-deep muck, while Gabriel waded several paces away, mud cresting at his chest. Reeling in the chain, Billy trudged through the bog. He found Ashley and hoisted her to the surface. She coughed and spat out a stream of brown sludge.

"You okay?" He thumped her back. More dirty water spewed, this time from her nostrils.

224

She sucked in a breath and rasped, "Find Walter."

While Billy pulled the chain from one side, Gabriel pulled from the other until they met where Walter had submerged. Each holding an arm, they lifted him toward the surface.

When his face broke through the mud, he opened his eyes and flashed a pain-streaked grin. "Was that a new thrill ride? Let's call it 'When Pigs Fly.'"

Billy laid a hand on Walter's mud-caked head. "I have a good mind to dunk you back in."

"No time." Walter set his feet and balanced himself. "Let's check on the soldiers."

Billy turned toward the chopper as it burned about thirty paces away. Flames roared within billowing clouds of black smoke. Probably no one survived, but they couldn't just ignore the men. "Gabriel, did you manage to hang on to the keys?"

"Got 'em." He held out a ring with several keys, all dripping muddy water. "Don't know which one'll work."

"Let's wade to dry ground first." Billy took a quick drink to soothe his aching throat, then locked arms with Walter and Ashley. "All together now!"

As they slogged, Billy called out their pace. "Left … right … left … right." With each step, they rose from the mud. His body no longer buoyed, pain ripped through his broken toes, but he had to go on.

When they reached the bog's shore, they sprawled across a field of dried mud. Gabriel unlocked his leg irons, then Billy's.

Billy struggled to his feet. "Give the key to Ashley and come with me!" He jogged with a limp toward the burning chopper while Gabriel half ran and half flew, slinging mud with his flapping wings. Heat from the raging flames made them stop about ten paces away from the wreckage.

Billy lifted an arm to block the scalding air. Four bodies lay near the fuselage and one inside the cockpit, barely visible through the blackened window.

"They're goners," Gabriel said.

Billy grasped his shoulder. "We'd be burning with them if not for you."

"Just reacting. No big deal." Gabriel laughed. "It's funny, but I did the same thing with Walter, Ashley, and Lauren the other day and vowed never to jump out of a plane carrying three people ever again. Good thing it was a helicopter and not a plane, or else I'd be a liar."

"Did I hear you say 'no big deal'?" Walter asked as he trudged toward them, Ashley at his side. "If that's true, then you won't mind carrying us all to civilization. You're the only one with wings."

225

Ashley looked to the east, her dirty brow furrowed as she crossed her muddy arms over her equally muddy chest. "That was a midair nuclear blast. The EMPs blew out the chopper's electronics."

"Electromagnetic pulses," Billy said. "I've heard of those."

"Which means we might not find much civilization. Even if some electrical equipment survived, nothing will run if the grid is down."

Gabriel slung the remaining mud from his wings. "I'll see if I can find a car someone will let me borrow, and I'll come back and pick you guys up."

"Look for an old vehicle," Ashley said. "The older the better. Newer ones have more electronic components, so they're more vulnerable to EMPs."

"Got it." Gabriel beat his wings and leaped into the air.

As he shrank in the distance, Walter sniffed the cold breeze. "I still smell that odor. It started right before the chopper blew all its fuses. Does an EMP smell bad?"

"Not that I know of." Ashley inhaled, then grimaced. "It smells like garlic ... and something else."

"Skunk?" Walter offered.

"I don't think so, but it's familiar somehow. It brings back dark memories." Ashley shivered. "It reminds me of Morgan."

"No wonder you're shivering. It's freezing out here, and you're thinking about the coldest heart ever to inhabit a body." Walter wrapped an arm around her and pulled her close. "Okay, so assuming Gabriel finds a jalopy that still runs, where do we go?"

"We try to contact Lois. She'll know where Lauren and Roxil are."

"But how? Even if we find a phone, if the grid's down, cell towers won't be working."

Billy eyed the helicopter. "Maybe we can salvage the radio. Ashley can rig the frequency."

"Not likely," Ashley said. "It was spewing sparks. But Lois might still be up and running. Last I heard, Carly's got Lois's mobile unit plugged into her car's power adapter. Even if the car gets fried, Lois can run on battery for a few hours. She monitors twenty-four different kinds of transmissions. If I can find a battery-operated ham radio, I can call her."

Walter shrugged. "No problem. There's got to be a thousand Radio Shacks. We'll find one. And maybe Gabriel can hunt down my bag full of weapons. It should be near *Merlin's* crash site."

"But that might be pretty far away," Ashley said. "We have to find fuel to get there. A gas station won't pump without electricity."

Billy shifted behind Walter and Ashley and laid his arms over their shoulders. "Ashley, Walter and I have literally been to Hell and back. You were locked up in your own hell for fifteen years, and in Second Eden you manufactured fuel cells from roof shingles, rubber bands, and twist ties."

227

"No, I didn't. I used the metallic—"

"Just listen." Billy pulled them closer. "My point is, we can do this. Even if we have to invent a radio that runs on Walter's bad breath, and even if we have to build solar-powered bicycles, we'll figure out a way to contact Lois and then find Lauren and the others."

Walter pumped a fist. "That's the spirit!" His brow wrinkled. "Hey! Who's got bad breath?"

"That awful smell," Billy said. "I heard you burp right before it hit. I figured it knocked out the chopper's circuits."

"Well, look who's talking, Dragon Breath himself." Walter pulled away with Ashley and spread out his arms. "Now put that torch to good use. We're freezing."

Jared sat on the RV's sofa and munched on a Vitamin C tablet, his fourth one this hour. Finding an open pharmacy had been a minor miracle. The infusion of vitamins definitely helped, as Mardon predicted.

With Marilyn still driving the RV, her wakefulness enhanced by a caffeine-enriched beverage, they had finally made it deep into the West Virginia mountains—only twenty miles from home where Larry and the secret file awaited.

Mardon fidgeted in the seat opposite Jared's. Ever since he joined them, he never stopped his anxious gestures—pulling on his sleeves, dabbing a handkerchief on his scarred face and scalp, and blinking every two or three seconds. "In conclusion, the candlestone weapons at Fort Knox are far more formidable than those at the Arizona prison. I haven't seen them myself, but the engineers were supposed to follow my designs, and they appeared to be a capable group of scientists. Elam's only hope will be to neutralize the weapons by stealth before he sends in any dragons."

"I agree," Jared said. "We'll try to contact Lois as soon as we get to Larry. It won't be long now."

"Speaking of Larry …" Mardon again dabbed his forehead. "Since your file contains genetic data, shall I assume that it is your dragon DNA structure?"

Jared swallowed the tablet remnants. "I'm not going to reveal anything more until the file is safely in my grasp."

Mardon smiled. "Yet you have already revealed the answer. If I had guessed wrong, you would have simply given a negative response."

"Not necessarily. I could be misdirecting—"

"There is no need to prevaricate," Mardon said, waving a hand. "Like you, I have been around for many centuries. I am not easily deceived, so we should both be completely straightforward."

"Spoken by the son of the most devious creature ever to walk the face of the Earth."

"True. I admit it. My mother is not the paragon of honest communication. Yet I must stand up for her one crowning virtue. She hates Arramos and would do anything to prevent him from achieving his goal—complete conquest of Earth and Second Eden."

Jared nodded. "Okay. I'll accept that for the sake of discussion."

"Another virtue that you might or might not accept is that my mother has always been loyal to me. Her rage at Arramos for disfiguring me cannot be overestimated, which is, of course, part of her motivation to destroy that wretched dragon."

"Then explain to me why she is helping Tamiel," Jared said. "Tamiel is in Arramos's service."

"She is bound to Tamiel because he holds her well-being in his demonic sway. She and I died long ago, but we both maintain our existence by the enactment of a magical spell that Morgan began and Tamiel controls. If he were to be destroyed, the power would transfer to Arramos. Since Arramos has no use for us, he would eventually terminate the spell, and our souls would travel straight to the judgment seat of God."

"So Semiramis is working for Tamiel in order to get close to Arramos."

"Exactly. In fact, she carries a potion that she hopes to pour over him. If she can get just a few drops on any part of his body, the solution will shred his scales and expose his dark heart. It will not kill him, but he will be powerless until he finds another host."

"Just a few drops?" Jared asked.

Mardon nodded. "It is extremely potent. In fact, if a dragon were simply to inhale it at close range, the fumes would disable him in seconds."

"What's in it?"

"Only she knows, but all of her destructive potions include an elixir that Morgan concocted back at the time of the first Eden. It contains a pungent concentration of garlic and camphor as well as a single strand of Samyaza's DNA."

"Morgan's husband? The Watcher?"

"One and the same." Mardon pulled on a sleeve. "His DNA is a catalyst that greatly increases the potency."

Jared stroked his chin. "Interesting."

"So back to your file." Mardon leaned forward. "I deduced that you plan to battle Arramos. In past engagements, you were the only dragon powerful enough to stand against him. Your warrior prowess is legendary."

"Again, for the sake of discussion, I will accept your deduction." Jared nodded. "Go on."

"I further deduce that the file contains your entire draconic genome, and you also stored a sample of your dragon blood in a secure place, most likely within proximity of your West Virginia home." Mardon leaned back in his chair, a smug expression on his face. "Am I right?"

Jared reached for the vitamin bottle on a counter to his left. Since Mardon had guessed everything flawlessly, it was hard to act nonchalant. "Suppose you are. Do you have a proposition?"

"Indeed I do." Mardon withdrew a finger-length vial from his vest pocket. Holding the rubber stopper at the top, he swirled the purplish contents. "My guess is that you hope to restore yourself as the mighty Clefspeare. Your original plan was to revert to dragon form in the way you have in the past, by energizing Second Eden's birthing garden, wearing a rubellite ring, and stepping onto the soils of regeneration. Yet you know that those soils have been overrun by volcanic debris, so now you are counting on using a candlestone to regenerate yourself, a candlestone coated with your dragon blood."

Jared opened the bottle and popped a vitamin tablet into his mouth. "It would take more than that. A candlestone regenerates a human body's vitality, but it doesn't transform that body from one species to another."

"Of course not. The candlestone is merely a catalyst. I assume you planned to transluminate yourself and have Larry restructure your DNA based on the dragon genome information in the file. Since Larry has proven his ability to disintegrate and reconstruct highly complex objects, you hoped he could do the same for you. Yet you weren't quite sure of the procedure's safety, because Larry's ability has never been tested on a living creature."

Jared chewed on the tablet—orange flavored. "Would you trust Larry's transluminating engine at this point?"

"No, indeed. When Ashley's prototype was still in its infancy, tests on males were a disaster, resulting in severe brain damage. Of course, she restored some males to a normal state, but only those who had been in light-energy form for a long while. Your son survived, but I hear that he was protected by Merlin himself."

231

"So you don't see a reason to assume that Larry's engine is any better than the prototype."

Mardon wagged a finger. "Since you were so quick to come to that conclusion, I assume you have the same fear, so my guess is that you hoped to retrieve the file and then search for Excalibur— the only remaining device by which you know you could be transluminated safely. And when I offered Excalibur to you on the proverbial silver platter, you agreed to travel with a man you thoroughly distrusted, which proves my reasoning and closes my case."

Jared blew out a long breath. "I have to hand it to you, Mardon. Your deduction skills are impeccable."

"Good. Good. I was hoping to build your confidence in me."

"So …" Jared nodded at the vial. "What's that for?"

"Oh, yes." Mardon pulled out the stopper and waved the vial in the air, then quickly put the stopper back in place.

The odor of garlic assaulted Jared's nostrils. Camphor pierced his sinuses. His eyes burning, he blinked away the sting. "One of your mother's potions?"

He nodded. "We both carry the potion that will strip Arramos's scales. This will enhance your ability to defeat him."

"Would it also strip my scales in dragon form?"

"Without a doubt." Mardon extended the vial toward Jared. "Another gesture to demonstrate my trustworthiness and seal our cooperation. If I had kept it, I could have disabled you with it after you transformed."

Jared took the vial and laid it on his palm. "I appreciate the token."

"It is much more than a token. It is also the key to your regeneration. This potion would destroy you in your dragon form, but I can strip out Samyaza's DNA and replace it with yours. Once that is accomplished, when combined with Excalibur's energy, the potion will replicate the biogenesis properties of Second Eden's birthing garden and regenerate you as Clefspeare. No need for a candlestone or a rubellite. No worries about a flawed restoration."

"That's good, because I lost my rubellite when I last changed into a dragon." Jared recapped the vitamin bottle and put it back on the counter. "Your ideas sound great in theory, but the step that makes me balk is—"

"The fact that you don't trust me." Sighing, Mardon nodded. "I understand. My reputation has been well earned. My history has the blackest of marks." He lifted his brow. "Is it possible that I may assist you step by step? Perhaps I will earn your trust, and you can send me away at any time should I prove to be unfaithful."

"You gave me Excalibur and the potion. That says a lot." Jared nodded firmly. "You may come."

Lights in the ceiling blinked off. The RV's engine died.

"Jared," Marilyn said, stretching out his name. "Something's wrong."

Jared grabbed his cane. "Just let it coast and pull over somewhere."

She gasped. "Look out the back window!"

To the west, a brilliant light spread out in the sky, filled with colors that arced in all directions. At the center, a mushroom cloud billowed.

"An atomic bomb?" Jared asked.

Mardon squinted. "It is, indeed."

Jared grabbed Mardon's collar and jerked him close. "What do you know about this?"

"I ..." Mardon swallowed. "I merely recognized it. I had nothing to do with it."

"Are you telling me you know nothing at all about this explosion?"

"Well ... I ..."

Jared roared, "Spill it!"

"I ... I helped Tamiel prepare a launch system that would ..." Mardon swallowed. "Would guide a nuclear missile through a portal to Second Eden."

"To Second Eden? Then you *are* the same monster you always were!"

"No. No. I rigged it so that it would miss its target by at least two kilometers. No portal is that big. And Tamiel said the portal was in a secluded area, so I hoped for the best." Mardon trembled violently. "I had to ... to obey him, but I did ... did what I could to prevent ... the loss of life."

233

"Coward!" Jared shoved him back to his seat. "This changes everything. We'll have panic, fears of nuclear war, travel bans. We might be stuck here for days."

"Maybe not." Still trembling, Mardon pulled on his shirt, straightening the fabric. "Since the blast occurred in the atmosphere, the potential loss of life is likely minimal compared to a ground explosion, and fears of a war and panic might also be minimized. We are quite far away from the zone of immediate danger, so if we keep traveling away from it, we might not be impeded."

Jared grabbed his cane. "What do you mean by *immediate* danger?"

"The mushroom cloud proved that the blast lifted material and created significant radioactive fallout. Since we are on the east side of the blast, prevailing winds will eventually carry it toward us. Our more pressing concern is that it generated electromagnetic pulses and disrupted this vehicle's electronic components. Such pulses could have disabled the electric grid and sent surges throughout the system."

"Is Larry in danger?" Jared asked. "His room is reinforced with thick concrete, and he has a massive battery backup with surge protection that would block a direct lightning strike."

Mardon tapped his chin. "Difficult to tell. Many factors to analyze. We'll have to wait and see."

The odor of garlic and camphor returned, though the vial remained capped. Mardon blinked and whispered, "Mother?"

Jared sniffed the vial, but the odor seemed to be everywhere.

Marilyn pulled the RV into an exit lane and stopped. "That's as far as I can go." She turned the key, but only a click sounded. "It's dead."

"How many miles to Castlewood?" Jared asked.

"About eight."

"That's a long hike."

Marilyn pulled the key from the ignition. "Especially for someone who can barely walk."

"I'm doing a lot better. If fallout is on its way, we don't have much choice."

"Hiking is too slow," Mardon said. "Jared would never make eight miles, and the fallout could easily overtake us." He lifted his thumb in a horizontal position. "But hitchhiking might work. Older vehicles or those not running when the pulse hit are more likely to have been spared the fate of your RV."

"Probably our only option." Jared looked at Marilyn, who had turned toward them. "Agree?"

"I don't trust Mardon farther than I could spit him," Marilyn said.

Mardon tugged on his sleeve. "I gave you Excalibur. I gave you the dragon elixir. I offer you my expertise to defeat Arramos. What more can I do to gain your trust?"

"Nothing." Marilyn pointed at him. "I'll be watching you like a hawk. With every step you make, every tweak of every genetic fragment, remember that you'll have me looking over your shoulder. If you harm Jared in any way, I will personally send you to your maker. Understand?"

"I understand." Mardon dabbed his scalp with his handkerchief. "I have seen the wrath of a woman who has been deceived, especially when a loved one is harmed as a result. You may keep a dagger at my back and feel free to plunge it through my heart if I step out of line."

235

15

CHAPTER

HEAT SEEKER

I sense danger," Roxil said as she descended toward a cloud-bank. "We should stay out of sight."

Lauren pressed her body against Roxil's back while Mom flew alongside and closed in. She had lifted off Roxil from time to time, giving her a break from the added weight. Even the most powerful dragons couldn't carry two people for so many miles without a rest.

When they dropped into the cloud, Mom settled behind Lauren and grasped a spine. Lauren faced the white streams of mist, cool and wet as they whistled by. Feeling invisible in the fog helped, though only Roxil could tell if danger had passed, but she stayed silent.

Lauren's scales tingled. An engine rumble entered her ears, growing louder by the second. "Roxil," she called, "I think I hear a jet."

237

Roxil curled her neck and drew her head close. "If it is military, I assume we cannot hide from a radar-directed pilot."

"Not likely."

"I hear it now," Mom said. "Roxil, your only advantage is low-altitude maneuvers—through a forest or around buildings. Maybe you could even land and hide. A jet needs a runway."

Roxil bobbed her head. "Prepare for a rapid descent."

Lauren and her mother clutched tightly to the spines. Roxil folded her wings and dropped. They plunged through the clouds and into open air. The ground lay a few hundred feet below, closing in quickly. Lauren's bottom rose from Roxil's scales, and her hands slipped toward the top of the moist spine. Mom jerked her back in place, and Lauren wrapped both arms around the spine and held on.

238

A jet appeared about fifty feet to the left and zoomed past. It arced to the right and began a wide circle. Roxil stretched out her wings and caught the air. Their plummet slowed.

Lauren's body pressed against the scales as if her weight had tripled. The ground now lay less than a hundred feet below with no sign of trees anywhere. Only a barn and a small lake interrupted the acres of grassy meadowlands. Roxil leveled out and headed toward the lake.

Something crackled in Lauren's ears, then a man's voice joined the noise. "Radar anomaly engaged. Dragon verified."

A second voice replied, "Deploy the heat-seeker. Those vermin supposedly have a furnace inside."

"Roger. Fox two."

A crack and a whoosh rushed into Lauren's senses. "Roxil!" she screamed. "A missile! It seeks heat!"

Roxil dove again. The missile zipped by overhead, barely missing them. As it careened in a sharp turn, Roxil zoomed toward the lake and beat her wings madly. "Hang on!"

The missile completed its turn and headed toward them again. The lake closed in, only seconds away. The missile narrowed the gap—two hundred feet … one hundred … fifty.

"Hold your breath!" With another sudden drop, Roxil plunged. Lauren sucked in a breath. They splashed into icy water. Roxil continued flapping her wings. They surged downward and stopped at a gravel-covered bottom where Roxil flattened her body.

Lauren's ears ached, like they were ready to implode. She looked up. The surface appeared to be about fifteen feet above, though the water's murkiness made gauging distance almost impossible. At least the cold water might send that missile seeking a different warm body. But how long should they stay submerged to be sure? Hugging herself, she shivered. Her mother wrapped her in her wings, but they didn't ward off the cold.

Finally, Roxil vaulted from the lake bottom and surged to the surface. When Lauren broke through, she slung water from her hair and scanned the skies—no sign of the jet or the missile.

239

Roxil paddled with her wings. Mom wrapped her arms around Lauren and flew with her toward the edge. As they drifted over the lake, water streamed from Lauren's hair and clothes, and wind knifed through to her skin. A barn stood only fifty yards away, a good place to build a fire and get warm.

After shaking out wings and wringing out hair and clothes, the trio gathered in front of the barn, opened a set of double doors big enough for a dragon to pass through, and walked onto a hay-strewn concrete pad. A dozen or more cows stared at them from surrounding cattle stalls. One let out a lamenting moo that spread like a contagion until five or six cows sang the same song.

"Maybe they're hungry," Lauren said. "They're probably normally out grazing this time of day."

Mom touched an empty water trough in front of one of the cows. "I'm sure they're thirsty, too."

"Judging from the lack of food and water," Roxil said, "perhaps the owners have met with trouble that prevented a morning release into the pasture."

Lauren grabbed a stable's locking bar. "I'm letting them out." She and her mother hurried from stable to stable and opened the gates. As the cows tramped from the barn, their hooves made an echoing clatter.

After the last cow exited, Roxil breathed over Lauren and her mother to dry them, but Roxil quickly grew tired and settled to the floor. "I do not understand why I am so weary. This is quite unusual even after carrying passengers. I apologize for my inability to make you warm and dry."

Mom stroked Roxil's wing. "Don't worry about it. We'll be fine."

"If you will collect some combustibles," Roxil said, "I should be able to start a fire. That will be beneficial for all of us."

After they had swept hay and parts of a broken stable gate into a pile, Roxil ignited the fuel. Soon, the fire blazed, and they all settled close to it. Lauren took off her shirt and wrung it out, leaving on a wet T-shirt that clung to her torso. Warmth spread over her body and chased away the chill.

Mom aimed her palms at the flames. "That pilot had to know that he missed his target. He might be back."

"Or perhaps," Roxil said, "he was called to a more urgent matter. With the state of affairs in this world, surely there is much more to look after than a solitary dragon and two women."

Lauren picked up the cool end of a short piece of lathing and stoked the flames. It seemed odd that these two were discussing the whys and what-ifs of the situation when they had come within a split second of death.

A minute or two passed with only the crackle of their makeshift campfire interrupting the silence. "So ..." Lauren pursed her lips. How could she say this without raising too many questions? "Since both of you have died, maybe you can tell me what it's like. I mean, what happens right afterward? Where did you go? What did you do?"

Mom set a wing around her. "A close brush with death makes one consider the afterlife, doesn't it?"

"I suppose that's part of it, but I came closer to death when I tried to jump into the volcano and the lava chased Albatross and me down the slope. I was super scared, but then I saw Joan rise into Heaven, so I knew for certain that there's an afterlife, and the fears just went away." Lauren shrugged. "I guess now I'm just curious. Was there a lot of pain? If so, did it last long? What was the first thing you saw? That kind of thing."

Roxil's eyes blazed through the smoky air. "I suffered great pain, though the physical discomfort lasted only a few seconds. The emotional pain was far worse. Since my own mate betrayed me, that thought tortured me for a long time. Of course, I went to Dragons' Rest, and I ruminated over the betrayal for centuries. The mental torture was ghastly."

241

Lauren nodded. "Betrayal is probably the sharpest dagger of all. I can't imagine how much it must have hurt."

"My physical pain was horrific," Mom said, "but it was like a flicker of flame that vanished in a comforting breeze. Unlike Roxil, I was given a view of Heaven right away, so every emotional wound instantly healed. The bliss was beyond description—better than a warm fire to ward off the chill, better than a cool drink of water after hours of working in the sun, better than a warm embrace after not seeing a dear friend for years."

She clasped her hands over her chest. "Heaven is an eternal fire that burns in your heart; it is living water that quenches your thirst forever; it is an embrace that never ends, because no one ever has to say good-bye." She let out a sigh. "My visit to Heaven helped me endure fifteen years in prison, because I knew those years were nothing compared to an eternity with Jesus."

"Did you see him?" Lauren asked.

Mom's eyes sparkled with tears. "Yes, Lauren. I saw him. He took me into his arms and hugged me." She wrapped her arms around herself. "I can still feel his embrace—warm, strong, and loving. There is no greater feeling in this world."

"Then you want to go back," Lauren said, nodding. "You're ready to leave this world and be with him again."

"Of course. After what I've seen, who wouldn't?" Mom tilted her head. "Why do you ask?"

Lauren shrugged again. "I don't know. I guess because I kind of feel that way myself, even though I haven't been to Heaven. Seeing Joan's face when she ascended was enough to make me want to follow her. She looked so peaceful, so content, like she had finished a great journey and was finally receiving her reward."

Mom patted her on the back. "Well, we need you to stick around for a long time. This world needs you."

"True." Lauren poked at the fire. "That much I agree with. I have to stop Tamiel."

"That's everyone's goal," Mom said. "But no one can do it alone. He's too crafty and powerful. We have to act as a team."

"He is powerful. I'll grant you that." Lauren scanned the barn. Maybe it would be best to change the subject. Her gaze drifted past a crib of corn. "Looks like we have food, and water's just a few steps away. Maybe we should spend the night here."

Roxil extended her head out the door and looked up. "Evening is approaching. We should check with Lois to see if we can stay here and still maintain our schedule. Since I am more exhausted than expected, I would be glad of a chance to rest a while longer."

Lauren tapped on her jaw. Static buzzed in her molar. "You'd better use your transmitter. I think my habit of killing electronics put mine out of commission again. Maybe it'll come back soon."

After a minute or so of conversation with Lois, Roxil focused on Lauren and her mother. "It seems that disaster has struck. That nuclear missile detonated in the air somewhere over Kentucky."

"So it was real, after all." Mom's shoulders drooped. "I wonder how many people died."

"Reports are conflicting, but since it exploded in the atmosphere, it didn't kill as many people as it could have, though it knocked out much of the electrical grid in this country. Lois is in the warehouse's stairway now, so she and Carly are safe, but she's running on battery again. Carly's going to search for a generator."

"That explosion is probably why the jet didn't bother to finish us off," Lauren said. "We weren't worth the trouble."

"The good news is that Lois has spoken to Elam, though their contact came before the explosion and she has not been able to reconnect with him. She believes he was out of the danger zone, so he should be safe. Since she sent him the sixth address, she hopes he will go there eventually."

Mom heaved a sigh. "We'll hope for the best."

"Indeed." Roxil stretched out on the concrete pad. "According to Lois, we will have to get an early start and fly quickly if we are to arrive in the morning hours, but after a good rest, I should be able to manage it."

"That's great, Roxil." Lauren halfheartedly poked at the flames. "Go ahead and get some sleep. I'll find more stuff to burn and keep the fire going."

"Excellent. I can get a meal in the morning. Perhaps I will be able to find a deer, or if that fails, maybe a farmer who has abandoned his cows will not be too angry about losing one." Roxil settled to her belly and lowered her head to the ground. Within a few seconds, she let out a rumbling snore.

Lauren blinked at her mother. "That was fast."

"I'm concerned about her," Mom said. "I could tell that her flight rhythm deteriorated just before we went down into the clouds. It was a sudden change."

"No use worrying." Lauren walked to the corn crib, picked up six ears, and found a metal pan in one of the stables. She set the pan and corn on top of the fire and watched the kernels swell. After a few minutes, several popped open and leaked juice.

"I love the smell of food cooking over a fire." Mom inhaled deeply, then wrinkled her nose. "Do you smell garlic?"

Lauren sniffed. Several aromas filtered in—wood smoke, corn, and a hint of garlic. "It's kind of weak, but I do smell it."

"If we could find it, we could add it to the corn. Butter and salt would be nice, too."

244

Lauren grinned. "Plenty of milk standing on four legs, but who wants to collect it and churn the butter?"

"I guess plain corn will have to do." Mom pinched the end of a cob and gave it to Lauren. "It's not too hot."

During their meal, they made plans to take turns watching the fire during the night while leaving the barn doors open just enough to draw the smoke away but closed enough to keep out the evening's cooling air. When they finished, they strolled outside and drank water from the lake, then returned and sat close to the dwindling fire, their clothes now warm and dry.

Mom slid hip to hip with Lauren. "Something's bothering you. I mean something more than being cold and having a near-death experience. You seem distant ... melancholy."

"Not really." Lauren picked up the lathing again. "I'm just focused. Tamiel's the cause of all this trouble, so I've been thinking about how to stop him."

"Any ideas?"

"Nothing new. I just have this feeling that when I see him, I'll know what to do."

"I've had that feeling a few times. It's a certainty, like you've been given something that no one else has, that no one else would understand, and they might think you're crazy if you tried to explain it."

Lauren nodded. "That's it. That's exactly it."

"It's all part of being an Oracle of Fire." Mom slid her hand into Lauren's. "Do you mind if I tell you something Joan once told me? She branded the words in my mind, and I whispered them to Ashley a hundred times to encourage her during our years in prison."

"Sure. I'd love to hear anything Joan had to say."

Mom looked upward as if searching for a memory. "Speak the truth. Live the truth. Be the truth. Never let the faithless ones change any of those three principles. Remember that you are an Oracle of Fire, as is every faithful follower of our Lord. For all true disciples possess the pure silver, purged of all dross, and the fire of God's love burns within, an everlasting flame that others, even those who give lip-service to the truth, will never comprehend until you are able to pass along that fire from heart to heart. As an Oracle, you will look through portals to their hearts, you will feel the heavy sadness of their lonely and dark estates, and you will possess crystal-clear vision that will allow you to see what will bring them deliverance from their sorrows. In trying to bring this deliverance, you will say and do things that will make them shake their heads in pity. 'That poor girl,' they will say. 'Her passion has addled her brain.' Your confidence, they will call arrogance. Your faith, they will call wishful thinking. Your purity, they will call self-righteousness. Your firm standing, they will call pride. Yet you will know, because of that fire within, that they are the ones dwelling in darkness, and you must touch your lighted wick to their darkened lamps."

Lauren let the words soak in. Surely if Mom or anyone else knew what she had in mind, they would think she was crazy, though she really did know what would bring everyone deliverance. Of course Mom wasn't dwelling in darkness, but this light had been given to only one Oracle of Fire—Lauren Bannister—and she had to be the one to carry it into battle. It seemed that Joan, her former companion, had spoken from Heaven and given the new Oracle her marching orders.

After a few silent seconds, Lauren breathed a quiet, "Amen."

16

THE FIFTH DOOR

M att parked the Mustang in front of a Japanese-style, one-story building. Its roofline curved into upward-pointing corners. Blinking red lights across the front spelled out Fantasy Pagoda. With no other cars in the lot, the sign provided the only indication that the store might be open. Downtown Lincoln, Nebraska, likely provided more regular customers for a business like this, but the recent chaos was probably keeping nearly everyone off the streets on this dreary afternoon.

He checked the phone's GPS screen. The caption for the address said, *The Fifth Door—The Fodder.* The address matched the number on the building, but how this place could relate to fodder remained a mystery.

As Matt stared through the emporium's dark window, his danger sense skyrocketed. "I don't like the looks of this place."

"I sense evil," Thomas said from the backseat. "If you must enter, find the key and get out as quickly as possible."

"I will. I just hope fantasy doesn't mean what I think it means."

Mariel piped up. "The fifth circle held the temptation of gluttony for food, a special kind of food concocted by Morgan that rendered those who consumed it vulnerable to the flames of a chasm. It's a good bet that this establishment offers to feed a different kind of hunger."

"That's what I was thinking," Matt said, "but not in so many words."

Thomas leaned forward and touched Matt's shoulder. "Be careful, Son. Normal temptations of the flesh are difficult enough, but there is a twisted evil emanating from that place. It is demonic … filthy … unnatural. An abomination."

Matt gazed into the old man's vacant eyes. Even without irises or pupils, they seemed to emote. "That's not exactly a confidence booster."

248

When Matt reached for the car door, Darcy grabbed his wrist. "Let me go."

"You? Why?"

"I know places like this. They're a profitable hangout, if you know what I mean. They're pretty much all the same."

"That's not the point. There's danger inside. I'm not sending a defenseless woman in there while I'm sitting out here cooling my heels."

Darcy's face reddened. "Listen, Matt, I've been watching you risk your life again and again while I've been on the sidelines like a good little cheerleader." Smiling vacantly, she shook an invisible pom-pom. "Yay, Matt! Go get 'em, tiger!" She shook her head. "Give me a break!"

"Don't play that game. You risked your life at the shark tank, and you voluntarily sat in that chair knowing you could die. You've been more of a hero than I have."

Darcy pushed her hair back and looked Matt in the eye. "There's more to it than playing 'who's the hero?' If I'm right about this pagoda place, I'll be in less danger than you would be. Trust me on this."

They stared at each other, both with firm jaws. Finally, Thomas broke the silent stalemate. "Let her go, Matt. If Tamiel set this up to tempt you specifically, then she probably is less vulnerable. Besides, if she needs you, you'll be just seconds away."

"All right. All right." Matt nodded toward the pagoda. "Prop the door open if you can, and if you get into trouble, scream."

She smiled. "Don't worry. I do a great banshee impersonation."

"I'm not touching that line." Matt opened both front windows and turned off the engine. "Now I'll be sure to hear you."

"Here goes." Darcy got out on her side and walked to the emporium's front entrance, a steel-and-glass single door. A sign hung over the glass with handwritten bold letters—Dancers Wanted. Male or Female.

Wearing camo pants and a thick, thigh-length coat, Darcy didn't look anything like the kind of woman they were likely looking for.

When she pulled the door open, propped it with a stone, and disappeared inside, Matt exhaled. "How long should we give her? My danger sensation is through the roof."

"Thomas will know," Mariel said. "We should be quiet and let him concentrate."

A brilliant light flashed somewhere in the distance, but the building blocked their view of the source. The blinking sign sizzled, then went dark.

Matt whispered, "That can't be good."

"Something terribly evil occurred," Thomas said, "but not yet where Darcy is. We should be patient."

A foul odor drifted through the car, something drenched in garlic and carrying an abrasive bite.

Matt's eyes watered. "Where's that smell coming from?"

"It's familiar." Mariel wrinkled her nose. "But I can't place it."

Thomas tapped Matt's shoulder. "Evil is ready to strike. You'd better check on Darcy."

"Mariel, can you drive?" Matt asked as he opened his door.

"Well enough to get away."

"I'll leave the keys just in case." He got out and strode toward the door. As he drew near, he slowed and tried to peek into the dark opening, but nothing took shape inside.

Someone grunted. Glass shattered. Darcy appeared in the doorway and grabbed the frame. A woman in a skimpy bathing suit clutched her arm and tried to drag her back inside.

"Let me go!" Darcy shouted as she tried to shake loose and reach for her knife at the same time.

"Stay with me, sweetness," the woman said with a sultry purr. "I want to show you something."

Matt leaped to help, but a bare-chested man wearing tight shorts pushed past Darcy and blocked him with a forearm. "Cool it, kid. Let's watch the catfight."

"Watch this!" Matt grabbed the man's wrist, spun him around, and shoved his backside with a foot, sending him stumbling head-long into the pagoda. He wrenched Darcy away from the bikini-clad woman and hustled with her toward the Mustang.

The woman called out, "Hey, honey! Look at this!"

"Don't look!" Darcy hissed as she pulled Matt to a faster pace. "I got the key. Let's just get out of here."

They hopped into the car. When Matt turned the ignition key, the Mustang's starter whined for a moment before kicking in. With tires squealing, they roared away.

Matt turned onto a downtown street. Every traffic signal and business window was dark, as if someone had pulled a plug that powered the entire city. People streamed along sidewalks, some with handheld radios to their ears. One man picked up a brick and smashed a storefront window, while another used a crowbar to pry a door open.

"More looting." Matt stopped a block away from the crowd and gripped the steering wheel tightly. "Darcy, pull up the next address. Let's get out of here."

Darcy tapped on the phone's screen. "I'd better not tell you what the sixth label says. It's ... well ... obscene."

"What kind of mind games is Tamiel trying to play? It's not like I have virgin ears. My drill sergeant used every word in the book."

Darcy leaned the phone against the dashboard. "Probably to upset your mother, not you."

"Right. Good point." Matt turned the car around and followed the GPS program's directions.

Thomas spoke up from the back. "May I suggest turning on the radio? When there is such chaos, some sort of major event has often taken place."

"Well, electricity is off everywhere. That's one reason." Matt turned on the radio and pressed the Search button. After a few seconds, the scanner stopped. A shrill signal emanated from the speakers, then a man's voice. "This is not a test. This is an actual emergency. A nuclear bomb has detonated in the atmosphere near the northern border of Kentucky, sending an electromagnetic pulse over the entire country. Two-thirds of the electrical grid has failed, and the failure is spreading. This radio station is running on backup equipment and a generator, so we will be broadcasting intermittently. Tune in for an update in five minutes." The radio clicked and fell silent.

"A nuclear bomb," Darcy whispered. "That puts everything in perspective."

251

Matt drove onto an interstate highway and tried to set the cruise control, but it wouldn't engage. "What do you mean?"

She gestured with her head. "That little wrestling match back there. Part of me was still wishing I could go back and give that witch a piece of my mind, but now ..." She let out a breathy whistle. "A nuclear bomb."

"I was going to ask." The bare-chested man's face came to mind—wide eyes and out-of-place smile. "What happened in there?"

She stared out the side window. "Let's just say that the place wasn't exactly what I expected. I don't want to go into details."

"Okay, so where did you find the key?"

Darcy pulled a beaded necklace from her pocket. A key dangled at the bottom, glowing violet. Each bead, about the size of a knuckle, had been painted with rainbow stripes. "It was hanging on a statue of a man."

"That was it?" Matt blinked. "Just hanging on a statue?"

She broke the key away from the necklace and let the beads spill to the floor. "Like I said, no details."

Matt glanced at the key while trying to pay attention to the road. "That's strange. Why would Tamiel make it so easy this time? He must really be in a hurry to get us to the sixth door."

"Tamiel expected you to go in, not me. Maybe it would've been harder for you."

Matt laughed under his breath. "Not to insult you or anything, but how could it have been harder for me? That guy was literally a pushover. And the girl looked like a beach bimbo. No problem."

"Well ..." Darcy hooked the key to the ring at his belt. "Can I ask you a personal question?"

"I guess that depends on how personal it is."

"Very personal." She glanced at the backseat passengers. "Maybe I'd better not."

Thomas cleared his throat. "I have to use the facilities."

"The facilities?" Mariel said. "You just went a little while ago."

"I drank two liters of water. I'm an old man with an old bladder. I have to go."

"You and your water. If you had fins you'd be a flounder."

Thomas cleared his throat again, louder this time, and spoke through the noise as if hiding the words. "Someone needs a bit of privacy."

"What?" Mariel blinked. "Oh! Of course. I see what you mean." She scooted forward. "Matt, if you can't find anything open, just pull over somewhere. He's not too proud to use a tree."

"Not too proud at all," Thomas said. "A tree is nature's toilet."

Matt nodded. "I see a good spot up ahead."

A few seconds later, he drove the car onto a widened shoulder, an emergency stopping place with a telephone attached to a pole. Mariel looked at a watch on her wrist. "We should return within ten minutes." She helped Thomas get out, and the two walked into a forested area. The afternoon sun, though fading, provided plenty of light.

"Thomas is a sensitive gentleman," Darcy said.

"Yeah, I picked that up." Matt turned toward her. "So what's your personal question?"

"Well, this might sound kind of dumb, but ..." She bit her lip. "Do you have a girlfriend?"

Matt's cheeks warmed. "No."

"Have you ever had one?"

The heat spread to his ears. "No. I'm just sixteen. Is that so strange?"

253

"Not really. I was just wondering. I mean, you've matured a lot since I last saw you, and you turned into a really handsome guy. Not only that, you're so ... chivalrous, I guess. So I thought girls might be flocking to you."

Images of Victoria came to mind. She and a couple of other girls did pay him a lot of attention at the school socials. "Maybe a few notice me. I guess none of them were really my type." He furrowed his brow. "Why all the questions about girls?"

"I'm trying to figure out what Tamiel had in mind for you in that place." Darcy slid her hand into his. "You know, back when we lived together, I treated you terribly, so I'm wondering if I turned you off to girls."

"Turned me off?" He pulled his hand back. "What do you have in mind?"

Darcy huffed. "I'm not coming on to you, Matt. For crying out loud!"

"Then what *are* you trying to do?"

"Chill for a minute. I'm just trying to figure this out." She picked up one of the rainbow beads and looked it over. "What I'm asking is if you have any feelings for girls in general. Romantic, I mean."

He gazed at her delicate fingers as they caressed the bead. "Well ... not really. I've been training and studying. That took up all my thinking time ... until recently. But there are two that seem pretty special now."

She looked at him and smiled. "Tell me about them."

"When you said *personal*, you really meant it."

"Just hang with me. Who are they?"

His cheeks flashed hot again. "This might sound weird, but I felt something for Lauren, before I knew she was my sister, I mean. ... Well, even after I knew, but—"

"Don't worry. You didn't grow up with her as a sister. It's not so weird." She tilted her head. "Who's the other girl?"

"As long as I'm spilling my guts." He breathed a sigh. "There's this girl on Second Eden who's pretty amazing. Her name is Listener. Strange name, I know, but she's strong, intelligent, passionate, a real fighter, knows what she wants, and ... well ... she's beautiful. But ..." He looked away.

She laid a cool hand on his burning cheek and turned his head toward her. Failing sunlight sparkled in her sincere eyes. "But what? Is she married or otherwise taken?"

"No, but she's in her late twenties at least. Someone on Second Eden said people don't mature as quickly there, so we're really about the same age maturity wise, but I don't know if I can ignore such a big difference in years."

"Of course you can! Like you said, you're really the same age." Darcy rubbed her hands together, her smile wider than ever. "This should be fun. I love playing matchmaker."

"Matchmaker? I'm too young for that."

"Details. Trust me, you'll be an adult before you know it. Besides, it might take time to convince Listener. *I* know you're a great catch, but she sounds like the type who isn't on the hunt at all."

"True. She's really independent. One man told me she was exasperated with her suitors for being too fawning." He gave her a curious stare. "Why are you so excited about Listener and me?"

"Three reasons." She lifted a finger with each point. "One, I didn't mess you up by being so mean to you. Two, I want to see you happy with this awesome girl. And three, it means Tamiel was wrong about you. The fifth door was meant to be a temptation for you, but it wouldn't have worked, because you're as straight as an arrow. And that means Tamiel isn't the oh-so-smart deity he thinks

255

he is. He's making mistakes, so maybe we can use them in our favor."

Darcy's meaning finally sank in. His ears heated up, worse than ever. Tamiel definitely assumed too much. "Okay, I'm all for exploiting his mistakes. Do you have any ideas?"

Darcy pointed out the window. "Look. They're coming. We can brainstorm."

"Sure, but ..." Matt laid a hand over one of his burning ears. "Can we leave out details of my love life? Or lack of it, I guess."

Darcy grinned. "Your secret's safe with me, Romeo."

When Thomas and Mariel reseated themselves and Matt drove the Mustang onto the highway, Darcy turned toward the back and clutched the top of her seat. "We need to brainstorm. First, what do you know about the sixth circle? Maybe that'll give us some clues about the sixth door."

Thomas's white eyes appeared in the rearview mirror. "It was Morgan's prison. She kept Shiloh, daughter of Sir Patrick, there for forty years."

"It was like a ghost town," Mariel added. "Shiloh was able to see visions of humans wandering there, but she couldn't communicate with them. They were the spirits of former dragons who actually resided in a parallel dimension."

Thomas nodded. "Bonnie fell from Morgan's abode into the sixth circle. Bonnie set Shiloh free, but in the process, she died of an electrical shock. Billy found her and carried her to the seventh circle. Eventually, with the help of Ashley and Excalibur, he found a way to resurrect her."

"A prison," Matt said. "Could Tamiel be holding someone prisoner behind the sixth door? I mean, he held you and Mariel at number three. Why would he repeat himself?"

"I assume," Thomas said, "that the parallel for number three was that you had to deal with a danger in the water while Arramos kidnapped Bonnie. Billy faced serpents in a swamp while Morgan kidnapped her." He shrugged. "Who knows? The parallel for number six might be someone's death rather than an imprisonment. Tamiel is an artistic sort. If he were to replicate such a death, he would likely attempt an exact parallel."

"Meaning?" Matt prompted.

"Bonnie basically killed herself in sacrifice," Thomas continued. "She used her body to block a portal's energy field so Shiloh could escape through it. If I were a gambling man, I would bet on Tamiel setting up a similar arrangement."

"A sacrifice to rescue someone." Matt tightened his grip on the steering wheel. "My mother would probably do it again in a heartbeat."

Thomas pointed at him. "Exactly. Tamiel is well aware of her sacrificial ways."

257

"Okay, so maybe we should dig into Tamiel's psyche a bit. What do you know about him?"

"Very little," Mariel said. "When he began chasing us and we learned his name, I conducted some research in Sir Patrick's archives. He is mentioned in some antiquities as a demon who appeared now and then before the great flood. They called him the Silent One, because, unlike other demons, he emitted no telltale sound. Every other demon gives off some sort of signal, but only Listeners can detect it."

"Listeners?" Darcy asked, glancing at Matt. "Is Matt's friend Listener one of them?"

"Yes." Mariel lifted her brow. "Matt, I didn't know you're friends with Listener."

"We met in Second Eden." He shrugged. "I didn't get to know her very well."

"She could be quite helpful," Thomas said. "Tamiel is able to create a shield of silence around himself and an opponent. The shield is a dampener of sorts that doesn't allow anyone inside its boundaries to hear anything. Since Tamiel has not yet employed that weapon as far as we know, perhaps he is waiting to unleash it at a deadlier opportunity. Since a Listener is immune to the shield's effects, as I said, having one around might be helpful."

Matt shook his head. "That's a pipe dream. Listener's on Second Eden so she's out of reach. Lauren's also a Listener, but I have no idea where she is or if she's even alive."

"In any case," Mariel continued, "Tamiel disappeared from recorded history after the flood and returned only recently."

"At least we have some clues," Matt said. "He'll probably set a trap and make it look like someone's in danger, you know, bait for my mother."

"Or someone else. We're merely guessing that your mother is the one in mind. Perhaps she, herself, will be the bait for someone else, someone like a heroic son who would do anything to rescue her."

"Yeah." Matt curled his fingers around the steering wheel, mentally strangling Tamiel with his grip. "That makes sense."

"It's already evening," Darcy said, "and the next address is still pretty far, so I guess Tamiel will send us an arrival time in the morning. Is there anything we can do between now and then?"

Matt looked at the radio clock—7:30 p.m. "We'll check into a motel and get some rest, but we should get up in the middle of the night and head to the sixth door before dawn."

Darcy laid a hand on her chest. "Tamiel said he could track me, so he'll know we're coming."

"Maybe he embedded a chip in you." Matt looked at her hair, but it was too thick to see through to her scalp. "Have you noticed any kind of sore spot or scar?"

She shook her head. "Nothing."

"Darcy," Mariel said, "with the technology these days, Tamiel might have used a micro-thin adhesive strip. No surgery needed, and you wouldn't even notice. So I can look you over tonight at the motel—that is, if you're willing."

Darcy nodded. "Sure. You can do that."

"And with electricity out everywhere," Matt said, "maybe Tamiel can't track us at all."

Thomas piped up. "No electricity means no working fuel stations. Gasoline is likely a valuable commodity right now."

Matt checked the dashboard. One hundred and seven miles to empty. "How far to the sixth door?"

Darcy squinted at the phone's screen. "Ninety-eight miles."

"Too close for comfort."

"Just ease up on the gas pedal, Son," Thomas said. "We'll make it. No need to chase after the hounds while they're sleeping on the porch."

Matt slowed the Mustang to sixty. Every fiber in his being begged to go the seventy speed limit, but that would be a stupid waste of gas. They had plenty of time. "Speaking of fuel ..." He nodded at the phone. "How's the battery?"

Darcy studied the screen again. "Getting low. We need to charge it, but how, if there's no electricity? Our adapter just has a regular plug."

"Look for a lighter adapter in the glove compartment."

"I didn't see one last time, but ..." Darcy popped it open, pushed aside a small flashlight, and rummaged through a pile of manuals. "Nothing."

"Chalk up another mistake for Tamiel," Matt said. "I don't think he planned for this power outage. He probably assumed we would charge the phone with the wall adapter every night."

Mariel extended her hand. "Let me see the phone."

Darcy reached it back to her. Mariel stared at it for a moment or two, tapping it now and then. Finally, she turned it off and handed it to Darcy. "I have the route memorized. I'll get us there, and we'll save battery at the same time."

"Just what we need." Thomas let out a throaty chuckle. "Mariel as a backseat-driving GPS unit." He shifted to a computer-like voice. "Recalculating. Recalculating."

Mariel batted him on the shoulder. "Oh, be quiet, you old geezer, or I'll recalculate you."

As the two bantered back and forth, Darcy smiled at Matt, her eyes wide with excitement, as if she looked forward to the next day's danger. She grasped his hand and caressed his knuckles with her thumb, then leaned close and whispered, "Someday, some lucky girl is going to get the best guy I've ever met, and I want to be there when she walks down the aisle dressed in white."

Matt's cheeks heated up once more. Why was she being so affectionate? Why the speculations about someone else's relationship and not her own? Darcy was only three-plus years his senior. Not that he would be interested, but plenty of men have married women who were that much older. If she thought he was the "best," why give up on the possibility?

Then an image of Darcy came back to mind—her stumbling out of Tamiel's grasp, still wearing her street-corner garb, layers of come-hither makeup smeared across her face.

He winced at the mental portrait. Maybe she had given up on the so-called "best" because of her past. Maybe she wanted him to have someone who could dress in white, someone who was his equal in inexperience, someone who could blush in his embrace. And such unselfish hope painted a picture of real love.

He concealed a sigh. Then why couldn't he trust her completely? It seemed that every time she tried to break down the wall between them, whether by words of kindness or acts of heroism, dark phantoms rebuilt the barrier.

Earlier she expressed joy that she hadn't "messed him up" by being so mean, but maybe she had, just not in the way she guessed. Somehow he still dangled from a window clutching a lifeline that Darcy controlled from a precipice. To this day her dark laugh cast a shadow over every glimmer of light. He was still her prisoner, swinging back and forth in the frosty air.

He shivered. It seemed that cold air finally drilled into his bones in spite of his normally impenetrable shell.

Darcy laid a hand on his arm. "Are you all right?"

Matt glanced at the rearview mirror. Thomas and Mariel both appeared to be nodding off. "Just thinking about some things. I'll be fine."

"Painful things?"

"Yeah. I guess so."

"Want to tell me about them? I'm a good listener." She smiled. "Maybe not the listener you want sitting next to you, but I'm here. I'll take good care of your secrets."

Darcy's words stabbed his heart like a rusty dagger. But why? How could such kind words hurt so much? It didn't make sense. Nothing made sense anymore.

Tears welled. *Stop it! Don't cry in front of her! Be strong! Control yourself!*

He bit his lip and swallowed. A single tear dripped, and he quickly brushed it away. "I think ..." His voice nearly squeaked. He took a deep breath and stuffed the emotions down where they belonged. "I think I'd better keep my secrets to myself, if that's all right."

"Perfectly all right." She drew her hand away. "Let me know if you change your mind."

"Yeah. Sure." He swallowed again. Change his mind? It seemed that a rope bound his mind, twisted and knotted, a rope that plunged into his soul and wrapped around his heart while he looked up into the mocking eyes of his betrayer.

He slowly clenched a fist. Why couldn't a trained fighter with a disciplined mind cast off this binding rope? It just hung on, ever tightening, like a hangman's noose. It seemed that no one could cut it and set him free. No one. Not even Darcy herself.

And soon they would again venture out together to meet another red dawn, maybe the most dangerous dawn yet. They had to be strong, an unbreakable unit. Otherwise, they might fail to locate the final keys, fail to unravel Tamiel's plot, and fail to save his mother. Somehow he had to break that wall of division and fully embrace Darcy. For Mom's sake, nothing else mattered.

CHAPTER

THE SIXTH DOOR

L eaning on his cane, Jared walked on Cordelle Road with Marilyn at his side and Mardon following a step behind. A new moon and powerless streetlamps left the neighborhood in near total darkness. Only a few stars peeked through a thin layer of clouds, and a chilly breeze drifted along his home street, making no sound to disturb the silence. It seemed that the neighbors huddled in their houses and shivered, both from the cold and from fear. With nuclear war possible and with the danger of radioactive fallout looming, who would be crazy enough to venture outside? At least the Enforcers had probably been stymied. The targeted children and their parents could rest more comfortably for a while.

Marilyn carried Excalibur under her arm, wrapped in a blanket. She pointed a flashlight at house after house, trying to find address numbers. Their own house, 1545 Cordelle, lay about two blocks ahead, not far to go.

263

Jared lifted his cane and tried to walk without it. Pain shot up one leg and into his back. Catching a ride on a National Guard truck to a nearby base had helped a lot, but walking two miles from there had taken a toll.

"Look." Marilyn set the beam on an ivy-covered mailbox with script numerals on the side. "Fourteen oh three. We're almost there."

"Time to douse the light," Jared said. "Familiarity should guide us the rest of the way."

A click sounded, and the beam disappeared, leaving the street in darkness. Mardon whispered, "Kindly lead the way, and I will listen for your footsteps."

"I'll tap my cane on the pavement. You'll hear that." Jared and Marilyn walked hand in hand, taking slow, careful steps. After a few minutes, he stopped and whispered, "I think we're in front of it."

"Stay here. I'll check it out." Marilyn pulled her hand away. Her footsteps clopped and soon faded. After about a minute, they returned, along with her voice. "You're right. There's one car in the driveway, Adam's Mazda. The window blinds are closed except for a small gap. I saw a tiny light moving around, like a penlight."

"Adam has a penlight on his key ring. If the government agents were still here, they'd have more powerful flashlights." Jared scanned the street for any sign of a moving car. "Maybe they flew the coop when the power went out. No need to monitor a computer that can't run."

"True, but we'd still better be careful. They might have left an agent behind in case the power returns."

Jared took her hand again. "Lead the way."

They walked up the driveway, bypassed Adam's car, and stepped in front of the door. To the rear, Mardon's footsteps clicked on the stone porch and fell silent.

Keys jingled. "Here goes," Marilyn whispered.

A muffled click rode the dark air. Hinges creaked.

A bright beam flashed on, blinding them. "Who's there?"

Jared blocked the light with a hand. "Adam?"

"Mr. Bannister!" The beam shifted to the entry room floor. "Get in here! Hurry!"

Jared and Marilyn followed the beam inside. Marilyn set Excalibur, still wrapped, on a nearby sofa.

As soon as all three had entered, Adam closed the door with a thump and focused the beam on Mardon's face. "Who are you?"

Mardon bowed his head. "A scientist the Bannisters are employing to help with a project they have in mind."

"Good enough for me." Adam waved the beam around the foyer. "I don't want to leave this on. It might attract attention." He clicked it off, darkening the room. A smaller light came on and illuminated his face. "They left one of their goon squad here. I tied him up in the hallway."

Marilyn touched a bruise on Adam's cheek. "You fought him?"

"Yeah. He's got a decent right jab, but I had a baseball bat, so ..." Adam shrugged. "I don't think he'll wake up anytime soon."

"Good work." Jared shook Adam's hand. "How's Larry doing?"

"I'm not sure. We had a huge power surge and then everything went out. I tried to start the generator, but when I turned the key, nothing happened. That's when the other two agents decided to leave."

Mardon lifted a finger. "I assume the generator was not in a shielded room."

Adam shook his head. "It's on the screened back porch. It needs ventilation for exhaust."

"Then the electromagnetic pulse probably disabled the electronic ignition."

Adam squinted. "What kind of pulse?"

265

"Electromagnetic," Marilyn said. "From a nuclear explosion in the atmosphere."

"Yeah. Everyone knows about the bomb. Before it got dark, people in the neighborhood were buzzing about it, going door to door to let everyone know about a fallout warning. Not everyone has a battery-operated radio to hear the official statements. Later, a National Guard unit came by and told everyone to stay inside, so the streets are deserted."

"A blessing in disguise," Jared said. "The other two agents probably won't return to bother us when we try to turn Larry back on."

"How are you going to do that?" Adam asked.

Jared walked to the window and peeked through the blinds. "Does your car still run?"

"Yeah. I started it right after I tied up the agent, but since fallout's coming, I decided it was best to stay here."

266

"Well, if you don't mind letting us borrow a couple of parts, between you and me and our scientist, I think we can rig the generator to use your car's ignition."

"Perfect! Why didn't I think of that?"

"Probably because your mind was on guarding that agent." Jared nodded toward the garage. "Shall we get my tools?"

Jared, Adam, and Mardon removed the Mazda's ignition, fashioned an adapter for it, and installed it on the generator. During the process, Marilyn held Adam's baseball bat and shadowed Mardon's every move. At first Mardon worked with jittery hands, but he soon calmed down.

When they finished, Jared turned the generator's key. The engine chugged to life, and the porch light flashed on. Adam lunged to the switch and turned it off. "Let's hope no one can hear the generator," he said. "Otherwise we'll have a line of neighborhood folks dragging extension cords over here."

Jared closed his toolbox. "Let's see if Larry's waking up."

All four entered the house and walked through the hallway alongside the computer room, heading toward the access door. Without windows in the corridor, no one on the outside could tell what was going on behind the thick walls that protected Larry.

Using his cane for support, Jared stepped into the dimly lit room, followed by the others. Power-supply cooling fans hummed, as if the room's collection of metal boxes and glass enclosures were warming up to sing a song.

Jared took a seat at the main control station's desk and looked at a flat panel screen mounted on the side of Larry's outer wall.

"Someone has entered," Larry said in his unflappable tone. "Identify yourself."

Jared spoke toward the computer. "Larry, this is Jared Bannister. I request special security clearance alpha, zeta, six."

"Voice print for Jared Bannister verified. Stand by for challenge questions."

Jared straightened in his seat. "I'm ready."

"Question number one of three. Where did you reside in the year twelve fourteen?"

"Dublin, Ireland."

"Correct. When you killed Andrew the merchant, what were his last words?"

"I need a drink."

"Correct. Where is your wife's birthmark?"

Marilyn raised her brow, her cheeks reddening.

"On her ..." Jared smiled. "Posterior."

"Synonym accepted. You now have security clearance alpha, zeta, six. One moment while I load the required software. Would you like some music while you wait?"

"Uh ... sure. Just not loud."

"Volume setting, level two."

While a soft piano played, accompanied by a bass and drums, Jared turned to Mardon. "How do you want to see the file?"

Mardon stepped closer. "A mapped image of both your human and dragon genome, please. Since I am well acquainted with both species' genetics, I will be able to identify what I need."

"Jared." Marilyn touched his shoulder. "Did you put this music into Larry's entertainment database?"

"No. Never heard it before." Jared turned to Adam. "Did you?"

Adam half closed an eye. "It sounds like jazz. I wouldn't have loaded it. I'm a heavy metal guy."

"I'm seeing red flags," Marilyn said. "Larry hasn't cracked a single joke."

Jared looked at the screen—blank except for a slight flicker now and then. "Why is he taking so long?"

268

The music ended abruptly. Larry's voice returned. "I am now ready."

"I guess he's okay." Jared scooted the chair closer. "Larry, since you're on generator power, let's skip any pleasantries. I'll just say that I'm grateful for your help, and I'm looking forward to working with you again."

"Before you proceed, my AI algorithms have generated a warning. If not for your clearance, which forced my main processor to load a secure checkpoint version of my operating system, I would not have noticed the software patch installed two days ago by user M one thousand. That user attempted to access your files seventy-two times during a three-hour period and also created a database that captured all incoming and outgoing communications."

Mardon raised a hand. "I did that from a remote site. Tamiel asked me to set up the monitoring system for the government agents."

"A different remote user installed the music I played for you," Larry continued. "I now realize that it sounded like diseased alley cats imitating Bob Dylan gargling with hot sauce."

An image appeared on the monitor showing a trio of singing cats. After a few seconds, an old boot flew at them, making them scatter.

Marilyn grinned. "Larry's back."

"Great." Jared adjusted a smaller monitor on the desk. "Larry, switch your communications to screen number two, then access my file and display the genome maps on the main screen."

"One moment." Both screens flashed. Two seconds later, a complex diagram appeared on the flat panel. Filled with labeled boxes within a colorful circle, it appeared to be gibberish.

Mardon leaned close to the screen and studied the map. As his eyes shifted, he nodded every few seconds. "Uh-huh. … Yes, I see. … This is quite enlightening."

Finally, he turned to Jared. "I have identified what I need. Now if you will agree to the terms we discussed earlier, I will help you restore the mighty Clefspeare."

Matt aimed the flashlight at the pavement, Darcy at his side. As they walked along the two-lane back road that led to the sixth door, barred owls hooted now and then, muffled by dense fog in the vast darkness. "Who blew the fuse?" one owl seemed to ask. Another asked the same question, but no one had an answer.

Something snapped in the woods. Matt stopped and swung the beam that way. The light fell on trees and dense underbrush. As he kept the radiant circle in place, nothing moved.

Darcy touched his arm. "Spooky, isn't it?"

"Especially when we don't know what we're heading into."

"Want me to turn on the phone and check the distance?"

"No. We can't risk it." He turned around and shone the beam in the opposite direction. Again it illuminated nothing but fog and pavement. Somewhere back there, Thomas and Mariel sat in the Mustang, parked on a side trail, waiting, as instructed. Since Mariel now held the micro-thin tracker she found on Darcy's skin, Tamiel would think everyone sat in the car waiting for the right time to drive closer. The phone might also carry a tracking device, so they had to leave it off unless absolutely necessary.

270

Fortunately, Mariel had allowed them to borrow her watch so they could keep track of time. The Mustang radio's clock was sufficient for her and Thomas. "Based on the distance when we parked," Matt said, "I'm guessing the sixth door is about two hundred yards ahead. It's a straight shot, so we shouldn't need the GPS."

Darcy pushed back her sleeve and looked at her wrist. "I can't see the watch."

Matt shone the beam on the face.

"Five forty-eight." She slid her sleeve in place. "We don't have much time."

He nodded. That meant they had barely more than an hour till they were supposed to arrive. When they powered up the phone earlier to check for messages, a text came in telling them to arrive at seven. "Let's get moving."

Matt flicked off the light. Darkness flooded everything. Even Darcy faded from view. "You'd better hold on to me."

She touched his elbow and ran her fingers down his arm until she reached his hand and grasped it. "Ready."

Keeping his stare straight ahead, Matt walked toward an imaginary point in the distance. At least the sound of shoes on pavement would keep them from veering off the path.

After about a hundred steps, several lights up ahead pierced the fog, apparently streetlamps. Soon, a building took shape on the right, then a driveway leading from the road through a gate attached to a tall fence topped with barbed wire. The building, a one-story brick structure, stood several feet inside the fence, no lights visible in a window on its front wall.

Matt stopped and pulled Darcy shoulder to shoulder. The streetlamps cast a dim light across her face. "A prison," he whispered. "Like the sixth circle."

She nodded. "How are we going to get in? Especially without being seen?"

"Not sure yet." He scanned the area. The lights were, indeed, simple lamps mounted on telephone poles rather than movable searchlights in watchtowers. No guards perched on rooftops or strolled the grounds. A generator was probably running somewhere, so an attendant of some kind might be inside, and he or she probably didn't expect any visitors.

Matt touched his stomach. No danger alert. Maybe a bold approach would be best.

"Let's go." He marched along the driveway and stopped at the gate. A professionally printed sign spelled out, Enter and Register at the Window. Customers Serviced Beginning at 7:00 am.

Matt gave the chain-link gate a slight pull. It dragged an inch or two along the pavement before stopping. A latch with a red LED clock held the gate closed. The clock displayed 5:59. When it changed to 6:00, something clicked, and the gate swung ajar.

"It's like an invitation," Darcy said. "Shall we?"

"I don't trust invitations from the enemy." Matt checked his danger sense again. Still nothing. "I guess we don't have much choice."

He and Darcy sidestepped through the gap and followed the driveway to a window at the side of the building. With a cash register on the inside, it looked like a ticket counter at a theme park. Just beneath a horizontal gap in the glass, a protruding wooden counter held a clipboard with a pen lodged under the clip.

Matt picked up the board and scanned the attached page while Darcy looked on. The column headings read, Name, Arrival Time, First-time Customer? Attendant Preference.

"Attendant?" he whispered.

Darcy shrugged. "Someone who takes you to visit a prisoner?"

"Then it would say Visitors instead of Customers."

"Good point." As Darcy stared at the page, her expression turned grim.

"What's wrong?"

She shook her head briskly. "Just a random thought. It's nothing."

"Suit yourself." Matt waved a hand. "Let's see where the driveway leads."

Still surrounded by fog, they walked past a parking area and onto a tree-lined path, paved with blacktop, wide enough for one vehicle but no more. As they continued, light from the streetlamps faded, allowing darkness to enfold them.

Darcy hooked her arm around Matt's and whispered, "I smell incense."

He stopped and inhaled. The air carried a sickly sweet aroma. "A religious ceremony?"

"Or to cover a worse odor. I burned incense if a customer smelled like ..." Her voice trailed off.

Matt lowered his whisper even further. "You don't have to mince words. I'm not squeamish."

"That's not it. The random thought came back. I'm starting to wonder ..." She shook her head again. "Never mind. If I make sense out of it, I'll let you know."

Matt turned on the flashlight and aimed the beam ahead. The path led to a group of small modular houses that appeared to be aligned in a circle, their fronts facing toward the center. Low and small, they probably held only one room, two at the most.

He flicked off the light. "Let's go."

Following his memory, Matt led Darcy to where he estimated the path likely intersected a gap between two houses. He stopped and felt for an exterior wall. When his fingertips touched a metal panel, he whispered, "Now to the front. Stay close."

Keeping his hand on the wall, he followed the surface around a corner to a door. Matt searched for a knob. His fingers brushed across a metal object that shifted with his touch. He grasped it and felt the shape. A padlock? "Check this out."

Darcy's hand joined his and fingered the closed lock and latch. "It *is* a prison. Someone's locked inside."

"And I didn't see or feel a window anywhere."

"I didn't notice one when the flashlight was on." She sniffed. "The incense is stronger. Where's it coming from?"

"Probably a roof vent." He pushed on the door, but it didn't move. "A prison door is bound to be pretty strong."

"Are you hoping to kick it down?"

"Not until I figure out if the prisoners should be here or not." Matt took her hand and led her toward the center of the circle. As they walked, their shoes made a swishing sound. He bent low and felt soft blades of grass. This area had been tended carefully.

Matt bumped into something hard. He bounced back, but Darcy kept him from falling. While rubbing his forehead, he turned on the flashlight. A thick wooden pole stood in the way, reaching a few feet higher than Matt's head, its base embedded in the ground. A pair of empty chains with cuffs on the ends dangled from connection points near the top, and another set of chains lay across the grass, attached to the pole at the base.

"A punishment arena?" Matt asked.

Darcy pushed his arm and guided the light over a pillory and something that resembled an altar, complete with a knee bench and elbow rest. "I'm not so sure."

"What else could it be?" Matt trained the light on the pole's dangling chains. "If we can find the key and get out of here, maybe we can avoid whatever Tamiel has in mind for us."

274

Darcy grasped his arm. "Matt, we can't leave. We need to set these prisoners free. They're not criminals."

"How do you know?"

"Just think about it and see if you come up with the same idea. Customers waiting in line. Houses with padlocked doors. Chains in a grassy plot. Incense."

Matt stared at the manacles at the ends of the chains. "A slave market?"

"Slaves for labor camps ... and other things."

"Women?"

Darcy nodded. "Maybe even children."

"Okay. I figured out the obscene word." Matt grabbed a chain and jerked it, but the pole stood firm. Rage burned. His throat tightening, he growled, "Monsters!"

"Then we have to break down the doors and get the prisoners out of here."

He took in a deep breath and exhaled slowly. "They open at seven. What time is it?"

Darcy looked at the watch. "Six thirty-three." Something beeped. "The phone!" She jerked it from her pocket and looked at the screen. "A text message."

"Read it. Quick."

She read the message out loud. "Change of plans. Arrive at the sixth door at exactly seven fifteen."

Matt took the phone and shut it off. "It must have some kind of wake-up mechanism when a message comes in."

"It didn't wake up last time. A text came in when I turned it on in the car, like it was waiting."

"True. Maybe he marks some messages with a higher priority level to make sure we get them right away." Matt pushed the phone into his pocket. "That might mean he figured out that we had to turn off our phone to save the battery."

275

"Doesn't it also mean our phone's always on, like in sleep mode? Maybe he's been tracking us the whole time."

"Not likely. If he knew we were sneaking out on him, he'd probably rub our faces in it, and he wouldn't give us a new arrival time if he knew we were already here. I get the feeling some geek's been helping him, like with the missile launch, but he's gone now, so Tamiel's flying solo." Matt shrugged. "Just guessing, but since he keeps changing plans, it's a good bet he's having trouble."

"So we're probably under his radar screen, at least for now."

"Right." Matt looked up. The first hints of a reddish glow flared across the sky. "Let's go."

The two ran toward the first house. Matt's flashlight illuminated the ground, making the going easier, though darkness still veiled the front door. When they stopped at the threshold, Matt lowered his shoulder and set his feet. Clenching his teeth, he thrust his body against the door. The lock clanked, and the frame made a splintering sound, but the door held firm.

Something shuffled inside. Indistinct whispers followed. A few seconds later, a woman called out, "What's going on? They told us no customers today."

Matt opened his mouth to reply, but Darcy touched his arm and whispered, "Let me."

"Right. A woman's voice." He backed away.

Darcy tapped on the door. "I'm here to rescue you. A friend and I are trying to break in to let you out."

After a moment's pause, the voice returned, spiced with a skeptical tone. "Why don't you just use the key?"

"Where is it?"

"Hanging near the door."

Matt swept the flashlight beam along the wooden frame until it illuminated a key hanging on a nail well above his head. He grabbed the key, shoved it into the lock, and released the shank.

Darcy opened the door and peeked inside. Incense rode a warm draft through the gap. "I'm Darcy," she whispered to someone in the shadows. "How many are in here?"

"Five of us," a woman said. "And a boy and girl. They're both four."

"How long have you been here?"

"Twila and I have been here five years. Three others for about a year. The kids have lived here all their lives."

Darcy put on a confident smile. "Well, get ready to leave. We'll be back to break you out."

276

"You'd better hurry," the woman said, her tone still skeptical. "The boss will be here at seven."

Matt spoke over Darcy's shoulder. "We have to unlock all the other doors. We'll go as fast as we can."

A pair of bloodshot eyes appeared in the darkness. "Who are you?"

"I'm Matt. I'll see you again in about two minutes." He grasped Darcy's elbow. "I'll run to each house and unlock the doors, and you'll come behind me and explain to everyone what's going on. Tell them they have two minutes to get ready and to be absolutely quiet. When I get back to this house, I'll lead them out and then go house to house and gather the rest."

The woman stepped out of the shadow. Her tied-back blonde hair allowed a clear view of her care-worn face. "And then where will we go?" she asked. "There's a fence all around."

Matt attempted a confident smile. "What's your name?"

"Anna."

"Okay, Anna, how tall is the fence?"

"Maybe twelve feet or so."

"Way too tall." Matt drew a mental picture of a high, chain-link fence and focused on the links at ground level. "Do you know of any weak spots? I mean, a loose place at the bottom?"

Anna nodded. "But it's not real loose. I tried to pull it up once, but it moved maybe two inches."

"That might be good enough. Between Darcy and me, maybe we can get you through."

"If you can't, we'll all get whipped." Anna turned and lifted her shirt in the back. Six red welts striped her skin from mid-back to waist. "Those were for scowling at a customer."

Matt curled his fingers into a fist. "I'll get you past that fence even if I have to bite through it."

"I guess we'll just have to trust you." She stepped back into the shadow. "We'll get ready."

Matt turned to Darcy. "Listen. We'll lead them to the fence, me in front with the flashlight, and you in back. We'll make a train with everyone hanging on to the person in front of them."

Darcy nodded. "Got it. When they're all safe, we'll come back to find the sixth key."

"Right. I keep forgetting about that."

Darcy patted his chest. "Because you have such a good heart."

"Or a forgetful brain." He set a hand on her back. "Let's go."

With the flashlight beam leading the way, Matt ran to the next house, grabbed the key from a nail, and unlocked it. While Darcy spoke to the people inside, he hurried to the third house. Now that the morning rays provided more light, he turned off the flashlight. Another red dawn had arrived. He had to make sure it wouldn't turn into a disaster.

Running as fast as he could, he unlocked the third door, then the fourth, then the fifth, sixth, and seventh. When he arrived at the next house, the lock was already loose. A crack in the door-frame proved that he had arrived back where he started.

He pushed the door open. Anna appeared in the glow of a candle she held shakily in one hand. Wearing a bulging maternity dress, she blew out the flame. "We're ready."

"Quietly now." Matt guided the occupants through the door-way. When everyone had exited, he snapped the lock's shaft in place and hung the key on the frame. "Let's go." He grasped Anna's hand and led the way to the second house, trailed by a line of four other women, two carrying small children. Everyone stayed perfectly silent except for the sound of feet brushing grass.

From house to house, Matt collected more prisoners—four to six women and at least one child at each stop, ranging from an infant to a six-year-old, though one of the "women" might have been no older than thirteen, barely more than a child herself. At each stop, he refastened the lock and set its key in place.

By the time he reached the final house, Darcy had already led its inhabitants outside. After he set the lock and hung the key on the nail, the newcomers joined the line—hand in hand in hand.

Matt pulled Anna closer. "Which way to the weak spot?"

Anna pointed toward the back of the compound. "It's about a hundred yards that way. There's some woods before you get there, so it'll be dark."

"Okay. Then we'll—" Matt's danger sense shot higher. Someone might be coming. "Let's hurry!"

He flicked on the flashlight. With the beam again shining in front, he pulled Anna. As the line of women and children caught up to his pace, he slowly accelerated. After passing between two houses, he tromped through scrub grass and thorny bushes. The safety of the forest lay about ten paces away for those at the front of the line, but those at the back were just now reaching the edge of the circle.

279

"To the left a little more," Anna whispered.

Matt turned that way and passed into a stand of thin pines. Like the head of a long snake, he weaved around the trunks, still leading the human train. Several seconds later, he reached a chain-link fence with barbed wire at the top, about a dozen feet high, as Anna had guessed.

While the others caught up, Anna crouched and pulled at the bottom of the fence. "See this?"

Matt inserted his fingers between the links and jerked as hard as he could. The bottom edge bent inward and created a gap about half a foot high. As he pulled, links uprooted from the ground, making the opening grow inch by inch.

"Children first," he grunted. "Maybe they can fit now."

Darcy grabbed the fence a few feet away from Matt's hands and pulled. As the opening continued to grow, women began shooing children through. Soon, the smaller women were able to fit, and finally Anna. She squeezed her pregnant body through, helped by the women on the other side.

Matt and Darcy released the fence. It flopped down, still loose. Anyone could probably use this escape hole now.

Back at the circle, an engine rumbled, and headlights swept across the thinning fog.

"The boss!" Anna hissed.

"I'll distract him." Darcy ran. Matt lunged to grab her but swiped empty air.

Anna pressed her face against the links. "You two better get out of here while you can!"

280

"*You* get out of here! All of you!" Matt rolled the flashlight under the fence and pointed in the direction he had parked the car. "Head that way. Near the road, you'll find a Mustang parked with two elderly people waiting inside. Tell them to come to the front gate and wait for Darcy and me. You and the others hide in the woods until we come and get you."

Women and children ran into the dim forest, while Anna stayed. "What are you going to do?" she asked, each eye peering through one of the fence's diamond-shaped holes.

"It's complicated. No time to explain." Matt ran back to the edge of the circle. A pickup truck sat at the opposite edge near the path leading to the gate, its headlights trained on Darcy. She faced the truck, her feet set and a hand on her knife's sheath.

A burly man wearing tight jeans and polo shirt hopped out of the pickup, a shotgun in his grip. "Who are you?" he shouted as he stalked toward her. "And what are you doing here?"

Matt ran around the back of the houses, glancing at Darcy between each gap. With the trucker's eyes on her, maybe he wouldn't notice a sneak attack.

She drew the knife and pointed it at him. "I am here rescuing the women and children you're holding as slaves."

"Some rescuer you are." He lunged and slammed the butt of the gun against Darcy's head. She dropped to her knees, a hand over the wound. "Didn't they tell you this whole place is fenced in? And we have a guard at the gate. I guess you must've snuck in before he got here."

Blood oozing between her fingers, Darcy glared at him but stayed quiet.

The man pressed the barrel against her forehead. "You're a pretty thing. I'm not sure if I should blow your brains out or put you to work here. You'd fetch double the usual price, at least while you're still young."

Matt charged from behind. He grabbed the man's hair, jerked him backwards, and snatched the shotgun from his grip. The second the man landed on his back, Matt shoved the gun barrel into his mouth. His teeth cracked, and he let out a loud moan.

"Shut up," Matt growled. "Not a word. Understand?"

His eyes nearly clenched shut, the man nodded.

Matt called to Darcy, "You okay?"

"Not really." She struggled to her feet. After sheathing her knife, she staggered to his side and braced herself on his shoulder. Blood trickled down to her neck. "I'm dizzy."

"Then lie down. I'll take care of this ..." A half dozen foul names stormed through his mind. He finally growled, "This piece of filth."

Darcy lay on the grass and curled on her side, facing Matt. "What are you going to do with him?"

"Just this." Matt swung the gun around and thumped the man's head with the butt. His arms fell limp.

"Wait here. I'll be right back." Matt laid the shotgun at Darcy's side, dragged the man to the closest house, and locked him inside. When he returned, he picked up the gun. "Feeling any better?"

She nodded. "A little."

"Stay put for now. I'll look around for the sixth key. It wasn't any of the ones that unlocked the houses."

The phone chimed in Matt's pocket. He pulled it out and read the text message aloud. "You are supposed to be at the sixth address by now, but according to my tracker you are still waiting close by."

Matt set the gun down and typed out a reply with his thumbs. "We're here. Maybe your tracker is broken. Did you lose your techno-geek helper?"

After about a minute, the phone chimed again. "Your deduction skills are better than I imagined. Proceed to the circle of houses at the rear of the compound. I will meet you there in a moment."

The phone beeped and blinked off. Matt pressed the Power button, but nothing happened. "Battery's dead."

"I guess you can ditch it."

"At least until later." He picked up the gun, laid it and the phone on the truck's front seat, and turned off the lights and engine. After pushing the keys into his pocket, he knelt next to Darcy and examined her wound. A two-inch gash ran across her skin just below her hairline. "Does it hurt much?"

"It throbs, but I'll be okay."

"Let me try something." He laid a hand over the wound and pressed his palm against it.

Darcy winced. "What are you doing?"

"I have healing powers. It's part of the whole dragon thing. I healed my mother by touching her." After a few seconds, he pulled away, leaving a smear of blood on his palm. "Is it any better?"

She shook her head. "But that's all right. You're probably exhausted."

"That doesn't explain it. I was exhausted when I healed my mother." He offered Darcy a hand. "Can you get up?"

"I think so." She grabbed his hand and climbed to her feet, still shaky but no longer teetering. "Tamiel will wonder why the truck's here."

"I'll think of something." Matt laid a hand on the hood. "It might be our getaway vehicle. Besides your knife, the shotgun's our last line of defense."

283

18

TAMIEL

During the next minute, Matt's danger sense rose steadily. Waiting for Tamiel felt like standing blindfolded in the middle of a highway. Eventually, a truck was bound to come along and flatten him into a pancake.

Finally, a winged humanlike figure appeared over the trees in the direction of the front gate. Seconds later, Tamiel's familiar form took shape. As his wings flapped, the breeze blew his black sweater and pants against his rail-thin frame, and his dark curly hair tossed about, sometimes spilling over his pale forehead.

While they watched, Matt edged closer to Darcy and unhooked the key ring from his belt loop. He slid three keys off and slipped them into her palm. "Hide these. Better to keep him guessing."

"Got it." She hid them in her pants pocket.

Matt pushed the ring into his own pocket, two keys still attached.

When Tamiel landed near the circular yard's center pole, he looked at Matt and Darcy in turn. "My agents tell me that the five keys are gone. I assume you have them."

Matt pointed a finger at him. "Listen, freak. I'm not giving you a scrap of information until you tell me what you did with my mother."

Tamiel folded in his wings. "Arramos took her to a safe place. I expect him to arrive with her very soon. She is unharmed, and the two of you will be reunited shortly."

"If you've hurt her, I'll …" He pressed his lips together. It was better not to lob an empty threat. "Okay, we got the keys, but they're hidden."

"A clever move. I hope they are close by." Tamiel glanced at the pickup. "Have you seen the driver?"

"He was here for a couple of minutes," Matt said. "I think he got a headache or something. Had to leave."

"He didn't protest your presence?"

"Annoyed, I think, but he seemed interested in hiring Darcy to work here."

"Is that so?" Narrowing his eyes, Tamiel took a step closer to Darcy. "What happened? That wound looks fresh. Did Matt hit you?"

"As if you care." Darcy covered the wound. "And no, he didn't hit me. I banged my head against something."

"Just get on with it," Matt said. "Why are we here?"

"To activate and obtain the sixth key, of course."

"Since you seem to know that we don't have it yet, you must have hidden it."

"Oh, it is hidden. Quite well, in fact. The hiding place will manifest itself soon." Tamiel pivoted, gazing at the houses one by one. "Are you curious about who dwells here and why?"

"We guessed prisoners of some kind." Matt nodded at the pole and pillory at the center of the yard. "And if they get out of line, you punish them over there."

Tamiel gave Darcy a probing stare. "So your traveling companion has not yet discerned what this compound is for. I thought the address label I chose would give it away." He shrugged. "No matter. We shall proceed with the next step."

"What next step?"

"I find it comical that you ask questions that I am obviously getting ready to answer. Your love of genre novels is the likely reason." Tamiel withdrew a phone from his pocket and studied the screen, then looked up. "My master should arrive in approximately thirty seconds."

Matt and Darcy looked up as well. The brightening sky still displayed its familiar reddish hue. Nothing appeared out of the ordinary.

"How strange." Tamiel checked his phone again. "He has always been punctual in the past. Perhaps one of his captives gave him some trouble."

Matt whispered to Darcy, "*One* of his captives?"

She gestured toward Tamiel. "Ask him."

"And get slapped with another genre-novel comment?" He shook his head. "We'll find out soon enough."

After several more minutes, Matt's danger sense heightened again, stronger than ever. Although every morning these days carried a sailor's warning, now it felt like a category-5 hurricane was about to blast through.

As if formed by one of the reddish clouds, a dragon emerged from the overcast sky and descended toward them. A woman dangled limply from its rear claws.

"Mom?" Matt whispered.

"No," Darcy said. "That woman has white hair."

Matt focused on the woman's head. Indeed, the apparently unconscious captive had long white hair and wore green pants and an orange shirt. "It's Sapphira. She's the queen of Second Eden. But that's the same dragon who took my mother. He has to be Arramos."

When the dragon arrived, it circled the yard once, then set Sapphira down gently near the center pole before landing in a trot. Heaving sparks-laden snorts, it settled to its belly and rested its head on the ground.

"Is that Arramos?" Matt asked.

Tamiel nodded, though not with his usual confident expression.

"Then where's my mother? And what's wrong with Sapphira?"

"We administered a drug that keeps Sapphira sedated. Regarding your mother, I will have to find out from Arramos." Tamiel waved a hand. "Come. We will speak to him, but I advise you to mind your tongue. He has destroyed many humans for displaying the slightest discourtesy. He is not nearly as forgiving as I am."

288

As they walked toward the pole, Darcy kept pace, still wobbling, though the bleeding from her head wound had stopped. He could easily prop her up, but it would be better for now to refrain from showing kindness. Since Tamiel assumed they were still bitter enemies, that assumption might be useful.

Darcy whispered to Matt, "Do you think he's really Satan?"

"I've been told that. We'd better watch our step." Matt leaned closer to her and kept his voice as low as possible. "Let's be the Matt and Darcy of old. Understand?"

She nodded and said nothing more.

When they arrived at the pole, Tamiel bowed to Arramos. "The time has come, Excellency."

"Indeed." Arramos's eyes seemed dull, a washed-out red, weak in comparison to the flaming pupils in other dragons' orbs. "After all these millennia."

"If I may ask, where is Bonnie?"

"I returned to the island, and she was gone. The shackles were open."

Tamiel stroked his chin. "Interesting. Did you try to follow her scent?"

"Her scent left the ground abruptly, so I assume she flew away. With a breeze blowing, I had no hope of tracking her."

Tamiel turned to Matt. "Does your mother know this address?"

Matt furrowed his brow. Did she? She had looked at the GPS map several times, but that didn't mean that she had memorized any addresses. If she managed to find his note at the farmhouse, maybe she knew it by now, but providing Tamiel with that information would be stupid.

"I see that Matt is unwilling to tell us," Tamiel said, "but let's assume that she either knows or will find out. She is a very resourceful woman."

"Resourceful and stubborn." Arramos's ears flattened. "I would like to know how she escaped. I detected no other scent, human or dragon. The manacles were opened without undue force, and the candlestones were still intact."

"Help from above, I assume, which means that she will come and fulfill the prophecy."

"What prophecy?" Matt asked.

"You simply can't resist the questions, can you?" Tamiel smiled. "In due time, young man. In due time."

"Whatever." Matt edged closer to Sapphira. She lay on her back, her chest rising and falling in an even rhythm. With silky white hair spilling over her shoulders and a smooth, ivory face shining in the growing sunlight, she seemed to radiate a holy aura.

"Excellency," Tamiel said, "you seem weary. Are you tired from searching for Bonnie?"

"That journey was a trifle. An unusual weakness has beset me." Arramos inhaled through his snout. "Something foul is in the air. It smells like one of Semiramis's potions."

"I noticed it as well. I have a theory about it that I will reveal when you and I are alone."

A growl rumbled from Arramos's throat. "Perhaps I have the same theory. I have long been wary of those who allow her to plot her schemes."

Tamiel shifted from foot to foot. "Well, in any case, are you strong enough to provide incentive for Matt and Darcy to refrain from interfering with what I am about to do?"

290

"I am." Arramos spewed a fiery rope that cracked like a whip on top of Matt's head. It snapped back, ripping hair and flesh.

"Augh!" Matt crouched and laid a hand on the wound. Heat from his scalp warmed his palm.

Darcy pulled back his hand. "Let me have a look."

Matt winced, both from the pain and from the fact that Darcy had forgotten to be the old Darcy.

"What a wimp!" She jerked him to his feet. "It's just a little burn. I swear, you're just as big a sissy as when we lived together."

Tamiel looked at Arramos and smiled. "Sibling love. Isn't it touching? Especially after he rescued her from death at the fourth door."

"I am not interested in their quarrels," Arramos said. "Let us proceed."

"As you wish." Tamiel lifted Sapphira and set her against the pole in a sitting position. Propping her up with his leg, he raised her arm and clasped her wrist with one of the dangling manacles. Then, as she tipped to the side, he raised her other arm and shackled it.

Sapphira sat with her head low and her arms stretched back, her body leaning slightly to one side, kept from falling by the chains.

"Now Sapphira's incentive." Tamiel walked toward a house, though not the one where the pickup driver lay. "I will return in a moment."

While Arramos watched Tamiel's progress, Matt looked Sapphira over. A tiny white tab adhered to her neck, similar to the one Tamiel had used on Mom to keep her knocked out.

He whispered to Darcy, "I'm going to insult you. I want you to slap me as hard as you can. Don't worry about hurting me."

Her brow arched for a split second, and she nodded almost imperceptibly.

"This is all your fault," Matt barked. "If you hadn't been such a witch, we could've gotten out of this mess. You're just a dirty little hooker. You'll never change."

291

"How dare you!" Darcy reared back and slapped him across the face. Matt faked a stumble toward Sapphira and fell against the pole.

"Stop the bickering!" Arramos lashed out again with a fiery rope that caught Matt's neck and sliced deeply. "My next whip will take out an eye."

Matt groaned. This one hurt even worse than the other. He grabbed the pole with one hand and removed Sapphira's tab with the other, palming it as he flipped her hair to cover the spot. She twitched but stayed silent.

"Get up!" Arramos shouted. "You have two seconds."

"Okay. Okay." Matt whispered to Sapphira, "Pretend to be unconscious and listen for my cues."

He climbed to his feet and held a hand over the new wound. No blood flowed. The fire probably cauterized the cut, or maybe his healing touch was working after all.

As he shuffled a couple of steps away from the pole, he spoke loudly enough for Sapphira to hear. "Why is Tamiel going to that house?"

Arramos gave him a scornful stare. "You will soon see."

"I'm just wondering if you're going to threaten someone to get Sapphira to do your bidding." Matt stepped in front of Arramos and faced him, though he furtively glanced at Sapphira every few seconds. "I mean, you could probably set that house on fire from here, couldn't you? Why bother hauling someone out and dragging them over here?"

Sapphira's eyelids fluttered. Bright blue orbs appeared for a moment before rolling upward and disappearing behind her heavy lids.

"Do not test my patience," Arramos said. "You are speaking as the fools do."

At the house, Tamiel removed the key from the nail. Now was the perfect time for Sapphira to launch an attack. He took a step closer to her and nudged her leg with his foot.

Sapphira's eyes opened again. She stared at the house and whispered, "Ignite."

Just as Tamiel opened the door, fire erupted from inside. As the house turned into an inferno and flames engulfed him, he covered his head with his arms and staggered back until he fell in the grass. His clothing smoked, but he seemed unharmed.

Arramos swung his neck toward Sapphira. She had already lowered her head and resumed her unconscious position. He then whipped his tail and slapped Matt, ripping his cheek with a spine. Matt fell to his bottom and held a hand over the newest wound.

"How did you do that?" Arramos roared.

"You didn't do it? I thought you said—"

"Do not play me for a fool!" Arramos lunged at Matt, knocked him to his back, and stomped on him with a sharp foreclaw. "Stay there!" With a slow beat of his wings, he skittered haphazardly across the ground toward Tamiel.

Matt dug the pickup keys from his pocket and tossed them to Darcy. "Start the truck! We'll make more distractions."

She caught the keys and ran toward the pickup. Arramos stopped next to Tamiel and batted with a wing at his clothing's hot spots.

Matt hissed at Sapphira, "Ignite the rest of the houses. No one's in them except the guy in charge here."

As Sapphira looked at him, her head swayed. "Which one ..." She spoke with a slur. "Which one is he in?"

Matt pointed. "That one."

Sapphira looked at a different house. It exploded in flames. While Arramos and Tamiel stared at the new inferno, Darcy hopped into the truck and started the engine.

A third house caught fire, then a fourth, though both eruptions were smaller than the other two.

Tamiel spun toward Sapphira and shouted, "Stop! Stop or Arramos will slay you all!"

Weak flames crawled along the roof of a fifth house. Sapphira called out in a strained voice, "I am trying to set Tamiel's clothes on fire, but something's wrong. Maybe my energy is spent."

Matt shoved the pole, then jerked on the chains to no avail. "Can you at least burn the pole where the chains are attached? I'll try to get you out of here."

"I don't think so." She heaved shallow breaths. "I'm too weak. I feel like there's a portal here. If I could open it, maybe we could

293

escape, but I don't have the strength. Opening a portal drains my energy."

Arramos launched toward Matt and Sapphira. Tires squealed. The truck shot out and cut him off. With a flap of his wings, he leaped into the air and vaulted over it. Darcy jumped out and aimed the shotgun at him. She fired. A spray of pellets riddled the scales on his flank.

He pivoted in the air, landed, and faced her, his head swaying. "Now you will die!"

She pumped a new shell into place and aimed at his head, shifting the barrel in time with his motion. "I've hit clay pigeons a lot smaller than your ugly snout."

"I am immortal. You cannot kill me."

"Maybe not, but I'll bet I can blind you for a little while."

"Stop!" Tamiel shouted. "Surrender or Billy Bannister will die!"

Matt raised a hand. "Keep the gun on him, Darcy. Tamiel's been threatening that for days, but I think he's bluffing. His whole scheme is unraveling. He probably doesn't even have my father."

"I still have him, you fool." Tamiel withdrew a phone and lifted it to his ear.

Darcy's eyes shifted toward him. She appeared to be thinking about shooting him, but the split second she turned, Arramos might fry her. At the same time, Arramos could easily break away from the stare down, but the slightest move would bring a barrage of buckshot that would probably cripple anyone, even an immortal. They were at a stalemate.

"Yes, Sergeant," Tamiel said, "I have a new order for you. I want you to break one of Billy Bannister's kneecaps right now."

"Wait!" Matt shot an open hand toward Tamiel. "Let me talk to him. If he's there, we'll surrender."

Tamiel shook his head. "I don't bargain. You will surrender on my terms."

Matt turned to Darcy. "Shoot Arramos, then Tamiel."

"No!" Tamiel shouted into the phone, "Break his other kneecap. Stand by for orders to kill him."

"Do it, Darcy!"

She fired. Arramos roared and staggered backwards, his wings over his eyes. She pumped the shotgun and spun toward Tamiel. Just as he dove to the ground, she fired again. Pellets zipped inches over his prone body.

Matt ran to Tamiel, set a foot on his back, and snatched the phone away. He pressed the phone to his ear. "Sergeant! Order countermanded! Do not break his kneecaps! I repeat—"

"Silence!" Tamiel shouted.

Every sound hushed. Matt tried to talk again, but not even a whisper came out. He backed away from Tamiel and mouthed to Darcy, "Finish him off!"

Darcy pumped the shotgun. Her brow furrowing, she turned the gun and showed Matt the empty ammo port.

Matt slapped the truck's hood and shouted, "Then get out! Now!" But the wall of silence absorbed his words.

Arramos, his scaly face bleeding from several holes, blew a fireball that slammed into the truck's windshield and rolled over the cab. With his toothy maw moving, he appeared to be yelling something, but Tamiel's blanket killed every sound.

Matt grabbed Tamiel, jerked him to his feet, and put him in a stranglehold while clutching a fistful of his hair. With a squeeze, he slowly closed off Tamiel's air supply.

"You really are a fool." Tamiel's words crackled like leaves on fire. The sound of Matt's heavy breaths returned. With a sudden burst of strength, Tamiel broke free, twisted around, and thrust the heel of his hand into Matt's chest.

As if thumped by a battering ram, Matt flew backwards and slid on the grass.

Darcy jumped into the truck. Tires spinning, she zoomed between Tamiel and Matt. She opened the passenger-side window and screamed, "Get in! Hurry!"

While Matt struggled to his feet, Arramos shot another fireball, a much smaller one that fizzled before it reached the truck.

Tamiel raised a hand. "Your Excellency. We still need these two humans. Please do not kill them."

"That witch nearly blinded me!" Arramos roared. "I have a pellet lodged in one eyeball!"

"We must exercise patience. Remember the goal. Rest and allow your fires to regenerate."

Arramos lowered his neck and scowled. "I still have plenty of firepower left. I have not yet tapped my reserves. Yet, I will restrain myself, but not for much longer."

Matt climbed into the truck. Every part of his body either ached, stung, or felt like it was on fire. The self-healing gift had been working, but it needed to kick into a higher gear. Passing out would be disastrous.

When he closed the door, Darcy shifted into reverse. "I'll get a running start and head right for Arramos." As she backed the truck, she twisted her neck to see through the rear window. "If he flies out of the way, I'll bump the back of the pole hard enough to break it."

"Just don't hurt Sapphira."

"Matt. I'm not stupid." She winked and pushed a button to roll up his window. "Hang on."

She shifted to drive and slammed down the gas pedal. The truck roared ahead. Arramos blasted flames at the tires, then grabbed Tamiel's shirt with a foreclaw and flew with him over the truck.

The tires exploded, and the truck skidded to a stop. To the rear, Arramos whipped his neck back to launch another blast.

"He'll ignite the gas tank!" Matt shouted. "Get out!"

They threw their doors open and leaped. Matt rolled through the grass, scrambled on all fours to Sapphira's pole, and looked back. A thin stream of fire slashed through the truck's gas hatch.

When Darcy joined Matt, he whispered, "Help me cover her." Kneeling, they both wrapped their arms around Sapphira and the pole, their backs to the truck.

The roar of fire heightened until it spiked to a thunderous explosion. A wave of heat blew across Matt's back, neck, and scalp. He cringed at the scalding surge. Darcy let out a soft moan, while Sapphira whispered, "Take courage, friends. It's almost over."

297

Seconds later, the heat eased. Matt looked at the two women in turn. "You okay? Darcy? Sapphira?"

Darcy nodded, the ends of her hair singed.

"I'm all right," Sapphira said. "But be wary. Tamiel is crafty. He convinced Arramos to spare you a moment ago. There must be a sinister reason."

The truck, still in flames, had blackened on the exterior. Arramos lay on his belly, heaving rapid breaths. Tamiel watched the smoldering heap from afar, as if waiting for Arramos to get his strength back. "I think he just doesn't want us to escape," Matt said to Sapphira. "He's keeping us here to do something for him. He knows we won't leave without you."

"And we haven't found the sixth key yet," Darcy said. "He wants us to get it."

"A key?" Sapphira looked down at her chest. "When I was leaning over, I noticed a key on a necklace. Someone must have put it on me after they knocked me out."

Darcy pulled a thin chain around Sapphira's neck and lifted a key from behind her battle tunic. It looked just like the other five, though it didn't yet carry a luster.

"Take it away a few steps," Matt said. "If it glows, it's the right one."

Darcy lifted the chain over Sapphira's head and, keeping her stare on Arramos and Tamiel, walked slowly backwards.

Matt covered his eyes as well as Sapphira's. "It's blinding. Just protecting you."

After a few seconds, Darcy called, "It's safe."

Matt lowered his hands. Darcy walked toward them with the necklace. A brightly glowing key dangled at the bottom, though its dark blue aura diminished as she drew closer.

Tamiel strolled toward them, followed by Arramos, who shuffled weakly. "Congratulations," Tamiel said. "I assume you removed the drug tab from Sapphira's neck, though you did it earlier than I had expected, which nearly upset my plans. Yet all is now well. You have successfully redeemed six keys from their corrupted habitats."

"Okay," Matt said. "At the risk of asking an obvious question, what are we supposed to do with them?"

"Retrieve the keys from where you have hidden them, put all six on the ring I provided, and press them together. Then I will give you further instructions."

Matt glared at him. "Look, I get the whole go-on-a-mission-to-save-the-world thing, and we helped some people, but now that I know you don't have my mother, I'm not doing anything you say until you prove there's a good reason for it. And don't give me that line about hurting my father. I figured out that you made everything silent to keep me from talking to your Sergeant, if there was really anyone there at all."

Tamiel nodded in an admiring way. "I have underestimated you far too many times. You are truly insightful. I also noticed that you have already emancipated the poor, unfortunate slaves here, likely including a means to penetrate the fence. You are clever, indeed."

"At least clever enough to ignore flattery from a forked tongue."

"Touché, Matt. I will get right to the matter at hand, and I provide this explanation only because I need your cooperation. Otherwise, I would have killed you long ago." Tamiel spread out his arms. "This entire compound was constructed at this site for the express purpose of creating this exact scenario. As I am sure you discerned, what was occurring here is perhaps the lowest form of cruelty. Murdered innocents are spiritually freed from their oppressors, but here women and children suffered daily pain, squalor, and cruel humiliation with no hope of escape. You might call this compound the capital of corruption, if I may mimic Abaddon's alliterative ways."

"Agreed so far." Matt nodded. "Go on."

"As the song of the ovulum weakened, corruption grew widespread. And where corruption abounds, correction must eventually take place. The Bible states that in the last days, when evil flourishes, a special person will open the abyss." Tamiel arched his brow. "Shall I quote the relevant section?"

"Will it matter?"

"Not to me. Again, I am laboring through these details because I wish to convince you that you need to cooperate. Not only that, your mother is intimately involved."

Matt heaved a sigh. "Go ahead."

"Must you?" Arramos asked, now looking stronger. "That book is an offense to my ears."

"I will quote only the relevant portion." Tamiel's irises turned reddish, matching the sun's tainted hue. "And the fifth angel sounded, and I saw a star fall from Heaven unto the Earth: and to him was given the key of the bottomless pit. And he opened the bottomless pit; and there arose a smoke out of the pit, as the smoke of a great furnace; and the sun and the air were darkened by reason of the smoke of the pit. And there came out of the smoke locusts upon the earth: and unto them was given power, as the scorpions of the earth have power. And it was commanded them that they should not hurt the grass of the earth, neither any green thing, neither any tree; but only those men which have not the seal of God in their foreheads. And they had a king over them, which is the angel of the bottomless pit, whose name in the Hebrew tongue is ..." He smiled through a dramatic pause. "Abaddon."

19

THE SEVENTH DOOR

M att clenched his teeth. Tamiel wanted him to react to
Abaddon's name, but giving this monster the satisfaction
would be like drinking acid.

Tamiel's eyes returned to normal. "For centuries prophets have
wondered who this star might be. Since it fell from Heaven, many
assumed a fallen angel, but I rejected that notion. Fallen angels
worked to bring about the behavior that incited wrath. Why
would one of them be chosen to deliver it? That duty would be
given to someone who possessed purity of heart, someone who has
the moral authority to unleash due punishment. Of course, I
immediately thought of your mother. As the purity ovulum who
was once in Heaven and then came back to Earth, she is a star
fallen from Heaven, a perfect fit. Although the text uses masculine
pronouns, it is mere semantics based on Greek noun gender. In
reality, the star could easily be female."

"So that's the prophecy," Matt said. "That's why you're sure she'll come."

"Indeed." Tamiel lifted his brow. "So now I hope for your cooperation. If you acquiesce, the people who have committed these horrendous acts will receive justice. I needed you to collect the keys, and now I need you to convince your mother to open the seventh door."

Matt took a deep breath to keep his voice calm. "I figured out why you needed me to get the keys. Someone like you couldn't do it."

Tamiel smiled in an unpleasant manner. "Someone like me?"

"Right. Corrupt to the core. Despicable. Evil incarnate. A buffoon who doesn't realize that he will eventually be fodder for Arramos's flames."

302

Tamiel shot out a hand and grabbed Matt's throat. As he squeezed, fangs extended over his bottom lip. "Your usefulness is wearing thin, Charles Reginald Bannister. If you wish to survive, I suggest that you choose to act in a civilized manner."

Barely able to breathe, Matt glared at him. Pressure built inside his head, ready to explode. Finally, he nodded and squeezed out, "If my mother approves."

"Good enough." Tamiel shoved him backwards. Darcy caught him just in time to prevent a fall.

Matt lifted himself out of her arms and caressed his throat. "It sounds like opening the door would hurt a lot of people. My mother wouldn't do it, even if they deserve what they'll get."

"She will once I explain the alternative." Tamiel waved an arm toward the eastern horizon. "As we speak, several nations are hurling accusations at each other regarding the nuclear explosion that has immobilized this country and sent a shock wave of fear sizzling from coast to coast. The world is on the brink of nuclear war that will slaughter billions of wretched humans. Although the vast majority contributed to the looming catastrophe by participating in the corruption, precious innocents will burn in agony without any idea why they would suffer such torture."

"So you'll tell my mother that opening the door will prevent a nuclear war? How is that possible?"

Tamiel's cocky grin reappeared. "It is not merely possible, Matt. Opening the abyss will certainly prevent a war. The creatures that emerge from the pit will see to that. Humans will not be able to continue their petty bickering when they are suffering to the point that they are begging to die."

"But if she doesn't open it, there's no guarantee of a nuclear war. I mean, who would want global annihilation? They'd be crazy to start it."

"My singular detonation will lead to others." Tamiel withdrew his phone and tapped the screen a few times. "My phone still works, so satellite receivers and relays must be up and running on generator power. If emergency-broadcast radio stations are also operational, I should be able to provide an update."

303

Arramos, his eyes now bright and fiery, lumbered closer and looked over Tamiel's shoulder.

Seconds later, a voice emanated from the phone's speaker. "When the president determines his course of action. According to sources, Russia, China, India, and North Korea have responded by mobilizing missile-carrying submarines and readying their ground-based ICBM weapons. Other reports claim that Israel has also readied its nuclear arsenal. With tensions this high, the slightest provocation might start the most dreaded event in history—global nuclear war."

Tamiel turned off the radio and looked at the screen. "We have arranged to provide that provocation in approximately fifteen

minutes. One of my agents will deliver an urgent communiqué to
the U.S. president indicating that Russia has launched twenty missiles aimed at various locations, including Washington, D.C., and
a supposedly secret command headquarters for land-based missiles.
If that location is neutralized, the U.S. will be hard pressed to
respond at all.

"Also, my agent has already infiltrated the computer warning
system with software that will affirm his claim, including ground
reports from CIA that eyewitnesses have verified the launches.
That should topple the first of many destructive dominoes."

A shiver crawled up Matt's spine. The beginning of the end of
the world was now only minutes away.

Darcy laid a hand on Matt's back and whispered, "I don't
think he's bluffing this time."

"I agree." Trying to slow his rapid heartbeats, he nodded at
Tamiel. "Okay. You've proven your point. But my mother's not
here. She can't open the door."

"We can still begin the process by revealing the seventh door."

"Where is it?" Matt asked. "You never gave us the password to
find the address."

"That's because the seventh address is the same as the sixth. I
didn't want you to learn that until this moment." Tamiel nodded
at Matt. "You may enter REFICUL to see the final address and
the label I assigned. Don't worry. It's not as, shall we say, descriptive
as the one I chose for the sixth address."

Matt scowled. "Forget it. I'm not playing your game."

"Pity. One of your novel's characters would have played right
along."

"Just get to the point!" Matt growled. "You're wasting time!"

"Very well." Tamiel gestured toward Sapphira. "If our Oracle
of Fire opens the portal that will unveil the seventh door, she can

forestall the nuclear war. I had hoped to simply threaten her by killing the resident slaves one at a time until she acquiesced. That would have enabled me to avoid this tedious explanation. Since I don't know where you have hidden the six keys, I cannot kill one of you as a way to persuade Sapphira."

Matt gave Darcy a furtive glance. She averted her eyes. If she had not managed to hang on to her three keys in spite of the commotion, she would have let him know by now.

"So …" Tamiel crouched next to Sapphira and shook one of her chains. "I have to resort to appealing to your innate sense of mercy. If you choose to open the portal, and Bonnie follows by opening the seventh door, people will suffer but not as terribly as they would in a nuclear war. Those who are servants of God will not be harmed, so the innocent will not suffer at all. I'm sure Abaddon will enforce that obligation dutifully."

Sapphira's eyes blazed like cobalt flames. "How dare you appeal to my sense of mercy! You feed on suffering. You relish death. You enjoy misery." Her brow dipping low, she growled. "And you talk of mercy, you foul beast."

305

"Here is mercy." Tamiel slapped her face. "It is merciful that I don't torture you further to force you to acquiesce!"

Darcy leaped and clawed at his eyes. He slammed the back of his hand against her face and knocked her away. She flew several feet and sprawled on the grass.

Matt lunged at Tamiel, but Arramos blasted a torrent of fire, blocking him. Holding up his hands to shield against the scorching heat, Matt backed away. "All right! All right! I get the point!"

When the jet turned off, Tamiel bowed toward Arramos. "Thank you, Excellency. I appreciate the help, though I could easily ward off the boy."

"Maybe next time I will let you try." Arramos snorted a plume of sparks. "Do not underestimate a furious opponent."

Matt crouched next to Darcy and laid a hand on her back. "Are you all right?" She didn't answer. When he leaned closer, she winked at him, then closed her eyes again.

Sapphira glared at Tamiel, a red handprint on her cheek. "Unchain me. I can't create a firestorm unless I'm free."

Backing away from Sapphira, Tamiel withdrew a key from his pocket and tossed it toward Matt. "You may do the honors."

"Coward." Matt snatched the key from the ground. He walked to Sapphira, bent low, and whispered, "Are you sure you should cooperate? He could be lying about that agent talking to the president."

"He's not lying," she whispered. "Watch him. When he lies, he rubs a thumb and finger together. While they were holding me in another place, he did it a couple of times, and he also did it while pretending to talk to the sergeant on the phone. It's like children who cross their fingers to excuse a lie."

"I didn't notice, but I'll keep an eye on him." Matt unlocked Sapphira's four manacles and helped her rise.

As she massaged her wrists, a breeze kicked up, making her snow-white tresses flutter on her shoulders. She rotated in a slow circle and gazed at her surroundings, but her eyes seemed to focus far, far away. "I sense something familiar on the other side of this portal."

"You are quite perceptive," Tamiel said. "The abyss lies on the other side. It is a path to Abaddon's lair, the valley where he keeps those souls Elohim deems needful of resurrection. Bonnie passed through there, as did her father, Billy, his mother, and a few others."

"And I've been there as well." Sapphira straightened and inhaled deeply. "I'm getting my strength back, but I still can't create a firestorm big enough to open this portal."

"I understand." Tamiel looked at his phone again. "You have eleven minutes to recover. If I don't contact my agent by then, he will push the first domino."

"But I'm not sure I'll be strong enough by then," Sapphira said. "You're the one who drugged me. Are you going to allow your own actions to destroy your chance to gain this world before it's reduced to a ball of char?"

"My dear Sapphira, if I were to delay my agent, I would have to tell him to await further contact before pushing the domino. If something were to happen to me during the ensuing time, I wouldn't be able to contact him. That's a vulnerability I wish to avoid."

"What are you afraid of? I tried to set your clothes on fire a few minutes ago, but I couldn't."

Tamiel patted his partially scorched shirt. "It's flame retardant. I anticipated your attack."

"And you also have a powerful dragon ready to protect you. Do you lack confidence in him?"

Tamiel laughed. "Well played, Sapphira. Very well played. After that master stroke of a question, it would be unseemly and perhaps even traitorous for me to doubt my master's protective abilities." He began tapping his phone's screen. "You have bested me on this point. I am sending my agent a message to stand down until further notice."

Matt gave Sapphira a firm nod. It really was a master stroke. Obviously she had a lot of experience dealing with monsters like Tamiel and Arramos.

"Still, I have one ace in the hole, as the saying goes." Tamiel slid his phone back to a pocket. "I gave the wait order, but I also created an unsent message to proceed with the provocation. All I need do is press a single key to send it."

Matt looked at Tamiel's fingers. They relaxed at his side.

"Very well." Sapphira cupped her hands and stared at them. A grapefruit-sized flame blossomed—orange, white, and blue ribbons swirling in a ball. "I feel more strength returning. It shouldn't be too much longer."

"Good." Tamiel walked closer, Arramos trailing by a step or two. Blood still oozed from at least ten pellet holes in his snout and just below his eyes, and his gait appeared unsteady. Whatever was weakening him seemed to be taking hold again.

For the next minute or so, Matt, Tamiel, and Arramos watched Sapphira. Her ball of flame grew slowly but steadily, spinning faster and faster. The flames crackled and sizzled, filling the yard with the din of a hundred campfires.

Matt glanced at Darcy. She still lay in the grass several steps away. Pretending to be unconscious was probably a good idea, but how might she use that ploy? They needed a strategy, something that could take advantage of their enemies' weaknesses.

The biggest weakness seemed to be in Arramos—his drooping features and loss of firepower. He mentioned smelling one of Semiramis's potions. Might her potion be the cause of his weakness? At the silo, Semiramis had said she was carrying a potion that would destroy Arramos. Since the nuclear explosion blew her into bits, could the potion have spread this far and weakened Arramos? No other explanation seemed plausible. But was this a good or bad outcome? If the potion hurt Arramos, it probably did the same to Makaidos, Thigocia, and Roxil. Three good dragons weakened versus one evil dragon? Not a good tradeoff.

Something chimed, barely audible in the fireball's noise. Tamiel pulled out his phone and read the screen. "Excellent. Bonnie Bannister has been spotted only ten miles from us. She is heading this way riding on a dragon." As he continued reading, his face grew paler. "Another female human is riding with her, but my agent doesn't recognize her."

"Perhaps not," Arramos said, "but I trust that you have discerned who she must be."

"I have. It seems that the pilot failed in his mission." Tamiel's smile looked nervous, forced. "While we're waiting," he said to Matt, as he pushed the phone into his pocket, "it would save time if you would retrieve the six keys from wherever you have hidden them and press them together. When your mother arrives, she will be able to open the seventh door without delay."

Matt eyed Tamiel's phone pocket. Just a touch of a button would start a holocaust. No sense in arguing with him now. Still, every good soldier knew that the squadron needed an exit strategy. Once he made the key and Mom opened the door, what then? Arramos would kill everyone. Only Sapphira had the ability to battle a dragon, but in her weakened condition, maybe not.

Still, Sapphira said something about using the portal to escape. Maybe they could jump through it and she could close it behind them. That plan might be sketchy, but it was the only exit strategy available.

309

He withdrew the ring and the sixth key. As he walked toward Darcy, he slid the key onto the ring. He knelt next to her and dug into her camo pants pocket. With his body blocking Tamiel and Arramos from view, she opened her eyes and touched her opposite pocket. A dark bruise on her cheek proved that Tamiel had really hit her hard.

Matt pushed his hand into the other pocket and retrieved her three keys. As Sapphira's flames continued their noisy song, he took a chance on a whisper. "Darcy, what are you planning?"

"Watching for a chance to strangle that creep."

Without another word, Matt rose and walked to Tamiel. After putting Darcy's keys on the ring, he pressed them all together. They sparked and crackled, and their glow brightened, each one emanating its own color. The metal grew hot ... too hot. Still holding the ring, he let them go, but they stayed together and melded into a single white key that emanated pulses of light, each pulse a different color—blue, orange, green, red, violet, and dark blue, likely indigo. A shimmer ran around its edges as if electrified, but it didn't carry a shock.

Just a few steps away, Sapphira waved her hands in circles. Her ball of fire swirled around her body and the pole. As the flames thickened, she faded, veiled by the flickering cylindrical wall.

Something black fluttered in the trees. A dark creature twice the size of a vulture sat on a high branch, though it seemed far too big for its flimsy perch. With leathery wings, fangs, and red eyes, it looked just like the drone that crashed through the window at the first motel.

As Matt let his gaze wander across the edge of the forest, more dark forms came into view—twenty, fifty, a hundred, all staring straight at him. Apparently Tamiel had called for reinforcements. This would be a good time to test Sapphira's theory about Tamiel's lying gesture.

"I formed the key," Matt said, "but it's still too hot to hold."

"I expected that. It's the reason I asked you to begin the process early."

Matt glanced at Tamiel's hands. His fingers remained motionless. "When my mother comes, she might have powerful allies with her. I mean, how else could she get free from Arramos?" He lifted his brow. "Do you still think Arramos will be enough to fend them off?"

Tamiel gave him a dismissive wave. "Apparently your mother has acquired the services of a single dragon. Let me remind you that my master is the most powerful dragon in existence. I need no other protection."

Matt glanced again at Tamiel's hands. On his left, he rubbed a thumb and forefinger together. Perfect. He was well aware of his master's weakness. This hole in Tamiel's armor might come in handy, part of a way of escape. When confronted with two powerful enemies, survival strategy called for getting the enemies to quarrel.

"Arramos mentioned something foul in the air that smelled like one of Semiramis's potions. I think it's weakening him. At least I could tell that he's worried about it. Since you didn't want to talk about it with me around, I assume it's a bigger weakness than you're letting on."

"Silence!" Arramos lashed out with another fiery rope, but it sizzled and died before it reached Matt.

"Interesting." Matt nodded slowly. "I wonder who could have sprayed a potion that would harm a dragon. None of us would. We want our dragons to come here safely. If it's one of Semiramis's brews, Tamiel is the only one who has access to it."

Tamiel's fangs reemerged. "You had best be silent. I had nothing to do with my master's weakness."

"Does your master believe that?" Matt asked. "He said he was wary of those who allow her to plot her schemes. That would be you, wouldn't it?"

"Arramos!" Tamiel pointed at Darcy. "Fire or no fire, you can kill that wench. I no longer have need of her."

"How dare you speak to me as if I am your scullery maid!" Arramos roared. "Perhaps I should consider whether or not *I* have need of *you*!"

"Excellency!" Tamiel gestured toward Matt. "This vermin is intentionally driving a wedge between us. In anger at his scheme, I directed hasty verbiage toward you. I apologize for my misdirected fury, but I was merely trying to defend our faithful relationship and unbreakable bond."

Arramos's brow bent into a deep scowl. "You are quick to recover, Tamiel, and I will overlook your ill-advised command, but if I were to kill that girl, it would appear that I am doing your bidding."

"I understand, and of course you are right." Tamiel turned toward Darcy. "I will gladly kill her myself."

"Wait!" Matt held up the key, now cool enough to hold. "If you so much as touch her, you'll never get this. I can hide it where you'll never find it, and the seventh door will stay closed forever."

Tamiel pivoted back to him, a wicked smile on his face. "I see that your fondness for that worthless prostitute has elevated. Have you decided to take a liking to members of the opposite sex?"

Matt's ears burned. "Just leave her alone, and I'll cooperate. I'm not saying anything more."

"Very well, but you will not be able to hold your cooperation over my head much longer." Tamiel stepped within reach and growled, "If you utter one more word that disparages my master or me, you will have signed death warrants for yourself and Darcy."

"Okay. Okay. Let's just get on with it." Matt averted his eyes. That little exercise nearly cost Darcy her life, but at least he had succeeded in raising Arramos's suspicions.

Tamiel turned toward Sapphira. "Is the portal opening?"

"Slowly. It feels like a door with rusted hinges, like it's never been opened before."

"That is a correct evaluation. The door on the other side of this portal is designed to keep intruders out and to bar its contents from escaping. No one has ever opened it, so the portal window that protects it has been sealed for thousands of years." Tamiel's fingers stayed motionless again. "Not only that, it is unlike other portals for a reason that I will explain soon."

As Sapphira continued waving her arms, she grunted with the effort, but the flames kept spinning, never slowing.

312

Matt gripped the key in his fist. What else could he do to fan the flames of suspicion? His gaze drifted across the drones as they perched lazily in the trees. They would do just fine. But he had to be careful. Darcy was still vulnerable. "Tamiel, I noticed your reinforcements."

Tamiel glanced at the forest. "Oh, those?" he said with a nonchalant air. "You need not worry about them. They are drones, completely under my control. They will attack at my command or withdraw whenever I wish. As long as you continue cooperating, they will stay where they are."

Arramos stared at Tamiel, his eyes aflame, but he said nothing.

"Just wondering." Matt reattached the key ring to his belt loop. "Since you said you needed only Arramos, I was kind of surprised to see them."

Arramos growled. "So was I."

Tamiel rubbed a thumb and finger together. "There are three dragons unaccounted for—Makaidos, Thigocia, and Roxil. Should they come, these drones are here to counter them."

"The drones would be helpful in such a battle," Arramos said, though his skeptical tone continued. "But they are stupid beasts. Unpredictable. I am quite capable without their help."

"Excellency, as soon as you showed signs of weakness, I summoned them. I did so to honor your exalted position, not to show distrust or belittle you. You are far too important to—"

"Your flattering tongue does not impress me, Tamiel. I introduced flattery to this world. I am the master of it." Arramos snorted. "But we can continue this conversation in private."

"Yes, of course." Tamiel shifted uneasily. "You will be glad to know that drones are also flying about watching for Bonnie Bannister." His eyes widened. "Ah! It seems that Sapphira is nearly finished with her task."

Matt smirked. Tamiel changed the subject in a hurry. Although the two enemies didn't come to blows, at least a second seed of discord had been planted.

Sapphira's flaming cyclone spread out into a curtain that stretched from one side of the yard to the other and upward to five times her height. She stood inches in front of the pole, her arms spread as if conducting the expanding flames.

The ground shook. A rumbling sound followed, like thunder, only deeper, rougher, like grinding stones. As if reeled in by a spring, the curtain of flames collapsed toward Sapphira's pole and wrapped around it, exposing a dark rocky cliff where the curtain had been. Leafy vines adhered to its surface, dense near the ground and thinning as they reached toward the top—a ledge about thirty feet up.

Sapphira staggered back and leaned against the cliff, panting. "I ... I did it."

Her knees buckled, and she drooped forward. Matt leaped and caught her. As he held her up, white locks fell over her eyes. She pointed at the pole and whispered, "Extinguish."

The fire shrank from top to bottom and sizzled near the ground. The pole broke at the base and toppled over.

Still holding Sapphira, Matt glared at Tamiel. "Okay. That's done. Now what?"

"We await your mother." Tamiel stepped up to the cliff and touched the vine-covered, rocky face. "As Sapphira can attest, there is no longer a portal here. It was designed to be pierced only once, and opening it dragged the realms together."

Sapphira pulled away from Matt and stood on her own. "I no longer sense a portal. He's not lying."

"At this point," Tamiel said, "I have no need to lie."

Matt checked Tamiel's hands. No finger rubbing. So much for jumping through the portal to escape. They would have to come up with a new plan.

Tamiel pulled a curtain of vines to the side, revealing a wooden double door. Sparks ignited near the left-hand door's upper left corner and burned into the wood. Like fiery termites, the sparks inched along and left a smoky trail. As the smoke cleared, revealing a letter *A*, a new splash of sparks erupted to the letter's right and began etching a second letter that slowly took the shape of a lower-case *b*.

Soon, sparks blossomed on both doors in two rows, sizzling as they gnawed deeply into the grain and veiled the upper portion of the doors in smoke. After a few moments, the sizzles faded, and the smoke blew away.

Matt read the series of block letters silently—Abandon All Hope Ye Who Enter Here.

"The quote is from Dante's *Inferno*," Tamiel said with a casual air. "It seems that Abaddon hopes to frighten away any pretender who would attempt entry without proper credentials." He pulled an iron ring embedded in the left-hand door, rattling a huge pad-lock that joined the ring to its twin in the opposite door. Dull yel-low, as if coated with rust, the lock shook with the rings. The door eased out an inch or so before being stopped by the lock. Bright light shone through a gap between the doors, as if a star blazed somewhere inside.

"Secure. As expected." While Tamiel broke more vines, appar-ently to make a permanent access to the door, he continued in a storyteller's cadence. "When Bonnie opens the seventh door, which I have deemed *The Forever Fall,* you will be able to see the abyss. As I alluded to earlier, for many centuries a powerful force has awaited this day to bring wrath upon those who have rebelled against God. This force dwells in ferocious anticipation and will swarm over the earth. It will bypass you because you are protected, but I advise you to stand back when it is unleashed."

"Is it safe to look inside?" Matt asked.

"I see no problem with that. The force within cannot leave until the lock is removed."

Matt stepped up to the door and peered through the gap. Inside, the light shifted at various spots, as if a hundred spoons stirred a cauldron of blinding energy. He backed away, blinking. "Nothing. It's way too bright."

"If you are satisfied ..." Tamiel gazed upward. "Now we will wait for the bearer of the song, that is, what's left of it."

Matt scanned the sky. A single drone flew across the reddish-blue canopy and alighted on a high branch. Could that have been the agent that spotted Mom? If so, she shouldn't be far away now. And who might the other female be? Ashley? Lauren? Either one seemed impossible.

316

He looked at the door and its dark, forbidding rings and lock. His eyes then wandered to the enigmatic words. Abandon All Hope Ye Who Enter Here. Although Tamiel assumed that Abaddon had prepared the statement as a scare tactic, that explanation didn't make sense. Why would anyone be crazy enough to enter? He would have to be out of his mind.

In any case, Mom would soon arrive and decide whether or not to allow a nuclear war or unleash a horrendous plague of torturing locusts. Either way, a catastrophe would explode across the world in just a few minutes.

CHAPTER

ALPHA DRAGON

Marilyn touched a handgun in a holster at her hip, probably for the tenth time this hour. Pacing the floor while watching a mad scientist work had that effect, especially when the only lights in the room emanated from Larry's monitors and the flashing LEDs on his panels. With eerie shadows shifting as Mardon moved, it seemed that at any second he might create a poisonous explosion that would kill her and Jared while he escaped just in time, cackling in delight.

In reality, Mardon stood at a table and painstakingly mixed chemicals derived from various household and garden products, as well as leaves and weeds from the yard. A pot of soil no bigger than a bowling ball sat on the floor under the table's edge, though he hadn't yet explained how he would use it. Sweat on his scarred brow indicated anxiety or fear, a good sign. He knew he was being watched.

"Are you sure you don't want a flashlight?" she asked. "Or candles?"

"I prefer working in a dim chamber. I created masterpieces of genetic ingenuity in such conditions ages ago."

Marilyn rolled her eyes. Whatever Mardon lacked in integrity, he made up for in confidence. In any case, he had proved his skill many times, and saving lights and candles helped the cause. With the generator low on fuel and Adam out searching for more, they couldn't afford to waste anything.

Jared stood next to Larry's light energy collection tube—a suction device Ashley installed years ago to mimic a similar unit she once had in an underground laboratory in Montana. Dressed only in gym shorts, he held Excalibur with both hands, the blade upright in front of his face. His body structure looked so unlike it did only a couple of weeks ago—muscle tone had atrophied, making his skin, now pallid and mottled, sag in places. Age spots covered his hands and shoulders, and body hair had turned gray from head to toe. The parasite and its toxins had devastated him. He was far from the robust and ruddy Jared Bannister of the past, even the recent past.

318

Mardon poured a single drop of thick brown fluid from a test tube. When the drop struck the clear liquid in a beaker, the solution sizzled. He picked up the beaker and swirled the contents. After a few seconds, it turned violet and settled.

"Excellent. Now for the most important step." He withdrew a vial from his pocket and pulled out a stopper. "When I add this potion, the contents in the beaker will strip Samyaza's DNA and make it precipitate at the bottom. I will be able to filter the combination, retrieve the original potion, and add Clefspeare's DNA. The resulting solution, however, will be volatile and short-lived, so we will have to work quickly from that point until we finish the transformation." He set the beaker down and turned to Jared and Marilyn. "In other words, we cannot pause and reconsider, and we will not have an opportunity to try again."

Jared nodded. "That's when I transluminate myself and Larry collects my light energy."

"And that's also when Mardon will have your life in his hands," Marilyn said. "I won't have a clue if he's taking care of you or try-ing to dispose of you." She patted her gun. "This is the only insur-ance I have. I think it will be sufficient persuasion."

Mardon mopped his brow with a handkerchief. "It is suffi-cient, I assure you. But please remember that my primary motiva-tion is to travel to Second Eden to be with Sapphira. If I fail to take care of Jared, I know that my hopes will be permanently dashed and I will have no future except for an eternity in the lake of fire. I wish to avoid that fate at all costs."

Marilyn shifted her hand away from the gun. "Fair enough, but explain the procedure step by step so I can follow your every move."

"Gladly." Mardon touched the suction tube. As bendable as a pipe cleaner and roughly the width of a vacuum hose, it extended from near Jared's back to a hole in Larry's front panel. "Jared's light energy will travel into a collection chamber within Larry. He will reassemble the energy based on Clefspeare's DNA structure using the program I wrote while you two took turns sleeping."

Mardon leaned back against the table. "A casual observer might think we should be able to use that DNA code to transform the energy into a full-fledged dragon, but the process is not that simple. Just as Second Eden's birthing garden uses special soil to feed and grow regenerated babies, and just as I germinated and grew spawns in an energizing soil, so must I feed a newly formed Clefspeare with a nurturing compound.

319

"My own soil, which created Sapphira and Acacia in the underground mines, was a slow grower, much too slow for our use now, but the soil in Second Eden proved to be much faster when energized by an Oracle of Fire or by Excalibur. When I was in Second Eden's birthing garden, I collected some of the soil and isolated the properties that allowed it to become a rapid regenerator."

He showed them the vial. "This potion is the result. It is dreadfully powerful, which allows it, in its purified state and endowed with demonic DNA, to destroy something that contains foreign DNA code, that is, a specific code that I program it to identify as an invading agent. In this case, I programmed it to attack the basic dragon DNA structure. When I remove Samyaza's code and replace it with Clefspeare's, it will not destroy but instead rebuild what it recognizes as its own, because Jared possesses code for both his dragon and his human form."

Mardon smiled. "The parasite I invented revived Jared's photoreceptors so they could leach his energy, but their revived state is a boon for us. With the parasite gone, the active photoreceptors will pass through to Jared's dragon form. You see, my theory is that wearing the rubellite in the Second Eden garden regenerated the photoreceptors during the transformation from human to dragon. Since we don't have a rubellite now, without revived photoreceptors, this process would be impossible."

"So," Jared said, "you're proud of making a parasite that nearly killed me."

"Not proud." Mardon dabbed his forehead with a handkerchief again. "Just pleased that we salvaged some sort of benefit."

"Whatever." Jared nodded. "Finish the explanation. What happens next?"

"After the translumination, it will be up to Larry to reconstruct Jared's light energy into a physical seed that we will plant in soil.

Then I will mix the catalytic potion into the soil. Regarding creating the seed, Larry has performed similar tasks with his Apollo engine, but he will have to do so with Jared's dragon encoding instead of his human encoding. That way, a dragon will be the result instead of a human."

"How long will it take?" Jared asked.

"Judging by the birthing garden's rate of reconstitution when it is energized, perhaps only seconds, but it's impossible to be sure. This experiment is the first of its kind. I have no empirical data. Yet I do intimately know the stages of development that all regenerated spawns pass through, so if the process is slower than expected, I can identify where Jared is in the growth spectrum and extrapolate to determine when he will reach a fully mature state."

"Tell me the stages now," Marilyn said, "so I don't have to depend on you if things go wrong. I'll also need to know when to move Jared. I don't think a full-grown dragon can fit in this room."

321

"Very well. You might remember Dr. Conner's secret laboratory. He had two doors that he labeled alpha and omega, yet you probably never learned why. They stood for the beginning and end of the regenerating spectrum. Alpha is initial germination, that is, the first time the observer notices anything sprouting from the seed. We used other Greek letters for the remaining stages. Delta means that limbs have sprouted. A river's delta might help you remember it. Kappa means that a head is evident. Think of a cap on a head. Omicron is the mouth stage when a little oval orifice appears. The parallel with the letter should be self evident. There is a significant leap to the next stage. Upsilon is when we uproot the spawn and place it in a growth chamber. From that point it simply grows until full maturity, that is, when it can walk or fly or do anything for which its body is designed."

Marilyn nodded. "And that's omega."

"Exactly. But since the growth should be quite fast, the spawn will uproot itself and need no growth chamber." He nudged the pot of soil on the floor with his shoe. "If all goes well, we should be able to simply watch the stages pass by in rapid succession."

"Assuming this works," Jared said, "how do I return to human form?"

"By reversing the process. Transluminate Clefspeare. Larry collects the energy and applies the human code to create the seed. Plant the seed in energized soil. And Jared grows from alpha to omega, but this time maturing as a human."

"But he won't be able to transluminate himself again," Marilyn said. "As Clefspeare, he is not King Arthur's heir."

"True. I had not considered that." Mardon tapped a finger on his chin. "Then we will have to call upon your son. He is an heir. Or perhaps Walter. Ashley could also build a device that mimics Excalibur. She has done it before."

"If we can find any of them." Marilyn looked at Jared. "Is that enough of a guarantee for you? Do you want to go ahead with it?"

"It's time to rid the world of Arramos once and for all." He nodded firmly. "Let's do it."

Marilyn stepped close and kissed him. As she drew back, she smiled. "I'll kiss you again when you're back to human form."

"I'll look forward to it." Jared tightened his grip on Excalibur and focused on Mardon. The blade began to glow. "I'm ready."

"Then we will begin." Mardon poured half of the vial into the beaker. The mixture turned black. Green smoke rose. After a few seconds, the liquid cleared, and a sooty deposit collected at the bottom. He poured the contents through filter paper and into another beaker, then threw away the black residue. With a pair of tweezers, he picked up a single white thread from a Petri dish. "This holds Clefspeare's DNA. You saw me dip this in the blood sample you saved and stored here. I isolated the necessary code, which now adheres to this sanitary thread."

He poised the thread over the new beaker and carried both to the door. "Marilyn, kindly accompany me to the hallway while Jared transluminates himself. We don't want to become random sparkles in the air, and I don't wish to lose the organic material on this thread."

"Larry," Marilyn said, "give us a call when you've collected him."

"I will choose an appropriate shout, perhaps an excerpt from Charge of the Light Brigade."

"That should do." Marilyn walked to the door and opened it for Mardon. When he passed through, she joined him in the hallway and closed the door. She spoke with a menacing hiss. "I suppose you have heard about the fury of a woman scorned."

The hand holding the tweezers trembled. "Yes. Of course."

"Good." She drew the gun and cocked the hammer. "That is nothing compared to the fury of this woman if a certain mad scientist causes the death of her husband."

"I will do my best. As I mentioned, this has never been—"

"Honor the Light Brigade, noble six hundred!"

Marilyn slid the gun back to the holster. "Let's go."

When they reentered the room, no one stood where Jared had been. Only Excalibur and a pair of gym shorts remained.

Marilyn stopped and stared. The vacancy felt like a deep void, as if someone had cut her heart out of her chest. But she had to go on. The empty room was expected.

She reached into a recess in Larry's front panel at waist level and withdrew a pea-sized white seed. Cradling it in her palm, she showed it to Mardon. "I've got it."

"Excellent." Mardon hurried to the table and dropped the thread into the beaker. The moment the thread touched the liquid, the solution erupted. Droplets splashed into Mardon's face. He

323

slapped his hands over his eyes. Screaming, he dropped the beaker. It shattered and spilled the solution. Sizzling and popping, the liquid flowed to the side of the table and dripped over the edge.

"Mardon!" Marilyn ran to the table and stared at the mess. "What do I do?"

He dropped to his knees and groaned, his hands still covering his face. "I need water! It burns!"

"Not until you tell me what to do!" Marilyn slid the pot under the drip and let the soil collect the solution. "I'm catching some, but a lot of it evaporated."

Mardon groaned again, louder and longer. "My eyes are on fire!"

"Do we have enough solution?" Marilyn shouted.

He shook his head wildly. "I don't know! I don't know!"

She knelt in front of him, grabbed his shirt, and jerked him close. "You left some in the vial. Can you make more?"

Keeping his eyes closed, he nodded. "But what … what I kept … I planned to use … to make Jared human again … I have no way … of getting more."

She shoved him backwards, leapt to her feet, and swept the rest of the liquid down to the pot. Her palm burned, worse than if she had laid it on a stove.

"I'll be right back." She pushed the seed into the soil and ran out of the room, down the hallway, and into the kitchen. She turned on the cold water and set her hand in the flow while at the same time rummaging in a cabinet for a container of some kind, any kind.

After snatching a stray plastic storage bag and filling it, she ran back to the computer room. Mardon lay on the floor, writhing on his back. She rushed in and poured the water slowly over his eyes.

"Blink to let the water in," she said softly, though the burning sensation on her palm made her want to scream. "We have to flush that stuff out."

Mardon's eyelids fluttered. Water flowed into his eye sockets and dribbled over the sides. "You are most gracious. I very much appreciate the kindness."

"Don't go overboard. I'd do the same for an injured dog." She emptied the rest of the bag and helped him up. "How are your eyes?"

"They are still burning, though not as badly." He blinked rapidly. "I see only fuzzy images. If not for your voice and the fact that I knew you were here, I would not recognize you."

"Not good for a scientist I'm counting on to restore my husband."

He felt his way to the table and found the pot. "Did you plant the seed?"

"Just a minute ago."

"Do you see any growth?"

She crouched next to him and scanned the surface of the dark soil. A tiny sprout, green and supple, slowly emerged. "Yes!" Her heart thumping, she caressed the thin stalk with a fingertip. "Is that Jared?"

"Clefspeare, to be precise. He is now an alpha dragon." Mardon ran his hand along the soil until his own finger touched the half-inch sprout. "He is very small, and I don't detect rapid growth. That means we have some difficult options to choose from."

"Like what?" As she rose, she helped him rise with her.

Blinking again, he retrieved the vial from his pocket. "One, we create more catalyst solution and risk being unable to restore Jared Bannister. Two, we wait for Clefspeare to grow, which is probably the safest option, though it could take a long time. Some of our spawns grew for a hundred years before we uprooted them and transferred them to growth chambers. Or three, we travel to Second Eden and transplant him into Second Eden's birthing garden. That soil is sure to be faster than what is in our pot. The babies are ready in months instead of years. And if Sapphira is there, she can energize the soil for even faster results. Your son or Walter could do the same with Excalibur."

Marilyn huffed. "A trip to Second Eden. You'd like that, wouldn't you?"

"Madam, are you suggesting that I intentionally—"

"I don't know. Maybe." She grabbed a fistful of her hair. "This is just too much! I have no idea what to do!"

"May I suggest another option? You take our alpha dragon to Second Eden yourself and leave me behind. My incentive to continue helping you remains, because I will still be short of my goal to get to Second Eden. And I know you will return for me because ..." He held up the vial. "I have the catalyst and the know-how to restore your husband. I assume you still have the DNA sample you took from Jared before we began."

"Yes, yes. Of course. And you're not getting it." Marilyn paced the floor in a five-foot circuit, checking the plant every time she pivoted. If it was growing at all, the difference was undetectable from this distance. Mardon's options made sense, as did his offer to stay, but all the facts and possibilities jumbled in her mind. "It seems like everything and everyone is going stark raving mad, including me!"

"Marilyn," Larry said, "my voice interpreter indicates that you might need help from an emotionless third party."

She halted in front of his screen and heaved a sigh. "Yes, Larry. I need all the help I can get."

"Sun Tzu, author of *The Art of War,* said, 'Keep your friends close, and your enemies closer.' Since

Mardon has proven himself many times to be an enemy, and since this latest attempt to prove friendship has failed, at least so far, I propose that you keep him close. You might need his help for Jared's restoration on short notice, and you will be able to monitor his activities for anything that suggests a departure from loyalty to your cause."

Marilyn set her hands on her hips. "Larry, that was amazing! So articulate and well thought out. And not a hint of a joke. I'm impressed."

"Serious times call for serious discussion, but if you are concerned that I have reverted to my monitored state, I am able to imitate the sound of flatulence."

"No. Please don't. That's not funny. It's disgusting."

"Then I will add a second quote—Your enemy is like spoiled ham. He comes from the backside of a pig, has turned rotten, and tastes terrible on a sandwich."

327

"Who said that?"

"I believe I just did."

Marilyn smiled. "Larry, thank you for the comic relief. I needed it."

"You are quite welcome."

Mardon shuffled closer, his hands wringing. "Does this mean that you will take me to Second Eden?"

"Yes, but it's not as easy as it sounds." She sat at the control station. "Larry, can you contact Second Eden so someone at the portal will watch for us?"

"I have already begun trying to use the frequencies the guards at the portal are likely to monitor, but the recent nuclear blast has created an enormous amount of volatility in the atmosphere. So far, the guards have failed to answer, and I have no way of knowing if they did not receive my message or simply were unable to reply. Unless I get a response soon, you will have no choice but to go there and hope for a good result. The latest reports say that fallout is light here, though far worse to our south. If you begin with a northern trajectory, the danger range will be minimal to moderate."

"Well, that raises the second problem. Transportation. We can get a vehicle, but we'll need gas stops. We don't want to run out halfway there."

"Very few fuel stations are open," Larry said, "and most of those are reserved for emergency and military vehicles. Success by a gas-powered vehicle is unlikely."

"Then we'll need to summon a dragon."

"Three dragons have tooth transmitters. I will begin attempts to contact them, but the atmospheric conditions could easily interfere."

"Thank you, Larry."

"And speaking of gas..."

"Larry," Marilyn said with a warning tone. "No flatulence."

"I was merely going to say that if Adam fails to return soon with gas for the generator, I will have to shift to power-save mode, and I will lose my ability to send messages."

"Can you keep sending messages for another half hour?"

"If I turn off all other input-output channels, then yes."

"Go ahead. If you don't get an answer in half an hour, you probably never will."

"Your conclusion is sound. If I receive a reply, I will restore the verbal interface and inform you."

Larry's monitor flickered off, and more than half of the lights on his panels winked out.

The room darkened. Marilyn turned toward Mardon, now only a silhouette in the dimness. He walked slowly toward her and reached out a hand.

"I'll get candles." She turned, but he grabbed her arm. "Don't touch me!" she barked as she jerked away.

"I was merely hoping for a guide back to the plant so that I may observe it while you obtain alternative lighting. With my diminished eyesight, I have lost my bearings, and the darkness makes it impossible to regain them."

"Okay." She exhaled loudly. "Sorry about the reaction."

"It's quite all right. These are anxious moments."

She grasped his upper arm and walked with him to the plant. Barely visible in the dark soil, the tiny sprout appeared to be no taller than before. "Shouldn't I take Jared ... I mean, Clefspeare, out into the sunshine, such that it is?"

329

"These plants require very little light. Ours grew in the depths of Hades. And if you take him outside, you will expose him to fallout, however little there might be, and you will not be able to hear Larry should he provide a report from Second Eden or the dragons."

"Okay. Then you can watch Clefspeare and listen for Larry while I get the candles." As she hurried from the room and down the hallway, guided by daylight from outside, prickles ran up her spine. Trusting Mardon with the precious plant felt stupid, but if he was going to be her only company on a long journey, she couldn't avoid trusting him. Keeping the plant safe was in his own best interests, at least until they arrived in Second Eden.

When she reached the kitchen, she pulled open a drawer and rummaged inside. Candles and matches were in there somewhere.

"Mrs. B?" Adam called from the rear of the house.

"In the kitchen." She grabbed two candles and a matchbook and laid them on the counter. "Did you find gas?"

"Yep." He walked in from the living room. "Enough for a little while. I already put it in the generator."

"Good." She lit a candle and handed it to him. "Please go to the computer room. Mardon's in there with—"

"Can't." He pushed the candle back into her hand. "I've been in the fallout. They say I'm supposed to scrub from head to toe." He grinned. "Unless you want me to glow instead of the candle."

"Go ahead. The tub's still full, and you'll find a wash basin and a scrub brush in the bathroom closet. I'll get you up to speed when you're done."

"Sure thing." Adam spun and hustled into the dimness of the hallway.

Marilyn walked back toward the computer room and touched the lit candle to the dark wick on the other. As the second candle flared up, an old memory returned—her wedding day with Jared. Years ago they had each carried a lit candle to a church altar and touched their individual flames to a unity candle. That day they became one flesh, inseparable, for better or for worse.

Even then she knew about his dragon/human genetics, but they had no idea that he would transform from one state to the other multiple times over the years. Her vows never included a phrase such as "whether dragon or human." The first time Jared transformed into Clefspeare, he became aloof. He even said, "Your husband is now dead, and Clefspeare lives again." That didn't sound like the keeping of such a vow.

She shook her head hard. *No! Stop thinking like this! If you don't, you'll never have the courage to save Jared! He is your husband, dragon or human!*

Now holding both candles in one hand, she stopped at the door to the computer room and gripped the knob. Why was it so hard to turn? Why was the sight of that weak little plant so hard to face?

Leaning against the opposite wall, she slid down to her bottom. She stared at the candles and imagined her form in one flame and Jared's in the other. Leaning the candlesticks toward each other, she brought the flames together and whispered, "Lord, please help us to stay as one." Her breath made the single flame shudder. Wax dripped to her jeans, but it mattered little. "Help Clefspeare grow, help him fight Arramos, help him win. Then transform him into Jared again and bring him back to my arms."

21

SACRIFICE

Lauren clutched a spine and studied a narrow road below. Roxil rose and fell more randomly now. Even after a good night's sleep, her energy had fallen dangerously low. Although she complained very little, she had mentioned a "blight in the air," an odor she had been unable to identify.

Both wings folded in for a moment, causing a sudden drop. When they expanded again, Roxil snorted a weak stream of sparks and flew on.

Mom, sitting only inches back, touched Lauren's shoulder. "Roxil needs another rest."

"Let's see if she'll agree this time." Lauren patted Roxil's scales and shouted, "You need a rest!"

Keeping her eyes focused straight ahead, she grunted. "Lois says we have less than a mile to go."

"Then we'll walk if we have to, which is better anyway. Maybe no one will see us. Besides, we can't have you crashing and breaking your bones."

"Or yours." Roxil angled toward the road. "Very well."

Seconds later, she slid along on a grassy strip to the right of the pavement. When she stopped, she let her neck flop to the ground. "Perhaps you should dismount."

Lauren slid off Roxil's back on the highway side, and Mom flew down on the other.

"Let's go ahead and walk," Mom said. "Roxil can come by stealth when she feels up to it."

"I do not have the strength to argue." Roxil pointed down the road with a wing. "Lois says the address is eight-tenths of a mile straight ahead. You should be able to find it easily. I will follow as soon as I can."

334

Mom grasped Lauren's arm. "Let's go." As they jogged along the right side of the pavement, Lauren took inventory of her body. Her arms felt okay, but her legs and buttocks tingled from the long ride on a tough-scaled dragon. It felt good to stretch them out.

She glanced at her mother. Mom limped slightly, lifting herself with a brief flap of her wings every few steps. With legs and wings tired, combining the two was probably the best way to keep the strain from taxing both.

After a couple of minutes, Lauren's back scales began to tingle. Mom's thoughts came through, calm and peaceful. *Father, thank you for watching over Lauren. Please take care of Billy and Matt.* Variations of these thoughts continued flowing, heartfelt prayers that melded with her waning song.

A moment later, other thought-voices filtered in—a man and a woman, quiet and nervous, their words too low to make out. Lauren grabbed her mother's arm and pulled her to a stop. "I hear thoughts." She scanned the forest to the right. "Somewhere that way."

Mom pointed at a narrow dirt path about twenty paces ahead. "Let's check it out."

They hurried to the path and followed it into the woods. Just as they passed the edge of the trees, a stripped-down car came into view. As they passed it, Lauren ran a finger along the frame. Equipped with only two seats, an exposed motor, and what appeared to be solar panels mounted on the back, it looked like a failed green-energy experiment. A duffle bag sat close to the rear of the frame, its top zipped and fastened with a small padlock.

The path turned to the left. Soon, a sports convertible appeared. "The Mustang!" Mom beat her wings and jogged ahead.

"Wait! We don't know who's in it!" Lauren sprinted, and they arrived at the front of the Mustang at the same time.

The driver's door swung open. An elderly woman stepped out and smiled. "Well, if it isn't Bonnie!"

"Mariel!" Mom half ran and half flew to her. "Where are Matt and Darcy?"

"They went to the sixth door early this morning." Mariel pointed parallel to the main road. "That way."

Mom leaned around Mariel and looked inside the car. "Hello, Thomas."

"Greetings." An old man waved from the backseat. "Mariel, stop wasting time and tell them where Billy, Walter, Ashley, and Gabriel went."

Mom smiled like a little girl at a birthday party. "Billy was here?"

Mariel nodded. "And a whole gaggle of women and children came by, escapees from a prison behind the sixth door. They were …" She glanced at Lauren. "They were slaves of some sort."

"Where are they now?"

Mariel ran her shoe along the dirt path. "This road leads to a warehouse at the back side of the prison where they keep a bus to haul prisoners for … well … big events, let's say. Ashley is driving the bus, now loaded with escapees, to a shelter; Walter's telling funny stories to the children; and Gabriel's flying overhead to watch for trouble. Billy's around here somewhere and—"

"Billy's here? Now?" Mom swiveled her head. "Where?"

"I'm right here."

Lauren searched for the source of the voice somewhere in the woods. Seconds later, Dad pushed between two bushes, his face bruised and bloodied; his shirt torn in front, revealing a long gash and smeared soot; and sleeves rolled up to his elbows accentuating muscular forearms and clenched hands gripping a military rifle. "I heard something. Had to check it out." He winked. "So who is this goddess-like woman with the lovely wings?"

Tears filled Mom's eyes. She spread her wings and flapped them gently. "Special delivery from a dragon courier. Whether escaping to the peak of Mount Hardin, journeying through the horrors of Hades, or waiting for fifteen years in prison, I am the woman who gave you her heart, and yours still beats in my bosom."

He laid the rifle on the ground and extended his arms. "Bonnie. My love."

"Oh, Billy!" She ran into his embrace, and they wept together, hugging in a gentle sway.

Lauren sniffed. A tear dripped. So beautiful. Real love. A forever covenant, for better or for worse, and they had suffered through the worst.

When they pulled apart, Dad smiled and reached for Lauren. "Come here, girl!" With a running start, she leaped into his embrace. As they hugged, he ran a hand through her hair. "I am so proud of you! When I left you in Hades, I was so worried. How could she handle being all alone in that horrible place? But what did you do? Cry in the corner like a baby? No, you helped save all of Second Eden!"

She pulled back and gazed into his sparkling eyes. "Well, I did cry a little, and I had a lot of help."

"We all cry, dear daughter, no matter how brave we are." He kissed her forehead. "And we all need help, especially at the gates of Hell."

"You and Mom are my inspirations." Lauren tried to smile, but her lips just trembled as she looked at them in turn. "I love you both so much."

Tears trickled down Dad's cheeks. "And I love you more than life itself."

"Much more," Mom said, her own tears flowing.

"Well …" Lauren stepped back. "I guess we have a lot to do."

"Definitely. And a lot to explain." Dad retrieved the rifle and leaned against the Mustang. "Since I have a couple of broken toes, I was elected to stay here and guard Thomas and Mariel. Word from the escaped prisoners is that they left Matt and Darcy at the prison, so I was just about to drive there to see what's going on. One woman named Anna said she stayed long enough to see Matt take down the prison boss, so she thinks they might be just fine, but we have to check it out. Thomas and Mariel think they should've been back here by now, even though Matt said to give him till noon."

Bonnie brushed away tears. "I think we should go."

"Just a minute. I have to move Ashley's solar car. We found an auto junkyard across the street from an electronics store. That's all she needed."

337

"Can we drive it?" Lauren asked. "I mean, Mom and I can go first, and you can come behind us with the Mustang."

Dad shrugged. "Sure. It still has some juice. Just turn the switch on the battery behind the seats. A lever attached to the right of the steering wheel is your accelerator. On the left is your brake."

"Sounds easy enough." Lauren curled her arm around Mom's. "Ready?"

She looked at Dad, then at Lauren. "Well …"

"On second thought …" Lauren slid away. "Ashley's contraption might be better off with only one person, and besides, Dad looks like he needs some tender loving care. Broken toes can be torture."

Mom smiled. "Go on ahead. We'll be right behind you."

"Someone has to check on Roxil," Lauren said to her father. "We flew here on her, and now she's resting at the main road back a little ways. Something's in the air that's weakening her."

"Thomas and I will stay with her," Mariel looked back at him. "Won't we, Thomas?"

"Yes. Of course. With a fire-breathing dragon as a companion, even a weak one, we should be well protected."

"Perfect. I'll get going." Lauren jogged to Ashley's makeshift car, turned on its electric motor, and slid into the driver's seat. She grabbed the steering wheel and pushed the lever on the right. The car eased forward, as quiet as a gentle breeze. The wheels, not much bigger than those on a child's wagon, rolled effortlessly along the dirt path.

When she reached the main road, she pulled back the accelerator lever and pushed another lever on the left side of the steering wheel. The car came to a halt. She looked to the left. A few hundred feet away, Roxil lay in the grass on the side of the road. From this distance, it was difficult to be sure, but her body seemed to rise and

338

lower in a normal respiration rate. To the rear, the Mustang's engine fired up. Mom and Dad would check on her in a few seconds.

Lauren breathed a whispered, "Thank you, dear friend. You are a most noble dragon." She pushed the accelerator and turned onto the road. As the car picked up speed, she looked back. The Mustang had stopped next to Roxil, and Dad was leading Thomas toward the dragon while Mom was walking with Mariel.

After a couple of minutes, Lauren arrived at a driveway leading to a fenced compound with a gated entry. She stopped the car, climbed out, and shook the gate. It rattled but wouldn't open. A small building with a service window stood nearby, probably the control station. Mom could easily fly over the fence and open the gate for everyone. Maybe waiting for her would be the smartest move.

The scales on her back tingled. Sounds magnified—a bird, a frog, and … a voice? Matt's voice? Yes, Matt was talking, but to whom? The tingles spiked. Like replays from a dark dream, another voice pierced her mind, the voice of a callous killer, from the hellish mouth of the demon who murdered her foster parents and Micaela, who kidnapped and tortured Mom, and who threatened to lay the world to waste. Tamiel. This beast who mocked God had to be stopped once and for all.

Lauren looked up. Three barbed wires ran in parallel at the top of the fence. It could have been worse. At least it wasn't razor wire.

She checked the road again. Far down the narrow pavement, the Mustang still sat motionless near Roxil. Settling a blind man and his companion with their dragon protector could take a while.

Letting out a sigh, she slid her fingers between the chain links and listened to Tamiel's grating voice—so cocky, so pretentious, so evil. He would kill millions, even billions. He cared nothing for life … or love.

She lifted the medallion and read the engraved words once again. *My gift to you. My life. It is all I have to give.*

She let it drop behind her shirt. No one else could stop that evil demon. No one. Waiting for Mom and Dad would be a mistake.

Lauren vaulted upward and climbed. Because they would try to stop her.

M att kept his gaze on the sky. Where could Mom be? She had had plenty of time to cover a few miles. A dragon wasn't that slow.

Tamiel's phone chimed again. He drew it out and read the screen to Arramos. "Another agent is reporting in. A flatbed truck recently turned onto our access road at the highway intersection. Something wrapped in a gray tarp is on the bed. The agent thinks the tarp moved, though the movement could be the wind."

"No one uses that road except for employees and customers," Arramos said. "This facility is supposed to be shut down for the day."

"It is. All regular customers were notified." Tamiel furrowed his brow. "Is a flatbed truck big enough to carry two dragons?"

"If they curled closely together." Arramos's ears twitched. "You are worried about Makaidos and Thigocia."

"Shouldn't I be? In your condition—"

"I know all about my condition!" Arramos snorted a plume of smoke. "If they are covered by a tarp, they are either hiding in hopes of a stealth attack, or they are suffering from the same malady and are too weak to fly. Either way, I do not wish to battle two of them, especially if Bonnie arrives on a third dragon."

"Yes, Roxil is a formidable warrior." Tamiel stroked his chin. "Elam is likely the truck driver, so Yereq might be with him as well. If the truck recently turned onto our access road, we still have at least twenty minutes before he arrives. Even if Yereq and all three dragons come, we can ward them off by threatening our human hostages. Therefore, we can complete this task, and you can be on your way."

"Very well. I am no coward, but I have not survived this long by being stupid. I will look forward to battling them when I recover."

"Of course. Of course." Tamiel pursed his lips and whistled a shrill warble. It oscillated through various notes in a narrow range. The drones bobbed their heads. "I have commanded the drones to watch for any signs of a dragon. They will warn us."

Matt kept an eye on Tamiel's hands, now clasped in front with the phone lodged between them. No sign of a lie, though he said only that the drones would give a warning, not that they would descend to join in a battle. With so many, they could be overwhelming, especially since, according to Enoch, their venom brought paralysis, death, or insanity.

Tamiel glanced at his phone. "If Bonnie fails to show within five minutes, I will send the order to push the domino, and we can leave long before the truck arrives."

Sapphira whispered, "Matt, someone's coming. Look in the trees next to the driveway."

Matt shifted his eyes. Lauren peeked around a tree, then quickly hid.

Keeping a straight face, he refocused on Tamiel. How could Lauren have gotten here? What might she be planning? With a powerful dragon and a crafty demon around, she couldn't possibly sneak up and hope to do anything helpful. Unless … Matt swallowed hard. She *could* do something helpful … and horrible. Simply touching Tamiel would kill them both.

Sapphira edged closer to Matt. "Here she comes."

Now out in the open, Lauren strolled down the driveway as if walking in a park, her head erect and her eyes straight ahead.

Tamiel looked her way, blinking rapidly. "Stay back!" he shouted, lifting his phone. "Or I will send a message that will start a nuclear war."

Lauren slowed her pace. As she entered the circular yard, she stared at Matt as if asking for verification. Behind Tamiel, Darcy slowly rose to all fours and crawled toward him.

"He's not lying," Matt called. "He really can start a holocaust."

Lauren halted within fifty paces. A stitched wound marred her forehead, blood trickled from jagged cuts on her chin and hands, and holes in her pants revealed bleeding skin on her knees. "Tamiel," she said, her voice clear and confident, "put down the phone. You know what I can do to you."

"And what *I* can do to *you*." He slid one step back. "Don't take me for a fool. Self-preservation is the strongest of instincts. You are wise enough to stay away."

"Wise or foolish, I'll let others judge that." Lauren resumed her confident march.

"Lauren!" Matt sprinted to her and grabbed her shoulders. "I know what you're trying to do, and I can't let you."

"This isn't your choice." She caressed his cheek. Her eyes sparkled on her battle-weary face. "I love you, Matt. You're the best brother a girl could ever ask for."

Tamiel pointed at them. "Arramos, if you would be so kind. Kill them both. Sapphira will collect the key from his charred body."

"My pleasure." Arramos reared his head back. When he whipped it forward, fire blasted forth from his mouth and nostrils. Sapphira slung a flaming ball that plunged into the orange flow, diverting it into the sky.

Matt pulled Lauren to a crouch. "Stay low!"

Sapphira heaved ball after ball. After the fourth one, considerably weaker than the others, Lauren broke free and crawled toward Tamiel. Matt scrambled after her, grasping at her ankles, but she kept jerking loose.

"Get away!" Tamiel shouted, now backpedaling quickly.

Lauren continued crawling under the barrage of flames. "In your dreams."

Just as Sapphira launched a fireball directly at Arramos's face, Lauren leaped up and ran at Tamiel.

"Lauren!" Matt shouted. "Don't!"

Tamiel set a finger over the phone's screen. "Let the billions die!"

Darcy lunged, snatched the phone from Tamiel, and slid on the grass, the phone in her hand.

Lauren never slowed. Her eyes fixed on Tamiel, she broke into a sprint.

Tamiel turned and ran. "Master! Rescue me!"

Arramos beat his wings and launched from the ground. Just before Lauren caught up with Tamiel, Arramos grabbed him and lifted him into the air, inches away from Lauren's lunging grasp.

"You coward!" Lauren shouted, her eyes following their flight. "Are you scared of a girl?"

Arramos orbited several feet overhead in a tight circle. "Your taunting is useless," Tamiel called as he dangled from the dragon's rear claws. "I am not a gullible fool."

Lauren stood underneath them, pivoting as she watched their orbit. "Maybe you aren't gullible, but a dragon who jumps to obey your every command certainly is. It looks like you're the master, and he's the slave."

"We work together." Tamiel spread out his arms. "He needs me to help him eliminate mankind."

Matt jogged to Lauren. Her verbal attack was brilliant, but dangerous. Arramos's ego had already been damaged. "You'd better cool it," he whispered. "He's liable to—"

"Arramos needs you?" Lauren laughed, her stare still locked on the flight path. "Arramos, the mighty dragon, needs a pipsqueak like you?"

"He is mighty, to be sure," Tamiel said, "but he needs my ingenuity. Who else could have come up with this brilliant plan to open the seventh door?"

Arramos roared. "I have had enough of your self-inflating ego! My own plan is sufficient." He opened his claws. Tamiel fell and landed in Lauren's outstretched arms.

She wrestled him to the ground. Holding his hands in hers, she pressed her cheek against his. Fire erupted over Tamiel's body and spread over Lauren.

344

Matt dove and pried Lauren free. He rolled with her in the grass, batting away the flames. When they stopped, he rose to his knees and laid her on her back. Breathing heavily, he straddled her and looked her over. The flames had been snuffed. They couldn't have done much damage. She would be all right.

He blew a few ashes from her face. "Lauren? Can you hear me?"

She blinked at him, her skin ghostly pale. "Is … is Tamiel dead?"

Matt looked toward Tamiel. The demon's body twitched in death throes and continued burning. As if prompted by the death of their master, the drones lifted into the sky and flew lazily away. Well beyond Tamiel, Arramos flew back and forth, spewing some kind of thick liquid from his mouth. The fluid landed on the grass in a series of dark swaths. After a few seconds, he lifted higher into the air and soared out of sight.

Matt caressed Lauren's cheek. "He's dead. You killed him."

"Good." She held a hand over his. "And now I'm going to die."

"What? No, no. I put out the fire. You're fine."

She shook her head. "I can feel my life draining. I think I ..." Her eyelids fluttered. "I have only a few seconds left."

"How can that be? You just—"

She set a finger on his lips. "It's time ... time to say good-bye, dear brother." Her faltering voice weakened to a bare whisper. "I hope to see you ... in Heaven someday. Please tell Mom and Dad that I love them ... and ... and good-bye."

Matt swallowed hard. Tears flowed. "I ... I can't say good-bye. I just can't."

"Then ..." She winced briefly. "Then will you kiss me good night?"

"Kiss you?"

She nodded. Her face paler than ever, she raised a trembling hand and touched her furrowed brow.

Matt brushed back her blood-matted bangs and kissed her softly on the forehead. When he lifted away, she smiled. "Good night, Matt. ... I love you ... and ... I'll see you in the morning."

Her eyes closed, and her head lolled to the side.

345

22

CHAPTER

To Open or
Not to Open

L auren?" Matt set a finger against her throat. No heartbeat. No
breathing. "Lauren!"

He set the heels of his hands on her chest and pushed—once,
twice, three times. "Darcy! Help me do CPR! I need a breather!"

Darcy ran to them and knelt at Lauren's side. "What do I do?"

He continued pumping at a rapid rate. "Tilt her head back…
Breathe into her mouth … twice … every time I stop." After the
thirtieth pump, he lifted away. "Now!"

Darcy tilted Lauren's head back, set her lips around hers, and
blew once, then inhaled and blew again. Lauren's chest rose with
each attempt, but when Darcy leaned back, the motion stopped.

"Get Sapphira over here," Matt said as he continued pumping
Lauren's chest.

Darcy turned on her knees and shouted, "Sapphira! We need
your help!"

While counting to thirty again, Matt gazed at Lauren's face—motionless, tinted blue, no sign of blood flow. No sign of life.

When Sapphira arrived, she knelt on Lauren's other side. "How can I help?"

"You're an Oracle of Fire. Can you see anything I can't?" Matt lifted away. "It's time to breathe again."

Sapphira blocked Darcy with a hand. "Let me." She bent low and pressed her lips against Lauren's. She inhaled through her nose and exhaled slowly through her mouth. As Lauren's chest rose again, Sapphira closed her eyes. She inhaled again, this time with her mouth, drawing out what she had just exhaled, making Lauren's chest sink.

As Sapphira straightened, she sighed, tears evident as she turned toward Matt. "Lauren is gone. Her soul is no longer there. You won't be able to revive her."

348

"No." Matt shook his head. "No, I have to keep trying." He set his hands on Lauren's chest again and began pumping. "She was fine ..." His throat tightened, pitching his voice higher. "She didn't burn. She barely got singed. She has to revive. She just has to."

Sapphira grabbed his arm, stopping him. "Matt. ... Don't. ... It's over."

Matt stared at her. As tears dripped to his cheeks, Sapphira raised a glowing hand and caressed his face with a warm palm. "Fear not, Matt. The Lord will carry her safely home."

"The Lord?" Matt rose to his feet and backed away, pointing at Lauren. "The Lord let *this* happen! She's my sister! He let my sister die!"

Darcy sprang up and grasped his arm. "She gave her life willingly to save the world. You would have done the same. We all would have. Sacrifice is what love is all about."

"Don't give me that!" Matt jerked away. "What would a prostitute know about love?"

Darcy's lips thinned out. "I know enough about love to ignore what you just said to me."

"Whatever!" Matt turned and staggered several steps away. His heart pounded, aching worse than any stab wound. Thoughts scrambled. Lauren was dead. *Dead!* His dear sister! After only a few precious moments with her, she had been ripped away from his arms, all because of that foul demon. She was so courageous, so loving. She didn't want anyone else to suffer at Tamiel's hands.

Matt gritted his teeth. And now how did her stupid brother respond to Darcy? Like a bitter fool who stabbed wildly at someone who didn't deserve it. That dark shadow was still in his soul, a demon of his own that even Lauren's love couldn't cast out.

He turned slowly toward Darcy and Sapphira, both now standing next to Lauren's body. "I'm sorry." He brushed tears from both eyes. "I was stupid. I acted like an idiot, and … and I'm sorry."

Darcy walked straight to him and embraced him. "I forgive you, Matt." She pulled back and clutched the lapels of his open jacket. "We'll get through this together. If you'll let me be your sister again, I'll do better. I promise."

"My sister?" The demonic shadow loomed again. *She wants to replace Lauren? A prostitute replace someone so pure, so holy? No. She couldn't. Impossible.*

Matt brushed away the thoughts and took in a deep cleansing breath. "Thank you, Darcy. I appreciate it."

An engine roared, closing in quickly. Seconds later, the Mustang barreled into the yard, slinging dirt. Before it came to a full stop, two doors flew open. Mom jumped from the car and flew toward Lauren. "Lauren! Are you all right?"

349

Dad leaped out, raised an automatic rifle to his shoulder, and swung it around, apparently searching for a target. When Mom landed at Lauren's side, she knelt and wept. Her body rocked in heaving spasms. "Lauren! ... My baby! ... Oh, dear God, why is she dead?" She sucked in a halting breath and cried on. "If only ... if only we hadn't taken ... so long to get here! If only ... she had waited for us!"

Matt shuffled slowly toward them. How could he comfort anyone, especially a grieving mother? His own heart had already been shredded. "Dad!" he shouted. "Arramos and Tamiel are gone. Mom needs you."

Dad ran toward them, still holding the rifle. "I'm coming!"

Matt stopped. Better to let him provide comfort, at least for now. He gave Darcy a light nudge with his elbow. "Do you ..." He swallowed, but his throat stayed tight. "Do you still have Tamiel's phone?"

"Right here." She withdrew it from her pocket, her own tears evident as she spoke with a shaky voice. "I was trying to check to see if he sent that message, but then ... you know."

"Did you look at the sent messages?"

She nodded. "Nothing there at all. Maybe he doesn't save them. Some kind of security setting."

The phone chimed. A message icon flashed on the screen. Darcy tapped it and read the message out loud. "Command acknowledged. Taking Russian missile verification to president. Expect full arsenal launch within the hour."

"Quick! Send a countermand! Tell him to stand down!"

"You do it." Darcy pushed the phone into his hand. "I wouldn't know what to say."

A flatbed truck rumbled into view. When it stopped between the remains of two houses, Elam jumped out and sprinted into the circle.

A giant man, presumably Yereq, leaped off the bed and lumbered behind him. Elam ran to Sapphira and gathered her into his arms.

Matt focused on the phone again and scanned the screen. Where was the New Message button? Ah. There. When he tapped the button, a text box popped up—Enter Password.

"What?" He stared at the request. "Why would he protect sending but not receiving?"

Darcy shrugged. "I guess he didn't care who read incoming stuff as long as no one could send a command in his name."

"How could we possibly guess his password?"

She took the phone back. "I'll try some guesses, like the one he said would unlock the seventh address."

"I don't remember it. My brain feels empty."

"I do. It's Lucifer backwards." Darcy punched it in. "Nope. I'll keep trying. Maybe search his body for a note. Since he was wearing flame-retardant clothes, something in his pocket could have survived." A new tear followed a track down her cheek. "You should go to your parents. Someone needs to tell them what happened."

At Lauren's body, Mom and Dad knelt together on one side, Mom with her hands covering her face, Dad with an arm around her.

"You're right." Matt jogged toward them, passing Tamiel's remains. Smoke curled up from his clothes. A misshapen skull and skeletal hands protruded from his shirt, all scorched. It seemed strange that a demonic spirit would have a body at all, much less one that remained visible after being burned to a crisp.

When he drew near, Mom looked up. She stretched out her arm as if begging for a morsel of bread. Matt ran the rest of the way, knelt on Lauren's opposite side, and slid his hand into Mom's.

"What ..." Tears pouring down her grief-ravaged face, Mom caressed Lauren's hand, a thumb rubbing the red gem in her ring.

"What happened, Matt?" She sucked in a breath and stared at him, her body shaking in time with suppressed sobs.

"She gave her life to save us all." While he told the story, the others began gathering around—Elam and Sapphira and Yereq. An old gray bus marked County Prison rattled down the driveway and rolled into the grassy yard. When it stopped, Walter and Ashley emerged and hurried to join them. Seconds later, Mariel got out of the bus and guided Thomas their way.

Soon, everyone congregated around Lauren's corpse. Bits and pieces of several stories passed from mouth to ear until everyone heard all the details, including how they found shelter for the former prisoners. Now Gabriel waited with Roxil, who was slowly recovering, and because of her improvement, when Walter and Ashley came along in the bus, Mariel and Thomas decided to ride to the prison with them.

When Ashley noticed the words etched on the seventh door, she told of her journey with Walter down a seemingly endless staircase that led to Sapphira's abode. All along the way, Dante's eerie phrase was engraved in Italian in the staircase walls. Larry had translated it based on an entry in a reference work, though she later learned that the work's English rendering was slightly off. This new etching translated it properly. She then theorized that a similar journey might await anyone who passed through the door.

Elam related his story about having to leave Makaidos and Thigocia behind while he hitchhiked with Yereq. The flatbed truck driver, a seventysomething war veteran, showed no fear of Yereq. In fact, he seemed thrilled to rekindle a bit of excitement in his life. After a conversation-filled drive of many miles, Elam dropped him off in a small town nearby and promised to make arrangements to get the truck back to him.

When everyone finished their summaries, including a word of concern about the recently departed drones, Darcy crouched next to Matt and slid the phone into his hand. "Nothing I tried works. I searched Tamiel's clothes and found a scrap of paper, but the numbers on it didn't work either." She displayed a wrinkled strip of paper pinched between her finger and thumb. "I tried it forwards, backwards, and scrambled a couple of ways. It's useless."

"Then the missiles are going to launch. Lauren didn't stop Tamiel from starting a war." Matt forced a lower tone to keep from squeaking. "Her sacrifice was in vain."

"Matt," Walter said, extending a hand. "Give me the phone and the paper. I'll try to patch into Larry and see if he can help."

Matt handed them over. "Think it's encrypted?"

"That's one possibility. If anyone can decrypt it, Larry can."

"Larry's back online?" Elam asked.

Walter began tapping the phone's screen. "Full speed, secure, and as painfully witty as ever. Ashley called Lois from the shelter and heard the news. Carly's fine, too. She and Lois are holed up in a warehouse somewhere in West Virginia." His brow arched. "Ah! I can make a call. Just no access to sending text messages."

353

While Walter worked on the password with Ashley and Larry, Matt drew his mother's hand close and kissed her knuckles. "Lauren said to tell you she loves you." He nodded at Dad. "Both of you."

"Those were her last words?" Dad asked.

"Not exactly." Her dying voice flowed to mind as if she were whispering at this moment. Matt bit his lip hard. It would take every ounce of restraint to deliver this message without breaking into sobs. "She said … 'I'll see you in the morning.'"

Mom drew her hand away and began crying anew. Dad rubbed her back and spoke softly into her ear.

"I have a solution," Thomas called from somewhere in the gathering.

Matt perked his head up. "The password?"

"No, no. I'll wager that no one will guess that." Thomas stepped closer, guided by Mariel. "I know a way to stop the missile launches and perhaps resurrect Lauren, both by the same method."

"You do?" Matt shot to his feet. "How?"

"According to those who can see, the solution is right before your eyes."

Mariel swatted him, her red eyes afire. "This is the worst time to play games." She waved a hand toward the seventh door. "Thomas says if you open the door and release the locusts, they will terrorize the people. No one will be able to launch the missiles."

"Tamiel mentioned something like that," Matt said, "but can the locusts get to Washington that fast?"

Thomas shook his head. "Washington is not the issue. The U.S. would be more likely to launch their ground-based missiles, because they are the most vulnerable to the supposed Russian attack. The submarine arsenal is hidden, so they are safe. This is merely a guess, of course. I have very little knowledge of nuclear defense procedures."

Matt nodded. "Well, a lot of the ground-based missiles are in this area; the locusts won't have far to go to disrupt the launches if the command centers are close by."

"What about Lauren?" Mom asked. "How would releasing the locusts resurrect her?"

Thomas turned toward the door, apparently guided by his sensory abilities. "Supposedly the seventh door leads to Abaddon's Lair. That is the realm of resurrections, though perhaps it is presumptuous to assume that God would guide Lauren's spirit there when so few have been chosen for resurrection. Still, an extraordinarily high percentage of Bonnie's relations have been so chosen,

I assume because of the prophecies surrounding her life and purpose, so maybe instead it would be presumptuous to assume that Lauren *wouldn't* go to Abaddon's Lair."

"Enoch said as much." Mom brushed away more tears. "One problem. Resurrected souls on Second Eden acquired a new body from the soils of the birthing garden, but resurrections here always had the dead body around, like with Lazarus and me and Billy." She lifted Lauren's limp hand. "Do you think we would have to carry her body into Abaddon's Lair?"

"Most likely," Thomas said. "It would be tragic to go there without her body and find out upon arrival that you need it. Besides, so far I have noted many close parallels with your journey through the circles of seven. This appears to be yet another. You died in the sixth circle. Lauren died at the sixth door. Billy carried you to the seventh circle. Now someone must carry Lauren through the seventh door."

355

"And here's another problem," Ashley said as she stepped closer, Tamiel's phone in hand. "I synched Larry, but he can't break in. He tried more than a thousand combinations of the number string. Larry believes the numbers have a pattern that suggests geographic coordinates instead of a password."

"Coordinates?" Matt reached toward Walter. "Let me see those numbers."

Walter gave him the scrap. "Larry says if they're coordinates, they point to a spot in the middle of the Indian Ocean."

Matt searched the numbers for... Yes, *4403* was there in the middle of the string. "They're Second Eden coordinates. Semiramis told me she put a deadly device in Second Eden, and she baited me with a string of numbers that were part of the coordinates. I thought it was just a ploy to get me to let her go, but I guess she was telling the truth."

"So we have to send a message to Second Eden." Walter took the paper. "We'll get Larry to work on it."

Matt inhaled deeply. Maybe Lauren didn't die in vain after all. If she hadn't killed Tamiel, they never would have found his note.

Ashley lifted the phone to her ear. "I have some good news. Larry spoke a coded message. Jared and Marilyn have been home. They're working on some kind of secret project, but Larry didn't want to risk giving the details. He just said they need transportation, so if we have a spare dragon, they'd appreciate it if we sent one their way."

"Check this out." Darcy pointed at a dark spot on the grass. "Arramos was spraying something here. It really stinks."

Dad limped over and crouched next to the blackened blades. "Male dragons have a scent gland they use as a marker."

"Enoch said the drones are trained to follow a scent," Mom said. "It's a good bet they'll be back."

356

"No use wasting time." Matt unhooked the key ring and looped it over his fingers. He then slid his arms under Lauren and lifted her. "I'm going through the seventh door."

"So am I." Dad straightened, wincing with the effort. "Bonnie, you and the others can go with Elam and Sapphira back to Second Eden to warn them about the device. The portal isn't very far and—"

"Dad, I can't let you go with me."

He cocked his head. "Why not?"

"Supposedly there's a bottomless pit behind the door. An abyss. Tamiel called it the forever fall. It's too dangerous. You need to be with Mom."

Mom rose and touched Dad's arm. "He's right. We should both go."

"We are wasting time," Thomas said. "Open the door and release the locusts. Otherwise it will be too late to do any good. Then you can look inside and decide who should go."

"He's right." Matt carried Lauren to the door. With broken vines framing the arch, a lock twice the size of a man's hand, and the eerie words spelling out a fearsome warning, the door seemed more formidable than ever.

"My mother has to open the lock. According to Tamiel, she's a star fallen from Heaven or something like that."

Mom took the key ring from his fingers. "I suppose we have no choice." When she grasped the melded key, the colors pulsed like a luminescent heartbeat. "I dreamed about these colors. Each of the seven ovula had one of them, but yellow is missing. All seven were necessary for the complete purity of the eighth ovulum."

"The lock is yellow," Matt said, "so it must be the last piece of the puzzle. Maybe you being the eighth ovulum is the reason you're the only one who can use the key."

She turned a tiny knob above the keyhole. When a blocking plate slid out of the way, she pushed the key into the lock. Her facial muscles straining, she grunted, but the key didn't turn in either direction. "According to the dreams I had about the colors, yellow stands for patience. I suppose that means we have to wait."

Matt shifted Lauren again. An urge to complain about the loss of time seemed overwhelming, but that might work against the whole patience idea. He shoved the urge away and stayed quiet.

Leaving the key in the lock, Mom stepped back. "While we're waiting …" She slid a beaded necklace up over her head and put it on Lauren. Now draped over Lauren's chest, the beads glowed, each with an individual color. As Mom fingered a yellow one, she blinked through a new cascade of tears. "I suppose we'll see if these beads really have resurrection power."

Soon, the yellow in the lock bled toward the key, turning the lock gray. The key ceased pulsing and slowly faded to transparency.

"It's invisible," Matt said.

"Just like the purity ovulum." Mom felt for the key, grasped it, and turned it. The lock clicked, and the curved shank popped up from the body. She shook the lock away from the chains, withdrew the key, and set the ring over Matt's fingers.

"When you are ready," Yereq said, "I will open it. It is better that I risk any initial danger."

Matt hiked Lauren's body higher and stepped back from the threshold. Now all that remained was to pull the rings and see what lay behind the mysterious letters—Abandon All Hope Ye Who Enter Here.

He nodded at the seventh door. "Open it."

23

THE ABYSS

Yereq grabbed a ring on each door, set his feet, and heaved. The doors gave way and swung open. Blinding radiance poured forth, a wave of pure light. Yereq ducked and jogged out of the burst of energy. Smoke followed in a billowing stream and intermixed with the light.

Matt backed away and readjusted his hold on Lauren. The sky darkened. Gloom settled over the yard. Soon, the stream of smoke stopped, and ashy particles gathered into individual clouds, fist-sized puffs that hovered in place, growing brighter and brighter. They slowly morphed into winged insects that emitted a deafening buzz.

One of the insects, an especially noisy one about two feet tall, flew closer to Matt and floated in front of his eyes, as if examining him with a probing gaze. This "locust" had a human torso, arms, and head, as well as an equine body and legs. A crown on its head, waist-length hair flowed around its body, and a long tail with a stinger at the end twitched as if ready to strike.

More locusts descended and buzzed around Mom, Dad, and the others. As the insects pulsed with light, they stared with reflective compound eyes.

The first locust slapped his breastplate, making a flesh-on-metal sound. With a louder buzz, it flew slowly back. The others followed, and the entire mass of clattering insects hovered in place. Numbering in the thousands, they faced the door as if waiting for something else to emerge.

A growl erupted from the dark opening, growing closer and closer. A dragon's head appeared, then its long neck and body. Sleek and black, this dragon looked more powerful than Makaidos or even Arramos. The locusts chattered wildly, as if cheering the dragon's arrival.

"Abaddon!" Mom took a step toward him. "I'm so glad you're here. My daughter died, and I was wondering if—"

360

"If I would raise her from the dead." Fire spewed from Abaddon's nostrils. "Your grief has addled your brain and made you overly presumptuous. I do not make such decisions."

Mom just stared at him, her mouth hanging open.

"What? Agape at an absence of alliteration? Astonished at an avoidance of amicability?" He set his snout in front of her face. "As I warned you, I have changed. I am not the dragon who played word games with you in the depths of the valley. I am now the dread angel of the abyss, and I must fly with my horde to bring wrath to those who rebel against the Almighty, and because of certain circumstances, I will have to hurry if I am to quell the coming catastrophe. I have no time to spend chatting about the soul of yet another one of your relations."

"Leave her alone!" Matt yelled as he stepped closer. "Just tell me if it's possible to get to that domain of yours, and I'll look for Lauren's soul myself."

"Ah! The Bannister I rescued from a drone a few days ago. I see that you have Bonnie's boldness and bravado."

Matt growled. "Just tell me."

"It is possible to get there, but the way is harrowing. You are far more likely to die than to succeed, especially if you are carrying such, shall we say, deadweight."

"That's not funny." Matt took in a deep breath. "If Lauren's soul is there, how would I find her?"

"Search the statues, search the streams, rely on the residents, deliver their dreams." Abaddon set his snout close to Matt's ear and whispered, "If you go to my abode, I warn you, go alone. Carry Lauren's body with you if you must, but hear this word of promise. If two living humans go, one of them will die. And speak my name to the guardians. It is the only way to survive. One of those guardians will not respect my name, so you will have to use your wits to pass." He beat his wings and lifted into the air. The locusts swarmed around him, and they flew away at an incredible speed. The smoke broke apart and began to diminish.

361

Matt laid Lauren's body on the ground and reattached the key ring to his belt loop. "Someone watch her. I'm going to have a look inside."

"I'm coming with you," Dad said.

They walked side by side, Dad limping heavily, and stepped through the doorway. Daylight, though muted by the leftover smoke, provided a view of a huge circular pit, maybe fifty feet across that spanned all but a narrow ledge around the perimeter.

Matt stopped at the edge and looked down. A stiff breeze funneled up and swirled, creating a tight vortex that tossed his hair and clothes. Pulsing red light below illuminated the rocky cylinder. Shifting shadows made it look like ledges protruded here and there from the sheer wall and then drew back in, like darting tongues of rock. Other shadows teased of the possibility that a door or a narrow passage in the rock might create an exit for an expert climber, but every hole and ledge might be imaginary. "Looks almost impossible to scale."

"And Bonnie couldn't fly down there," Dad said. "She can handle some pretty rough winds, but not if they're spinning like that."

"Someone could rappel. The wind doesn't affect a rope climber that much."

"True, but a climber could go down only so far. We'd never find enough rope to explore everywhere. It looks thousands of feet deep."

Matt pointed at one of the larger shadows that appeared for a moment then vanished. "That could be a hole of some kind. Maybe Yereq could lower me that far with a rope."

"Lower *you?*" Dad shook his head, laughing under his breath. "Oh, no. You're not going."

"But you're crippled. You can't rappel with broken toes. I'm not in the greatest shape, but I'm self healing. I'll be fine soon."

"Lauren's my daughter. She's my responsibility."

"What about *my* responsibility?" Matt pressed a thumb against his chest. "If I had been quicker, I could've stopped her from grabbing Tamiel. It's my fault."

"She was bound and determined to give her life to kill Tamiel. No one could have stopped her." Dad laid a hand on Matt's shoulder. "Listen, Son. Your mother is already grief-stricken. Lauren's death probably crushed her song. If she loses you ..." He shook his head. "I don't know if she could survive."

"She could. Mom's strong. And besides, what if *you* die? That would be even worse. I can't comfort her like you can. I barely know her. You two were separated for fifteen years. I'm not about to let you leave her now."

"Not about to let me—" Dad cleared his throat. "It's not your decision. You'll stay here while Yereq lowers me with the rope, then—"

"Abaddon told me something."

Dad narrowed his eyes. "What?"

"Didn't you see him whisper in my ear? He told me a secret that'll get me past their guardians."

"Okay …" Dad dragged the toe of his shoe across the rocky floor. "Let's hear it."

Matt shook his head. "I can't. I mean, I won't."

"You won't?" Dad glanced back at Mom. She knelt next to Lauren, whispering with Sapphira. When he turned back to Matt, he spoke in a stern but calm voice. "I understand your feelings about this, but as your father, I demand that you—"

"Demand?" Matt pressed his lips together hard. The urge to yell at this man, this newly minted father who would pull parental rank on a son who was little more than a stranger, sent a hot shudder from head to toe. But he couldn't spout off. That would be like barking at the drill sergeant—rude, disrespectful, and worthless. "Give me a minute to think."

363

"Go ahead. I think we both need to cool off."

Matt pivoted toward the abyss. What could he do? Everyone would probably agree with Dad, that a teenager should give up his secrets and let the experienced warrior go on the dangerous journey. Yet, wasn't it love that motivated this warrior to make the demand? Of course it was. And maybe love held the key to convincing him to relent. But could a son who barely knew his father come up with the right words? Maybe, but it would take a dose of his mother's eloquence, the best key to his father's heart.

"Dad," Matt said as he turned around. "I'm sorry about getting so hot about this. You have every right to make demands of me, but I need to explain something." He wrapped his arms around his father and held him close. "You have a warrior's spirit, a heart of gold. There is no way you could ever let your son go on this dangerous journey, to take your rightful place as protector of your precious daughter. That is a father's duty. I understand that." He pushed back and looked into his father's misty eyes. "I inherited the same spirit, the same heart. I am a warrior. I love Mom, but you're the one who bonded with her, and I just met her a few days ago. She needs you a lot more than she needs me. You know it's true. Stay with her. Be her guardian. Remember, Arramos is still on the warpath, and she's bound to be one of his main targets. You can protect Mom a lot better than I can. Chances are, I won't be able to resurrect Lauren, but you can keep Mom alive. And if you die, she'll die inside. After fifteen years of waiting for the two of you to reunite, don't let that happen."

A tear trickled from Dad's eye. He sniffed and looked away, his voice cracking. "You are truly the son of your mother."

"Then will you ..." He dragged his shoe along the same line his father had. "Will you let me go?"

Dad refocused on Matt and nodded. "Let me break the news to your mother. I'll try to use some of your words, but it's better if they come from me."

Matt tried to smile, but his lips wouldn't move. The terror of the abyss ripped away any hint of satisfaction. "Let's see if we can find a rope."

For the next few minutes, Matt, Walter, Ashley, Elam, and Yereq hustled around in search of anything that might be of use for Matt's journey. At the bus's depot behind the prison fence, Yereq found a long rope and ripped away a crawl-space access door that could be used as a lowering platform. From the makeshift car, Walter retrieved a duffle bag containing a stash of weapons he had brought from the military prison in Arizona. Elam discovered an electrician's climbing harness, while Ashley pulled blankets from the only remaining house.

Since Thomas sensed a growing danger, Dad stood guard over the women while they worked on the harness and blankets to fashion a way for Matt to carry Lauren. Mom retrieved the flame-retardant cloak from her suitcase and padded the harness with it, saying he might need flame protection for a portal jump.

Matt used the prison's restroom facilities, drank plenty of water, and ate three snack bars. When they reconvened in front of the seventh door, Walter strapped a belt around Matt's waist and attached two semiautomatic pistols, four extra ammo magazines, two hand grenades, and a knife in a sheath. He also clipped a flashlight to a pants loop underneath the belt. When he finished, he slid the scrap of paper that contained the device coordinates into Matt's shirt pocket. "In case you get in touch with Second Eden before we do."

365

"Thanks." Matt adjusted the belt, taking note of a water bottle someone had slid into a pouch. Since the strap was too wide to pass through his pants' belt loops, the heavy load made the belt hang low, and the buckle seemed ready to pop loose. He would have to be careful.

Yereq held aloft a four-foot-by-four-foot board attached to a rope at the center. Ashley gave it a push, making it swing. "As you can see," she said, "it's going to take a lot of strength and skill to keep from falling, especially with Lauren strapped to your body, but it's better than just hanging on to a rope."

Sapphira and Darcy tied the harness around his abdomen and fastened it at his chest and waist. Mom looped a rope from his back, between his legs, and up to an attachment point at his chest, then tied it in place. "Is that all right?" Mom asked.

Matt pushed the rope to a comfortable spot. "Yeah. It's good."

"There's something I have to tell you before you go." She slid a finger behind a strap at his chest. "Sapphira told me some of the things you said when Lauren died."

"Yeah … well, I can explain that—"

"No need to explain. The Lord *did* let Lauren die. That's a fact."

"What then? Was I not supposed to get mad? She was my sister. If God let her die, then—"

"Shhh." Mom touched Matt's lips with a finger. "Just let me tell you what's on my mind."

Matt gave her an apologetic nod. "Sure. Go ahead."

"You lost your sister, and it broke your heart. It broke mine, too, and we're both sobbing in our souls. And no wonder. She was an amazing young woman. Even though we knew her for such a short time, she was more precious to us than any treasure." Mom bit her lip and swallowed hard a few times. A new tear slowly coursed down her cheek. "With all our grief, can you imagine what it would be like to lose someone you have loved and cherished for uncountable years? Can you imagine what it would be like to watch your son, your only son, die a cruel death at the hands of people who should have loved him?"

Matt looked into her eyes, seemingly alight with a flickering flame. Obviously this was going to be a Jesus talk, but that was fine. "No, I guess I can't imagine it."

"Neither can I." She inhaled deeply, as if gathering courage. "Matt, we don't have much time, so I have to be blunt. I hoped to tell you this in another way, but now I feel like I have to step up on a soapbox and preach a sermon. I hope you don't mind."

"No, Mom. You can say anything you want. I'm listening."

"Okay. Here goes." Mom slid her hand into Matt's. "God loves us so much, he allowed his only son to die for us on a cross. I'm

366

sure he watched in agony and suffered far more than we do over Lauren. But he let it happen anyway. Why? So something good would result, something so wondrous, it was worth the torture. Jesus died so we could spiritually die with him, so that the poison of sin could be purged from us, body and soul. And once we died, we could be resurrected to a new life, free from bondage to those evil things we couldn't purge ourselves, a life of liberty and life that casts away every shadow, even the most stubborn phantoms that once stalked us, wrapped us in chains, and never let us go."

Matt swallowed. A phantom? Yes, how well he knew the phantom, the one that kept injecting poison every time Darcy tried to heal the rift between them. He glanced at her, but she had walked several steps away, her back turned. "So … um … how does it happen? … I mean, how does a person die like that?"

"By faith." She pressed a hand against his chest. "From the depths of your heart, soul, and mind, you have to believe in God and what he has done for you, turn away from your sins, and surrender to Jesus. Reject hate and embrace love—love for God, love for others, especially for …" Mom's face twisted into a mournful mask. "Especially for …"

367

"Especially for Darcy." Matt nodded. "That's my phantom. I understand that. But I've tried to get rid of it, and I can't. I just can't."

"I know. I know." Tears flowing, Mom took his hands and ran a finger along each palm. "He bled for you, Matt. People who hated Jesus drove nails into his hands. Yet he forgave every repentant soul, even those who were once his enemies." She kissed the heel of his hand and whispered, "That's real love. And real love forgives. There is no need to hold on to pain and bitterness. Jesus can set you free."

His own tears welling as he looked into her eyes, Matt enfolded her hands in his. "Thanks, Mom. I'll be thinking about it. I promise." He lifted his brow. "Pray for me?"

"With all my heart." She pulled back, her chin quivering. "I guess you'd better go."

He kissed her knuckles. "I'm ready."

Yereq picked Lauren up and hoisted her high enough to let her slide feet first into the harness. While Ashley tapped on Tamiel's phone, the other women worked on strapping Lauren securely to Matt's back.

When they finished, Ashley slid the phone into one of Matt's pockets. "I programmed it to use the frequency for our tower in Second Eden. If you manage to get there, maybe it will help. Also, your mother wrote an electronic note that explains how to translate the resurrection book. If you find Abaddon's table, look for the book, a glass egg, and a vial. If those are all there, then you're good to go. Her note is on the screen right now. The battery's almost fully charged, so it should last a long time."

Matt shrugged to get Lauren to slide down a bit. When her body shifted into place, he nodded. "Got it."

After a tearful round of good-byes, Matt walked to the abyss. Yereq stood there, his feet set wide apart next to a coil of rope and his two powerful hands clutching the fibrous line. Several paces behind him, the rope led to the Mustang where he had attached the end to the front bumper.

At the other end, the platform dangled a foot or so below the pit's edge. For some reason, the flat slab of wood seemed familiar. Probably nothing. Just a bout of déjà vu.

With everyone watching from a few steps away, Matt turned toward them and gave them a weak smile. Mom folded her hands as if in prayer, her arm curled around Dad's. Dad offered an affirming nod. Walter pumped a fist. Darcy drew the closest and blew a kiss.

Matt dropped to all fours and grabbed the rope. As he scooted backwards toward the platform, Lauren's weight dragged him down until he set his feet firmly on the board, one at each side of the rope.

"Let me know when you have your balance," Yereq said, "and I will begin lowering you."

Matt shifted his weight from one foot to the other. The board teetered but not too much. This was definitely doable. "Okay. Slow and easy, Yereq. I want to look for exits on the way down."

"Call if the descent is too fast."

The platform lowered. As Matt dropped with it, his chest and head descended below the pit's lip. As light grew dimmer and reddish, only Yereq's bearded face stayed in view.

Matt looked at the surrounding wall—rugged stone at this level, no sign of holes or tunnels, though below, the pulsing radiance continued painting shadows, then erased the dark silhouettes and painted them again. The spinning wind constantly pushed him to the side, but his weight combined with Lauren's kept them from flying around.

369

When he reached a depth of about thirty feet, a rocky ledge fell open to his right, like a castle's drawbridge dropping over a moat. Above the protrusion, a low recess led into darkness. "Yereq! Hold it there!"

The rope stopped. As Matt reached for the ledge, his danger sense heightened. Something terrible lurked nearby, but not in this pit. It seemed to come from above.

"Yereq? What's going on up there?"

"The sky is filling with creatures Darcy calls drones." Yereq looked away, though he remained visible from chest to head. "There are hundreds of them. They will be upon us in seconds."

"Then pull me up. Quick."

A dark-winged beast leaped onto Yereq and sank fangs into his neck. Yereq let go of the rope with one hand and swatted the drone away. The platform dropped a foot. Matt nearly tumbled off. He set a hand on the ledge and steadied himself, but the rocky protrusion lifted, forcing him to let go. It then sealed the opening with a crackling thud.

Yereq reset his grip and began reeling Matt upward, "Drones are chewing the rope!"

Shouts and demonic squeals streamed from above. Only twenty feet to go.

Yereq vanished under a blanket of beating wings. The rope slipped from his hands. Something snapped. Matt plunged, clutching the useless line. Then, the descent slowed. A wild scream erupted from above, a woman in horrible pain. Had the drones attacked Mom? Sapphira?

Matt replanted his feet on the platform. A new stony projection opened at eye level. He grabbed it with one hand and brought the drop to a halt. Now about a hundred feet below the surface, he looked up. Darcy lay prostrate. Half of her abdomen jutted over the edge of the abyss, her arms straight down and her hands desperately holding the rope.

More hot air blew from below and swirled past. Hadn't he dreamed this exact scene? Didn't Darcy let him fall, laughing as he plunged? What could it all mean?

A sudden gust slammed the platform and Matt's hip against the wall. The belt flew loose and fell into the abyss, taking the weapons and water with it. The wood cracked and broke into pieces.

Matt held to the rope, set his feet against the wall, and clutched the ledge with straining fingers. He couldn't swing up to it, not with Lauren's body adding extra weight. "Hang on, Darcy!"

"I'm trying." Her throaty cry pierced the dark pit. "Matt! I can't hold on much longer!"

Explosions boomed somewhere above. More shouts rang out, angry and warlike.

He released the ledge and grabbed the rope with both hands. "I'm trying to … get to this hole … before it closes." Straining with all his might, he climbed hand over hand to the opening's level, his feet stepping up the wall. With a leg thrust, he pushed off and swung toward the ledge. The moment his feet landed, Darcy screamed. The rope reeled downward.

A stretched-out call zoomed at him from above. "Matt!" Darcy plummeted past him, the rope still in her hands.

"Wrap it around your waist and hang on!" He dropped to his stomach, twisted the rope around his wrists, and pulled his sleeves over his hands. The projection began to rise. Matt slid backwards into the darkness as if being swallowed. The rope twanged and jerked him forward. The force nearly pulled his hands from their sockets, and the rope cut into his palms in spite of the protective sleeves, but the projection's angle kept him from being slung into the void with Darcy.

The "drawbridge" slowly lowered again. Gasping for breath as he hung on, Matt belly-crawled to the edge. Below, crisscrossing shadows seemed to jab a dangling human form as it swayed in the cyclonic updraft.

"Darcy!" Matt battled for breath. His hands and wrists burned. "Can you hear me?"

A shaky "yes" floated up from the void.

"Is the rope around your waist?"

Another weak "yes" rode the hot rising air.

"Hang on." Matt pushed up to his knees, lifting Lauren and pulling Darcy at the same time. Biceps screamed. Sweat poured. His palms grew slick, but he held on. Failure was not an option.

With a thrust, he planted one foot on the projection's floor, then pushed up to the other. Both hands still gripping the rope, he backed up, step by step, grunt after grunt. His leg muscles ached, but they gave relief to his arms as he labored through the torturous reverse march.

When he reached the opening in the pit's wall, he walked onto the drawbridge again, pulling the rope along the way, then trudged backwards once more. After repeating the process several times, Darcy's head appeared. She threw an arm over the ledge, then the other.

Matt lunged and grabbed Darcy under her arms. With Lauren pressing down on his back, he summoned every remaining ounce of strength, heaved Darcy onto the ledge, and helped her crawl into the recess.

With their weight removed from the projection, it lifted and shut them in. Pressure crushing his lungs, Matt unclipped the flashlight from his belt loop and flicked it on. At least that had stayed put when the belt snapped, as did the phone in his pocket. The flashlight slipped from his numb fingers and spun on the ground. As the beam arced, its radiant circle illuminated the walls of a small cave.

Darcy sprawled on her stomach and clawed at the stony floor, groaning. Matt lowered himself to his side next to her and let Lauren's body rest. He gasped for air, but his lungs wouldn't draw it in. Too much strain. Too tired to inflate. His head pounding, he turned over a little to put more weight on Lauren. Something released in his chest, and air slowly seeped in.

After nearly a minute, the pounding stopped. Air flowed easily. He reached out and slid his hand into Darcy's. His fingers touched something warm and moist. Sweat, maybe? "Are you all right?"

"I ... I think so. I just hurt my palms while holding the rope."

She pulled her hand away and pushed up to her knees. Her dirty, wet shirt clung to her abdomen. "Are you?"

"Yeah." He slid his arms out of the harness, unhooked the groin loop, and knelt upright. "What happened? I saw the drones attack Yereq, but that's all."

"Those things were everywhere." Darcy pushed sweat-dampened hair from her forehead and sat down. "Sapphira blasted them with fire while your father and Walter carried Thomas and Mariel to the Mustang and shut them inside. Then they shot the drones with rifles and even threw hand grenades, and your dad blasted fire at them. All that stuff worked for a while, but they just kept coming and coming, clawing and biting. Anyone they bit just collapsed in a heap."

She sucked in a long breath. "When Yereq let go of the rope, I was the closest, so I just leaped for it and hung on."

"I'm glad you did." He rose and pushed on the projection, now tightly closed, but it wouldn't budge. "I don't think I have the strength to open it. I guess I could put Lauren back on again, and our combined weights might dislodge it, but I can barely move."

"Rest a while. Maybe it'll open up again on its own."

"Good thought." Matt sat cross-legged in front of her, grasped her wrists, and turned her hands up. Bloodstained rope burns cut deep gashes in her palms. Like a firebrand, the image burned in his mind, and Mom's words returned, reverberating like a distant echo.

He bled for you ... bled for you ... bled for you.
Real love forgives ... forgives ... forgives.
Jesus can set you free ... set you free ... set you free.

When the voice died away, he whispered, "How much does it hurt?"

She flexed her hands and winced. "It's pretty awful. I think one of the cuts goes to the bone."

"Maybe I should try to heal you."

She pulled her hands away. "I'll be all right." Her head drooped. "I mean, it didn't work before."

Matt gazed at her sorrowful pose—shoulders slumped, head low, blood and sweat smeared over nearly every inch of bare skin. She had been so heroic, so sacrificial. Once again she risked her life to save his, asking no questions, expecting no rewards. And now? Now she probably just hoped the pain would go away, untouched by his clumsy hands.

More words returned to mind, this time Enoch's, as if spoken by the prophet himself. *You have healing hands that will seal horrific wounds ... your touch will be of no use unless all barriers to love are broken. If there is the slightest stain of contempt for your patient, love will be squelched, and your touch will be nothing more than the abrasive scrape of a hardened callous.*

374

Matt bit his lip. Tears welled. As images flashed of Darcy hanging on to the rope while drones attacked her vulnerable body, it seemed that the rope binding his heart unraveled and plunged into the void, pulling a dark phantom with it. "Darcy ..." He carefully lifted her hands with his fingers. "Darcy, I need to tell you something."

She raised her head and looked into his eyes. Blood dripped from her hand wounds and pooled in his palms, intermixing with his own blood. "Yes?"

He swallowed. "I hated you for so many years, I couldn't—"

"For good reason. I was a real—"

"Shhh." He leaned his forehead against hers. Their noses nearly touched. "I know what you *were*. I wouldn't let you be who you *are*. I guess I'm saying that I couldn't forgive you. I should have, but I didn't. And now I'm saying that I do … forgive you, I mean." He drew back and gazed into her eyes, twin orbs sparkling in the flashlight's glow. "Will you forgive me?"

"Oh, Matt! I do! I do!" She rocked forward and threw her arms around his neck. "I'm so sorry! I'm so, so sorry! If I had been a decent sister—"

"What's done is done." He grasped her wrists and gently pushed her back. "It's time to stop the bleeding." He turned her palms up and set her hands on her lap. "Will you trust me?"

She nodded. Tears dripped to her cheeks. "Do whatever you need to do."

Matt laid his palms over hers and pressed down. His skin heated up. Darcy grimaced but stayed quiet. Soon, she began humming a familiar melody.

" 'Amazing Grace,' " Matt said.

She stopped. "Is that all right?"

"Perfect. Keep it up."

Smiling, she continued humming, this time louder. As the tune echoed in the tiny chamber, Matt added words. "Amazing grace, how sweet the sound that saved a wretch like me." His throat caught. He couldn't force out another word. But that was all right. He had said all he needed to say.

After a few minutes, Matt lifted his hands. Red stripes still crossed Darcy's palms. "Maybe a little more—"

"No, Dr. Bannister. I'm fine. Look." She brushed her hands together. Dried blood crumbled and drizzled to her lap. "You healed me."

He glanced at his own palms. The cuts, shallower than Darcy's, had also healed.

375

"Thank you." She grabbed his shirt, pulled him close, and kissed him tenderly on the cheek. "I hope that's enough payment. I don't have any money."

He smiled. "A sister's kiss is worth a lot more than money."

"Speaking of sisters ..." Darcy nodded at Lauren. "Have you rested enough?"

"Right." Matt picked up the flashlight and fastened it to his belt loop. "We have to get out of here."

CHAPTER

THE BOTTOM
OF THE ABYSS

Darcy helped Matt refasten Lauren to his back. When they
finished, they pushed against the closed "drawbridge."
With each thrust, the lip budged a few inches, allowing Matt to
set a foot higher on the incline and push again. Soon, they were
able to crawl up the slope, and their combined weights eased the
projection down.

When it settled to its horizontal position, Matt rose and
stepped to the edge. Above, no one appeared at the top of the pit.
The sounds of battle had ceased, but who won? How many survived?

He shouted, "Can anyone hear me?" His words echoed once,
then faded. "Hello? Dad? Walter?"

Only the whoosh of the breeze replied.

Matt picked up the rope and studied the sheer wall and the distance to the top—much too far to climb or toss a loop, especially with no one to catch it. "Looks like we're stuck."

A car horn blared a short burst—once, twice, three times, then three longer bursts, then three short ones again. After a brief rest, it repeated the same pattern.

"That's an SOS in Morse code," Matt said.

"Must be Thomas and Mariel," Darcy said. "Maybe the drones are still around and Mariel's calling for help. They're afraid to get out of the car."

"Can't blame them for that. But if we could contact them, they might be able to find another rope and haul us out with the Mustang."

"No use wishing for two old folks to face those drones." Darcy shuddered. "I guess that sign on the door really meant what it said."

378

"Abandon all hope ye who enter here? It's from Dante's *Inferno*."

She nodded. "I've read it."

Matt looked at their little cave. "I didn't search for a way out the back side. It looked too low and narrow to get through, especially with Lauren on my back."

Darcy shrugged. "Can't hurt to look. This opening has to be here for some reason."

"If we move, this door will close, but I guess we can open it again." After retreating into the cave and removing Lauren from his back, Matt dropped to hands and knees and crawled deeper in. Although the ceiling angled lower, enough room remained for a belly crawl. Far away at the end of a dark tunnel, a glow flickered, dim but very real.

"I see a light." He crawled back and sat with Darcy. "I'll have to go first and drag Lauren after me. You can follow behind her and make sure she doesn't catch on anything and nothing scrapes her head and face."

"Will do."

For the next couple of minutes, Matt and Darcy tied the rope to Lauren's harness and legs, then tested it to make sure it would drag her feet first in a straight line. When they finished, Matt pumped his elbows in a crawling motion. "Just watch what I do and copy me."

Darcy nodded. "I get the picture. Go ahead."

"I'll give the line a sharp tug when I get to the end." Holding the rope in one hand, he squirmed into the tunnel. As the passage tightened, he lowered himself to his stomach and slithered through. Of course he had done this a hundred times in training, but never after the kind of torture he had just suffered. And Darcy? She had suffered far worse; and she probably never army crawled in her life. This wouldn't be easy for her.

With every elbow push and leg thrust, the glow drew closer and brighter. After another minute, he pushed his head into a larger chamber, dimly lit by a lantern sitting on a flat-topped boulder, too dim to give away the dimensions of the room or any other details.

379

Extending his arms, he crawled down the wall about four feet until his hands touched the floor and his legs cleared the hole. He then climbed upright and picked up the lantern by a handle on top. It squeaked loudly, apparently rusted at the hinge where the handle pivoted.

The lantern cast an undulating glow on uneven stone, from a ceiling just over his head to the side walls—bare rock except for the hole he had come through. In the direction opposite the hole, the chamber led into darkness.

Matt set the lantern near the tunnel and jerked on the rope. A reply tug jerked back. Grabbing the rope with both hands, he locked his elbows and walked slowly backwards. He stopped at times while Darcy freed Lauren from a snag, but she glided smoothly for the most part. After a few minutes, Lauren's feet appeared.

Matt dropped the rope and grabbed her ankles. He pulled, grasping higher on her clothes as she inched forward. Finally, her head came into view. He slid his arms under hers, lifted her out, and laid her on the ground.

One second later, Darcy's head emerged. Matt helped her crawl the rest of the way until she stood.

"Any problems?" he asked.

"Not too many." She brushed off her clothes and examined a scrape on her elbow. "I donated a little more blood for the cause, but I'm all right."

She teetered to the side. Matt caught her arm and pulled her upright. "Are you sure you're okay?"

"Just a dizzy spell. I'm probably dehydrated."

"Let me check something." He picked up the lantern and held it close to her neck. Although sweaty and smeared with dirt, her skin seemed free of injury. He pulled her collar down in the back, revealing twin puncture wounds, red and raw. His throat tightened, but he kept his voice calm. "Looks like a drone bit you."

Darcy covered the wound with her hand. "I thought I felt something."

"Maybe it didn't inject any venom. I mean, it's been a while. It probably is dehydration. We've been sweating like crazy."

She massaged the wound. Her skeptical expression gave away her doubts, but she said nothing.

"I can try to heal you, but when I worked on my mother's bullet wound, I had to push my fingers deep into the damaged tissue. I can't heal what I can't touch."

"And venom flows all through my bloodstream, so …" Darcy's voice trailed off.

"Yeah. It's a long shot. But I have to try." Matt set the lantern down and laid a palm over the two holes. As before, his skin warmed, as did hers, though not painfully so. Soon, the heat faded, and he lifted his hand. The two holes had sealed, leaving only pinhead-sized abrasions. "The bite looks a lot better."

"Great. Let's hope for no venom." She lifted his hand and kissed his knuckles. "Thank you again."

"You're welcome." He unclipped the flashlight from his belt loop. "I guess we'd better see where this room leads."

She pointed at the lantern. "You can take that and save your batteries."

"Whoever left it here might want it back." He turned on the flashlight and pointed the beam into the darkness. "Abaddon mentioned that I need to get past some guardians, and I don't want to make any of them mad."

381

Another squeak emanated from the lantern, then words. "Do you know Abaddon, young man?" The flame flickered in time with the speaker's cadence, and its voice crackled, more masculine than feminine.

Matt looked at Darcy. She gave him an I-have-no-idea kind of shrug.

"I do. We both do." Matt crouched near the lantern and searched the curved glass for a face, but no eyes or mouth appeared, just a wavering, two-inch flame. "Who are you?"

"I have no name." The flame popped and sizzled. "I am a humble guardian in service to Abaddon."

"Do you just sit here in this chamber all the time, or are you mobile?"

"I am as mobile as the one who wishes to carry me. Otherwise I stay here to guard this access point."

"Guard it? How can a lantern guard this place? Anyone could just walk right past you."

"So you think." The flame shot through the top of the glass to the ceiling. Eight fiery appendages stretched out and created a mesh that blocked the way deeper into the chamber.

Matt straightened and backed away. "Okay. I get the picture."

The flame shrank until it returned to its original size. "Since you know Abaddon, you may proceed, but you should carry me so that I can give you further instructions soon."

"Just a minute." Matt dropped to his side next to Lauren and, with Darcy's help, put the harness back on. When they had refastened everything, he climbed to his feet, Lauren again on his back.

The flame crackled. "Is the girl on your back dead?"

Matt nodded. "She died just a little while ago."

"Collecting dead people is a strange hobby."

"No, I don't collect dead people. We came here to resurrect her."

The flame curled as if forming a question mark. "Do you know how?"

"Not exactly. I have some instructions from someone who's been here. I know about Abaddon's book and the eggs."

"That will not be enough, but if you will carry me, I will show you the way."

Matt reclipped the flashlight and began gathering his towline. "We'd better hurry."

When he and Darcy finished looping the rope, Darcy slid her arm into the coil and carried it on her shoulder. Matt picked up the lantern. "Now what?"

The flame grew until a slender flickering protrusion rose out of the glass and pointed into the darkness ahead. "That way."

As they walked, the lantern's glow slowly shrank back into the glass, though it still illuminated the passage—nothing but a tunnel of rock with a dark recess here and there. If any of those alcoves led anywhere important, this guardian didn't seem interested in mentioning them.

After a few moments, Matt spoke to the flame. "Is there a way to the surface? We have to check on our friends."

"That is a strange question."

"Why?"

"You just arrived, and you cannot resurrect the girl at the surface."

"Right, but ..." Matt suppressed an exasperated sigh. How could he recount everything that led up to their arrival? Maybe something short would do. "We ... uh ... I guess you could say we fell."

The flame curled again. "With a rope and a dead girl?"

"It's kind of hard to explain."

"You need not explain, for it is none of my business, but I will again warn you that no resurrection is possible at the surface."

When they neared a fork in the tunnel, the lantern's flame hissed. "Stop here."

A pair of five-foot-wide passages with head-high arches angled away to each side. The passage on the left sloped downward, and the one on the right ascended.

The fiery arm lifted from the glass again and pointed to the right. "That way is certain death." It then shifted to the left. "That way ..." The flame crackled. "Maybe you will survive, but your chances are low with the burden you carry. Still, it is the only way to resurrection."

383

"But does one of them lead to the surface?"

"Perhaps this one." The pointer indicated the right-hand passage again. "A predator lives there. No one who has ever gone that way has survived to tell me where it leads, but I have heard screams of terror and crunching bones, so I recommend avoiding it."

"Is there a safe way to the surface that you know about anywhere? We're willing to travel a long distance."

The flame shrank and quivered. "If you are willing to travel straight up, then you may ascend the walls of the abyss. That is the only way I know. But if you do, leave me here. I am not foolish enough to want to go."

"We can't climb. Especially not with Lauren on my back."

The little flame seemed to nod. "The abyss is likely far more dangerous than is the predator."

384

Matt glanced at the knife still sheathed at Darcy's hip. That wouldn't be enough unless this lantern really didn't know what it was talking about. It obviously had never been in that passage to see what lay within. "Have you heard the predator recently?"

"No. I have not heard it in a very long time. Few explorers travel through here."

"Matt," Darcy said, "we don't even know if it's possible to get to the surface, so it doesn't make sense to face a dangerous predator. Besides, you came here to find a way to resurrect Lauren. You were going to leave everyone behind anyway without knowing what would happen to them. Mariel and Thomas are smart. They'll figure out what to do."

"Blaring an SOS in the middle of nowhere isn't exactly my idea of a good strategy." Matt turned on his flashlight and aimed it into the predator's tunnel. Leaving that mystery unsolved felt like abandoning a fellow soldier on a battlefield, but it would be stupid to fight a battle that had no clear benefit. They had to help Lauren.

"You're right." He nodded at the lantern. "Thanks for the advice."

"Just do not curse me when you face the dangers. I leave you to your journey. But first, kindly return me to where you found me. I sense that something is happening there that I must attend to."

"I'll be right back." With the lantern in hand, Matt jogged to the tunnel site. He waved it from side to side, scanning the walls. No hole appeared. "Where is our tunnel? Did I take a wrong turn somehow?"

"We are in the right place," the flame said, sizzling more than ever. "I feared this outcome. Since Abaddon departed with his destroyers, all accesses to this domain are closing. My responsibilities have ceased to be."

Matt set the lantern down. "What will you do?"

"I will also cease to be." The flame withered. "I am a servant without a soul. I have completed my duties, and now I will disperse and be no more."

The flame shrank and winked out. Matt cast the flashlight beam on the lantern. Cracks ran along the glass and metallic fuel holder. Then, it crumbled to dust. Liquid spilled and sank into the stone.

Matt exhaled. What a bizarre ending to a guardian's existence, but there was no time to dwell on it, especially if accesses were closing.

A pebble dropped from the ceiling. He pointed the flashlight upward. Above, a jagged crack ran along the stone. As one end of the crack slowly crawled toward a side wall, the gap widened. More pebbles fell, along with sand and grit.

Matt turned and hustled back, his flashlight darting from floor to ceiling to walls. The stone seemed stable here. No use telling Darcy about the lantern or the closing accesses. Why spread fear? All they could do was keep moving forward.

385

When he rejoined her, he aimed the light into the left-hand tunnel. "We'd better get going."

After shifting Lauren's body to a more comfortable position, he ducked under the arch and followed the beam into the passage.

Darcy stayed close behind. "Matt, I didn't want to say anything while that guardian was around, and it might not be important, but ..." During the pause, her words echoed in the darkness.

"Go ahead." Matt waved the light back and forth, illuminating the narrowing rocky passage, now about four feet wide. "It doesn't look like anyone's around to hear you."

"I'm worried about the drone bite. I'm getting dizzier, and I'm not thinking straight."

Matt stopped and shone the light on her chest, close enough to illuminate her pallid face. No cracking sounds emanated from walls or ceiling. Maybe it would be safe to pause for a moment. "Your thinking was pretty sharp just a minute ago."

"I get flashes. Sometimes I feel like a genius and then I'm in a fog, like my brain is on a roller coaster."

"Well, I want to heal you, but like I said before, I can't heal what I can't touch, and my power can't go inside a person unless I have a source of energy poured over me, like dragon fire, but I have to be wearing something flame retardant."

She looked at the harness on his back. "Like the cloak?"

"Right. I wore that when I healed a baby. Karrick blasted me with fire while I ..." Matt's mind drifted to the chamber where he left the lantern. He whispered, "The guardian's flames."

"I'll get him. You wait here." Darcy opened her hand. "I'll need the light."

He tightened his grip on the flashlight. "There's something I didn't tell you. When I took the lantern back, the tunnel we crawled through was gone. The lantern said accesses to this place are closing, and then he just crumbled and disappeared. Then the ceiling started cracking. I think the way we got here might collapse."

"You mean this passage itself might be closing, like squeezing us out from a tube of toothpaste?"

Matt gazed into her eyes. They seemed wild and unfocused. "I hope not," he said. "I haven't noticed a problem between there and here. Maybe since the little tunnel we crawled through got sealed, the rest of the passage will stay in place."

"Oh. That's good." She looked at the beam, still on her chest. "Anyway, while I'm thinking clearly, I just want to make sure you know that I think you're amazing, and ..." She refocused on him. "And that I love you." She drew him into a tight embrace, her arms around his neck. "Maybe I'm already on the brink of insanity right now, but I needed to let you know my feelings before I go over the edge. I really do love you."

387

Matt returned the embrace and rubbed her back. She had expressed her feelings earlier. Had she already forgotten? Maybe insanity really was encroaching. Still, Darcy seemed pretty lucid. Maybe she could win the battle if the drone didn't inject too much venom.

When they separated, Matt slid his hand into hers. "I love you, too, Darcy. I'm glad you're at my side."

Her eyes misted. "Thank you, Matt. That means a lot to me."

As they gazed at each other, pangs of guilt swelled in Matt's throat. His conscience hurled mental stones. *You didn't tell her about Abaddon's prophecy. If you go to his lair, one of you has to die.*

He slung the thoughts away. Warning her now might drive her even closer to insanity. And what good would it do? There was no turning back. "We'd better go." Still holding Darcy's hand, he aimed the light deeper into the tunnel and walked at a brisk pace, listening for signs of collapse. Lauren's body seemed heavier now. The straps had loosened, making her ride lower and shift more— far less secure.

Darcy adjusted Lauren from time to time and tightened the straps. That helped, but she could do nothing to overcome the aches in his muscles and the stinging pain throbbing in cuts, scrapes, and deep bruises. His healing gift was probably working hard, but constantly getting new wounds had to be overtaxing it.

Their shoes crunched gravel. Their breaths came faster and shallower. The sounds seemed hollow and muted, no longer echoing. The tunnel went on and on, ever downward. Even if they wanted to turn back, Lauren's weight combined with Matt's exhaustion would make the long climb impossible. They had no choice but to press on.

While they walked, Darcy chatted about her life after Matt went to military school. She left home when she turned seventeen and took a bus to Las Vegas where she hoped to get involved with a stage show, either singing or playing piano. Although she got bit parts here and there, and made pretty good money playing piano at bars, it wasn't enough to pay the bills. That's when she turned to, as she put it, alternative sources of income.

As she related each tale, her tone and cadence altered from frenetic to slow and methodical and back to frenetic. The roller coaster carried her on a ride she couldn't seem to stop.

After what felt like an hour, a light appeared in the distance, reddish and pulsing, similar to the glow in the depths of the abyss. At the end of the passage through a chest-high arch, a new chamber came into view, now about twenty paces away. Inside, an indistinct shape pulsed with red light, and its bright flashes made it impossible to focus on it for more than a second.

Something skittered across the entry from left to right, something dark, nimble, and the same height as the opening. It appeared to have more than four limbs, but its speed blurred the details.

Matt halted. "Did you see that?"

"It looked like a spider." Darcy's voice sounded like that of a frightened child.

"I'll check it out. Help me get Lauren off."

"Sure." She held Lauren while Matt unfastened the straps and shrugged her down his back.

When they had laid Lauren carefully on the floor, Matt flicked off his flashlight, drew Darcy's knife from its sheath at her belt, and handed it to her. "Just in case," he said.

She held the knife in an open palm. "I'm kind of nervous about using this. I mean, the insanity thing." Her voice had returned to normal.

Matt smiled. "I'm not worried. I think you can beat that venom."

She slid the knife back to the sheath and nodded. "Be careful."

"I'll do my best." He tiptoed to the end of the tunnel, set a hand on the right side of the arch, and leaned out in front of the opening. Inside, a curved, reflective wall surrounded a rectangular column, creating a cylindrical chamber around it. The rectangle appeared to have dozens upon dozens of tiny hexagonal openings. It looked more like a giant honeycomb than a support column.

The column pulsed with a heartbeat rhythm. With each throb, scarlet radiance shot out through the hexagons and formed a ring of energy that struck the mirrored wall and bounced back. The echoing ring collided with the column in a vibrant splash of sparks that shot upward and disappeared just in time for the next throb.

Bending low, Matt crept toward the room, but his head struck something solid, though nothing stood in sight. He extended a hand and pressed his palm against a transparent barrier, perhaps a window—perfectly clear and invisible.

He pushed his fingers under the barrier and lifted. Something that felt like a panel slid upward, but its size and shape were indiscernible. While holding the panel up with one hand, he extended his other hand underneath and felt for the opening's barriers. The hole appeared to be rectangular, big enough to crawl through.

Matt squeezed past the opening and lowered the panel back in place. On this side, instead of a window, the panel appeared to be a mirror, slightly curved as it melded into the continuous mirror that encircled the room.

Staying in a crouch, he scanned the chamber. That multi-legged creature was nowhere on the floor or in sight on the glassy walls. The mirrors continued upward until they faded in the darkness above. The creature could be hiding in the higher reaches, lurking and watching.

He rose and walked toward the central column. When it throbbed, a new ring of red light passed through his body. The radiance tingled, raising goose bumps across his skin, but it seemed to do no harm.

When the radiance bounced off the wall and struck his back, the tingle returned, not as strong and shorter lived. He turned to the wall. Directly in front, his reflection stared back, but the curvature in the mirror created a continuous reflection that showed his body at every possible angle as it stretched around the room. The mirror also reflected other portions of the wall, which showed his body at another angle as if standing behind the first image, and another image stood behind that one, and another behind it, and on and on into infinity. It seemed that thousands of copies of Matt Bannister stood watching him and each other.

The honeycomb pulsed again. When the wave passed by, his closest reflected image vanished in all directions, though the farther reflections remained intact. When the radiance bounced back, the collision with his body erased every image but a distant one directly ahead. It stared at him as if alive and sentient. Scarlet light flew upward and dissipated, and the surrounding images returned.

Skewed reflections of himself and the honeycomb swirled. Dizziness swam through his senses. Matt shook his head hard. It wouldn't take long for this bizarre room to drive anyone insane.

He blinked. Insane? A good reminder. He had better check on Darcy.

Keeping his focus on the ground, he hurried to the panel, lifted it, and crawled underneath. Since the spiderlike creature never made an appearance, it would probably be safe to bring Lauren and Darcy in. Maybe another panel lay hidden in the wall somewhere, an opening that would lead to a new passageway.

391

Still a bit dizzy, he jogged to Darcy. She crouched, combing Lauren's hair with her fingers. "Don't worry, Lauren," she crooned in a lilting voice. "We'll get you resurrected very soon. Matt loves you, so he'll never give up."

"Darcy?" Matt stooped next to her. "Are you all right?"

She squinted at him. "Don't I look all right?"

"You look fine. It's just ..." He shook his head. "Never mind. Just help me get Lauren."

For the next two minutes, they once again hoisted Lauren onto his back and strapped her in. Matt led Darcy to the panel, opened it, and squeezed through on hands and knees. Once Darcy had entered, he closed the panel and walked slowly to the honeycomb.

He and Darcy stood together and turned toward the surrounding mirror. "My guess," he said, "is that we might find another movable panel like the one we came through. We can split up and start looking."

A voice came from somewhere above. "There is no need for such a wasteful activity."

A recent splash of red light shot into the cylinder's upper reaches and bounced all around until it blended into an amorphous wave of upwelling radiance. Clinging to the wall, a dark humanoid crawled down, headfirst as if her hands and bare feet adhered to the slick surface. With two sets of arms, she looked like a black Hindu idol. A tight bodysuit, as dark as her skin, covered her from ankles to neck to all four wrists, spoiling the imagery.

When she reached the floor, she stood upright. No taller than a preteen, she walked gracefully toward Matt and Darcy, her expression more curious than challenging. "Who are you?" she asked with a girlish voice. "Why are you here?"

CHAPTER

JADE

The honeycomb continued pulsing. Red light bathed the four-armed girl in crimson, as if washing her in a bloody fountain. Jet-black hair streamed over her shoulders and down to her knees. The bodysuit accentuated the curves of a fully mature woman, belying her preadolescent face and voice, and an oval stone embedded in her sternum radiated a soft green light.

"I'm Matt." He nodded at Darcy. "And this is Darcy."

"Excellent. I chose the correct language. I thought you looked like Earth Americans." She gave a head bow. "My name is Jade. I am Guardian of what you probably call the abyss, a name that conjures nightmarish images of darkness, an eternal plunge into the unknown, and an eruption of hellish creatures from its depths." She laughed as if amused with her own words. "Although Abaddon's armies did indeed fly from here, that is a one-time event. The abyss is not designed to be a place of nightmares or even the slightest of fears. It is a passageway to every wondrous daydream, to every corner of every world, even to fantasies you could never imagine. It is mysterious, to be sure, but it poses no danger to anyone who is wise enough to solve its puzzles and avoid its pitfalls."

Matt kept his stare locked on Jade. Her bright eyes and smile dressed her in a friendly aspect, but the abyss speech sounded like a propaganda oratory, as if she were a devoted worshiper of this place.

"You're so pretty!" Darcy touched Jade's ebony cheek. "Do you live here?"

Jade grasped Darcy's wrist with one of her left hands. "It is best not to touch a guardian without asking permission."

"Oh!" Darcy pulled her hand back. "I'm sorry."

Matt narrowed his eyes. Darcy seemed to be at a low point in her roller-coaster ride. Maybe a bit of stimulus would give her a boost. "Jade, in Abaddon's name, I ask for passage to his lair. We need to resurrect the girl I'm carrying on my back."

"In Abaddon's name?" Jade laughed gently. "Abaddon is a powerful ally, but he is not my superior. I will do whatsoever I choose." She walked around to Matt's back, reached up to Lauren's face, and touched her forehead, her graceful movements visible in the mirrors. "She is beginning to deteriorate. You have very little time."

"I know. That's why I—"

"Why you are in such a hurry." As the honeycomb continued sending pulses of radiance over Jade's body, she seemed to float along the mirrored wall, like a warped shadow stretching and reshaping itself. "What makes you think her soul is in Abaddon's Lair? Very few are sent there for resurrection, perhaps one in a billion, or even fewer."

"She is Bonnie Bannister's daughter. Does that name mean anything to you?"

394

"Of course. The Oracle of Fire, the purity ovulum, the one who sings the hope of all the Earth." Jade ran a hand along Lauren's arm. "So this must be Lauren, the girl who created a miniature abyss in the museum room."

"Yes, she's Lauren." Matt grasped Darcy's shoulder and gave her a shake. "Mom told you that story, right, Darcy? The museum room?"

Darcy blinked, as if waking up. "Yes. The museum room. I know about that. The tree-of-life story."

Jade smiled in a pleasant way. "The tree of life created a reflection of this place—the Sanctum of the Abyss. The central column is the sanctum's heart, the hub of every world—Earth, Hades, Second Eden, and other worlds you likely have not heard about. Lauren's replica of this place was not the first. There is also a pool in the Bridgelands that displays some of the worlds."

Jade laid her palm on the pulsing column. Under her touch, the red light faded to black, and darkness spread across the surface, as if the connected hexagons bled into each other. Sections of the mirror reflected the change in a shadowy crawl along the glass. "This is the heart of inter-world navigation. It monitors portals as they are created, opened, and closed, and I am able to alter trans-portal activity from this station."

"So what world are we in now?" Matt asked.

"Under normal circumstances, this place is in no world at all. It exists in a neutral plane in the midst of all worlds. But because of events occurring on Earth, this junction has been transported to Earth's plane in order to await the outcome of your people's transgressions. If Earth is terminated, then I will—"

"Terminated?" Darcy said, her eyes dull. "You mean, like destroyed?"

"That is exactly what I mean." Jade looked upward. "The entire universe we symbolically call Earth might be swallowed into this bottomless pit and enter a state of cosmic neutrality. In essence, it will cease to exist."

Darcy blinked several times. "So are we at the bottom of the bottomless pit?"

Jade laughed. "That is a logical conundrum to your mind, because you are unable to perceive this place from a higher plane. If someone were to fall into the pit, he would plunge without reaching the ground upon which we stand. He would transport from world to world, always falling and never landing, an eternity of terror. In that sense, the pit is bottomless, though you and I stand at its base."

Matt peered at the column. "So can this contraption send us to Abaddon's Lair?"

"Not on its own. I merely adjust openings and closings. I do not have the power to open a portal myself. Someone with supernatural abilities, such as Sapphira or Acacia, is able to do it. The flames of the tree of life also possess that power. Beyond that, I know of only one other form of energy that is able to pierce the veil between portals—life energy. An inhabitant of one of the worlds must contribute his life force to the effort."

Matt hid a swallow. Abaddon's deadly promise stormed back to mind. "And I assume that person would die."

"Of course. One cannot contribute his life force and also expect to keep it. That is illogical." Jade pinched Matt's sleeve. "If your garments do not burn easily, jumping through the open portal should be safe as long as you cover exposed skin."

"We brought a cloak for that in the harness." He scanned the room again. The red pulses continued to wash over his body as well as Jade's and Darcy's. The multiple reflections stretched out and skewed, painting warped portraits of all three as they appeared and disappeared in time with the honeycomb's heartbeat.

Darcy walked to the wall and touched the mirror. "Am I at a carnival? This is a funhouse, right?"

"Darcy!" Matt strode to her and shook her arm. "Fight the venom! Snap out of it!"

She stared at him, her mouth partially open. "Matt," she said in a wispy voice. "Help me. I'm swimming in a stormy sea. I need … I need a lifeline. The waves are … washing over me."

He gave her another shake, harder this time. "Darcy! I'm here! Don't give up!"

She wagged her head vigorously, then squinted. "Matt. Where did the water go?"

"Don't look at the mirror." He led her to the column where Jade stood, all four hands reaching out.

"Allow me to hold her. I have a clarifying effect on humans."

Matt guided Darcy into Jade's grasp. Jade pulled her close and stroked her hair and back with two of her hands as she looked up into her eyes and whispered, "Embrace reality, child of Earth. Close your eyes and focus on my voice. Allow peace to filter into your senses and extract the chaotic noise and fractured thoughts that assault your mind. Only in this way can you hold to your sanity."

Edging closer, Matt focused on Jade's voice. Something magical infused her tone—peaceful, confident, ageless. His own confusing thoughts leaked away, allowing room for clarity … and a potential plan. "How does a person donate life energy to open a portal?"

Jade continued petting Darcy and hummed between phrases. "First, we locate the world you wish to visit. We will be able to see into that world to verify its identity. Then I determine the hole in the sanctum's heart to energize. I activate that hole's intake ability so that anyone who touches it will be drained of his or her life energy. Another option is to draw life energy through a portal window from a willing donor, though physical passage through that portal will be impossible until after the donation is complete. The sanctum's heart then uses the energy to open the portal. The energy contributor dies almost immediately."

"What happens to that person's body and soul?"

"The body disintegrates, and the soul goes to God, unless, of course, the contributor is one of the few who is sent to Abaddon's Lair for resurrection. Without the body, however, the only possible resurrection would be in Second Eden's birthing garden."

"Besides opening a portal, is there any way we can get to the surface?"

"Under normal circumstances, one could retrace his steps to find his way back to his starting point, but not in this case. Abaddon is one of the wisest creatures in any world, and he predicted that your need might arise, so he allowed your passage. Now that your journey has commenced, the path you took has been sealed. You may not retreat."

"Right. I noticed that the hole we came through is gone."

"As is much of the passage you traveled. Soon it will all collapse." Jade looked up. "Of course, you may climb the abyss from here to the top. It is a dangerous venture, especially if you continue to encumber yourself with Lauren's body. If you slip and fall, you will suffer the eternal plunge, which is far worse than death."

"I think we'll avoid that option." Matt pointed at the honeycomb. "Can you locate the portal to Abaddon's Lair for me? I want to see what's going on in there."

"Of course." Jade gently pushed Darcy toward Matt. "She is calm now, and her sanity has returned for the moment. Make sure she avoids looking at the mirror."

Matt enfolded Darcy in his arms. "Keep your eyes closed. I'll let you know what's going on."

"Thank you, Matt." She nestled closer and laid her head against his shoulder. "I heard what Jade said about contributing life energy. I hope you're not planning to do that."

"The thought crossed my mind. If I die, you'll have to figure out how to resurrect Lauren. My mother's instructions are on my phone, so—"

"No!" She pulled back and glared at him. "Matt, I can barely keep my mind from taking a hike down loony lane. There's no way I'd be able to do it. I wouldn't be worth a nickel."

"Okay. Calm down." He pushed her head against his shoulder. "Just close your eyes. I'll see what Jade comes up with. Maybe I'll get another idea."

Jade walked to the wall and touched the mirror at eye level, her hands in the positions of the four corners of a four-foot-wide square. As the green stone in her sternum grew brighter, the glass within the square darkened, first to gray then to black. When she lifted her hands, the square remained. Like night becoming day, the blackness faded, leaving behind a transparent window.

399

"If memory serves," she said as she crossed one pair of arms over her chest, "this should be the portal to Abaddon's Lair. Come and look."

Matt whispered to Darcy, "Follow my lead and keep your eyes straight ahead. You'll see a square window. Focus on that."

"Okay."

They walked to where Jade stood. Two arms still crossed, she gestured with a third arm toward the window. "Abaddon's resurrection chamber."

Matt took a step closer and peered through. Within a dim room, a stone table stood at a distance that appeared to be only a few steps away. About ten feet long, five feet wide, and four feet high, the table held several wooden mounts, all empty except for the tallest one, which supported a large, glass egg. Three short, thick candles sat near the egg, two of them burning with disturbed flames and providing the room's only light, while a thin line of smoke rose at a sharp angle from the third candle, apparently snuffed by a breeze.

A finger-length vial lying on its side rolled slowly back and forth between two of the candles, and a foot-tall hourglass sat nearby, its sand trickling slowly to a small pile in the bottom half.

Near the table's edge, a page fluttered on a huge book that lay open on a four-footed stand next to a quill-like pen perched in an inkwell. A dull banging sound, like wood against wood, permeated the chamber, rhythmic and distant.

"There must be quite a breeze in there." Matt narrowed his eyes and tried to focus beyond the table. As his vision adjusted, the far wall took shape where shutters swung open and closed over a window. "Do you know where that window leads?"

Jade shook her head. "I do not spy on Abaddon's domain. I leave his business to him, and he leaves mine to me, but I once visited this room, and I am certain that it was as motionless as death. There was no open window."

"Abaddon told me he was sending Second Eden refugees home from his world. Maybe that open window is a passage of some kind."

"While you ponder this mystery, I will locate the correct spot on the sanctum's heart so that you will have the opportunity to donate life energy if you so choose." Jade walked to the column and spread her four hands over the surface, covering most of the side facing the portal. She drew her fingers slowly toward her

400

palms, then pulled her hands back until only the end of an index finger touched the surface.

When one of the hexagons blackened under her finger, she stepped away. The hole remained black while the rest continued pulsing red. "If you touch the sphere at this spot, it will drain your life energy and open the portal."

Darcy stared at the sphere, her eyes again turning distant and vacant.

Matt grasped her shoulders. "No, Darcy! Don't even think about it. You're not going to open the portal."

"I know," she said in an expressionless tone. "You need me. I saved your life. I help with Lauren. You can't do this by yourself."

"Exactly. So we have to find another option." Matt looked at Jade. "There are other portals, right? Other ways to get to Abaddon's Lair?"

"There have been other portals, but when I searched the sanctum's heart for the location of the portal you hope to open, I found only one other." Jade touched the edge of the square leading to the chamber. "I now suspect that the shuttered window on the wall is that portal. Because Lauren created it with the tree of life, it required no protection for passage from either side, but now it is what you might call a fire-escape portal. When escaping a burning building, a person hurries through but would not dare go back. With this portal, people may pass from Abaddon's Lair to the tree's chamber without harm, but coming back requires protection. My guess is that Abaddon altered it to a one-way passage to ensure that the refugees do not return."

Matt set a hand on the square. It felt like glass, though his fingers didn't leave a smudge. Since it spanned from knees to forehead, it would be easy to step through once it opened, even with

Lauren's body still on his back. "How long will this stay here? I mean, when will I have to decide what we're going to do?"

"It will last about ten minutes, but I can easily make it again. Creating a viewing window to any world is a simple matter as long as a portal already exists. It requires no energy just to look and listen."

"I understand." Matt studied the objects in the room—the book, the vial, the egg, everything necessary to resurrect a soul. Everything except the soul itself. It would be crazy to sacrifice himself and send Darcy to resurrect Lauren when they didn't even know if Lauren's soul was there.

After a few seconds, strange sounds drifted through the window—first a scraping noise, like stone on stone, then a grunt, low but feminine. The combination continued in the same order, scraping and grunting, drawing closer with each repetition.

402

"Do sounds pass through both ways?" Matt asked.

Jade shook her head. "Sounds travel from there to here, though perhaps someone who possessed Lauren's gift of hearing could detect sounds from either world."

Soon, a woman came into view, her back toward the portal window. She dragged a dark humanlike statue, tilted at an angle so she could wrap her arms around its shoulders. A spyglass swung at one hip and a scabbard at the other, both attached to a belt wrapped around a form-fitting beige tunic and loose black trousers.

Every few seconds, she set her feet, heaved the statue a yard or so, and repositioned her arms and feet to pull again. With each heave, dark pigtails swayed against her back. When she turned to the side, a small glass egg floated into view and hovered close to her nose.

Matt whispered to Darcy. "That's Listener. I told you about her."

Darcy stared, her mouth agape. "What is that egg? It's flying, but it doesn't have wings."

"Her companion. All residents of Second Eden have one. It's like an external conscience. I don't know how it flies."

"Sir Barlow!" Listener shouted as she set the statue upright. "Do you need help?"

"Coming, Miss!" A new scraping sound followed in the wake of the first. Seconds later, Sir Barlow entered the room, dragging another statue. With a scabbard and a pistol attached to his belt, he looked ready for a battle.

He set his statue next to the first one. "I apologize for the delay. For a moment, it seemed to have a mind of its own, but I suppose my own mind has deteriorated in this strange world of rapid transformations. As they say, a mind is a terrible thing to haste."

"Haste?" Listener narrowed her eyes. "What a strange phrase."

"It is, indeed, Miss. I think it has to do with overtaxing one's mind, but I am not certain. For my part, I simply try to employ idioms to fit into a new environment, as the idiom states, to become birds of a feather."

"I have heard that one." Listener strode to the book on the stand and flipped to a page near the back. "Where did Abaddon say the instructions are?" The shutters banged, and the breeze blew the pages toward the front. Listener gave the book a sour stare and began flipping the pages again.

"I will take care of it, Miss." Sir Barlow hurried to the window. He peered through the opening and called out, "Tamara! We are back in the resurrection chamber. We will come through soon."

A feminine voice replied from far away. "Thank you. I will … take these … children to … to Second Eden." Her cadence kept faltering, an obvious speech impediment. "I'll see you … when

403

you get here. ... And thank you ... for the flowers. ... They are lovely."

"My pleasure, though they are not as lovely as you are." After bowing, he closed the shutters, and locked them in place.

"Wasn't that sweet?" Darcy whispered to Matt. "So Tamara and Sir Barlow are romantically involved, just like your mother dreamed."

Sir Barlow hurried back to Listener and used one of the burning candles to relight the third. "Even if the book has instructions, I believe this effort is doomed to fail. Neither of us has a drop of dragon blood in our veins, that is, ever since one of your companions left."

Listener drummed her fingers on the table. "I don't care if we have a one percent chance of success. We're not going to leave these souls here. Abaddon told me face to face to get every last soul out, so I'm going to bust my backside to get it done."

"True, Miss, but in our world, the idiom 'every last soul' refers to living people, that is, the Second Eden refugees, not to literal souls. Very few idioms are literal. I should know. I am an expert on their proper use."

"I'm not going to take any chances." Listener looked at the hourglass, her brow furrowing. "We don't have much time left."

While Listener flipped through pages, Darcy touched the window. "Matt," she said, her voice now well above a whisper. "She's so perfect! She's tough, assertive, and responsible."

Listener looked up from the page and faced the portal window. "Did you hear something?"

Sir Barlow gazed in the same direction. "Nothing unusual, Miss. Perhaps the hiss of the candle wick I just lit, but it is as quiet as a mausoleum here."

"I heard a woman's voice." Listener walked around the table and headed directly for the portal. When she drew close, she stopped and set her hands around the window's perimeter and let out a slight grunt. "This mirror is anchored to the wall. I can't pry it loose." As she stared at the portal again, her reddish-brown eyes sparkled.

Darcy gasped. "Matt! Listener is beautiful! Just like you said, like a goddess from storybooks!"

Listener cocked her head. "What is this? A mirror that compliments your looks?"

"Well, Miss …" Sir Barlow walked closer to the portal. "I assume you're hearing things that I cannot."

"This mirror just told me that I'm beautiful. It said something about storybooks."

Sir Barlow raised a finger. "Ah! There is a storybook in my world about a wicked queen who looked into a mirror and asked who is the fairest in the land, and the mirror always told her that she was the most beautiful until a certain girl blossomed into womanhood and became fairer. This enraged the queen, so she—"

405

"Never mind," Listener said. "I remember now. I heard that story from Walter." She detached the spyglass and looked through it at the window. "How strange. I see a faint pulse of red light and shadowy silhouettes. Maybe this bizarre mirror world has many fairy-tale objects."

Matt called out, "Listener! Can you hear me?"

She lowered the spyglass. "I thought I heard Matt."

"Matt?" Sir Barlow looked over Listener's shoulder and peered at the window. "Matt Bannister?"

"Yes, of course. Do you know another Matt?"

"I beg your pardon, Miss, but since you heard a voice from a mirror, I couldn't be certain that you weren't referring to a floor mat or some other kind of mat."

"Don't be silly." Listener reattached the spyglass to her belt. "Matt, I heard you speak. Can you hear me?"

He leaned closer. "I can. I'm at some sort of portal-viewing window. I'm trying to get through so I can resurrect Lauren."

"Resurrect Lauren? So she's ..." Listener's chin quivered. "How did she die?"

"It's hard to explain, but she died killing Tamiel. She sacrificed herself to save the world. I'm carrying her body, and I need to open this portal so I can bring her across for resurrection."

"What makes you think her soul is here in Abaddon's Lair?"

Matt shifted his shoulders to adjust Lauren's weight. "Since the souls of so many of my mother's friends and relatives came here for resurrection, we thought maybe hers did, too."

Listener relayed Matt's words. As Sir Barlow listened, a tear trickled down his swarthy cheek. "Well, I must say that explains a lot."

Listener blinked at him. "What do you mean?"

406

"When that statue resisted, I thought I heard a voice from inside it, but I was certain it had to be my imagination. As I said before, my mind is deteriorating. I assumed the voice was merely a symptom."

Listener grasped Sir Barlow's arm. "What did it say?"

"It was the strangest thing, like an echo that repeated again and again in a soft, feminine whisper, 'I'll see you in the morning.'"

"I'll see you in the morning?" Matt swallowed. "Are you sure?"

When Listener repeated Matt's question, Sir Barlow shook his head. "I am not one hundred percent sure of the exact words, but I believe it was something to that effect."

Matt began unfastening Lauren's harness. "That's good enough for me."

"What do you mean?" Listener asked.

"I've been told that to open the portal someone has to feed energy into a controller in this place I'm standing. Now that I know Lauren's soul is there, I can supply my energy and send

Darcy across with Lauren's body. My mother gave us instructions, so the three of you can figure out how to resurrect her."

Listener furrowed her brow. "Who is Darcy? The woman I heard earlier?"

"Yes. She's a friend of mine. I'll let her explain when she gets there."

"And you won't come with her?"

"No. I'll let Darcy explain that, too." While Matt shrugged and pulled his arms free from the harness, Darcy helped him lower Lauren to the ground. As her chest passed by Matt's hip, the beads in Mom's necklace glowed, each one pulsing its own color in time with the sanctum heart's rhythm.

"The key." Darcy touched the ring on Matt's belt loop. "Remember? We think it energizes the beads somehow."

"Right." When they had settled Lauren on the floor, Matt detached the ring and set it on her chest. When the nearly invisible key touched the necklace, the beads pulsed with radiance. "The key ring will have to go with her."

"But Matt, you can't—"

"Listen." He pulled the cloak from the harness and handed it to Darcy. "When the portal opens, throw the cloak to Sir Barlow and ask him to put it on and carry Lauren across. Then he can throw the cloak back to you so you can pass."

Darcy dropped the cloak to the floor. She shook her head slowly, then faster and faster. Finally, she pressed her palms on the sides of the window and shouted, "Listener! I'm Darcy." Her voice rose and fell as she struggled to spit out her words. "I used to be … um … Matt's foster sister, but I wasn't a good sister … I was an evil witch … but that's not important … at least not anymore. … We made friends again."

Matt grabbed her arm. "Darcy! Don't! Just let me—"

"No!" Darcy jerked away. "I can't let you! I *won't* let you!" She turned again to the window, her voice now steadier. "Listener, Matt is planning to sacrifice his life to open the portal. Someone has to give his life energy to open it, and whoever does that will die."

"If I may," Jade said in a calm tone as she picked up the cloak. "As I mentioned earlier, it is possible for the sanctum's heart to collect energy through the window. If one of them were to volunteer, I could arrange the transfer."

While Listener whispered the message to Barlow, Matt shook his head. "Lauren's my sister. I'm the one who should sacrifice for her. Sir Barlow and Listener aren't related at all."

Sir Barlow cleared his throat. "Listener has informed me of the quandary, and I would like to volunteer. You see, Matthew, only someone who has dragon blood can interpret the resurrection instructions, and since Listener lost her dragon essence years ago, you are the only one who possesses that qualification." He smiled, revealing an uneven set of teeth. "I have lived a good, long life of more than fifteen hundred years. I am ready to die for such a cause as this."

Darcy pressed so close, her nose nearly touched the glass. "But what about Tamara? You can't leave her."

Again Listener repeated the message.

Sir Barlow's smile wavered. "It will be painful, but we will see each other again in Heaven." He shrugged. "Besides, I have been transluminated. If I were to return to Earth, I would be nothing but light energy, so I am clearly the best candidate. Tamara will understand."

"But you won't even get to say good-bye." Darcy's voice rose to a lamenting wail. "Sir Barlow, you can't leave her without saying good-bye!"

Matt grasped Darcy's arm and gave her another firm shake. "Calm down. You have to focus. Don't lose your grip."

She turned to him, her eyes wide. After heaving several breaths, she spread out her hands as if trying to hold down a rising tide. "Okay, I'm in control now, but I can't let you or Sir Barlow throw away your lives. Tamara needs him, and Lauren needs you."

"Darcy, this isn't about who needs who. Sir Barlow is a soldier who understands that when duty calls—"

"Duty? This has nothing to do with duty. This is all about love." Darcy broke away and staggered toward the sanctum's heart, lurching to each side as if tossed by a ship on a stormy sea.

Matt lunged for her but tripped over Lauren's body and fell. "Darcy! No!"

She pushed her finger into the black hexagon. Matt leaped up, slung his arms around her waist, and pulled, but her finger stayed put.

As she leaned against Matt, she writhed and cried out, "Ah ... ah ... ah ..." After each pain-streaked gasp, she sucked in air and gasped again.

409

Still trying to pull Darcy away, Matt called out, "Jade! Stop this thing!"

"It is impossible." Jade glided to them and looked on stoically, the cloak draped over two of her arms. "Even if I could stop it, she would die. Once the siphoning begins, the leaking cannot be plugged. Her life would spill onto the floor instead of into the sanctum's heart."

Matt pulled Darcy close, her back against his chest. "Darcy ..." As he fought for breath, a vise clamped his throat. "Darcy ... why? Why did you do this?"

Breathing quick shallow breaths, she leaned back and pressed her cheek against his. "You don't ... don't need me anymore. You have ... Listener. She's per ... perfect for you. ... Perfect. It's no wonder you ... you think she's so ... so amazing."

Tears trickled down his cheeks. He swallowed past a painful lump. "I didn't want to trade you for Listener. Barlow would have done it. Gladly done it."

"Someone needs Barlow. No one needs me. ... No one." Her body twisted. She let out a long wail. When the spasm loosened, she looked at him, her eyes now clear. "It's not ... insane to ... to give your life ... so another can ... can live." She caressed his cheek. "Good-bye, Matt. I love you." Her body dissolved into sparkling particles that filtered through his grasp and rained onto the floor, leaving behind a pile of clothing and shoes.

"Darcy!" He dropped to his knees and scooped a handful of the dwindling sparks. His arm shook, making the particles spill from his hand. A swirling gust picked up the clothes, uncovering Mariel's watch and the Cracker Jacks ring. As the twisting breeze strengthened, it caught the watch and ring and began lifting them into the vortex.

Matt snatched the ring from the swirl and clutched it close to his chest with both hands. The other items rushed upward in the spin and disappeared in the darkness of the cylindrical chamber. His vision blurred by tears, he opened his hands and stared at the ring—a band of cheap metal, not worth a nickel ... yet priceless.

He rewrapped his hands around the ring and cried out, "Darcy!" Sobs broke through, heaving gasps as he whispered, "I love you, Darcy. ... I'm so sorry ... I treated you the way I did. I wish ... I wish I could've gotten ... to know you better. We could've ... we could've been friends."

Something patted Matt on the back, and Sir Barlow's voice flowed gently, much closer than before. "I apologize for interrupting your grief, Matthew, but you'd better come quickly. The four-armed lass says the portal will close soon."

Matt looked up and blinked through a flood of tears. Sir Barlow stood a step away, Lauren's body over his shoulder. The entire chamber seemed to spin. The honeycomb's blackened hexagon cast a narrow red beam on the window leading to Abaddon's Lair, like a beacon pointing the way.

After pushing the ring into his pocket, Matt climbed to his feet, took a step, and teetered to the side. A pair of strong hands grasped his arm and steadied him. "It's me, Matt. It's Listener. Let's get out of here."

He planted his feet, but his knees still felt weak. "Thanks."

Listener, now wearing the cloak, released him. Her companion floated close to her ear, flashing blue. "Can you walk?"

He brushed tears away with a sleeve. "I think so."

"Good." Listener draped the cloak over Sir Barlow's head and spread it across Lauren. "Let's go."

Sir Barlow stepped onto the window ledge and hopped down to the floor of Abaddon's Lair. He laid Lauren's body on the floor, tossed the cloak back to Listener, and helped her and Matt climb into the chamber as they ducked together under the cloak.

411

When all three had made it through, Matt shed the cloak and looked back. A window hung on a wall, providing a view into the sanctum. It looked so strange—a hole into another world. The heart within continued beating and sending scarlet pulses to the mirrors. The chamber seemed to pull his own heart back. He had brought Darcy there and now had to leave her behind—a fallen soldier on a battlefield who would never go home. Abaddon's prophecy had come true. If Darcy had not fallen into this journey, Sir Barlow would have given his life energy to open the portal, and Darcy would still be alive.

Jade drew near from the other side. The green stone again brightening, she set her hands at the four corners and began pushing them toward the center. "Farewell. Although you lost the presence of a courageous companion, I hope this journey brings you the desires of your heart." The window closed, leaving behind a mirror and a reflection showing Matt, Listener, and Sir Barlow, all staring with tear-filled eyes.

"Matt ..." Listener touched his shoulder. "We need to get started. Her body—"

"I know. It's going to rot." He exhaled. That didn't come out right. Too harsh. He had to control his grief. Listener deserved better. "I'm sorry. I just—"

"It's okay. Don't worry about it." Listener pointed at the hourglass, its sand now about one-third spilled into the bottom compartment. "Abaddon said when the sand runs out, this place will crumble and disintegrate. No one remaining here will survive. It fluctuates sometimes, but based on its current rate, I'd say we have about thirty minutes."

"Thirty minutes." Matt nodded. "No time to waste."

Listener touched the table. "Sir Barlow, lay her over here, please. I'll clear the way."

"Certainly, Miss." After Listener moved the glass egg and candles and set them on the floor, Sir Barlow laid Lauren gently on her back, her head near the hourglass at one end of the table. From his tunic pocket, he withdrew the key ring along with the transparent key and set it on her chest near the necklace. Once again the beads pulsed with a multicolored hue. "How long ago did she die?" he asked.

"A couple of hours," Matt said. "Why?"

"As one who has carried a number of corpses from the battlefield, I usually have a good feel for how long a warrior has been dead, based on stiffness, odor, and color. I would have guessed that Lauren expired only moments ago. Her body is quite limber and well preserved."

412

"That's good news." Matt took in a deep breath and let it out slowly. Grief for Darcy felt like someone had drilled a hole in his heart, but he had to pull himself together or he would lose another sister.

He withdrew Tamiel's phone from his pocket, stood at the end of the table near Lauren's head, and propped his elbows on the surface. When he slid his thumb across the screen to unlock the phone, Mom's note appeared. "My mother wrote these instructions. Let's see what happens."

"One moment." Sir Barlow walked over to the pair of statues standing several paces away. He wrapped his arms around the closer of the two, dragged it within Matt's reach, and set it upright. It appeared to be feminine, but it displayed no identifiable features. "This is the one housing Lauren's soul. Or at least we assume so."

Matt looked at the second statue, tears still blurring his vision. "Could the other one be holding Darcy's soul?"

"No, lad. It was already here before Darcy died."

"Oh. Right. I should've remembered."

Sir Barlow patted Matt on the shoulder. "Have no fear, Son. I will run out to the river and conduct another search. If Darcy's soul is out there, I will find her."

"Thanks, Sir Barlow. I really appreciate it."

While Barlow hurried out of the chamber, Listener positioned herself in front of Abaddon's book. "I'm ready. Just tell me what to do."

"I'll try. This is like waking up in a foreign country. I have no idea if it will work or not."

"You need a confidence boost." Listener laid a hand on his cheek and turned his face toward her. "Matt, Darcy said something about you thinking that I'm amazing. Did you tell her that?"

413

As heat rushed in his ears, he nodded. "I did."

"Well, I think you're amazing, too. Your heroism is an inspiration to me." She kissed his cheek. As she drew back, her pigtails swayed in time with her companion's affirming nod. "You can do this. Together, *we* can do this. You, Sir Barlow, and me. With help from the Father of Lights, we can do anything."

Matt stared at her. Listener's sincere eyes and determined expression washed over him like a cleansing shower, soothing and invigorating. For the first time in days, a sense of peace bathed his mind in spite of the crushing grief. Yes. They could do this. With God's help, how could they fail?

He withdrew Darcy's ring from his pocket and slid it onto his pinky. "Okay," he said with a new spark of energy. "Let's bring my sister back from the dead."

414

26

CHAPTER

LIGHTS IN A
DARK WORLD

Billy lay on his stomach, his cheek against cool grass and his eyes closed. Every muscle ached—stiff and heavy. Nothing would move. It felt as if an elephant had been sitting on him for hours.

A car horn sounded, once, twice, three times. Then it paused before repeating the three blasts, though these were longer. After another pause, the car honked three more times, returning to the shorter notes.

Forcing his eyelids open, he looked around. Loved ones lay scattered here and there—Bonnie, Walter, Ashley, Elam, Sapphira, and Yereq—all motionless. Matt and Darcy were nowhere in sight. An assault rifle lay close by, and the Mustang sat idling a few steps away. Two drones perched on the fabric top, their fangs protruding. Inside, Mariel sat in the driver's seat and Thomas in the back.

415

Mariel leaned on the horn again and repeated the nine honks in the same sequence. When she finished, the pattern finally made sense—SOS in Morse code. At any moment those drones could claw their way into the car.

Billy stretched out a tingling arm and touched the rifle with a fingertip. He nudged his body to the side just enough to push the finger around the trigger frame. Slowly, he inched the rifle toward his body, praying that the drones wouldn't notice.

Fortunately, Mariel kept blaring the horn, maybe to distract the drones. After nearly a minute, Billy had pulled the rifle within reach of both hands. Now if he could summon enough strength and mobility ...

He thrust his body to the gun, grabbed it, aimed at the drones, and squeezed the trigger. Cracks sounded. Bullets flew and slammed into the beasts.

They squealed, leaped up, and flew away, dark blood dripping from their bodies.

The Mustang's driver's door popped open. Mariel climbed out and walked toward Billy as quickly as her old legs could carry her. She knelt at his side and grasped his arm. "Do you want to try to get up?"

Billy nodded. While she pulled, he climbed stiffly to his feet, still clutching the rifle. Blackness flooded his vision, and the burnt houses swayed back and forth as if spinning on a horizontal yo-yo. "Check on the others. I have to get rid of this dizziness."

"On my way." Mariel hurried toward Bonnie. "Your wife first."

The words felt like a splash of cold water. The dizziness fled, though when he followed Mariel, his legs felt like tree trunks rooted in a muddy marsh. As he slogged, Bonnie's form clarified. She lay on her stomach, her wings splayed.

Mariel knelt and pressed two fingers on Bonnie's throat. "I feel a pulse. She's alive."

"Thank God." Dizzy again, Billy sat on the grass next to Bonnie and cradled her head with a hand. "Can you check the others for me?"

"Will do." Mariel rose and hobbled toward Elam.

Billy slid his hand into Bonnie's and compressed her fingers. "Bonnie? Can you hear me? It's Billy."

She shifted and groaned quietly but said nothing. Billy pushed her collar down, revealing two pairs of fang marks, red and dirty. "Those drones packed a punch," he said, hoping his words would draw her back to consciousness. "I think I got bitten only once, so maybe that's why I was the first to recover."

"Elam's alive," Mariel called as she helped him sit up. "He'll check on Sapphira while I see how Walter's doing." Like a nurse conducting triage, Mariel hurried from body to body and announced each patient's condition. Walter and Ashley were both awake but too dizzy to stand, though Walter had risen to a sitting position. Since Yereq lay closest to the seventh door, Mariel walked toward him last of all.

Billy called out, "Has anyone seen Matt or Darcy?"

"Last I saw," Walter said, "Matt was still hanging from the rope in the pit. At least five drones were attacking Yereq, and when they knocked him out, Darcy grabbed the rope. The weight jerked her in. I had three of those buzzards on me, so I couldn't do anything about it."

Billy forced his legs into an awkward, stomping jog toward the abyss. As he passed by Mariel, who now knelt next to Yereq, she looked up, tears in her eyes. "He's dead, Billy. Yereq's dead."

"Dead?" Billy paused for a moment, then shook his head. He couldn't deal with that right now. "I'll be back."

He hurried on and stopped at the edge of the abyss, careful to keep from falling in. Far below, a red light pulsed. Shadows appeared and disappeared on the walls, and rocks jutted out and then withdrew, but there was no sign of Matt or Darcy. Did they fall into oblivion? Only a miracle could have saved them.

Dizziness again stirred in his brain. He dropped to his knees and stared at the void. Might it be possible to search down there?

A hand grasped his shoulder. "I know what you're thinking, buddy."

Billy looked up. Walter stood at his side, a small coil of rope in hand. "This is all we have left. Climbing down there is suicide. Even if Matt did the impossible and managed to find a passage in the wall, which one was it? Will it even open up again? It's like guessing where lightning is going to strike next—one in ten trillion chance you'll get it right."

"Walter, I have to try. He's my son. I've already lost my daughter."

"I know. That's why I brought the rope." Walter dropped the coil on the ground. "We've beaten tougher odds than that before."

Ashley limped to the edge of the abyss and looked into the depths. "I sense someone down there, two people actually. Their minds are anxious, filled with pain."

"That seals it. I'm going." Billy extended a hand over the hole. The upwelling wind churned the air in a tornadic swirl, still strong and erratic. "Without Yereq to hold the rope, someone will have to drive the Mustang back and forth to raise and lower it."

While Billy and Walter fastened the rope to the bumper and checked it for signs of weakness, Ashley and Mariel helped Elam, Sapphira, and Bonnie shake off the venom symptoms. Then Billy, Walter, and Elam took turns dropping into the abyss and searching for a passage, using a flashlight they had found on the prison bus.

After an hour or so, Gabriel and Roxil returned, Roxil now recovered from the mysterious blight. They tested the vortex in the abyss and concluded that no winged creature could withstand it. Gabriel then drove the flatbed truck to its owner, planning to search for a longer rope and then fly back.

Since the dragon blight had been erased, Ashley used Elam's phone to send a text message to Lois. If Lois successfully received the message, she would call Makaidos's tooth transmitter and attempt to guide him and Thigocia to the seventh door. The text seemed to go through, but Lois didn't answer.

When Gabriel returned with several sections of rope, he joined in the effort to probe the abyss. Now able to go deeper, they found many passages, but they all led to dead ends.

Although Ashley announced that she no longer sensed anyone in the abyss, Billy descended for one final try. After swinging into a recess, he sat on the floor and flicked on the flashlight. The recess's door closed and crimped the rope, but that didn't matter. Experience with dozens of other recesses proved that it would open again soon.

419

Still holding the rope, he guided the beam to the back. A low tunnel led several feet deeper, ending at bare rock. He sighed. Nothing. No escape that way.

While waiting for the door to open, he leaned against a side wall. Everything ached, especially his broken toes. He slipped a shoe and sock off and aimed the beam at the two little toes, both bent and swollen. They would heal eventually, but like many wounds, they might flare up throughout his remaining years, however few they might be.

With the beam illuminating the rocky floor, several dark spots came into view. He shifted closer and touched one of them—tacky, somewhat fresh. He shone the light on his fingertip, now red. Blood?

His heart thumping, he drew a knife from a belt sheath and used the blade to scrape as much blood as he could. After stowing the knife deep in his shoe, he tied the shoe to his belt. Soon, the door dropped open. He crawled out onto the projection and gave the rope a hard tug. "Haul me up!"

Billy clutched the rope and rode the Mustang's pull to the top. When he reached the surface, Walter and Gabriel hauled him to solid ground.

"That was quick," Walter said as Bonnie and Ashley joined them. "Did you find something?"

"I think so." Billy retrieved the knife from his dangling shoe. "Ashley, have a look at this."

Ashley squinted at the blade. "Looks like blood."

"I found it in one of those shallow caves. There was no way out, but maybe it means one of them didn't fall right away."

Ashley took the knife. "I'm sure we can find DNA samples for both Matt and Darcy, but I don't have any equipment here to do a comparison." She blew hair out of her eyes. "Without electricity, maybe I can't do it at all."

"Let's call Larry," Bonnie said. "He'll know what's available."

"If I can get through." Ashley pulled Elam's phone from her pocket and walked away.

"While you're doing that ..." Letting out a groan, Billy lowered himself to a sitting position and extended his bare foot. "I need to rest a minute."

Bonnie sat next to him and held his hand. "Blood is good news and bad news."

"Right. Someone's hurt, but the location means that person rested there. He or she was safe, at least temporarily." He shrugged. "Who knows? Maybe a portal opened up and let someone through. Stranger things have happened."

"I can't argue with that." She leaned her head against his shoulder. "I refuse to give up hope."

"Same here." Billy read the words on the door—Abandon All Hope Ye Who Enter Here. Maybe that message would intimidate most who saw it, including himself back in the days of the seven circles, but not anymore. After what they had been through, this was just another bump in the road. They would find Matt and Darcy ... somehow.

Framed by the scarlet rays of the setting sun, Ashley walked toward them, her expression grave. "No messages are going through at all. Looks like everything's shut down. Civilization is history. I guess Abaddon and the locusts have had their way."

Elam and Sapphira approached, walking hand in hand. "Then we're on our own," Elam said. "It's probably best to go back to Second Eden, assuming the portal's still open."

Sapphira snapped her fingers and created a fireball in her palm. "If not, I'm getting stronger. By the time we get there, I should be fine. I'll open it again."

421

"We cannot leave immediately," Roxil said. "We should give Yereq the burial he deserves. Doing so would provide the added benefit of giving Makaidos and Thigocia more time to arrive, assuming they are coming."

"Right on both counts." Bonnie leaned over and examined Billy's broken toes. "And a little rest will do our warriors some good."

Walter found a shovel at the bus depot. He, Elam, and Gabriel took turns digging a hole—shallow but acceptable. When they finished, Roxil lifted Yereq's huge body and laid him gently at the bottom. With the company gathered around the burial plot, Sapphira spoke of her love for the gentle giant and how she nurtured him when he was just a weakling spawn. She wept at times, some tears from fond memories and others from the bitter pain of loss.

Elam suggested honoring all of their fallen allies, especially those who had perished recently, seeing that they had not yet received proper memorials. He began with a eulogy for Valiant in which he recounted the great leader's faith, passion, and love. Roxil recalled Legossi's brilliance in battle, her sacrificial courage, and her unsurpassed warrior's heart. One by one, they added their thoughts about departed heroes—Acacia, Merlin, Naamah, Karen, Eagle, Abraham, Angel, and others.

Finally, Billy ended with a tribute to Professor Charles Hamilton, who died while saving people from Devin's fury. Without exception, the heroes had risked life and limb in sacrificial valor. Most succeeded in saving lives. A few failed, though their willingness to spill blood for the sake of others infused courage in those who remained. Without these brave souls, Arramos and his minions would have triumphed long ago.

Yet, no one mentioned Lauren, Matt, or Darcy. It seemed that a silent vow had passed from mind to mind that these loved ones still had hope for life or resurrection. Eulogizing them would feel like a faithless act.

A few minutes after the memorial, a gibbous moon rose at the horizon, hazy and blood red. While Roxil smashed the instruments of torture at the center of the yard, Elam and Gabriel added lumber from the remnants of the houses while the others tended to wounds.

After Billy and Roxil ignited the pile of wood with their fiery breath, everyone, including Thomas and Mariel, seated themselves at the fire. Bonnie found snacks and soft drinks at the guard house and passed them around.

Soon, two dragon silhouettes appeared in the moon's disk. Moments later, Makaidos and Thigocia descended and slid to a stop at the circle. Everyone rose and gathered around them. Again summarized stories flew back and forth until the two dragons had been updated on the recent events. According to Makaidos, since they had lost communications with Lois after her summons to come, he and Thigocia had to stop and ask directions from various police and military personnel. Although many refused to help and even became belligerent, the dragons received enough information from others to find the address.

Makaidos lifted his head and looked at the sky. "It seems that nuclear war has been averted, at least for the time being, but during our flight here, we witnessed great suffering. This world is quickly being swallowed in a whirlpool of judgment. I suggest that we go to Second Eden and allow the Maker to have his way. I do not think we can be of service here any longer."

"You're probably right." Elam patted Thigocia's scales. "Who knows? Maybe Matt and Darcy found their way into Abaddon's Lair and are even now working their way toward Second Eden. Matt's only form of communication is tuned to Second Eden's frequency, so we're better off waiting for word from him there."

Makaidos bobbed his head. "Then we will go to the portal."

Billy climbed to his feet. "Okay. We have several modes of transportation, but I'm guessing that bus guzzles gas like Walter eats hamburgers. Gabriel told me the bus shack has a gas tank and some plastic containers, so we'll fill them up and load as many as possible. Thomas and Mariel should ride in the Mustang, I can drive the bus, and Walter and Ashley can drive her solar-powered car, assuming that the battery's charged well enough to run at night."

"It should be," Ashley said. "We'll see how far it can go."

While Elam, Gabriel, and Sapphira discussed their travel options with the dragons, Billy grasped Bonnie's hand and whispered, "I said I would drive the bus, but I didn't mention that I have to stay here on Earth."

423

"I know. You're going to West Virginia to find your father and mother. You also have to check on Walter's family, Adam and Carly, and a few others." She compressed his hand. "And I'm going with you."

"It'll be a dangerous journey—corruption everywhere, suffering from coast to coast, nuclear war threatening. Not only that, your song might get snuffed out. And you won't be in Second Eden if ... I mean *when* they get word from Matt."

"I know, but even though this doesn't feel like my world anymore, I still love these people no matter how corrupt they are. They need the Lord, and they need my song. Besides, we were apart for fifteen years. Nothing's going to separate us again."

Billy smiled. "I was hoping you'd say that."

For the next several minutes, they gathered the gas containers, filled them to the brim, and stowed them—some in the Mustang

424

and some in the bus. After everyone settled on their travel plans and said their good-byes with handshakes and tearful embraces, Makaidos, Thigocia, and Roxil flew away with Gabriel riding on Makaidos. Now that the tooth transmitters no longer worked, Gabriel planned to fly between the conveyances to deliver messages back and forth. A few moments after the dragons departed, Elam drove the Mustang toward the prison exit with Sapphira, Thomas, and Mariel aboard.

As the Mustang's engine faded, Billy, Bonnie, Walter, and Ashley watched it disappear in the dimness of late evening.

"I guess we'd better stay close," Walter said as he climbed into the driver's side of the solar-powered vehicle. "Ashley found enough hairs in the Mustang to do the DNA testing, so we're good to go. Of course, I have to be her lab assistant. She said if I left her side for a minute, she'd tear *my* hair out."

Ashley slid into the passenger's seat. "I did not!"

"Well, you thought it." He tapped her forehead with a finger. "It leaked out right there."

"Oh, did it?" She swatted his arm playfully. "I'm the mind reader, not you."

"If you say so." Walter turned to Billy and displayed a grenade on his palm. "This is an egg laid by a very special chicken, guaranteed to cause explosive gas in whoever eats it. It's the only one I have left, so if you want it …"

Billy waved a hand. "We'll be all right. I don't think a prison bus is going to attract much suspicion. You two are a lot more vulnerable."

Ashley gave Walter a light shove. "Cut the comedy. Their hearts are broken."

"I know. Mine, too. Laughing is keeping me from crying." Walter bit his lip and looked down for a moment. When he refocused on Billy, tears welled in his eyes. "Listen, Billy, I don't know about you, but this whole end-of-the-world thing isn't like any danger we've ever faced. I mean, nuclear war. It doesn't get any worse."

Billy tilted his head. "What are you saying? You don't want me to stay here?"

"Not even close. I'm saying I wish I could join you. It's going to be a wild ride." He grasped Billy's hand and gave it a hearty shake. "Check on my family. All right?"

"Already planning on it. We'll get them all to Second Eden if we can."

"Good. If you don't show up there soon, I'm coming after you. Got it?"

Billy nodded. "Got it."

After a final wave, Walter drove the vehicle toward the prison exit. As it faded in the darkness, the solar engine's purr slowly diminished. Seconds later, every sound died except for the rustle of a slight breeze brushing through the nearby forest.

Billy took Bonnie's hand. "Ready to go?"

She turned toward the abyss and sighed deeply. "It feels like leaving a burial site after a funeral."

"I know what you mean." Billy kissed the back of her hand. "So we go in faith and leave our children in God's embrace."

Her lips trembling, Bonnie nodded. "We go in faith."

Billy and Bonnie strolled hand in hand to the bus's door. Billy guided Bonnie's wings through the narrow opening while she climbed three stairs to the floor level. Bonnie settled on the bench directly behind Billy as he sat in the driver's chair. Soon, he navigated the rattling bus out of the prison and onto the access road.

Bonnie hummed for a while, then added words.

426

> By faith we stand in dangerous lands;
> By faith we walk in the dark.
> By faith we know that light will arise;
> By faith we search for a spark.
>
> O God of my song, let me shine a true light;
> Let me be a lamp for their way.
> Let me glow from the valleys to the tops of the hills;
> Let me reflect the light of new day.

Billy joined in. As the dark countryside passed, they repeated the verses again and again. Tears flowed. Sobs shook their pain-streaked words. Yet, soothing comfort massaged their hearts—God's spirit, riding with them every mile.

During a break between verses, Billy glanced back at Bonnie and whispered, "It's going to be all right."

She scooted to the space next to him and crouched. Tears shining on her cheeks, she grasped his hand and held it tightly. "I know. Maybe not in this world, but ... I know."

Billy drove on. Yes, this dark world was no longer theirs. A brighter world awaited. But for now, hand in hand, they had to try to rescue those who longed for the light of day.

427

When you buy a book from **AMG Publishers**, **Living Ink Books**, or **God and Country Press**, you are helping to make disciples of Jesus Christ around the world.

How? AMG Publishers and its imprints are ministries of **AMG** (***Advancing the Ministries of the Gospel***) **International**, a non-denominational evangelical Christian mission organization ministering in over 30 countries around the world. Profits from the sale of AMG Publishers books are poured into the outreaches of AMG International.

AMG International Mission Statement

AMG exists to advance with compassion the command of Christ to evangelize and make disciples around the world through national workers and in partnership with like-minded Christians.

AMG International Vision Statement

We envision a day when everyone on earth will have at least one opportunity to hear and respond to a clear presentation of the Gospel of Jesus Christ and have the opportunity to grow as a disciple of Christ.

To learn more about AMG International and how you can pray for or financially support this ministry, please visit **www.amginternational.org**.